ON HIS
TERMS

Madison Quinn

Madison Quinn

To everyone who supported and encouraged me to write this is for you.

To my amazing editor and beta readers, this wouldn't have been possible without you!

And finally, to my readers, without you I wouldn't have had the courage to take this leap.

Thank you for encouraging and pushing me to tell Nicholas and Kenzie's story

On His Terms

Table of Contents

On His Terms

Prologue

"I'll come by around four to pick you up for the dinner tonight. Be sure you are ready on time. The last thing I need is to show up late again to a dinner. Wear the blue dress I picked out for you, hair up, minimal make up and no jewelry other than your ring. Understood?"

"Yes, I'll be ready by four."

"Good."

With that the door closes, no good-bye, no kiss, nothing, just the firm click of the door latching. I'd be lying if I didn't say I was looking forward to tonight, not that I'm looking forward to the tasteless dinner and boring conversations. It's been so long since I've been out of the house besides running errands or going to the grocery store. I miss meaningful adult conversations; I can't remember the last time I talked to someone about something other than the upkeep of the house or the weather.

I had hoped to get my hair cut and colored before the dinner tonight, but unfortunately he decided we shouldn't spend the money on my hair and that it was fine the way it was. I know it's not fine... I have split ends because my hair hasn't been trimmed in over a year. The highlights I once loved have nearly faded away leaving an odd coloring to my hair. I know better than to argue, so I just nod and don't bring it up again. I don't have much money of my own and even if I did, I wouldn't dare go against what he says and get my hair cut.

Although I'm tight on time, I decide to soak a few extra minutes in the bathtub before getting ready for dinner. I wish I had more time to enjoy the tub, but the few minutes I have right now must be enough. The alarm on my phone dings, letting me know I have less than half an hour before he comes home from work to pick me up.

I quickly get out, dry off and head into our large walk-in closet where the blue dress I was told to wear is waiting for me. If it were up to me, I wouldn't be wearing this dress. Don't get me wrong—it's a beautiful dress—it's just not my style. In my opinion, the front is cut too deep which ends up catching everyone's attention and naturally their eyes stay focused on my chest when they talk to me. The dress has a pretty high slit on the side as well, going nearly up to the top of my thigh which again seems to attract people's attention. Despite all of this, I know why he chose this dress: it's because of the back that is high, and leaves none of my skin showing so no one can see the bruises or the scars that are left there.

I somehow spent more than ten minutes getting changed, which means I have fifteen minutes tops to get ready because I'm expected to be ready even if he gets home a few minutes early. I quickly gather my hair into a quick up-do before curling a few pieces that fall near my face. Next is my make up, I chuckle to myself remembering he said minimal make up since it's going to take a couple coats of foundation to hide the still-yellow bruise on my cheek. I would rather use more make up than risk someone asking about the bruise in front him. The consequence of letting someone see it would be far worse than him thinking I used too much make-up. I'm slipping on my heels when he walks into the bedroom; I don't know how he does it but he can sneak into the house without me ever hearing him.

"Are you ready yet?" he asks.

"I just need to grab my purse."

"I said no jewelry, didn't I?"

"Yes, I don't—"

Slap

I feel the sting before I have time to prepare myself and the force of it has me falling against the bed. As he storms out of the room I quickly glance over my body trying to find the offending piece of jewelry. My engagement ring is still on, but I'm not wearing a watch or necklace. My hands run over my ears and I immediately cringe—I forgot to take out my diamond earring studs I normally wear. I quickly remove them and toss them into my jewelry box before rushing out into the living room where he is waiting for me.

"If we're late because you can't follow directions, you will be punished."

He walks out the door without waiting for my response. I quickly lock up the house and go to the car where he is already waiting for me impatiently. The ride to the restaurant is quiet and awkward, and I know better than to say anything to him when he is a mood like this. It's better for me to let him make the first move than for me to approach him before he has cooled down. If he hits me in the car on the way to dinner, I risk a bruise showing up before the night is over, ruining the perfect image he needs to maintain with his business associates.

"I don't think I told you how beautiful you look tonight," he takes my hand in his as we walk into the restaurant looking like the perfect couple he wants others to believe we are. No one could ever know that underneath this strong exterior is a man who frequently loses control at home and can't control his temper.

"Thank you," I whisper.

"Make me proud tonight, baby," he kisses me on the cheek, squeezing my hand tightly, although I'm not sure if it's meant to comfort or warn me. I take all his gestures as warnings. I learned a long time ago that with him everything is a warning... a promise of what is to come if things don't go his way.

The night is just like all the other business dinners I've attended. My role is simple: stand, smile and make small chat when someone speaks to me. I am not to share any opinion I have about business, politics or religion since these are often hot button topics. Instead, I have been provided with a list of topics that are considered safe, meaning that I can discuss them with someone but only if they bring up these topics first. I am never to approach anyone, never to start up a conversation with someone unless they have approached me first.

"You look beautiful tonight, Kenzie," Ms. Smith says I sit down next to her.

"Thank you, you look stunning in that dress," I complement her.

"I think I recognize yours... didn't one of the celebrities wear it to an awards banquet a couple months ago?"

"Yes, it's the very same one."

"You are such a lucky woman, Kenzie! To have a wonderful man who adores you and buys you such expensive clothing!"

"I am very lucky," and playing the perfect fiancée, I lean over and kiss him on the cheek. He looks at me with approval, as if that was the response I was supposed to give.

Dinner is boring as they typically are: the men talk about business while the women talk about the nonsense of some reality show that they are all watching. We don't have a television in our house so I can't contribute to the conversation. Even though this is boring as hell, I would rather much be here than at home.

"I'm going to get a drink, would you like something, dear?" he asks.

"No, I'm fine, thank you," I'm still slowly sipping my one glass of wine—the only glass I'm permitted to have when we are out. He doesn't like to take the chance that I drink too much, forget the rules and embarrass him.

"So tell me, Kenzie, how is your garden doing this year?" Mr. Ryan asks, surprising me that he remembers that I even have a garden since we've only spoken about it once or twice. Thankfully though, gardening is one of the topics that have been deemed safe so I can talk freely about it.

"We had some issues with rabbits trying to eat my pepper plants, but I used a homemade spray that has seemed to work well at keeping them away. The plants are slowly starting to come back so I'm hopeful that I'll still be able to get a few vegetables off it this year."

"That's wonderful! We had an issue with deer last year and they completely ruined my tomato plants—"

"Oh no!"

"Wasn't much we could do to save them but we tried this expensive spray that my wife found in the garden store and after the second bottle they finally left the plant alone. But by then it was too late; I think we only had two or three tomatoes on that plant the entire year."

"I'm sorry, next time try an egg wash. It helped keep the deer away from our apple trees."

"An egg wash?"

"Yes, I have a gardening book at home that recommended it. I was doubtful but it worked like a charm. Just reapply the mixture every few days and the deer will stop coming around because they don't like the smell."

"That's a wonderful idea! I will have to tell my wife about it when I get home tonight."

"She's not here with you?"

"No, our youngest developed a fever this morning and we didn't want to leave him with a sitter."

"Poor thing, I hope he feels better."

"Thank you."

I sense him behind me before I even feel him. I can't read his expression when he sits down next to me. I recall every word that I just spoke and can't come up with anything that would anger him. I find myself hoping that he isn't angry at me but that something happened when he was getting a drink to change his mood. No matter what the reason though, I know he will take his anger out on me tonight when we get home. He always does. His job is stressful, something I can never understand, he always tells me.

"Gentlemen, if you will excuse us, we need to be going," he pulls my chair out like the perfect gentleman.

We say our goodbyes and head out of the restaurant in silence. The ticket is given to the valet who quickly brings up our car. The ride home is as quiet as the ride there was. His knuckles are white from gripping the steering wheel so tightly, his lips are pressed into a firm line conveying his anger and displeasure with me.

"I thought the chicken was good."

"Shut up."

Nope, clearly not cooled down yet. I can't figure out what I did wrong but I know he's mad at me for something. I'm left with no choice but to wait until we get home and hope that at some point he alerts me to my wrongdoings. He's always quick to point out my mistakes, my flaws, so I'm sure I will know very quickly what it was that I did. I just have to hope he gets his anger out quickly. His outbursts usually only last for a few minutes, before he storms out of the house to go to a bar. He'll come back a few hours later, drunk and apologizing for what he did. The bruises will heal in a few days and during those days I will walk on eggshells, not wanting to anger him again and risk further damage. He's already broken a couple of my ribs; that was pain I hope to never feel again, so I do my best to not to anger him after an episode.

We pull into the garage a few minutes later and my anxiety is heightened, knowing what is about to come. There's no avoiding his reaction, his anger, right now. There's no point in arguing with whatever he thinks I did: I've learned the hard way that only angers him more.

"Was I not fucking clear when we left the house today?"

"You were," I whisper.

"The moment I fucking leave you... that fucking moment you chose to flirt with the vice president of the company? And you fucking do it in front of me?!?!?"

Slap

"You're a fucking slut! I can't take you anywhere! He's a fucking married man with a wife and sick child at home! Don't you ever think about anyone other than yourself?"

"I'm sorry."

Crack

On His Terms

His fist hits my face hard. I fall against the coffee table, catching my side before I finally land on floor. I want to argue with him, I want to tell him I wasn't flirting, that we weren't doing anything wrong but I know better than to say anything.

"Am I not good enough for you? Do I not give you everything? I bought this fucking house for you! I hate the yard, the area, I hate everything about this fucking place but I bought it because you liked it. I pay for everything you need, you don't have a want in the world that I don't meet and this is how you thank me?!?!?"

His kicks my ribs, hard, knocking the wind right out of me. It's the same side where my ribs were broken before. I don't need an X-ray to tell me they're broken again, as the pain I feel when I try to take a breath is all the confirmation I need.

"His eyes were all over you! They were glued to your fucking small tits and you did nothing to redirect him! I bet it turned you on when he looked at you, didn't it? Did you want him to fuck you?"

"No!" I whimper as he kicks me hard again in the same spot.

"You're a fucking liar," he yanks my hair, pulling me from the floor and there is nothing I can do but following him as he nearly drags me across the room.

My back is slammed up against the wall, picture frames fall and shatter from the force. His eyes are dark with rage, darker than I've ever seen them. He is angry, furious even, and for the first time I'm petrified. He has scared me before but I always knew he would never take it too far but now I'm terrified that he won't be able to stop. My eyes search the room, looking for what I don't know, but as I try to move from him, he pushes me against the wall, my head slamming hard against it.

"I do everything for you and you are nothing but an ungrateful slut who thinks she can flirt with the first man who says hello to her after I leave the table! Is it because he makes more money than I do?" His hand is around my neck the moment I open my mouth to answer. His grip is tightening, slowly cutting off my air supply. "You are a piece of shit! I should have known you would turn out just like your mother! My father was right: you are no better than she is! She was a fucking slut just like you are! Why I ever thought you were different is beyond me."

His grip on my throat is tightening again, the room is slowly going black around me and in that moment I know... I know he's going to kill me.

"Fucking bitch."

Chapter 1
Kenzie

"I'll see you tomorrow, Kenzie," Ruth calls.

"Bright and early," I chuckle as the door closes behind me.

It's nearly noon and I've already worked seven hours today. I have a couple of hours before I need to rush to my second job which I'm hoping to spend napping. By the time the day is over I will have worked about 12 hours, just like yesterday and most of the other days this week. I work four to five mornings a week at a place that I absolutely love. Most people probably wouldn't find working in a bakery enjoyable, but since starting there, I've discovered how much I enjoy baking—something I never did before. When I first applied to the bakery, they were looking for just a cashier. However when they were short staffed one day, the owner asked me to whip up a batch of cookies and ever since has split my shift between baking and the register. Unfortunately as much as I love that job, it doesn't come close to paying the rent so I also work a second job as a personal shopper in a high end department store. The pay isn't the greatest either and I don't particularly enjoy what I do, but it helps to pay the bills. The people I meet can be stuck up and often act like they're better than you are, but every once in a while I will meet someone who is decent.

I don't work in the neighborhood I live in, even though it would be much more convenient and wouldn't require me to take a subway and bus each way to work. The reality is, the area I live in is a dump and there really are no decent paying jobs there. My options would be limited to corner stores and gas stations, neither of which is safe, so instead I spend 30 minutes commuting on the subway and bus—sometimes up to four times a day—so I can make enough money to return to the crappy neighborhood.

My apartment is in a rundown building, covered in graffiti. Like any other day there are people hanging out on the front steps already getting drunk or waiting to buy drugs. I ignore them and they ignore me; it works for everyone involved. My apartment is small: basically the living room and bedroom are the same space with a small "kitchen" area against one wall. There is a small fridge with a freezer, a very small sink and a hot plate. The bathroom is just off the living room/bedroom and is just big enough for one person. If you are sitting on the toilet and someone were to open the door, they would hit your knees. I've tried to make my space as warm and comfortable as possible: I've spent money I really didn't have to paint the walls and buy small items that make it feel more like a home. No one but me sees it but the small touches make me smile when I come home and it reminds me that this is my own space, a space where no one can control what I do.

"Hello?" My phone rings the moment I sit down on my daybed.

"Kenzie, it's Nancy. "

"Hi Nancy, how are you?"

"I'm in a bind. We're incredibly short staffed and I just received a call from one of your clients insisting that they need a dress tonight and that you are the only one she trust—"

"Bridget?"

"Yes," she chuckles. "The only thing is, she insists she can't wait until you are scheduled to come in because she needs this dress *tonight*. I know you're not scheduled to come in until four…"

"What time does she need me?"

"No later than one thirty."

"I'll be there."

"Thank you, Kenzie! She said she will make it worth your time."

"I'm sure she will. I'll see you shortly."

And like that, my plan for taking a nap is gone although, knowing Bridget as well as I do, she will definitely make it worth my time, that is always appreciated since money is tight. I quickly start a pot of coffee knowing I'm going to need it if I'm going to make it until closing tonight and stay awake on the bus ride home.

I've worked as a personal shopper for a few months now even if landing the job was pure luck because I'm hardly qualified for something like this. I was killing time between an interview at a coffee house and waiting for a bus when I decided to walk around the store to escape the rain. Why I chose *this* store was beyond me because there was no way I could even afford even a scarf in a place like this anymore. At one time this was the type of store I shopped in regularly, it was all part of the world I knew. Walking around I was surprised I didn't miss this from my former life but instead it made me realize how much my life has changed since then. A few minutes later I noticed an older woman impatiently waiting at a counter desperately trying to get the cashier's attention but the cashier was busy with a long line of people. I happen to walk by her when she mumbled under her breath about useless staff who probably wouldn't be able to tell her if the item was this year's design or last year's.

Flashback

"I'm sorry, I didn't mean to eavesdrop but did you have a question about that purse?"

"Yes, I doubt you would know but I need to know if this is from this year's collection or if you just routinely stock out of date designs?" she asks, her voice full of disregard and annoyance.

"Ma'am I can't tell you what this store stocks, but I can assure you that the purse you are holding is from this year's catalogue. If I remember correctly, it was only released to stores within the last 60 days—"

"Are you sure?" she asks.

"Ms. Wilder, I am so sorry—" a woman quickly approaches us, giving an evil eye to the cashier who still appears to be overwhelmed with her customers.

"Apparently you don't value my business," the woman I now know as Ms. Wilder says. "This young lady came to my rescue and assisted me. I want her to be my personal shopper or you will lose my entire account—"

"But—"

"Get me the manager now!" Ms. Wilder hisses.

"I... Um... Ms. Wilder?" I ask nervously.

"What is it?" she snaps.

"I don't work here, so I can't—"

"You will by the time I leave."

"Ms. Wilder," an older man dressed in a perfect suit approaches us.

"Mr. Goodman, nice to see you again," she shakes his hand and smiles.

"You're looking lovely as always, Ms. Wilder. How can I assist you this fine afternoon?" he sends me a withering look, obviously trying to figure out what I'm doing here.

"You see, my usual personal shopper over there," Ms. Wilder glares at the woman who is just behind Mr. Goodman. "Showed up late yet again for our appointment, leaving me to find the purse I needed for the gala tonight. I wanted someone to answer a very

important question and could not find a single one of your staff members who could spare a couple of minutes to help someone like me. I'm sure I don't need to remind you, that I very large account with your store—"

"Of course not Ms. Wilder, I cannot apologize enough—" he quickly interjects.

"I have decided to give you one final chance at keeping my account but you blow this and I'll take my business somewhere else."

"Of course! Anything you want Ms. Wilder—"

"Fire her," she glares at the woman.

"Done," he gestures for her to leave them which she does in tears.

"Hire this lovely woman and assign her to my entire account," she gestures at me.

"Ms. Wilder, this is highly unusual—"

"I'm sure by now you know that I'm a very unusual woman Mr. Goodman," Ms. Wilder argues.

"If Ms—" he looks at me questioningly.

"Rose... Mackenzie Rose," I nearly whisper trying to find my voice in the confusion that is unfolding before me.

"If Ms. Rose has time, I would love to discuss the personal shopper position that recently became available."

"Thank you, Mr. Goodman," I confirm.

"Then that settles it. I will call tomorrow to schedule my first appointment with Ms. Rose."

I chuckle remembering Bridget that day and the type of woman she is. One who knew exactly what she wanted and went for it. Today is no different: she needs me earlier and I am here earlier. She has a very large account with the store, as in multiple people on the account easily spending thousands of dollars a week on high end items. Her account pretty much makes up my entire customer basis because it is that large. If I work on a day where someone on her account isn't scheduled, I assist with any walk-ins or cover for one of the other personal shoppers. However, it's clearly known that anytime I'm working, if Bridget or someone on her account comes in, they become my priority.

Bridget is the only reason I even have this job—typically you needs years of retail experience before you can even be considered for a personal shopper position at a high end establishment like this. While I've had plenty of work experience, nothing comes even close to something like this. However, living the lifestyle *he* kept me in, has for once worked in my favor. I know all the designers, the current trends and even what celebrities wear because that's how I was expected to be dressed in. That was the only reason I knew the answer to Bridget's question that day.

"Kenzie, thank you again," Nancy greets me as soon as I enter the staff area.

"It's not a problem Nancy, I'm glad to help out."

"Ms. Wilder will arrive in the next thirty minutes or so. She needs a floor length gown for an art gala tonight. Although she didn't specifically request it, I'm sure she will need accessories for the gown."

"Of course, I will have everything waiting for her when she arrives. Is her usual room available?"

"Yes, it's reserved for you to use today."

"Perfect."

"Later today she added a new client to your schedule—"

"A new client?"

"Someone new she recently added to her account. As usual she insisted that you are the only one who can assist him."

"Of course," I chuckle, knowing that any of the other workers here are more than capable of helping Bridget. Most staff here have far more experience in personal shopping than I do.

"You'll be providing him with several outfits according to the list: a ball gown, three cocktail dresses and several casual dresses. I emailed you the list and size information this morning."

"Great, thank you."

I quickly go through the store and pick out several gowns that I think Bridget would appreciate. Over the last few months I've gotten to know her very well, including the types of clothing and colors she prefers. Small things like colors and the high heels she likes are things to be a successful personal shopper. We are supposed to save them time so it is expected we know exactly what they want. I'm finishing hanging the last of the gowns when Bridget appears at my door right on time as always.

"Ms. Wilder, how are you today?" I greet her.

"Kenzie, dear, how many times I have I told you to call me Bridget?"

"Of course, Bridget, how are you?" I quickly correct myself. To my knowledge I am the only one here who is permitted to call her by her first name.

"If it wasn't for you I would be screwed," she sighs dramatically. "My incompetent assistant forgot to put the art gala on my schedule. I only learned about the event when one of the organizers contacted me about the schedule for tonight. Can you imagine how I sounded to her, not even knowing the event was tonight? I was mortified!"

"I am so sorry, that must have been terrible for you."

"Devastating! Luckily I was able to mumble through the conversation before I fired my assistant on the spot. Then I called here only to find out that you weren't scheduled to be in until the time I needed to arrive at the hair dresser for the only appointment time they had available today. I cannot thank you enough for coming in early as I'm sure you had other things to do today."

"It's fine Bridget, really it wasn't a big deal. I was just getting home so the timing was perfect."

"Getting home? Don't tell me you actually had a date this morning?"

As always Bridget assumes if I'm not at work, it must be because I'm seeing someone. Little does she know is dating is the furthest thing from my mind; just the thought of opening myself up and falling in love again is something that terrifies me. I don't think that I could ever trust someone like that again.

"No, I worked this morning—"

"Nancy said you weren't scheduled to work until this afternoon? Was she not aware that you worked this morning?"

"I work at a bakery in the morning which is why I only work evenings here."

"You work two jobs?" she sounds mortified that anyone would work more than one job.

I have no idea how much she thinks I make here but it barely covers the rent on my little apartment. The bakery paycheck covers my utility bills, food and the little clothing I have. The paycheck from here covers the rent on my crappy little apartment and my student loan bills that I will probably forever be paying off at this rate.

"I do, but enough about me! Let's show you the dresses I picked out for tonight. We don't want you to miss your hair appointment."

With the focus back on Bridget, the topic of my finances and why I work two jobs is avoided. Over the course of the next hour she tries on the gowns and accessories I selected before finally choosing the one I knew she would pick.

"This is perfect, Kenzie! You have outdone yourself as usual!" she gazes at herself in the mirror taking in the complete outfit.

"Once again your timing was perfect, this collection only arrived at the store this morning. It hasn't even made it to the floor yet—"

"It's perfect for the gala," she confirms.

"If you want to change, I will have everything wrapped up for you. I assume we're charging this to your account?"

"Of course."

The dress, undergarments, shoes and jewelry are packaged and waiting for Bridget when she steps out of the dressing area. Normally I would have the items delivered to her condo but even she knows with such a tight schedule tonight, delivery isn't an option and adds a risk she doesn't need.

"Kenzie… how many hours did you work this morning at the bakery?" she asks out of the blue as we are walking out to her car.

"Um… about seven," I'm taking back by her question as I assumed the topic of my employment was long forgotten.

"And you arrived here at what, one?" I nod. "What time will you finish tonight?"

"I am scheduled until closing so I should clock out around ten—"

"So you're working 15 hours today?" she quickly does the math in her head.

"About that."

"Is this typical for you?"

"Not really," I'm very uncomfortable with the personal questions but can't figure out how to end the conversation without insulting her. If I do anything to jeopardize her account, I will lose my job on the spot and there is no way I would be able to afford my apartment without this job. "Some days I work both jobs but other days it's just one or the other."

"I see," she pauses. "One last question, do you enjoy what you do?"

On His Terms

"I enjoy meeting new people and helping them find the perfect outfit," I answer vaguely.

"That's what I thought," she seems to be thinking about something but quickly shakes her head when we arrive at her car. "Thank you again, Kenzie, for your help, I truly appreciate you coming in early today for me especially after working this morning."

"Have a great time this evening, Bridget."

Chapter 2
Kenzie

"Kenzie?" Nancy calls for me as I'm putting the last items on a hanger in the private room I was assigned for the day.

"Sorry, Nancy, I was just gathering the remaining items for Ms. Wilder's new client," I explain.

"Oh good, because he's here now—"

"Now? I thought he wasn't due until four?" I glance at my watch, feeling the need to confirm that I haven't lost track of time.

"He wasn't, but apparently his plans have changed and he was hoping to pick up everything now, if it's ready."

"Of course, just let me organize everything and I can show it all to him."

Apparently nothing in my day is going as planned especially taking that nap I desperately needed earlier. I fight back a yawn and push through, realizing I still have several hours left to work today. Tomorrow I'm only scheduled to work at the bakery in the morning, so as long as nothing else changes, I'm planning on spending a few hours in bed catching up on sleep. Today is the third day in a row I'm working both jobs and although I'll be thankful for the increase in hours when I receive my paychecks, right now I'm wishing I had time to take a nap before coming in.

"Ms. Rose, this is Mr. Thompson... Mr. Thompson this is Ms. Rose, she handles all of Ms. Wilder's accounts," Nancy introduces me to the middle aged man next to her dressed in an obviously very expensive business suit.

"Mr. Thompson, it's nice to meet you."

"And you."

"If you need anything, I'll be out front," Nancy leaves.

"I understand from Ms. Wilder that you need several items for a business trip. I've organized several options for you however, if something is not to your liking, I can add more."

"Thank you, I appreciate you picking out all of this... I admit I have pretty lousy taste is women's clothing."

"You just let me know colors and styles you like or dislike as we go through the options and then, as I get to know you a little better, the choices will become less each time you need something. You will find with fewer choices we will easily have the perfect outfit for you quickly. Since this is our first meeting, it's going to take a little longer as I gathered items that most of Ms. Wilder's clients seem to favor."

We spend the next thirty minutes going through each of the items that I had chosen for Mr. Thompson. I learn very quickly he wasn't joking when he said he has lousy taste in women's clothing. In fact he barely says anything as I explain each item and seems unfazed by the designers I mention. By the end though, he agrees to a few of the items but I can't tell if he picks them because he likes them or because he just wants to get out of here. Typically I can read people and by the end of the first meeting I will have a fairly good idea of what they will like going forward, but Mr. Thompson still stumps me.

"Will there be anything else you need?" I ask as I zipper everything into the garment bags.

"I don't think so," he says nervously. "I'm taking my... girlfriend on a business trip with me so I wasn't sure what she would need. I think this will cover everything though."

"Is this the first trip she is accompanying you?"

"Yes," he admits. "I travel a lot for business but rarely bring someone with me."

"I'm sure everything will go smoothly. You have a good selection of clothing options for her–there is something here for casual dinners and others if you need her to attend something more formal."

"You're right... I think you have everything covered."

"If you think of something you need, just call the store before your trip and I'll have something ready for you."

"Thank you, Ms. Rose," he shakes my hand as he leaves.

I arrange for the items to be delivered to the address Bridget had put on file for Mr. Thompson before Nancy tells me to take a dinner break. Since I wasn't originally scheduled to work so many hours today, she gives me an hour instead of the standard half an hour to grab some food. Seeing as I'm struggling to stay awake, my first stop is going to be to the overpriced coffee shop, which is just within walking distance of the store. Having packed my meal as usual, I grab my lunch bag and umbrella before heading out. When the wind blows the rain onto me, I'm left wishing I had a grabbed a jacket when I left my apartment this morning.

I'm only a block away from the coffee shop when the sidewalk becomes increasingly crowded as people rush home from work. I'm forced to the edge, left walking too close to the curb but the crowd gives me no option as people just seem to push their way through to get where they want to go. Despite everyone else being in a hurry, for once I'm not… having an hour for a dinner break is far more time than I need. I'm going to grab my coffee, hopefully find an empty table where I can eat my sandwich and read the book I brought along. I love getting lost in a good book but most days like today I don't have much time to read except for my break. Tomorrow…

Splash

A shiny black car swerves dangerously close to the curb, blaring its horn, splashing me with water and drenching me from the waist down.

"Shit!"

"Excuse me… Ms… " a gentleman in a dark, *dry*, suit exits the driver's side of the car and rushes over to me. "I am so sorry—"

"It's fine," I shake my head sighing. Is it possible to catch a break at all today?

"No it's not," another gentleman gets out of the car, this time from the back seat, and walks over to where the I'm trying to brush the dirt and water from my clothes, not that it's doing much good. This man is dressed in a very expensive dark grey suit with an equally expensive blue tie. He runs his hands through his unruly brown hair as his blue eyes meet mine. He looks right at me, almost as if he is looking through me. My eyes land on his feet, not being able to handle the way he is looking at me.

"I cannot apologize enough," the first man says. "The guy in front of us slammed on his brakes without warning and I had to swerve to avoid hitting him. I didn't expect the puddle to be so large and certainly didn't expect it to hit you like it did."

"Really, it's not a big deal." It's a partial lie because really I'm now stuck spending my dinner break buying a new outfit with money I really don't have. "Accidents happen."

"Please, let me take you somewhere to buy you something to wear," the second man says. "I don't want you getting sick—"

"That's very nice of you to offer, but unfortunately I'm on my dinner break from work, so I don't have much time. I'll run and grab a change of clothes before I head back to work... it's fine really."

"Here," the second man takes a few bills from his pocket and hands them to me.

"No—" I push against his hand.

"Look, it's our fault that outfit is ruined, so at least let me pay for you to get a new one—"

"It's really not necessary—"

"It is," he takes my hand in his, opening my fist up so he can put the bills in it before wrapping my fingers around it. "Please, take the money, it's the least I can do considering we've probably ruined your evening."

"It's not ruined," I giggle at the big deal he is making over this. "Really, it's fine. These things happen. Thank you for offering to replace the clothes but really—"

"Good bye, Ms... "

With that both men walk away from me, cutting me off mid-sentence as I'm left standing on the sidewalk with a handful of money that I was trying to give back. The first man opens the back door for the second one, who turns and smiles at me before getting into the car. It's only then that I realize they both came out of the car without an umbrella and are now probably just as soaked as I am. I shake my head at the irony, given that they were the ones who splashed me and yet ended up getting soaked themselves.

I quickly shove the money into my purse, not wanting to stand in a crowd openly holding money and risk drawing attention to myself. I glance at my watch, realizing I barely have enough time to grab my coffee before I need to head back to the store. I'll never have time to eat my dinner, although it's probably not a bad thing, since I realize in the chaos of everything my lunch bag had fallen to the ground and was now lying in the offending puddle that splashed me.

Despite everything, I return to work in a better mood then when I left. The fact that there are still decent people in this world makes me smile. The driver of the car that splashed me could have easily kept driving, yet he stopped and physically got out of his car to apologize. He didn't simply roll his window down and yell an apology like most would. Instead he and the person he was with, both took the time to get out of their car and walk over to me. As if an apology wasn't enough, they insisted on paying to replace my outfit that again was beyond what I expected from.

"Oh Kenzie! What happened?" Nancy rushes towards me as soon as I open the staff entrance.

"A car swerved to miss hitting another car but instead hit a large puddle right next to where I was standing," I shrug.

"Take as much time as you need to get cleaned up," she checks the schedule. "It looks like you have a little while before your next appointment. You'll probably need to purchase something else to wear, though. I don't think you'll be able to clean those pants enough in the restroom."

"I know," I sigh, not really wanting to spend money on something I really don't need. "I'll find something and change quickly."

I clean up as much as I can in the staff restroom before heading onto the main floor of the department store. When you work in a place like this, image is everything. We're expected to wear clothes from the store we work in and our physical appearance is said to be a direct representation of the store. Therefore, I need to be quick in grabbing an outfit and getting off the main floor before too many people see me in my grime covered pants.

"Much better, Kenzie," she smiles taking in my new outfit. "I'm sure you must feel better to be out of those wet clothes."

"I do," I agree. "There's nothing worse than walking a few blocks in a pair of wet pants."

"I can agree with that," she laughs. "When I first moved here I left to get to work in a hurry and forgot my umbrella. The weather report said there was only a fifty percent chance of showers so I took a chance. I ended up walking six blocks in a pair of soaking wet jeans after getting caught in a sun shower."

"Oh no!"

"Ever since then, I carry an umbrella, even if they're not calling for rain."

"Well, hopefully this will be the last time I get caught like this. Here are the tags for my skirt and pantyhose that I need to purchase."

"With your discount, your total is $73.98."

I reach into my purse for my wallet, when my hand finds the cash that the man in the black car gave me. Hoping it covers at least half of the cost of this outfit, I pull the bills out and begin counting them. I force myself not to curse aloud when I realize the man gave me $200... me a complete stranger on the street, and he hands ten $20 bills like it was nothing to him.

On His Terms

"Kenzie?" Nancy pulls me from my thoughts.

"Sorry, here you go," I give her $80 in cash, hiding the rest in my purse until I'm able lock it back up.

"Here's your receipt, I'm sorry I can't give you any more time—"

"No, it's fine. I'm going to put my stuff away and then I'll get started pulling selections for my next appointment."

Thankfully the rest of my day doesn't get any worse and by the time I leave, the rain has completely stopped and my shoes have dried. Half an hour later, I'm home, completely exhausted, but home. I consider making something to eat, but the need for sleep quickly becomes a priority. I lock the front door, set my alarm on my phone and fall asleep still in the new clothes that I bought earlier today, having no energy to change.

Chapter 3
Nicholas

"Fuck!" I slam another magazine on my desk. "Melody get a meeting with Alex and my PR department in an hour. Move whatever you have to, just make it happen!"

I'm used to my face being on magazines… the paparazzi have been hounding me ever since I made my first million. Apparently becoming a millionaire at such a young age is newsworthy, which would have been fine if it were a one-time article. When I made my first billion it became even worse and now not a week goes by without my name appearing in some article or on some magazine cover. Typically they are business related articles and magazines, which doesn't bother me, as they often refer to me as the shark of the financial world.

Lately though the articles have become personal, attacking me on a different level that I don't understand. Why do they care who I'm fucking? What does it matter whether or not I'm seen with a woman on my arm or different women at different events? My business decisions do not change based upon who I'm fucking, so why is it necessary to attack my personal life? The magazine on my desk today is the icing on the cake:

Playboy Nicholas Parker… Can't keep a woman happy but can manage hundreds of employees? What is he hiding that prevents women from spending more than a night with him? How could so many people trust him with their investments while no woman can trust him in her bedroom?

The article shows several pictures of me attending various events over the last three months, each time with a different woman. Typically I don't pay attention to this junk, but when Carter, my head of security, brought it to me after finding it in our staff lounge earlier today, I lost it. I can't have my employees questioning my ability to run the company or the clients who trust my employees with billions of their dollars questioning my ability to make sound financial decisions.

Skimming the article in this magazine, the author states they are unable to speak with any of the women in the pictures. The women I'm seen with have already signed an NDA, so they would be in violation of it if they said *one word* to the media. They know I would have them in court within 24 hours at most. Of course the author speculates that this is because I'm hiding something and am just paying them off to keep quiet.

I never take them to more than one event with me because I don't want to give them mixed thoughts on what they are to me. The last thing I need is a woman thinking long term and commitment, when that's the last thing I want or need right now. However, my plan appears to be back firing because now the reporters are questioning why I'm with different women at events. Apparently six different women over the course of three months is considered excessive as far as the paparazzi is concerned. I'm damned if I do and damned if I don't. When I *don't* go to events with women, they question my sexuality... when I *do* go to events with women, I'm a playboy who can't manage his own company. Why the fuck they can't just focus on the financials of my company and leave me hell alone is beyond me.

"Mr. Parker, everyone is in the conference room when you are ready," Melody alerts me.

I take the magazine into the conference room next to my office, where my public relations department is waiting along with my vice president Alex Clark. Alex has been in the news as well, but nowhere near the amount or with the scrutiny that I have been. Alex married his high school sweetheart who accompanies him to nearly every event or business dinner so they tend to leave him alone. They never question Alex's ability to hold his position at Parker Financial Services, but suddenly because I'm not in a "committed relationship" I can't operate a multibillion dollar company—a company I started from the ground up with barely a penny to my name?

"We will not be leaving this room until we have a clear plan of action as to how we are going to address this!" I slam the magazine down on the table, beyond pissed off and frustrated. The entire PR department jumps but of course, Alex who is no doubt used to my outbursts by now, doesn't even flinch. "I've spent the last hour combing through this magazine and ten others just like it online that are now all calling me a playboy and questioning my ability to run this company. I followed your fucking advice and this is where it got me!!!"

"Mr. Parker... our advice—" Ms. Murphy begins.

"Did we not have a meeting less than three months ago when these pieces of crap were ruining my reputation?" They all nod in response. "I can have Melody pull the recordings from that meeting, but I guarantee they will show that you advised me to bring women to public events. Did you not?"

"Yes Mr. Parker, we did," Ms. Murphy agrees.

"It was less than three fucking months ago that the paparazzi were publishing headlines that I was gay and afraid to come out of the closet because it would ruin my business or that I had some secret sexual fetish that would ruin me and that was the reason I was hiding my sexual preferences. *Your* advice was to be seen with women at public events to eliminate the rumors that surround my sexual preferences. I did that! Fucking three months later we are back here!"

"Mr. Parker, with all due respect, we did not expect you would bring a different woman to every event—" Mr. Snyder says.

"What the fuck do you want me to do? I can't fucking sit here and let them question my ability to run my company and in turn handle billions of other people's money, based upon whether or not I'm in a relationship with someone. Everyone around this table knows I am not in a committed relationship right now nor do I plan on being in one in anytime soon. I keep my private life private for a reason! I don't fucking date because I don't want the paparazzi to see me out with different women and then gossip about them as well. This magazine, right here, is the exact reason I don't fucking date!"

I'm fed up and don't know what more to say as I sit in the chair at the head of the table and listen to my PR department scramble how to fix this. Two years ago this wouldn't be an issue… two years ago I was pictured in magazines with the same woman at event after event. I was never called a playboy, my sexual preference was never debated and no one believed I had anything to hide. No one questioned my ability to run my company and handle billions of dollars. Just another fucking example of another thing she took from me… how the fuck I was blind for so long is still a mystery. I don't believe in making the same mistake twice; hell will freeze over before I ever consider trusting someone the way I trusted her. I won't give someone that power over me ever again.

The conversations around me are about how to fix the story that's already out there. The suggestions: demand they recant the story, release a statement clarifying the situation, ignore the story. None of these suggestions tell me how to prevent this exact story from occurring after the next event requiring my attendance. Unfortunately, being such a big name in the financial industry and wanting to keep customers happy, I attend a lot of public events. Business is not always done in a board room… sometimes it's done at charity events, golf outings, boxing events… Hell I even once had papers signed at the opera.

I spend more time at public events than I ever wanted to but I realize public image is everything to some people, which is why having my name dragged through the mud is unacceptable. The people I shake hands with on the golf course need to know that the decisions I make are the right ones and that they should have confidence in me. Articles like this blow my integrity with people and will make them second guess their decisions.

"Enough!" I interrupt the continued chaos. "Do whatever you need to do to make this article disappear but right now we need to focus on how I can prevent the next article from questioning my ability to manage PFS just because I have a different woman on my arm. If I show up without someone, they are back to assuming things about my sexual preferences which for some reason, they believe has some fucking impact on my ability to manage other people's money."

"Parker," Alex speaks up after being silent this entire meeting. "The solution is clear. Find a woman and bring her to all your public events."

"Fuck Alex! Did you not hear me when I said I am NOT in a relationship right now nor do I plan to be in one?!?! Where the fuck do you propose I find someone who wants to drop everything and go to events weekly, if not more often with me? Fuck, in the next month I have at least seven or eight events that I need to attend... I don't even want to go to these things, so how the fuck can I find someone else to go?"

"Hire someone," he answers simply.

"Alex," I can't help but fucking laugh at him because I don't know what else to do. "Yes, that's the perfect solution. I'll drive around downtown and find a prostitute, offer her cash to accompany me for the night and then every night I have an event, I'll pick her up at the same street corner."

"Well... it solves two issues as far as I can see," his face is red from laughing so hard at me. "The press will stop calling you a playboy because you'll only be seen with one woman. And, they will stop wondering what it is you do with all your money."

"Right, because then they will have pictures of me paying a prostitute for her services."

"Well, you asked for ideas."

If anyone else at the table suggests I hire a hooker I would have their ass fired on the spot, but Alex is different... he has always been able to get away with things that I don't let anyone else get away with. Alex has been my vice president for years now but beyond that, we went to college together and have been best friends ever since. He was one of the very first employees I hired when PFS began expanding beyond what I could handle by myself. Alex works almost as many hours as I do and has put it many late nights working side by side with me. I spend more hours with him than I do anyone in my life... well maybe except Carter since he is with me constantly and even has his own living quarters in my penthouse.

Melody, my personal assistant, has been with the company for four years now, reporting directly to me for the last year. Prior to her I can't even remember the number of personal assistants I went through on a yearly and sometimes monthly basis. Alex still jokes with me how I scared away one assistant so quickly she left to get breakfast for a meeting only to drop the muffins off with Carter before telling him that she quit effective immediately.

Melody coming on board has been a godsend, she doesn't take things personally when I am short with her and she knows exactly how I like things. She has a way of making me more productive by having everything ready for me before I even know I need it.

Asher the head of IT makes up the remainder of what I consider the key members of my management team at PFS. Without him, investments could have gone differently and bad financial decisions could have been made because his staff have ways of finding things out about people and companies that no one else can find out.

"Short of hiring a prostitute, what ideas do we have for moving forward?" I bring the discussion back to the topic at hand.

"Sir, we think it would be in your best interest to find a woman who can accompany you to the majority of these events and when she is not available, to go alone or with a family member," Mr. Snyder recommends.

"So we're back where we started," I sigh. "I go with family members or alone to events and there are whispers, I go with women and there are whispers. You need to come up with a better solution because I refuse to have people questioning my management ability based upon who I do or don't bring to events. Fucking find me another solution!"

With that I storm out of the room and leave the PR team to discuss other options, although I know the reality is there really aren't any other options. I wish there was a way to get the paparazzi to just leave me alone but short of buying out every media outlet in the country, I don't see that option being realistic.

At one point I had my legal team demand a gossip site remove a story about me and issue a statement that they reported false information. The day after it was issued, another media outlet published a different story about me, this time speculating on why I make charitable donations to certain organizations and not to others. In that moment I realized no matter what I did, there would always be stories out there about me. I stopped wasting my resources having my legal team send requests for companies to recant their stories.

"Mr. Parker?" Melody knocks on my door.

"Come in, Melody."

"I just wanted to remind you that I am off tomorrow—"

"Yes, it's on my calendar."

"You have an early morning meeting where we usually provide breakfast so I have already placed an order with a local bakery. However someone will need to pick the order up—"

"Can't they just deliver?"

"This bakery does not offer a delivery service, Mr. Parker."

"Why the fuck do we do business with them if they don't deliver? Do you know how much time we could save if you didn't need to run out before meetings to pick up food? Surely there are other bakeries in this city that offer delivery?"

"Yes, there are numerous bakeries within a few blocks of the office. However you know those muffins that you love?" I nod. "They are from *that* bakery. And the freshly made donuts that are a hit at each of your meetings? Also from *that* bakery. Your meeting tomorrow morning is with Connors and Associates and according to Mr. Connor's PA, he has a soft spot for this bakery's banana nut muffins which, of course, I ordered for tomorrow morning. Now if you don't have anyone who can pick up the order, I can cancel it and find a bakery that will deliver—"

"That won't be necessary. I'll get Carter to stop by on our way in," I concede once again realizing why it is I value Melody so much.

"Will you need anything else before I leave?"

"No, enjoy your day off Melody."

After a couple more hours of work, I'm sitting in the back of the Audi SUV that Carter is driving back to The Accord Towers. Without asking, Carter again takes the long way, slowing just past the little coffee shop where only a couple of weeks ago, we splashed a beautiful young woman who has haunted my thoughts ever since. I don't know what it was but there was something about her that captured my eye. Her long brown hair was pulled into a neat ponytail, her makeup was very light and minimal allowing her natural beauty to show through. Her outfit was simple but dressy: a pair of perfectly fit tan dress pants was complimented by a form fitting black button up blouse.

I can't remember ever having women try to refuse money that I gave them. Normally that's all they want me for. That's what they expect from me: they expect me to give them money and buy them things. This woman was completely different in that she tried to give the money back to me! No matter what I said, she insisted paying for new clothes wasn't necessary but Carter and I both knew it was our fault that she would have to buy something new. Carter has worked for me long enough that verbal communication is not always needed; a quick glance between us confirmed that we were both thinking the same thing. As I pushed her hand with the money away, Carter and I both turned around to head back to the car, leaving her with the money in hand.

Madison Quinn

Ever since that evening, I have found that woman entering my thoughts at random times. I don't know what it is about her but something is making her stick in my head. A couple of days after we spoke to her, I asked Carter to drive past the area on the way home. He was of course confused because this area was in the opposite direction but when I asked him to slow down as we approached the coffee shop, I think he figured out why I asked him to go this way.

Thus, every night on our way home, we go pass the coffee shop. We haven't seen the woman from that incident on any of our drives past. I know the chances are slim of seeing her again but I still don't ask Carter to return to his usual route. I'm not sure what I would do if we saw her tonight, or any other time for that matter. I have no desire to start a relationship and I doubt she would be interested in what I have to offer.

If I could find a way to just fuck her, it would probably get her out of my head but I certainly couldn't walk up to her on the street, introduce myself and then ask her to come back to my place for a quick fuck, could I? Something tells me that even if I could get away with that, she would never agree to it. One look at her and I could tell she isn't the type to have a one night stand with someone. She's the type who wants it all: the husband, the house, the white picket fence with 2.3 kids running around in the backyard.

Chapter 4
Kenzie

Beep Beep Beep Beep

I blindly slap my alarm clock, groaning when I see that time says it's four am. My muscles whine as I push myself into a sitting position and demand at least a few more hours of sleep. I worked more than twelve hours yesterday and despite that I couldn't fall asleep until close to midnight, thanks to my incredibly loud neighbors who thought it would be a good night to have a party. I think the only reason I finally fell passed out was from pure exhaustion because the noise level certainly didn't decrease.

Thankfully today I am only working at the bakery so by early afternoon I should be back at home where I can hopefully take a nap. I swear if the department store calls me this afternoon I may be tempted to ignore the call because I don't think I could make it through another twelve hour day even if I wanted to. Although the tip Bridget left me after calling me in early the last time she needed something made the long day very worth it. Perhaps if she calls I will go in after all, well maybe if I can at least get a small nap in.

I take a fast shower even though my body begs me to stay in longer and let the hot water ease some of my sore muscles. As much as I would love to, the building has a very limited supply of hot water and I know from experience if I spend more than eight minutes the water will turn ice cold without warning. After learning that the hard way, I now set a timer for seven minutes so there's no chance of ice water coming out of the shower head before I'm finished. There's nothing worse than having that happen while you still have a head full of shampoo. Quickly dressing in a pair of jeans and my bakery shirt, I make myself a bowl of hot oatmeal for breakfast. I'm not a big breakfast person, but I know I need to put something in my stomach before I start my shift. There are days when it can be so busy that I don't get a break until my shift is over and by then I would be starving if I didn't eat before I started working. By the time I finish eating and my coffee is done brewing, it's nearly four thirty, meaning it's time to leave.

"Good Morning Ginny," I greet the owner as I walk in.

"Morning Kenzie, how are you?"

"I'm good, thanks. What can I get started on?"

"Actually, I need to talk to you, if you have a moment?" I nod. "Please come to my office."

I follow Ginny back to her office… in the eighteen months I've been working here I haven't been in her office, except for the day she interviewed me. I have butterflies in my stomach for some reason. I know the outcome of this meeting is not going to be a good one… I just know it. I fear what Ginny is going to talk to me about but there is no avoiding it.

"Kenzie… there's no easy way for me to say this," Ginny takes a deep breath and briefly pauses. My heart is beating so loudly I'm almost certain she can hear it. "I've decided I'm going to retire and my daughter has invited me to come live with her in Texas."

"I'm so happy for you Ginny! I know how much you've missed your daughter since she moved."

"I have and she called me last night to let me know she is expecting, so by moving in with her, I will be able to see my grandbaby whenever I want. I can't imagine living in New York and having her and the baby so far away."

"Congratulations!"

"I'm going to sell this place and while I'm going to tell the new owners how wonderful each of my staff members are, I can't guarantee they are going to keep you on once the ink dries."

"I appreciate you putting in a good word for me."

"Kenzie, I wish I could do more to protect your job—"

"I understand. Don't worry about me, I'll be fine."

"I can't help but worry about you, you know that. If the people who end up buying this place are morons and end up letting you go I will give you a glowing recommendation to wherever you want to go next. I'll do anything I can to help you… you've come so far—"

"Thank you, but I promise I will be okay."

She squeezes my hand across the desk and I can see the concern in her eyes. Along with a few other entry level, minimum wage paying jobs, my interview with her was set up by my case worker on my second day in New York. Ginny and I clicked almost instantly; she never asked me any questions about my past or why I moved here. She knew where I was living at the time of my interview and knew who scheduled me for the interview but she never brought it up. She instantly became like a mother figure to me—she was the type of mother I always wish I had. She makes sure I have enough hours scheduled each week and always offers any extra shifts to me instead of one of the girls who work the register. She's the type of person who cares about everyone and doesn't ask for anything in return.

"I'll keep you updated on the sale of this place, but right now my attorney is reviewing offers so we are probably still a couple of months away from one being accepted and the paperwork completed."

"Thank you, I appreciate you telling me about this."

"Please don't tell the other girls. I'm not ready for everyone to know just yet. I worry some of the others might jump ship and leave just you and me working all these hours."

"I won't say anything."

"We have a catering order I need you to work on this morning; here's the order information. Someone will be by around 7:30 to pick it up."

"No problem, I'll make sure it's ready."

I try not to focus on what Ginny told me; there's not much I can but wait and see where things fall when the bakery eventually sells. I'm not going to start looking for another job because I would much rather stay here. I know all the recipes by memory, the register is easy to use and I really like the area. We are surrounded by large office buildings in a very busy section of the city which means everyone is always on the go. There are several stores within walking distance that I can hit if I need something before catching my bus. Even though it wasn't a tough decision, I very quickly decide to stay on with Ginny and see what happens. If the new owners decide to replace all the staff, then I will find another job. I'm pretty certain that the experience I have gained here will help me get a job at another bakery.

"Kenzie!" Ginny comes around the counter a couple of hours later.

"Someone is here to pick up the PFS catering order—"

"UGH they're early," I sigh, glancing at my watch. "Give me a few minutes, the banana nut muffins are just about ready to come out of the oven."

"No problem, just bring it up front when you're done."

At least half of Ginny's business is probably catering for the local businesses in the area. Although the chain places offer delivery to the offices, most of the customers are loyal to Ginny because they love certain items we make. Whether it's the handmade donuts, the warm croissants, the personalized breads or the flavorful muffins, it seems everyone has their favorite that keeps them coming back. PFS, for example, probably places an order with us at least two to three times a week. I can put money on it that, because while certain parts of the order will change, there will always be an apple cinnamon muffin in the order. Clearly, whoever does the ordering for them, loves that type of muffin; I assume the order changes either based on meetings they are having or who in the office want to order from us.

"Order for PFS?" I call as I walk into the front of the store.

"Over here," a deep voice calls me.

I stop in my tracks when I turn around and recognize the man who answered me— it is no other than the man who drove into the puddle that drenched me a few weeks ago when I was on my dinner break from the department store.

"Ms... it's nice to see you again," he greets me.

"And you," I place the box down on the counter. "I wanted to thank you and the man you were with again for replacing my clothes that day. It was too much—"

"I'm sure whatever you were given was not just meant to replace your clothes but also for the inconvenience of having to spend the remainder of your break shopping instead of taking time for yourself."

"Had I known how much was there I never would have accepted it! It was far too much money—"

"As I recall, you didn't accept the money. I believe my boss gave it to you and had to walk away when you tried to give it back repeatedly," he smirks.

"Well... yeah I guess I did," I laugh.

"What were you doing on break so far from this place anyway?"

"Oh, I wasn't on break from here. I work another job... I was only a block or so away from there when you..."

"Ruined your outfit?"

"It wasn't ruined, just wet and dirty," I point out. "Really it's fine. It all came out in the wash so it wasn't a big deal at all. Please thank your boss again for me, I appreciate that you both stopped and didn't keep driving like most people would have."

"Speaking of, I should get going. He has a big meeting this morning where these are needed for. It was nice seeing you again Ms...?"

"Kenzie... Kenzie Rose."

"Take care Ms. Rose—"

"Wait... do I get to know your name?"

"Carter," he replies over his shoulder while walking away.

It was very unexpected to see Carter here today, but I can't help but wish it was his boss who came in for the catering order. I don't know what it is but ever since that day I haven't been able to get the other man who was with Carter off my mind. Of course he was absolutely gorgeous, but there was something else about him that has kept me from forgetting him. I have no idea who he is but even if I did, I know I would be way out of his league. The car he rode in easily cost more than I pay in yearly rent.

Plus he had a driver... only people with incredible amounts of money pay for someone to drive them around in their personal car. People like that never give someone like me a second glance; the only time I talk to people with that much money is when I'm dressing them at the department store. It wasn't that long ago when I shared drinks and meals with those types of people... I cringe at the memory that I allowed to slip into my mind; memories that I've tried so hard to keep buried. Besides even if by some miracle he decided to even give me the time of day, I don't think I could ever trust someone again. If you can't trust someone completely, what type of relationship can you ever hope to have? I've learned what relationships are like without trust and I'd rather spend my life alone then to experience that again.

"Kenzie, we need more glazed donuts," Ginny thankfully pulls me from my pity party to remind me that I'm here to work.

"Coming right up!"

The rest of the morning is thankfully very busy which doesn't give me any time to take another unwanted trip down memory lane. Once everything is prepared for the lunch rush, I grab a cup of coffee to go and clock out. Surprisingly I'm not as exhausted as I expected to be by now, so I decide to do a little window shopping before I catch my bus home. I can't afford very much in this area of high end shops, but I still enjoy window shopping...

Ring Ring

"Hello?" I answer my phone nervously as the number on the screen is not one that I recognize. There are only a few people who know my phone number which is how I like to keep it. Since it's a prepaid cell phone, my name isn't tied to this phone number anywhere that someone can find it. While that should reassure me, I still get very nervous when a number calls that I don't recognize.

"Kenzie? This is Bridget," the voice on the other end says.

"Bridget? Oh… hi."

"Look, I'm sorry to call you but I need to speak with you and was hoping you could meet me later today?"

"Oh, I'm sorry Bridget but I'm not scheduled to work. I'm sure if you call the store—"

"I need to speak with you outside the store actually."

"I'm sorry?"

"Can you meet me around four today?"

"Ummm… I don't know."

"I have a business proposition I want to discuss with you. Meet me for dinner, listen to my offer and if you're not interested, then no harm done. I promise you that whether or not you accept my offer will have no impact on my account at your store. If you don't accept my offer, I won't pull my account or ask for someone else to be assigned to my account if that's what you're worried about. You have my word, Kenzie."

"Okay… thank you. I suppose I can meet you today, I'm not working this evening."

"There's a Brazilian steakhouse on 7th and Main, do you know it?"

"I'm familiar with the area, so I'm sure I can find it."

"Great, I'll meet you there at four today. The reservation is in my name."

"I'll see you then."

Nicholas:

"Mr. Parker?"

"What?" I snap.

I'm desperately trying to focus on responding to this arrogant ass who has been dicking me around on a decision for the last month. If I don't concentrate on my response, I'm likely to tell him that he has his head up his ass if he thinks the shares in his company won't plummet with the announcement of the merger next month.

"She works there."

"Who? Who works there? What are you talking about Carter?"

On His Terms

Now he's just pissing me off too. If you're going to interrupt me at least make it something worth my while; otherwise wait until I'm not fucking busy.

"Ms. Kenzie Rose."

"Carter… seriously what the fuck? What are you fucking talking about? Who the hell is Kenzie Rose?"

"The woman from outside the coffee shop… the one we inadvertently drenched during the rain storm."

"She… she works at the bakery?" I'm shocked, I never thought we would find her again. I even had Carter and Asher check security cameras in the area but none were able to give us a clear picture of the mystery woman who has haunted my thoughts ever since.

"Yes, she had prepared the order for today's meeting. We're running early if you want to go in—"

"No, just drive to the office."

"Sir?

"PFS, Carter."

I can't help but glance out the window at the bakery as Carter pulls away. Part of me wants tell him to stop the car so I can go in and meet this Ms. Rose properly. But then her image is in the front of my mind once again and I'm reminded that there's no way that I could ever be what she wants or needs. I'm reminded that she isn't the type of woman who is just going to want to fuck me, that she isn't the type of a woman for a one night stand. I'm not the type of guy who can do anything more than a one night stand or a quick fuck… not again.

Chapter 5
Kenzie

I have no idea what to wear tonight to meet Bridget or even what she wants to meet with me about. I've racked my brain over and over again, trying to figure out what she could possibly want to discuss with me outside the store and still can't seem to find anything that makes sense. Initially I assumed it must have something to do with shopping for her at other locations besides just the department store but then I realized that everything she has pretty much comes from our store.

I checked the website for the place we are going to meet and it seems like a pretty dressy place which is exactly what I expected of Bridget. I pick out a dress that I've worn to work a few times; I doubt that anything else I own would be appropriate for this type of place. The restaurant is located pretty much where I thought it would be, about a four block walk from the nearest bus stop that will bring me to the subway line I need but the area it is in is pretty safe so I'm not worried about walking back to the bus stop after our meeting. The menu was posted online as well but no prices were listed, leaving me only to assume that dinner would likely cost half of my paycheck if I were to go there on my own. I take some of the cash I keep hidden in case of emergencies and toss it into my purse in the event that I need to grab a cab or pay for something.

My stomach feels like there is a knot in it, whether it's from nervousness or anxiety, I don't know. I hope that I know her well enough by now that she will keep her word and that no matter what happens tonight, I won't lose her as a client. She had said this wouldn't be an option but I can't help but worry that it *could* happen if she doesn't like my response tonight. It may not be the best job in the world but without it I wouldn't be able to pay all my rent so I value it for that reason alone.

When the bus stops, I slowly get off and make my way along the busy sidewalk. My stomach feels like a brick is sitting in it and I'm practically shaking with nervousness. I try to calm myself down but I can't seem to stop my body's natural reaction. I'm not so much nervous about the actual proposition she has in mind but more so about the consequences if I decline the offer. I try to push those thoughts out of my head and desperately try to find something else to focus on during the short walk to the restaurant.

"Good evening miss… can I help you?" I'm greeted by an older gentleman in a suit as soon as I walk into the restaurant.

"Yes, I'm here to meet with Ms. Wilder, I believe she has—"

"Ms. Wilder has our private room reserved. Please follow me," he cuts me off and quickly leads me through the busy restaurant. Despite it being fairly early, I'm surprised at how busy this place is. It seems most people here are having business meetings as there are folders, notepads and laptops at almost every table. I suppose this place was a good option for conducting business dinners… the tables are far enough apart that you wouldn't feel like someone could eavesdrop into your conversation and the food would surely impress any guest based upon the reviews written online.

"Ms. Wilder, your guest has arrived," I am led into a small dining room where Bridget is seated at a table that looks rather large just for the two of us.

"Kenzie, it's so nice to see you again," she stands to greet me as soon as I walk in.

"Thank you Bridget, it's nice to see you too."

"The waiter will be in shortly with your meals."

"I hope you don't mind, I took the liberty of ordering for both of us so we can focus our time on discussing business. The food here is delicious but if you don't like what I ordered please let me know. The chef will make anything you want, even if it's not on the menu."

"I'm sure whatever you ordered will be fine Bridget, I'm not a very picky eater," I assure her.

"While we wait for our food, I need to ask you to sign this," she hands me a folder with what appears to be a legal document in it.

"What is this?" I ask.

"It's called a non-disclosure agreement, an NDA. Please read through it carefully. I want you to understand what you are signing. Essentially by signing this document you agree to keep anything we discuss here between the two of us. You cannot go home and tell your roommate about this discussion—"

"I live alone so you don't have to worry about that." It would be much easier if I had a roommate, financially speaking of course. The idea of living with someone, sharing my space with them… I just couldn't do it. I couldn't trust someone that much.

"It also means you can't talk to anyone about this at the store what we discuss tonight."

"I understand."

I spend the next few minutes reviewing the NDA which seems pretty straight forward. It warns that I can be sued if I discuss the contents of this meeting with someone, especially if the information is then leaked to the media. My curiosity is peaked even more as I wonder what Bridget could want to discuss that would require such a high level of confidentiality. Immediately, I toss out the idea that she wants me to be a personal shopper for her at other stores, not that it was a very good idea to begin with.

A waiter quietly brings in our salads and entrees, setting them in front of us before Bridget nods, dismissing him. She pours us each a glass of wine from the bottle that has been opened and is on the table with us. I take a deep breath and sign the NDA, closing the folder before taking a sip of the wine she just poured. I haven't had a glass of wine or really anything containing alcohol in the last year and a half; not that I haven't often wanted something but more because I was focused so much on saving money and just surviving.

"Do you mind if we discuss things while we eat? I've had a busy day and ended up missing lunch today so I'm famished," Bridget asks.

"I don't mind at all." I'm secretly relieved because I'd rather get the reason for this meeting out in the open than dragging it on much longer.

"Kenzie, I want you to keep an open mind with what I'm about to offer you," she warns and I nod in agreement as the anxiety in me rises even higher. "As you know, I run a very successful consulting firm here in New York. What you don't know is what my services entail. I work with very successful business men and women across the tri-state area who, because of their busy lives, finds dating to be either undesirable or something they don't have time for. This is where I come in: I set them up with men and women who match the qualities they are looking for."

"Like a match maker?" I ask completely surprised.

"Sort of... I *suppose* you could call me a match maker. However, unlike most match making services out there, my ultimate goal is often not about wedding bells and happily ever after. That doesn't mean that some of my clients haven't ended up married, of course, but the primary objective of the match is not compatibility for life."

"I'm sorry. I'm a little confused. If you're not looking for a husband or wife for someone, what's the point in the match?"

"Company, companionship and sometimes even friendship—what most people want out of life. The people I work with are very successful individuals in their respective industries. Often times they work 60, 70, even 90 hours per week with little to no time for their personal lives. They have sacrificed those personal lives for their success and this is something they accepted long ago.

"However, sometimes they just want to go to dinner with a lovely woman and have a conversation that doesn't revolve around the stock market or the latest merger. They don't want any type of commitment and because of their success, they always worry that someone is only with them for money so they never trust anyone completely. I pair them with someone that I think they have something in common with or that I think would be a good match for them. The two have dinner, go to a play, see a movie or more often than not go to social events together. You would be surprised how many business deals are ironed out over social events with husbands and wives present."

"I'm actually not as surprised as you would think," I mumble aloud.

"Oh?" she asks but when I don't comment she continues. "I've known you for more than a year now so I'd like to think I know the qualities you possess. I am confident that you would be a good match with several of the men, or women if you prefer, that I work with. I would like to offer you the opportunity to join my consulting firm."

"Ummmm... this is a lot to take in. Can I ask you a few questions?"

"Of course, ask anything you want. You've signed the NDA so I feel comfortable speaking freely with you about this."

"What exactly is expected on a date?" I ask cringing at the word date. Can you even call it a date if you are being paid to be there and the person is paying for your service?

"It depends on the context. Assuming it's not a business-social event, think of it like two friends going out together. You eat, chat about whatever you want: sports, the weather, aspirations in life... really anything. If you are accompanying someone in a business-social situation, you would likely have met the person ahead of time and he would have outlined what he was looking for at that event. Usually they need you to play the doting girlfriend role: hold hands, maybe dance if the event calls for it, and just make small talk with the other guests. They will have briefed you ahead of time on the key players and given you their opinions on business or political topics."

"How long do these... arrangements typically last?"

"I have some staff who have been meeting with the same client for years now. The press, without a doubt, assumes they are a couple but in reality they only see each other for business events and the occasional dinner beforehand. I have other clients who will ask for someone to go to dinner with once every few months when they are in town traveling for business. It really depends on the client and how well they click with my staff."

"What about... physical contact? Is that an expectation—"

"Absolutely not!" Bridget slams her hand down on the table between us. "I do not run a prostitution ring, Kenzie! Beyond holding hands, any physical contact is limited: a hand on the small of your back when you walk into the room, an arm around your waist when discussing something with another couple, etc… At most, a kiss on the cheek at the end of the evening. There is nothing beyond that—it is spelled out in the contract all clients and employees sign stating their will be no intimate contact between the two parties unless they both terminate their contract with my firm."

"I'm sorry, I meant no disrespect. I just had to know. I could never… that's just something I couldn't do."

"It's a common misconception; escort businesses have been given a bad name by companies who disguise themselves as providing escorts, when they really provide prostitutes. My clients have no problem finding a woman to be intimate with them, what they come to me for is something more than sex. They want someone who they can spend a few hours with who won't expect flowers the next day or a diamond ring on their finger in a week. Sometimes all they want is to conduct business but the people who they are conducting business with assume there is something wrong with them because they don't have a wife, girlfriend, husband or boyfriend to bring to dinners."

"Why me?" I blush when I realize I asked the question aloud.

"Kenzie… whether or not you know it, you're beautiful. You have this innocence about you that I know many of my clients will find endearing. You're not the type of woman who dresses incredibly sexy or tries to get into a man's pants for his wallet. From what I can tell, you haven't had any plastic surgery; the natural look is very appealing to most of my clients. You're polite but can handle yourself when necessary as well. These qualities are highly sought after for business events. My clients want someone who can hold polite conversations with their business associates but can also hold their own if they need to leave their side for a few minutes."

"I…"

"I'm sure these are qualities you don't even see in yourself, but I've made it my business to get to know everyone I come in contact with. I think this could be a good opportunity for you … you wouldn't have to work two jobs any longer and could afford to move out of that crappy neighborhood you live in—"

"Wait… how do you know where I live?"

"I ran a background check on you, of course, dear," she answers as if it's nothing. "Before I approached you about this opportunity, I needed to know if you would hold up to public scrutiny. It's possible you would be photographed at events with clients and I needed to know what the press could dig up on you."

"There shouldn't be anything…" I try to figure out what could be on a background check about me.

"There wasn't anything to worry about. Looks like you had bad luck a few years ago: a tumble down the stairs landed you in the emergency room with several broken ribs and a gash on your arm requiring stitches—"

"You could access my medical records? That's confidential!"

"For the right price anyone can access anything, Kenzie," she sighs. "I needed to make sure that I knew everything that the press could find out about you."

"Shouldn't that be my choice? I haven't accepted your offer!"

"Yet," she corrects. "You haven't accepted my offer *yet*. Kenzie, I know this feels like I invaded your privacy, but I didn't know much about you before I ran these background checks. I doubt the store ran detailed background checks, but even if they did, it wouldn't be as in depth as mine. I needed to know you were trustworthy before I even could approach you about this."

"I... I don't know what to say, Bridget," I sigh heavily. What she says makes sense but I'm still angry that she could access my medical records. However I'm relieved that even if she accesses all of them, she won't find anything else. There is nothing there to raise suspicion, nothing to make someone take a second look...

"Will you consider my offer? I have men and women who work for me don't have to work other jobs to pay bills. This could get you out of your apartment and into a place where you wouldn't have to worry about walking out your front door at night or that the police might barge through your door at any moment because your neighbor is dealing drugs. You wouldn't have to scrimp and save every penny. You wouldn't have to work ten, twelve or fifteen hour long days."

"I don't know, this is a lot to take in."

"Take some time, think about my offer. If you agree, one simple date could pay your rent for a month."

"Seriously?" I ask dumbfounded that she could be offering me that much money.

"Yes," she says straight faced. "Depending on the length of dinner, assuming it's just the two people, you could earn a minimum of $500 per hour. Most dinner dates will last at least two hours, sometimes longer. Then you figure in a movie, play or opera afterwards and your dinner now lasts four to five hours which means you earn a minimum of $2000. After the first date, your rate is increased by $100 per hour. After the first month, the rate is increased further. Social or business events have different rate ranges based upon the number of people in attendance, the expectations the client has and if publicity is required—"

Madison Quinn

"Publicity?"

"Sometimes, clients want to publically be seen with a date at an event. If this is required, the price is higher because it puts you in newspapers and magazines."

"I see."

"All of your expenses are covered, any clothing that is required for dates or events is charged to my account. As you know I have many accounts at different stores throughout the city; you simply pick out an outfit and charge it to my account. The outfit is yours at the end of the night."

"So the clients at the store...?"

"Clients and employees, all of them," she confirms.

"Wow..." I don't know what else to say.

"Kenzie, take a few days and think about my offer. Think about the doors it could open for you. Think about what you could do with extra money in your pocket every month. My staff have returned to school, are raising children on their own, helping to pay for medical bills for sick family members or even just paying off debts. Think about what you really want to do with your life. Do you want to work two and three jobs forever?"

"No," I whisper.

"Here is a contract, take it home and read through it. Call me in two days with a decision. If I don't hear from you in 48 hours, I will have your answer."

Chapter 6
Kenzie

Holy Shit… holy shit… holy shit.

That's all I can think about on the cab ride home. Bridget insisted on paying for a cab when she learned I arrived by bus and subway. I don't mind taking public transportation but I guess to someone like her, it's a foreign concept. I can't imagine what this cab ride must be costing her, since I don't live remotely close to this area of the city but when I tried to object, she wouldn't of hear it. So now I'm sitting in the back of a cab that is weaving in and out of traffic repeating holy shit to myself hundreds of times. I'm holding the folder tightly in my hands, almost afraid to open it to look at the contract that she says is in here. I can't possibly read a contract when I haven't even digested what she just told me. As I think about the people on her account that I have shopped for in the last year I suppose it makes sense. There are girls I dress for formal and business casual events, men who are dressed in suits and fitted tuxes and of course the gentleman that was shopping for a business trip the other day and needed clothes for his "girlfriend."

"Ma'am, is this the correct address?" The cab driver pulls me from my thoughts.

"Yes," I confirm after glancing out the window at the graffiti covered building in front of me.

I thank the cab driver and head up the steps to the entrance of my building just as the cab pulls away. There is a guy drunk or high leaning against the door, he's passed out and doesn't even move as I approach him. I cringe at the thought of stepping near him but as I clear my throat to get his attention, he doesn't even flinch. My hand grips the knife in my purse fiercely as I take a step forward, prepared to defend myself if this low life suddenly moves.

I quickly rush through the door, closing and locking it behind me the moment I enter the stairwell. The door is supposed to be locked at all times, residents are the only ones who should have a key but of course the door is rarely locked and I've seen people who don't live here entering the building without bothering to ring a bell. Other than a few derogatory comments thrown at me when I first moved in here almost a year ago for the most part whoever is outside leaves me alone. I still carry the knife in my purse at all times though, because I can never be too careful.

I quickly enter my apartment, shutting and locking the deadbolt behind me as I turn on the lights. It's nearly ten o'clock, I'm not sure where the night went but I guess I was at the restaurant a lot longer than I thought. I'm too tired right now to think about what Bridget said or to even consider reading the contract. I have a full day tomorrow, working both jobs so I need to get to bed soon.

I know I need to find a couple of hours tomorrow to review the information that Bridget sent me and to really process what she told me. My initial thought during dinner was that she was crazy, that there was no way in hell I would consider her offer, that I have too much pride to do what she is suggesting. But as I sit in my crappy apartment in this shitty neighborhood with no real future ahead of me, I have to admit that I would be crazy to not at least consider her offer.

Despite the neighbors loud arguing next door, I quickly manage to fall asleep, vowing to focus things tomorrow in whatever spare time I might have. I sleep soundly until the alarm buzzing wakes me up several hours later. I'm thankful whenever I sleep through the night… my nightmares have become fewer but when they hit, they usually prevent me from going back to sleep. On days like today where I have to work both jobs, I'm thankful when I do sleep through the night.

"Good Morning, Kenzie," Ginny greets me as soon as I walk through the back door of the bakery.

"Morning."

The morning passes by slowly, unlike most mornings in the bakery. I can't seem to focus; my mind constantly wanders back to the conversation with Bridget last night. The one thing that continues to stick in my head is the amount of money she was offering to pay me for a couple of hours' worth of work. Today I will bust my ass, work 12 plus hours and by the time the day is done, I will have earned around $150 before taxes. Around $150 for 12 hours of work… whereas Bridget is offering me almost 5 times that amount per hour. Am I stupid for not agreeing to it right away?

I could work only a few nights a month and have all my current bills covered. Add in a few more days and I would be able to afford a small apartment in a decent area of New York. But what type of job security is there in this type of… business? Would there be enough work to cover my rent every month? What happens if business slows down? Does this type of business slow down?

As the morning wears on, I realize I have far more questions than I thought was possible. The more questions I have the more I realize that I'm actually at least half way considering this offer. I have to admit the thought of not struggling as much financially is what is driving me to at least think about this and not just say hell no to Bridget. I've always wanted to go back to college; I looked into taking online classes years ago but I was *forbidden* from doing so. What if this job could pay enough to allow me to begin taking classes again? Bridget said some of her staff were paying their way through college by working for her. Could I do something like that?

"I'll see you tomorrow, Kenzie," Ginny calls as I punch out for the day.

"Have a good day, Ginny."

A subway and bus ride later, I'm back in my crappy apartment eating a bowl of instant noodles cooked on a hot plate for lunch. Not the healthiest option, but when you only have a few extra bucks to spare, crappy food always wins over healthy food. As I wait for my food to cool, I decide to make a list of questions for Bridget.

1) Safety:
   a. How will my safety be ensured?
   b. What kind of background checks are performed on the clients?
   c. Will *dates* always occur in public places?
   d. What options do I have if something happens on a date?
2) Communication:
   a. I don't want clients knowing where I live... how is that handled?
   b. How are the dates set up? Does the client call me directly?
3) Pay:
   a. How many hours per week is typical?
   b. Are there times during the year when business slows down?
   c. Can most girls maintain an average number of hours?
4) Publicity:
   a. How will reporters/press not tie me back to your company?
   b. How do I respond if I'm approached outside of a date and asked how I met someone I was seen with?
5) Clothing:
   a. I don't believe I can shop where I work. Are there other options?
6) Control:
   a. Will I be able to refuse a date?

As I look over my list of questions I'm satisfied that I have covered most of the key areas. Question one is a big one for me, I need to ensure that no matter what happens I will be safe at all times. I can't see myself going to some stranger's house to meet him for dinner no matter how clean his background check is. I know all too well, things can get left off background checks and sometimes not everything is reported to authorities, even when it should be. I could never trust someone so completely, that I would take them at their word that the person I'm meeting wouldn't hurt me. Could I ever go to someone's house alone even, if we went out several times?

I don't know… I need Bridget to realize that I have more trust issues than most people do and that's not something I'm willing to compromise on. Dates in public places I can deal with, there are options. If I felt threated I would have no problem making a scene to ensure my safety. Given what Bridget has told me about her clients, they would probably be on their best behavior in public because they wouldn't want to make a scene. Unfortunately, people can put on a great front in public and become the devil in the privacy of their own home as I've learned.

I don't know much about contracts but it seems pretty straight forward to me. The contract addresses my communication question: it specifically states all requests for dates must go through Bridget and prohibits staff and clients from setting up their own dates. I like this idea actually—it gives me the opportunity to say no without worrying about hurting the other person's feelings.

The contract further states that an addendum will be signed for every date. A sample addendum is attached to the contract which again seems pretty straight forward. The addendum lists the rate per hour for the date, the expected length of the date with a note that this may vary, but if it is going to exceed an additional hour the client is obligated to inform the agency of the change.

It also requires me to list what physical contact I am agreeable to. The options are pretty neutral which is what I would expect since the contract prohibits any sexual contact. Those include: hand holding, kiss on the cheek, kiss on the lips, hand wrapped around waist, hand on hip and dancing. I prefer no kissing on the lips, however I could see if a client is trying to show that we are romantically linked they may feel this is necessary. I decide to discuss that with Bridget and determine if it's something that can be changed after meeting with a client.

While working at the store, I can't help but look at the clients on Bridget's contract differently. With my mind somewhat more focused on work than it was this morning, the night goes by faster than I expected. When I'm on break I decide to call Bridget and see if she is willing to meet again to discuss her proposition.

"Good evening, Kenzie," she answers on the first ring.

"Hi Bridget… I hope I have caught you a good time?"

"Of course, I'm just in between meetings so I have a few minutes."

"I was wondering if you would be available to meet to discuss… things further?"

"Let's see, I'm free around eight tonight?"

"Oh, I'm working right now so tonight won't work."

"Ten tomorrow morning?"

"Sorry… working at the bakery tomorrow morning and the store in the evening."

"Okay, how about we meet for lunch at one tomorrow? I'll text you the address of a place as soon as I get a reservation scheduled."

"Thank you, I appreciate your flexibility with my schedule."

"I look forward to our meeting. Have a good night, Kenzie."

I feel relieved when I leave work at the end of my shift. I am confident that if Bridget can answer my questions to my satisfaction and guarantee my safety then I will try this whole earn-money-for-pretending-to-be-someone's-date thing. There are weeks when I work more than 60 hours like some of her customers do and during those weeks there is no way I could find the time to date even if I wanted to.

The next morning I wake up to my phone ringing which is odd because my alarm is set for four in the morning so the idea that someone is calling before that awful hour is concerning.

"Hello?"

"Kenzie? Dear, it's Ginny. Is everything okay?"

"Hmmm… what time is it?"

"Almost six dear… you're always here—"

"SHIT! Ginny, I'm so sorry, I overslept I'll be there as soon as possible."

I glance at my alarm clock and immediately realize why it didn't go off… apparently I have no power. I quickly wash up in the bathroom sink before throwing on clothes and heading to the bakery. Since my building the only ones without power I assume that once again the landlord didn't pay the electric bill. He does this a few times a year, leaving us without electric for a few days before paying the bill again. It makes for a difficult few days as there is no hot water to shower with and no way to cook a hot meal but considering he doesn't live in the building, I don't think he cares very much.

Chapter 7
Kenzie

"I have a reservation with Ms. Wilder," I inform the server when I enter the Italian restaurant Bridget texted me the details for earlier this morning. I had enough time to run back to my apartment and change into something more suitable for a place like this after my shift ended at the bakery this morning. Of course the electricity was still turned off at the apartment, not that I expected anything different. I had already left a voice mail for the landlord about it, but I don't expect to hear back from him anytime soon.

Luckily I'm more prepared than I was the first time the building lost electricity for three straight days when the landlord chose not to pay his bill once before. Now I have several candles, a flashlight with extra batteries, instant coffee (which tastes gross but at least will give me my caffeine fix until I can get to a store), canned tuna fish, bottled water and frozen bread. It doesn't make for the most appetizing meals, but there's only so much you can prepare without electricity.

"Yes, she is in our private dining room already," he leads towards the back of the main area to a much smaller room than the one we met in the other day.

"Kenzie, so nice to see you again," she greets me the moment I walk in.

"You too, Bridget. Thank you for squeezing me in, my schedule was tight today."

Unlike our last meeting, we both spend a few minutes looking over the menu before placing our orders with the wait staff. I feel much more at ease today than I did the last meeting.

"You had some questions?" Bridget starts as we wait for our meal to be served.

"I did. My first question may seem simple but it's a deal breaker for me. I need to know that I will be safe on these *dates*. I mean no offense, but I can't just take your word that these men aren't dangerous and won't hurt me."

"Kenzie... " She sits back in her chair, clearly caught off guard. I've thought a lot about this over the last day and a half, my safety absolutely must be my first priority. I may not live in the safest of areas, but those are dangers I can handle. I cannot and will not be put in danger by Bridget's offer. I will not allow the past to repeat itself.

"I can certainly understand your reservations about the natural risk involved when you meet someone you don't know. If anything, the way I handle things puts you in a much safer position than if you met some random guy on the street or online and decided to go on a date with him. I do not advertise my services, meaning the average Joe on the street cannot walk into my office and request a date with one of my staff. Clients are by referral only and their net worth must be over five million dollars or I won't even speak to them. All clients go through the same background checks as my staff, and I expect nothing less of them because they have a ton of money."

"I won't agree to meet someone in a private setting," I note. "I don't mind meeting someone in a room like this, but it absolutely must be in a public setting. I won't agree to dates in someone's apartment or in their office after everyone has left."

"Is this firm or is it something you are willing to negotiate after you have a few dates with someone?"

"I'm not sure. I guess for now its firm but maybe later I would feel comfortable negotiating?"

"That's fine. I only ask because sometimes clients ask for someone to accompany them on a business trip. For example, I believe you met Mr. Thompson the other day?" I nod remembering meeting him. "He was picking up clothes for the woman that I arranged to accompany him on a trip to the Virgin Islands. This is not unusual, but I will say that very rarely will these trips be a *first* meeting. Typically both parties have met each other several times before hand and feel comfortable enough with each other to go on a trip like this. We insist clients reserve suites at the hotel and provide us with confirmation of the reservation. Each suite must have at minimum two separate bedrooms and bathrooms giving each person their privacy."

"I hadn't considered business trips. I suppose that's something I would be willing to consider later, but I think other than those, I would prefer meetings to occur in public places."

"Perfectly understandable."

"How much control do I have?"

"You have complete control. You may decline a request once it's presented to you. You can terminate the contract at any point and walk away without any repercussions. I will not force you to go on a date or to a social event; you need to decide if the person requested your company is a potential match for you in a social situation. You have the *final say*."

"What are my options if something goes wrong during a date?"

"I am available at all times to both my clients and my staff. I have never received a call that something was wrong on a date or that the client acted inappropriately. But in the event something like that does happen, you simply call me and I will handle the situation even if it means I come to where you are."

"Good."

"What other questions do you have?"

"I don't want clients knowing where I live; I prefer to have that private—"

"Clients are not given your address, phone number and key information is blacked out of your background check that is given to them. Typically both parties agree to meet at a certain location, sometimes it's even my office if it is an event that the client wants to arrive with the *date* to. They will not pick you up at home or drop you off there at the end of the evening. Not only does it protect your privacy but it saves the chance of lines getting blurred especially at the end of the night."

"Thank you. I appreciate you settling my fears. When we met you mentioned that some of your staff are only working for you and not working other jobs. I'm trying to wrap my head around the financial aspect of this now that you answered my questions about safety. To be honest Bridget, I need to know if this is something I can steadily rely on to pay my rent every month or if this is something that will provide me only with spending money."

"That makes sense, especially given what I know about your current financial situation." Why do I get the feeling her background check likely included my bank account balances? "Let me put it this way, I have a long waiting list of potential clients—more than I can accept right now because I don't have enough staff. Staff decide how many events or dates they want to attend per week, some decide to only attend one and some attend two to three. It also depends on the requests; some of my clients have a standing arrangement with a staff member in that they request that staff for every event they attend. Many of those staff average two events per week, often bringing in close to five thousand dollars a month depending on the type of event. What it boils down to Kenzie, is how much you earn and how often you work is complete up to you. For some staff, this is simply spending money to pay off a few bills. For others though this is how they pay all their bills. What is it you want?"

"I don't know," I admit honestly. "I like the idea of not working so many long hours but I'm nervous to suddenly give it all up. I enjoy the bakery where I work and I could probably continue working there while I figure this out. If I signed the contract, though I don't think I could continue working at the store. I think it would be awkward to dress men and women who are essentially my coworkers or men who I could end up on a date with. However, giving that job up is a little frightening to me."

"Understandably so. I don't normally do this but I'll make you a deal. If you sign a contract with me and then find it isn't for you for whatever reason, I will give you a glowing recommendation at one of the many stores I have accounts with or companies I do business with. I will guarantee you a job within two weeks of you terminating your contract with me."

"Why would you do that?"

"I want to help you. I can tell you haven't had an easy life and for whatever reason you don't trust easily. You remind me of myself when I was younger and I guess that makes me want to see you succeed. I promise if this doesn't work out for whatever reason, I will ensure you have a job and are not left on the street. Why don't you try one dinner date with a client and see how it goes? If you decide after that date it isn't for you, we terminate the contract and never look back. If you decide this isn't as scary as the thoughts going through your head right now, then I will show your profile to other clients for potential dates. What do you say?"

"One date... I... I suppose I can agree to that."

"Good, I really think you will see this isn't as bad as you are thinking Kenzie. What other questions do you have?"

"How will I not be tied back to your company? I mean, if I'm photographed with a date and the press runs a background check on me won't they see that I'm on your payroll?"

"They might. However, if they look into my company they will see that we are a consultation firm working with large and small companies across the state. You will be listed as a consultant which is a very broad title. In all the years since I started this company up, I've never had a reporter question exactly what it is someone does for me or what exactly consultation services we provide."

We talk for another hour or so as we finish our lunch and at the end I have decided to stick to our agreement and try one date through Bridget, figuring I don't have much to lose. I won't quit one of my jobs until I'm sure this is going to work out.

"Thank you again for squeezing me in, Bridget, and for answering my many questions. I appreciate the time you took."

"I have to admit I was surprised to hear from you. I was worried I scared you off with the contract the other night. I'm glad that wasn't the case and that you decided to give this a chance. I don't think you're going to regret it. I'll be in touch soon with a potential dinner scheduled and a profile for you to approve."

Madison Quinn

The next few days go by slowly; the electricity remains off in my building but I hardly notice because I end up working even more hours than originally scheduled. Bathing is the most inconvenience of all: while I have water in my apartment, I don't have hot water. I wash my hair using gallons of water that I let get to room temperature before using. It's better than trying to shampoo my hair in the shower which now lasts less than a minute as I quickly wash before I freeze too much. I'm getting tired of eating tuna fish sandwiches for meals, but I would live with it if it meant being able to take a hot shower again. I think the longest we went without electricity was nine days—if it doesn't go longer this time it should be turned back on in the next few days.

Chapter 8
Nicholas

"Mr. Parker, may I have a moment?" Melody knocks on my door.

"Quickly."

"I have a Mrs. Bridget Wilder on the line requesting a meeting with you to discuss an upcoming charity gala you are attending, how would you like me to handle the call, sir?"

"Bridget Wilder?" I pause surprised that she would be calling to request a meeting with me. "I believe she sits on the board with my mother for the charity; she probably wants to solicit a donation for the event. Squeeze her in where you can but for no more than half an hour. I don't want to get trapped listening to how much some charity needs my donation for hours on end."

"Yes sir."

Usually my mother handles the requests for this charity since she's on the board but I know she has been very busy lately with another one that she's trying to raise money for. I think it's odd that Bridget would request a personal meeting with me to discuss the donation though, typically a phone is all that is needed, given that I regularly donate to most of the charities my mother is sitting on the board, for including the one that I am scheduled to attend next.

My thoughts are quickly diverted as my outlook calendar alerts me to another meeting that is starting in a few minutes in the board room. My day is filled with meetings, conference calls and reviewing reports just like every other day. I love what I do; I love analyzing trends in the market, helping companies succeed and even trying to predict what the market will do next. As is the case most days, before I know it the sun has set and I'm the last person in the building besides Carter. I leave PFS, return home for a late dinner and then spend a few more hours in my office. This routine is what my life consists of lately; the only change is when I have an event or business dinner to attend. It may seem boring, but the long hours are what have made PFS the success that it is. It wouldn't be anywhere near as successful if I only worked the typical eight hour day that most employees in America work. Instead, I average ten to twelve hours in the office each day plus another three to five hours per night at home.

As is the case most nights, sleep doesn't come easy for me. When I finally manage to fall asleep, I find my thoughts focusing on the beautiful brunette with the stunning eyes Carter and I met on the street months ago. Only this time I don't picture her as she was that day on the sidewalk, instead she is standing naked in front of me, her hands bound behind her back with a simple red piece of silk. She's waiting for me, her body is calling out, begging for my touch. Her nipples are hardened as the anticipation of what is about to happen arouses her even further.

I take a step towards her, not able to keep myself from touching her for another moment, but the space between us increases. Another step towards her, yet she is further away than she was moments ago. I quickly take three steps forward, my hand reaching out to touch her but again she remains just out of reach. Frustrated, I run to her but this time she completely disappears and I'm left standing in a cold dark room with a dirty mattress on the floor in the corner of the room.

It's nearly three in the morning and I find myself wide awake. I contemplate going for a run, but I really don't want to wake Carter up. I shouldn't give a fuck... I pay him to be available when I need him, but even I'm not that cold hearted to wake him up in the middle of the night and pull him from the warm bed he shares with his woman.

I've never experienced what he has—I've never slept in the same bed with a woman. My nightmares have always prevented me from being able to do that. I remember once when I was little, my parents took us somewhere... to this day I can't remember where we were going or why but we were in a hotel room and Austin and I had to share a bed because there were only two beds in the room with my parents taking the other one. I don't remember the nightmare that night and can only assume it's a variation of the one I have every night. What I do remember is waking up to find Austin wrapped in my mom's arms crying and my dad rushing into the room with a bag of ice.

Apparently during my nightmare I had given him a black eye and nearly broke his nose when he tried to wake me up. Both of my parents were quick to tell me that it wasn't my fault and Austin forgot what happened, instead making up stories that he would later tell his friends about how he was injured. I have never forgotten that day or the way my parents looked at me when I woke up. They weren't angry but their eyes were filled with pity though. Since that day, I have vowed to never give them a reason to look at me like that again. That was the last time I ever slept in the same bed with someone. Every trip after that my parents made sure to reserve a room with an extra pull out bed or a rollaway for me.

"I'd like to leave in ten minutes for a run," I notify Carter a little before five which is what I have decided is an okay time to wake him.

"Yes sir, I'm ready when you are," he responds quickly, obviously knowing my preference for early morning runs.

Our run pattern varies from day to day; Carter insists that I don't run the same route regularly, as he is afraid it puts me at risk. Any pattern we take has us running past Sweet Dreams Bakery recently. Carter started this after he learned who the beautiful woman was that we inadvertently drenched and where she works. I haven't gone into the bakery, but I find myself glancing at the window every day hoping to get a glimpse of her. A few times I have seen her at the register, other times she either isn't working or is in the back.

Carter purposely slows down when we approach the bakery knowing that I'm going to look for her but he doesn't say anything. It's one of the things I appreciate the most about him: he keeps his opinions to himself unless I specifically ask him about it. Like now, as I barely get a glimpse of her brunette hair through the window of the bakery, I'm sure Carter is wondering what the hell is wrong with me and why I don't just go inside. We would have a convenient excuse for going in: we could need bottled water, a cup of coffee or even breakfast but of course we never go in.

I don't know anything about her, but I know I could never be what she needs. The way she looked at me that day with her big, innocent brown eyes, I knew that I was no good for her. She is the type of woman who wants to bring a guy home to her parents, who wants and expects to be romanced by a guy and one who expects long term commitments when she goes out. She wants everything I can never give her. The only thing I can offer her is a fantastic, hard fuck one night and maybe a call when I need a release again. One look at her and I know that she would never settle for something like that, so why even bother?

"Sir?" Carter pulls me from my thoughts when we somehow end up back in the foyer of the condo. How we ended up here, I have no clue. Apparently I let my thoughts of Ms. Rose distract me for the last three miles of our run.

"We'll leave for PFS in twenty. Can you ask Julie to have my breakfast ready in ten?" I request.

A quick shower and even quicker breakfast has me at PFS long before most of my employees. I'm typically the first person here but every so often someone will beat me to it, like today. Alex works nearly as hard as I do, putting in close to the same number of hours I do at PFS. Minutes after I arrive, he barges into my office setting a cup of coffee in front of me before he sits down. We don't have a standing appointment, but this has been our routine for the last year or two when we are both in the office at the same time.

"You did it again, Parker," he sighs.

"Who did I piss off this time?"

"No one in particular... except a few reporters," he tosses the latest gossip magazine on my desk.

"UGH... what bullshit is it this time?"

"You're on page three."

I thumb through the first few pages before I find a picture of myself taken just two nights ago at a benefit at the local children's hospital. The headline reads **"What is the billionaire playboy hiding?"** I quickly skim the story speculating yet again that I am hiding something related to my sexuality which is the reason I can't keep a woman. The reporter goes further than most, hinting that my last relationship with *her* was simple a façade designed to keep the dogs off my trail so I can keep my secret hidden. While *she* provided no comment to the press regarding our relationship, the reporter goes so far to state it is because I must have bought her silence, likely coming with a hefty price tag since she has refused to comment on anything after our breakup more than two years ago.

"Damned if I do, damned if I don't," I sigh in frustration.

"We need to discuss the shipping company," he quickly recognizes that I'm done discussing this garbage. "I'm hitting a brick wall with them; I think they might respond better to you. Maybe you can set up a dinner or something to wine and dine them? We've been at a stale mate for the last couple of weeks over this, they always seem to respond better to you—"

"I'll call them and if they are agreeable, I'll have Melody arrange something at The Summit in a couple of weeks. I want you there though; you were responsible for bringing it this far, just because they want to be a pain in the ass at the end doesn't mean your work isn't recognized. I want it known to them that you were responsible for everything until this point."

"Thank... thank you Nicholas. I appreciate that," he is clearly surprised—I don't give out compliments often but in this case Alex has done everything on this including going above and beyond what they have asked for.

"I'll read this over but I'm sure you have everything aligned."

"Mr. Parker, your eight o'clock is here," Melody interrupts us a short time later.

"Let me know if you need anything else," Alex says as he leaves my office.

"Mrs. Wilder it's nice to see you again," I greet her as Melody closes the door.

"It's Bridget, but it's nice to see you as well, Nicholas," she shakes my offered hand before sitting in the gestured chair.

Since we were old enough to understand, my mother has brought us to various charity events and insisted that we find ways to give back to the community. Since I'm usually too busy, my giving back tends to be in the way of a large donation check. My parents organize various events, even hosting a few at their house. I've known Bridget for several years through those events and meetings with my mother.

"I understand you wanted to talk with me about a donation for the New Beginnings Gala next weekend? I've already confirmed my donation with my mother, but if there is something else that you need—"

"Actually, this isn't about that gala at all," she hands me a folder and when I open, it I see if contains a non-disclosure agreement. My interest is immediately sparked as to what Bridget could want to discuss that would require we both sign an NDA. I quickly review the document which is pretty standard, and then present her with one of my own NDAs. Although these are usually reciprocal, I don't take anything for granted, and insist that whenever I sign an NDA the other party signs one of mine as well.

"Now that we have that out of the way, what's this meeting really about, Bridget?" I ask.

"I've seen the tabloids and the numerous articles written about you, Nicholas." I cringe. "I've known you long enough that I don't believe any of the things that have been written about you. I know the constant focus on your personal life must be getting to you and I'd like to offer a possible solution."

"I'm listening."

"We know each other in the charity circuit, but we probably know very little about each other on a personal level." I nod in agreement. "As you probably know, I run a successful consulting business targeting large corporations through the tri-state area. What you likely don't know, is that my consulting services specifically target men and women in your current situation."

"I'm sorry, I'm not following," I have no idea what she is talking about. If this is a sales call I will kick her out of my office in the next two minutes and without a concern that she is a friend of my mother. I do not accept sales visits and to do so under the disguise of a charity event is just wrong.

"I'd like to help you with your media problem—"

"I already have a full public relations department, Bridget," I point out.

"I'm sure you do," she agrees. "But I can offer you something they can't. You see, my client list consists of many, highly successful men and women who are often publically criticized for their personal lives or lack thereof. These are men and women who don't have time to date, or don't want to date, but find themselves needing someone to accompany them to charity events, business dinners, award ceremonies, etc... That is where I can help you... "

"Help me how?"

"Between us and the NDAs that we both signed, my consultation business essentially arranges for acceptable dates men and women who need someone to be by their side in the public eye."

"You're a match maker?" I can't help but laugh.

"No, my goal is not love, romance and wedding bells. Essentially, I would provide you with a woman who would attend all your events with you to get the media off your ass. She would expect absolutely nothing in terms of romance. The only contact you would have with her would be on these prearranged dates. You wouldn't have to worry about her wanting you to call her the next day, or that she is going to start calling you every hour and demanding your attention. Think of it as a business transaction: you pay for her to accompany you to a dinner, gala or whatever else you might need her for your business."

"What does she get out of it?"

"A paycheck," she answers simply. "The fee you pay to me covers her clothing for the event, her hourly pay and of course overhead charges associated with my services."

"How would this be any different than what I'm doing now? I've taken women to events and the media still rips me apart… "

"You've taken *women* to these events. What I would propose in your situation is that you require an exclusive agreement be signed—"

"An exclusive agreement?"

"I'll back up… if you agree to my services one of the first things I would do is provide you with a profile of a woman that I think would be a good match for you. This is someone that I think would fit the look you want in the public eye but also that I think you could talk to. While it seems trivial since we're not talking about love and romance, having a common ground to talk to someone about is important, seeing that events are sometimes long and boring." I nod in agreement.

"Assuming you were interested in the profile I provide you, I would schedule a private date for the two of you to meet. I recommend, especially with you being in the media's eye right now, that this date occur somewhere private and away from the press. Think of the dinner as a get-to-know-you meeting. You are not charged for this first meeting. If you find that this woman is someone you could see yourself attending events with, then I would recommend you insist on an exclusivity agreement. Essentially this means that this woman would not be available to any other clients. This would prevent her from being seen with someone else at other events, which would of course reflect negatively on you in the press."

"Mr. Parker, your nine o'clock is here—" Melody interrupts us.

"Ask Alex to meet with them," I quickly dismiss her.

"What type of women does this sort of thing? How do I know I can trust them not to run to the press?"

"All staff sign the same NDA you signed; if they dare say a word to the press, I will destroy them legally and personally. They are paid very well for their silence. In the twenty years I have been running this business I have never had a staff member go to the press with a story. As for the type of women who do this, you would be surprised. I have a few attending graduate school, students in medical or law school, single parents and I have a few who are down on their luck and just want to better their lives. They all go through a very extensive background check including information that comes with a very hefty price tag. They will stand up to any media scrutiny, so if you are concerned that the skeletons in their closets would be found out, don't be. If I can't find the skeletons, no one can."

"I would insist on my own background check."

"Prior to the first meeting, I will release only very basic information to protect their personal information from being known to anyone who requests a first meet with them. If you both decided this arrangement would work for you, I would then provide you with the full background checks that I completed; most clients find my checks to be more than they need."

"I would need to have my security team review your information, I may still need to run my own checks."

"If mine are not sufficient, we can discuss it at that time. There is protected information in the background check that my clients usually prefer their clients not have access."

"What sort of protected information? If the press can obtain the information then I need to be able to."

"Mostly, their address and contact information including their emergency contact. Most of my staff prefer this information to be kept confidential so they have some privacy. It also keeps this arrangement more formal and prevents clients from being able to see or contact them outside of the agreed upon times."

"That wouldn't be an issue with me, I guarantee that. I can agree that if I need to run my own background checks, my security team will exclude her address and contact information in the final report that I receive."

"I think I can agree to that."

"What are the expectations at the end of the... evening if we attend an event together?"

"The end of the evening?" she looks confused. I do really not want to spell it out to her but if I have to, I will. "OH! There is a clause in the contract that both parties sign indicating there will be no intimacy between the client and staff member. Any physical signs of affection, such as hand holding, kissing, dancing, etc... are agreed upon and noted in the contract. It is expected those signs of affection would only be shown when other people are present, since this would likely be for appearances only."

"So how would this work? I would pick her up at her house, bring her to dinner then drop her off at the curb at the end of the night?" I can't help but think it all seems rather cold, but at the same time I find myself considering the proposition.

"You would never pick her up at home or drop her off there. Assuming you needed to show up together at an event, you would have a prearranged meeting location where you would pick her up. This could be my office, your office or any other public place. You would drop her off at the same location at the end of the night. If arriving together is not as important, she could meet you there."

"I see."

"The arrangements don't have to only include charity events and business dinners: if you wanted companionship—"

"That won't be necessary," I interrupt quickly.

"I understand. This is a sample contract including a price list for your review. As I stated, any clothing and accessories that are required for an event are at your expense. I would send you a bill which would include the receipt from the store where everything was purchased. These items do not come cheap, as anyone seen with you would be expected to wear certain things—"

"The cost wouldn't be an issue," I get what she's trying to say and I know she's right. The media expects that if I'm seen in a high end designer tux, then my date for the evening is also seen in an equally high end gown.

"Do you have any other questions, Nicholas?"

"How would the women not be tied to you if the press dug into them? Certainly their financial history would show you as their employer? How would they not tie me to you? I would expect questions would be raised."

"Yes they would. And if they dug into my business, they would see that we are a consulting agency providing a variety of services to successful businesses up and down the east coast. All of those companies will verify my relationship with them should anyone ask. As far as your relationship with me, it could be played off as a business relationship."

"I don't want PFS to be tied to your services," I quickly decide. While it seems like she has thought of everything, I can't risk PFS's reputation on finding a solution for my personal life.

"Normally I don't give clients another option," she pauses as she thinks. "However, since you and I have known each other for so long, I will provide you with an option I don't give other clients. I have an off shore bank account set up. If you decide to sign the contract and we go further with this arrangement, you would transfer funds into that account. Since it is an off shore account, you're aware that it is nearly impossible to track any money in and out of such an account. Even the account holder information is held in confidence."

"That would be acceptable."

"So tell me, are you interested in signing a contract with me? If so, I have a profile of a woman available right now for you to review…"

"I'd like to have my security team run their checks on your company. No offense, but I need to be sure that any information about what you really do is truly buried. If it checks out, I will sign the contract but I'm only agreeing to the initial meeting. If I don't like how it feels, our contract is terminated at that moment."

"Of course, I'll leave you with this file to review as I'm sure when your team performs their review, you will sign the contract. This young woman is newly signed to my company as well and has not yet met with anyone. I warn you though, I expect her to be signed to an exclusivity contract very quickly as she is a natural beauty that I think will appeal to most of my clients. You will note the file does not include a photo or any identifying information. Her basic physical description is provided, however the other information is kept confidential until your first meeting. This is protection for both of you, neither of you can have preconceived notions of the other or start searching online for one another. Her background check is included in the file for your review as well."

"Thank you, I will review the file and will be in touch."

"I appreciate your time, Nicholas and I look forward to doing business with you."

HOLY FUCK is the only thing I can think when she leaves my office. I need to have Asher dig into this because if anyone can find anything *he* can. This almost seems too good to be true; it's the perfect solution for getting my press off my ass about my personal life. I read through the contract expecting to find a catch, but everything seems very cut and dry. The prices are high, higher than I initially thought, but given the arrangement, I can't say I'm surprised. On one hand I can't believe I'm considering this, but on the other hand the thought of having the focus back on the success of PFS and off my sex life is very appealing.

Madison Quinn

I could be seen with a beautiful woman in public, one that wouldn't expect romance being with me. I wouldn't have to worry about her developing feelings for me after accompanying me to a few events.

After reviewing the contract for the third time, I decide to take a look at the profile Bridget provided me. Although there is no picture of the woman, I can at least learn about the type of women who would do something like this. I can only image what Bridget must pay them for their services which just reinforces to me that they are money hungry like most women I meet. Although, for once I don't care; the expectations of the evening are laid out in the contract. Hell, it even says that they cannot request I pay for anything outside of the actual date itself and the items I reimburse Bridget for. I don't have to buy gifts or feel pressured to do so.

Chapter 9
Kenzie

"Hello?" I answer the phone that is waking me up on a rare day that I have off from both of my jobs.

"Good morning, Kenzie, this is Bridget. How are you?"

"Oh hi, I'm good. And you?"

"Very good, thank you. I'm calling because I have a profile for you to review. If you're going to be home today, I'll have a courier service bring it to you."

"Yes, I'll be home today."

"Wonderful, it will arrive in the next hour. Now, just so you're not surprised, the profile won't contain any identifying information meaning there will be no picture. At this point, you are just reviewing the information to see if he is someone you would like to meet. If you agree to meet him, when I call you back with the date arrangements, I will provide you with his full name. He has reviewed the same information on you and would like to meet you if you are interested in meeting him."

"Okay…"

"I'll tell you a little about him if you have a few minutes. Unlike most of my clients, I have known this gentleman for several years now. He is a very successful businessman who works far too many hours and as a result has zero personal life. Because of his success, he is invited to many different events including charity galas, fundraising dinners, political events and then of course, there are the dinners associated with his own business. I do want to let you know however, he is going to require whoever he decides to contract with to sign an exclusivity contract—"

"Why would he insist on this?"

"In his case, he needs someone by his side for publicity. You can't be seen with him in one picture on a website and then a week later be on the arm of another man at a different event—"

"OH! I see… that makes sense."

"I don't know too many specifics about what his commitments will be, but I think it's likely to be at least weekly events with a chance of up to two to three times per week."

"Really? That many?"

"For men who are this successful, this is pretty typical."

"Can I ask… what happened to the last girl he contracted with?"

"Nothing… like you, this will be his first meeting. He is a brand new client to me."

"I see."

"Once you review the profile, give me a call or text me to let me know if you are interested in scheduling a meeting. Be sure to look over your schedule, because I expect the meeting to occur this week."

"Thank you, I'll call you later."

I decide to wait around for the courier before heading to the laundromat a few blocks away. I pack everything up, and once the courier arrives, I throw the large envelope into my bag and head out. I hate walking there, especially carrying a large bag of clothes but there isn't really another option, considering my building doesn't have its own washer and dryer. It's a pain, but at least the weather is nice today.

After I throw the clothes into the washer, I take the file out of the envelope and discreetly begin reviewing it. There isn't much to review though; like Bridget, said there was no identifying information, only his initials NP. Other than that, it's basic information: he works in the financial industry as a manager, he enjoys spending time on his boat and he lives in Manhattan. There is really no information about him as a person which is kind of disappointing. I don't know what I expected but I guess more along the lines of his likes, dislikes, favorite foods, etc…

There's actually more information about the type of woman he is looking for: someone who can attend social events and business dinners, must be comfortable meeting new people, must be able to remember key players, must have an open mind in business and politics, must be willing to sign an exclusivity contract, must be willing to be photographed and be available evenings and weekends when needed. I think I meet most of those requirements.

I decided a few days after meeting with Bridget that if I agreed to this arrangement, I would stop working at the store after the first date. I enjoy working at the bakery the most and if I had to choose a job to keep, hands down it's the bakery. Plus, I don't like the idea of interacting with coworkers or former dates while at the store. I think it would be awkward and uncomfortable for both of us. It's risky with the bakery because I don't know what's going to happen after the sale of the business, but I'm confident that if I don't stay on with the new owners, that I can find another job at another bakery, especially with Ginny's recommendation. Besides, the hours at the bakery are less likely to conflict with events that I would be requested to attend. I see very few business deals being done at five or six in the morning.

Taking a deep breath, I send Bridget a text message saying I agree to meet NP; I'd be lying if I said I wasn't nervous. I still can't help but question if I'm making the right decision and if I can trust Bridget whom I barely know. She has addressed all of my concerns and I have insisted that all meetings occur in public so I think there's less chance of getting hurt. I know if I ever want to improve my life, I need to make some changes and the only way to do that is to earn more money. I hate that I'm working so many hours and barely making ends meet.

I would love to be able to go back to school, afford a nicer place and maybe take a trip or something one day. Right now my focus is always on working enough hours to pay my bills and then to put a little money aside in the event that one day I might need to leave quickly or if one of my jobs fell through, I would have a safety net at least for a little while. I cross my fingers and hope that for once I have met someone I can trust.

He wants to meet you, tonight 6pm at The Summit. Reservation will be in my name. Go to Stacy's on Third, she will provide you with everything you need for tonight. It will be charged to my account. Good Luck, Kenzie. –Bridget

Holy crap! I didn't expect anything to happen so fast! I quickly throw my clothes into the bag and head back to my apartment. I only have a couple of hours to find something to wear for tonight and then get ready. Of course, The Summit is nowhere near where I live, so I will need to transfer routes to get over to that area of the city. I've never been there, but I saw it advertised in magazines at work; it's one of those places you could only dream of having enough money to eat there.

Less than an hour later, I arrive at Stacy's on Third which is what I expected: a high end, very expensive, boutique. When I mention Bridget's name, I'm immediately assisted by the owner who ushers me into a dressing room and starts throwing dresses at me. It feels very different to be on this side of the dressing room; usually I'm the one finding expensive, beautiful clothes for women who are getting ready for a night on the town.

"Oh that's it! It will be perfect!" Stacy pulls me from my pity party when she steps into the room just as I finish putting on a dark blue dress.

"I'm going to—"

"Bridget told me where you're going when she called me earlier. Rest assured Miss, this dress is perfect! We will pair it with some jewelry and shoes with a small heel but you won't need anything else. I recommend you wear your hair up, have a few pieces fall around your face and curl them. Minimal make up, you're a natural beauty anyway so you don't need that stuff caked on your face."

"Th... thank you," I'm stunned by her compliment.

"Shall I wrap everything up for you?"

"Yes, please."

By the time I'm back to my apartment, I have less than hour before I need to take almost the same trip to head to dinner. If nothing else, I'm grateful that the electricity in the apartment has been turned back on. I don't know how I would manage getting ready without electricity. If I decide to move forward with this arrangement after tonight, I'm probably going to need to come up with a contingency plan for getting ready when the electricity is turned off again at least until I can hopefully afford a new apartment... one at least where the landlord doesn't randomly decide to turn off the power.

I take one final look in the mirror before it's time to leave. I barely recognize the woman staring back at me. On one hand she looks vaguely familiar... she looks like the woman I've been trying so hard to forget used to look like. But, there's something else I see that I never saw in that woman. I'm not sure what it is exactly but it's definitely there and it's different from the woman who let *him* walk all over her. I shake my head, vowing to not think of *him* tonight, to not think of that life again. I may not live in a fancy house and have a lot of material things like I used to, but I'm happier now than I think I have been in my entire life.

"Good Evening, may I help you Miss?" I'm greeted the moment the elevator doors open to the restaurant.

"I'm... I'm meeting someone, the reservation is under Bridget Wilder," I take a deep breath desperately trying to calm my nerves.

"Yes of course, the other party has not yet arrived but I will show you to your private dining area for tonight."

As we walk through the dining room, I try to take everything in. The large dining room is even more stunning than the pictures in the magazines. There are floor to ceiling windows that line two full walls overlooking the city. I wish I could get closer to them to take in the full view but I realize if I don't keep up I'm going to lose my guide to the room. Just before we reach the back corner of the dining room, I take a final peek around the room and send a silent thank you to Stacy who dressed me absolutely perfect for tonight.

"Miss, your other party should be here shortly," he opens the door to the private dining room, ushering me in.

"Thank you."

The private dining room is small with only a handful of circular tables throughout the room, but what captures my attention are the windows along the wall. Just like in the main dining room, the windows line the entire small wall. My feet bring me to them almost instinctively; I gaze out at the beautiful view before me. Being on the top floor, the restaurant sits higher than most buildings providing an unobstructed view. I've never seen the city from this high; it's truly breathtaking. I'm told the view from the nightclub that is part of this restaurant just one floor down is equally stunning. Most likely a view I'll never see, but I try to take in as much from this view as I possibly can, vowing never to forget it.

I'm so lost in my thoughts I don't realize that someone else is in the room with me until they clear their throat. I turn around and am shocked at the man who stands before me. I never expected to see him again... and never in my dreams did I think he would be the man I was meeting tonight. I knew the chances of our paths crossing would be very slim. When he stepped out of the car to personally apologize for soaking me, I knew in that moment I would never see him. I knew right then that we were from two different worlds. I always hoped that sometime we would run into each other again, but I wouldn't have thought of him needing a service like this.

"Umm.... hi," I nervously walk towards him, praying I don't trip over my own feet as my legs suddenly seem weak.

"It's nice to see you again Miss...?"

"Mackenzie... well Kenzie. It's nice to see you again...?"

"Nicholas," he shakes my offered hand. The moment our fingers touch, a jolt of electricity goes through me, almost like static electricity but stronger. The look in his eyes tells me he felt it too.

"Would you like to have a seat?" he gestures me to the table behind me.

"I... I want to thank you again for paying for a new outfit—" I nervously begin.

"Don't... it was the least I could do," he interrupts.

"I'm not sure... how this works exactly. I've never done this before," I admit after an awkward moment of silence.

"Neither do I," he chuckles. "Why don't you tell me about yourself?"

"Okay," I take a deep breath trying to calm my nerves. "I currently work at a bakery in the mornings and for now as a personal shopper in the evening."

"Did you grow up in New York?"

"No, I've lived here for the past two years."

"Where did you grow up?"

"On the west coast; how about you? Did you grow up in New York?"

"I was born in New Jersey, but I've lived in New York most of my life."

"What is it you do?"

"You don't know?"

"Should I?"

"I guess not," he chuckles. "I'm often recognized from the tabloids stories, so I just assumed… Reporters love to try to destroy me whenever they can."

"Sorry, I can't say I read many tabloids."

"I'm the CEO of Parker Financial Services, PFS for short. We are one of the largest companies in the investment and financial management world. We offer not only investment services but financial advice to large businesses seeking to grow or are struggling where they currently are."

"Why would the tabloids have an issue with that?"

"The business articles written about me are typically very on point with what my company does. The tabloids though like to destroy my personal life. I'm sure you will see the articles if you google me and then you'll know what I'm talking about. That's one of the reasons I'm actually meeting you tonight."

"What exactly are you looking for? I mean, I know what your profile told me but… "

"I need someone by my side at events, dinners and probably even just an occasional date to keep the reporters off my ass. Apparently being seen without a date, or with various women at different events, is a sign of my inability to manage the hundreds of people that I currently employ. I've tried everything and my PR department can't think of anything that we haven't tried to throw them off. I don't know if Bridget explained, but I'm going to need someone to sign an exclusivity contract, meaning—"

"She explained. I can't accept dates with other men."

"Exactly. I need the media to think we are a couple so they get off my ass and let me focus on my business."

"I understand."

"Can I ask you something?"

"Of course."

"Why are you doing this? I mean, clearly in my situation I have a problem and this is a perfect solution. If you don't mind me asking, what's in it for you?"

"If I can be honest, it was a hard offer to not consider. As I said, I currently work two jobs most days of the week but despite that, I barely make enough money to pay my bills. I would love to go back to school one day, but I don't want to take out more student loans and live in debt the rest of my life. There are other things I want to do and Bridget's offer seemed like a good way to earn enough money to do those things."

"I see."

"Sir, ma'am, your dinner," the waiter places large plates in front of both of us.

"Bridget must have ordered for us, if you'd prefer something else we can send it back," Nicholas offers.

"No, it's fine. It smells delicious."

We spend the next hour slowly getting to know each other over dinner; the initial awkwardness is now gone. I learn that Nicholas lives and works in Manhattan but that his company takes up most of his time. From the sound of it he often works as many hours as I do when I work both my jobs. He is honest in saying that he doesn't have time to date woman and is not interested in dating at this point of his life because he knows he doesn't have the time. He describes recent events that he has been to, I think to let me know what I can expect if we decide to move forward with this arrangement. Nothing he says about the events raise a concern for me; it sounds a very similar to things I used to attend with *him*.

"Kenzie, I want you to know that sometimes these events can be rather boring. It's a lot of business discussions, contracts being negotiated and spreadsheets are being reviewed. It's not going to be fun—"

"Nicholas, I… I have an idea of what to expect. I… I've been to these types of things before."

"Oh?"

"I can mingle with guests and will not require your undivided attention. I understand that your focus is on these events and not on the company you're with. It's fine."

"They won't all be like that," he quickly explains. "Sometimes these events are just social events that I need to make an appearance at. A charity fundraiser, a hospital dedication or a park unveiling—those types of events would probably be more enjoyable.

Of course I still find them to be a waste of my time, but I'm obligated to attend. The food is usually half way decent, sometimes there's dancing and there's always good drinks."

"It's fine, really."

"I'm going to speak with Bridget tonight, Kenzie, but I want you to know that I'm going to tell her that I would like an exclusivity agreement with you. I wanted to let you know now so you an opportunity to think about it. If you agree, I have a charity event this weekend I would like you to accompany me."

"I…"

"Take the time you need tonight to think about it, I'm sure Bridget will call you tomorrow."

"Thank you."

"Can I walk you to your car?" he asks as we ride the elevator to the main floor. Carter joined us as soon as we left the private dining room. I've confirmed that Carter is not only his driver but his bodyguard as well.

"Oh… I didn't… I took the subway here. There's a stop a couple of blocks away."

"Carter will take you home—"

"No! I mean, that won't be necessary. The subway is fine, I take it often and know the stops and transfers to get home."

"Shit, I'm sorry, I forgot that part," he nods at Carter who immediately flags down a cab. "The cab will take you wherever you need to go."

"Nicholas, that's not—"

"Please, I can't let you get on the subway at this hour of the night. Let the cab take you home. I won't know where you live, but will at least know that you arrived there safely."

"Thank you, I appreciate that."

"Good night, Kenzie," he whispers as he pecks me ever so lightly on the cheek.

"Night, Nicholas."

Chapter 10
Nicholas

"Carter, I want a full background check on Mackenzie Rose first thing tomorrow morning," I request as soon as the car pulls away from the club.

"Sir, we already have a full background check on her. We can review it once we are back at the condo."

"Why do you have a background check on Ms. Rose? I don't recall requesting one."

"You didn't, sir," he confirms. "After I learned her identify at the bakery, I had Asher run a full background check on her. At the time… sir… well, I wasn't sure of your intentions, therefore I thought it would be beneficial to have it ready if you ever decided to make contact with her."

"I see. Were you aware that I was meeting her tonight?"

"Not exactly sir. I attempted to obtain that information from Mrs. Wilder but she refused to provide me with any information. Without knowing who you were meeting tonight, maintaining security measures were going to be difficult. I had Asher monitoring the club's security cameras beginning half an hour before your scheduled meeting. It wasn't until we left PFS, I received a text alerting that Asher identified the woman you would be meeting with after recognizing her from the background report."

Mackenzie was the last woman I expected to be the woman Bridget arranged for me to meet tonight. When I thought about what type of woman might decide to become an escort, I never once pictured Kenzie as that woman. I'm still not entirely sure what I think about her and this situation; everything about her until now has told me she is not interested in money, yet her reason for becoming an escort *was* money. Of course she has dreams which require money and I was pleased to learn it was education related and not something crazy like plastic surgery or to buy a bigger house.

It's still hard to wrap my head around the thought that she is the type of woman who would accept money in exchange for a date. I can't help but wonder if her innocence is all some act, but at the same time that innocence was there the night we met her on the sidewalk after the rain storm. If I believe her, she had no idea who I was that night or even tonight, although I'm sure as soon as she gets home tonight she will be on google, finding out everything she can about me. She will not only learn that I'm one of New York's youngest billionaires but she will also have the opportunity to read everything the media has written about me including when they rake my name through mud over my personal life. Ever since the plan my PR department came up with backfired, I have been attending events solo which of course the media still thinks means I'm hiding something but at least I don't have to hear about why I bring a different woman to each event.

I'm hoping this arrangement with Bridget is the solution to my problems with the media. I hope that once they see I have the same woman attending events with me, they will forget the idea that I'm hiding something and will stop digging into my personal life. Asher has completed full background checks on Bridget's company and as far as they can know, she only provides consultation services to different companies along the east coast. They weren't able to find any trace of her running an escort service or any other type of business. If it was out there, they would have found it. Besides Carter, no one knows about my arrangement with Bridget. Asher believed he was doing a background check for a possible new customer I later changed my mind about. I try to keep my personal life separate from my work life and this is one of those things that no one at PFS needs to know about... hell *no one* needs to know about.

"Carter, my office," I request as we enter the condo.

"Yes, sir."

He disappears into his suite off my condo before coming into my office with a manila folder which I can only assume contains the full background check of Mackenzie Rose. Carter is very good at his job and this is just another example of knowing what I needed before I knew it. I should have known he wouldn't take me past the bakery every day on our run without having completed a full check on her.

"Sir," he hands the folder to me. I quickly take it but before I can open it I am reminded about what Bridget said about certain information needing to remain confidential and my promise not to access the information through the background check. I'm tempted to just say fuck it; that I need to know everything about Mackenzie if I'm going to move forward with this arrangement. Surprisingly though, I hand the file back to Carter electing not to learn the information that Bridget said her staff require remain private.

"I'm not supposed to know her address, phone number and emergency contact information," I sigh. "It's part of the arrangement so we both maintain our privacy."

"I see," his face shows his surprise.

"Tell me what's in the file. I can't know exactly where she lives, but does she live in the city? Does she have any roommates that I need to be concerned will find out about this arrangement?"

"Sir, she lives alone according to the information we were able to obtain. She rents a very small, studio apartment in a less desirable neighborhood—"

"Less desirable meaning what exactly?"

"Let's just say sir, that I would not be comfortable going into that area without being armed—"

"It's that bad?"

"Even with an increase in police presence around that area, the crime remains very high."

"Why the fuck does she live there?"

"Sir, she has less than a couple hundred dollars in her bank account, so I doubt she can afford something in a better area of the city at least without a roommate."

"She works two jobs and can't afford something better than that? Are the rent prices that high in this city?"

"Yes sir, they are. She pays over a thousand dollars a month in rent for her studio apartment, now adding in her utilities and transportation costs, she likely doesn't have much left at the end of the month. She likely takes at least the subway and/or buses to work as there is no indication she owns a vehicle… that cost alone adds up."

"Okay, what else? High credit card bills? Other debts?"

"No credit cards, she has a small student loan balance but she has been paying it fairly regularly. It looks like she stopped on paying for a few months a couple of years ago and was granted a financial hardship reprieve; however since that expired, she has been making regular payments."

"I didn't think she went to college."

"She only had one semester left before dropping out."

"I see. What else can you tell me?"

"She appears to have moved around a lot as a child, there are many different addresses and schools on record for her. Her mother is deceased, no father is listed on the birth certificate—"

"Is there anything alarming in her file that I need to be concerned about the press finding out?" I quickly interrupt Carter. Hearing all these details about Kenzie's personal life makes me again feel like I'm invading her privacy. I guarantee Bridget's background check isn't this thorough, but I think this is one of those situations that the less I know the better. This is important information for Carter and Asher to have but none of it will impact the events that Kenzie attends with me.

"Nothing that I can find sir. I'm curious as to the reason she left Denver and how she ended up in New York as it appears she has no family anywhere in the state or even on this coast. However there is nothing here that suggests the reason she left is something for us to be concerned about. She has no criminal record, not even a parking ticket, and pays her bills on time every month."

"Thank you Carter; that will be all."

To: Bridget Wilder
From: Nicholas Parker
Subject: Meeting

Bridget,
I am confident that after tonight's meeting both parties are in agreement with the contract moving forward. I would like to review the background report before signing the contract. If both parties are still in agreement, I would like to request our next meeting occur at the New Beginnings Gala this Saturday night. I will contact you later this week to confirm the arrangements.

Nicholas Parker, CEO
Parker Financial Services, Inc.

I reworded the email several times to Bridget, trying to sound vague without disclosing the information about the contract or what services I'm discussing. Going forward I will have to find a better way to communicate with her regarding this arrangement. I think it will end up best if we have these discussions over the phone rather than leaving something in writing. I contemplate requesting Asher provide me with another email address that I would only use for communicating with Bridget, however I still worry about it being tied to PFS. Above all, I will protect PFS and would rather the press destroying my personal life than risk doing something that would ruin everything I have done to build it from the ground up.

A few minutes later my email dings indicating I have a new email. I'm tempted to ignore it and instead focus on the financial spreadsheet that was sent to me just before I left to meet Kenzie but instead, I open my email and see that I have an email from Bridget.

To: Nicholas Parker
From: Bridget Wilder
Subject: Re: meeting

Nicholas,

I am pleased to hear that your meeting tonight was successful. I will have the file couriered to your office first thing tomorrow morning. If the other party is in agreement, I will include a draft contract for your review. The effective date of the contract will be Saturday.

Bridget Wilder
CEO, Wilder Consulting

When I arrive at PFS the next morning, I find the courier has already delivered Kenzie's background check and a draft contract as promised by Bridget. I pleased that both were in there, as it means that Kenzie has decided to move forward with our arrangement as well. Although I thought last night was a success, I worried that she would change her mind after she read the shit the tabloids wrote about me. As soon as I suggested she google me, I immediately regretted the words, but since she knew nothing about me personally or professionally, google seemed like the best way for her to access the information quickly.

Later, when I finally have a few minutes of down time I open the file containing the background check that Bridget sent me:

Full Name: Mackenzie Rose

Age: 25

Occupation: Personal shopper/Bakery assistant

Bank Account Balance: Checking account: $127.93
                      Savings Account: $53.54

Education: High school graduate, college credits

Residence: New York City

Political affiliations: none

Religious affiliations: Catholic, not a member of a church currently

Driver's license: None; previous license from Colorado state expired

Assets: None

Marital Status: Single, never married

Mother: Avery Jones *(Smith) deceased*

Madison Quinn

Father: Unknown

There's isn't much more to her background check exempt a list of previous employers which include a coffee shop, a restaurant and a bank. A brief medical summary was included, indicating that there have been no major medical issues in her life. She was in a passenger in a car accident once and then fell down a flight of stairs requiring an emergency room visit but nothing suspicious.

I review the draft contract next. It's similar to the one that Bridget presented me when she first discussed this arrangement with me. This contract has been drafted with my name and Kenzie's, with an effective date of this Saturday for the gala as Bridget indicated it would be. The contract is pretty straight forward: all arrangements must be made through Bridget, contact between parties cannot occur outside of prescheduled dates and times, physical contact is limited to basic touching and light kissing, there is no set number of dates/events and either party can terminate the contract at any time.

The last part makes me a little nervous; I need this contract to remain in effect for at least several months so the media gets the idea that Kenzie and I are a couple and they get off my ass about my personal life. What happens if Kenzie cancels the contract after a couple of dates? I will be in the same situation I'm in now only the media will probably rip me a new one for being able to keep a woman for, a short period of time. As I down my glass of scotch, I decide to sign the contract, even with the risk of this backfiring. Weighing the pros and cons of the situation, if Kenzie decides to end the contract quickly, the PR department will just have to find a way to put a positive spin on it so I don't look like an even bigger ass to the media. The risk of not doing something, letting my integrity be further destroyed, is too big of a risk. If things go well after a few dates with Kenzie, I will find a way to insure that she realizes that staying in the contract is in her best interest.

Kenzie:

"Bridget, it's Kenzie; I'm returning your call from earlier. I apologize but I was working at the bakery this morning—"

"Of course, I apologize for calling you then. I've made a note in your file to only call in the afternoon; hopefully I'll remember that."

"It's fine Bridget, really."

"I'm calling to confirm the details for the New Beginnings Gala tomorrow night. I understand you have already obtained your dress and accessories for the event."

"Yes, I have everything."

"You have an appointment at the salon tomorrow at one, again the expense will be charged to my account so there will be nothing for you to take care of while you're there. A car service will be outside of you apartment—"

"Wait, I thought we were meeting at your office?"

"You are meeting Mr. Parker here, Kenzie. The car service is from me, not Mr. Parker. I don't see it being feasible for you to take the subway to get to my office in a ball gown. It doesn't seem practical therefore, I have arranged a car service to bring you to my office. The same car service will meet you here after the gala to bring you home. I will not be here as I will be getting ready to attend the gala as well. However my security team will meet you and Mr. Parker in the lobby before and after the event. Mr. Parker's driver will transport you and Mr. Parker to the Gala and back to my office when it's over. Did you receive my email yesterday?"

"Yes, I've reviewed the information you included about Mr. Parker and where he stands on various topics."

"You don't have to agree with any of his beliefs or stances, however what is key is that you do not verbally disagree with them while at an event. If they start talking about something you disagree with, either keep it to yourself or excuse yourself to use the ladies room."

"I understand, Bridget."

"The back story, should anyone ask, is that you and Mr. Parker met at a coffee shop a couple of months ago and have maintained contact with each other since."

"Okay."

"Oh and Kenzie, Mr. Parker's parents are hosting the event so his family will be in attendance. They are unaware of this arrangement."

"Of course."

"Good luck, Kenzie, and try to enjoy yourself. I will be there if you need me but otherwise I will not act as if we know each other."

"Thank you Bridget."

Chapter 11
Kenzie

"You're a fucking bitch! You can't do anything right, can you?" he screams at me.

"I'm… I'm sorry," I cry as he grabs my hair in his hand and pulls it hard so I fall onto the floor.

"I ask you for one fucking thing! One thing! Is it too much to ask for a hot meal to be on the fucking table when I get home? I work all day to keep a roof over your fucking head, to keep food on the table and what do I fucking get in return? A fucking cold dinner?"

SLAP

I wake up covered in sweat, my heart beating erratically as I frantically look around the room expecting *him* to be standing there. When my brain finally catches up to reality, my breathing finally begins to slow down as I realize *he* isn't here and can no longer hurt me. I haven't had a nightmare in a couple of weeks; they seem to come at random times and always without warning.

Tonight's nightmare was more of a flashback, as most of them are. It was the night he hit me for the first time. I remember every detail as if it were yesterday. He left that morning requesting I have dinner ready when he gets home, as was the request every day before he went to work. He told me that day he would be home by 6:30 and that he expected dinner to be on the table when he walked through the door. I did just that: I had dinner hot and on the table by 6:25 in case he was early. He didn't come up home until after eight that night and then was mad because dinner was cold. His screaming and yelling at me was nothing new—it had started a couple months ago but that night he slapped me for the first time. I still remember being in such shock that he hit me.

I need tonight to be absolutely perfect; the last thing I need is my shitty past distracting me. I need to be at the top of my game tonight. I need everything to be perfect. If tonight is perfect then I can quit working at the store and begin saving money so I can get out of this crappy apartment and into a safer neighborhood. Since meeting Mr. Parker earlier in the week, I've found myself starting to consider a future beyond this dump. I even looked into taking a few online classes from the local community college but I haven't decided what I want to work towards yet.

Stop getting ahead of yourself, Kenzie.

I mentally criticize myself, I just need to focus on today. If I get my hopes up about the future, something will happen, my plans will be ruined and leave me nothing but disappointed again. It's nearly five in the morning and although I would rather still be asleep, I know it's highly unlikely that I will be able to fall back asleep after that nightmare. Whenever they hit, if I try to go back to sleep, I typically end up right back in the middle of it again. I learned years ago it was better to just stay awake than try to fight it and go back to sleep. It's funny, I can't recall a time in my life when nightmares weren't an issue. Maybe when I was really little... it's hard to remember when they started but I know they were there even before *he* came along. After *him*, the nightmares were there, only now nightmares fall into one of two categories: before or after *him.*

I'm nervous about tonight but I'm also confident in my ability to fit in. I went to the library earlier this week after Bridget confirmed that Mr. Parker had decided to move forward with our arrangement. I googled him and as he mentioned I would, I found many business articles written about him and PFS. I was floored when I learned that he is considered New York's most eligible bachelor and even more so when I learned that he was also a billionaire, despite being only a few years older than me. I knew he had money; I doubted many people could afford Bridget's prices but I had no idea he had *that* much money. The business articles written about him were all very complimentary and from what I read, everything about his business seems legit.

In addition to the links to hundreds of business articles, I found nearly as many links to tabloids that had written stories about Mr. Parker. Nearly every article tried to connect his business life with his personal life. A few speculated that if he continues to be unable to maintain a relationship with a woman his company will likely go under in the near future. Despite reading all of the articles, I still can't figure out how the reporters are making the connection between his dating life and his business decisions.

What I did find interesting is that up until two years there weren't any negative tabloid stories published about Mr. Parker. He was pictured in several articles with a beautiful blond on his arm; some referenced the woman as his girlfriend while others called her his fiancée. Then she is no longer in pictures with Mr. Parker and that's when the negativity started.

My phone dings, alerting me to a message. I've set alerts on my phone when something new is written about Mr. Parker. I don't want to get caught off guard if something big happens that I should know about. So far in the last few days nothing has been published other than a business article highlighting a deal he recently closed on. Today's link sends me to a tabloid site that I've come to think is the one out to destroy Mr. Parker or PFS, based upon the crap that they write.

"Who will Mr. Parker bring to the gala tonight? Another nameless woman who will leave him after tonight? Or will he attend the event solo, yet again? What is Mr. Parker hiding and how is it related to PFS?"

Although I've only met Mr. Parker twice now, it doesn't really seem like he is trying to hide something. Since I'm not exactly a detective I guess he could be and I wouldn't know. Everything I read online about Mr. Parker and PFS plus the information that Bridget provided me, suggest that there is nothing illegal occurring.

After reading everything I could about Mr. Parker and PFS, I researched tonight's event. I didn't want to show up and have no idea what the gala was raising money for. I learned that New Beginnings is an agency that focuses on bringing quality prenatal services to women in low income neighborhoods. Unlike many programs, they continue providing services until the child begins attending school. New Beginnings provides home visits, nutrition care, post-partum screening for the mother and ensure that the child sees a pediatrician regularly.

I learn that Mr. Parker's parents have been hosting fundraising events for New Beginnings for the last ten years when it was started. Tonight's event is an annual fundraiser that typically raises more than a quarter of a million dollars for the charity. I also read that there will probably be roughly 200 guests in attendance tonight, everyone from politicians to successful business men who will make large donations to support New Beginnings.

I spend the afternoon at the salon, my hair is trimmed and highlighted before placed into a half up half down style which Bridget recommended to compliment my gown. After my hair is done, I have a manicure and pedicure, plus get my eye brows waxed before my make-up is applied. I've never attended an event of this magnitude and I'm very grateful that Bridget scheduled all of this for me today. Business dinners, dates and small events I can handle but I don't think I would be able to get myself ready for something this large by myself. By the time I leave the salon, even I'm shocked at the woman I see before me. I look elegant, sophisticated and somehow the salon made me look like I should be attending an event where people in attendance easily earn in a month what I earn in a year. I decide to splurge and take a cab back to my apartment rather than the subway. Although it cost an arm and leg to go this far, it's worth it as to not mess up my make up or hair while on a train.

When I finally reach my apartment, I have less than thirty minutes to get changed before the car service Bridget organized is scheduled to pick me up. I take my gown out of the garment bag and place it on my bed before getting out the undergarments and other accessories needed for tonight. The gown is black with sequins sewn in allowing the light to shimmer off of it. The dress is form fitting on the top but loosens at my hips so it falls to the floor.

On His Terms

I fell in love with the gown the moment I tried it on but had sent a picture to Bridget just to make sure it was appropriate for the event even though the sales woman working with me insisted it would be fine. She, of course, confirmed the dress was perfect and insisted I had to wear it tonight.

I still don't understand why Bridget felt I needed to purchase all new undergarments; it's not like Mr. Parker will be seeing any of them. Bridget said something about it would make me feel sexier and therefore more confident. I agreed to appease her, once again grateful that I'm not the one having to pay for all of this. I didn't catch the price on the gown, but I know the bra and panties cost a several hundred dollars together. Then there were stockings, shoes and jewelry that were added in with the gown to complete the outfit for tonight. It's funny, I've been dressing women for events just like this for the last year and a half but never once considered how much really goes into the outfits or the price of everything.

By the time I am strapping my shoes on, the alarm on my phone indicates that it's time for me to leave. I grab the silver clutch and wrap before peeking out the window to confirm the car service has arrived. It's not hard to determine which car outside is for me. A sleek, obviously fairly new sedan stands out in front of my crappy building with a man dressed in a suit waits in front of it. The car obviously is unique among the usual curbside wrecks and doesn't belong in this type of area, so it's pretty safe to say the car is for me. I glance at the bathroom mirror one last time, making sure that everything is perfect before I lock my door and head downstairs.

"Ms. Rose?" the gentleman at the car greets me as soon as I step outside.

"Yes," I confirm.

"I am here to take you Wilder Consulting," he opens the door and I immediately slide across the leather seats.

"There are water bottles in the cooler at your feet if you're thirsty."

The ride to Bridget's office doesn't take long but as we approach, I get more nervous as each minute passes. So much rests on tonight: whether Mr. Parker knows it or not, he holds the key to my future. If everything goes well tonight and he still wants to move forward with this arrangement, I will finally have extra money to change all the things in my life I've wanted to change. If tonight doesn't work out and he decides I am not the type of woman he needs for this type of an arrangement, I don't think I will move forward in working with Bridget. I think it would just be a sign that this business opportunity wasn't for me.

"Ms. Rose, we have arrived," the driver pulls me from my thoughts before I've even realized the car has stopped. "Take the elevator in the lobby to the fourteenth floor where your party will be waiting for you."

The lobby of the building is simple but elegant, a security guard at the desk nods in my direction but doesn't question why I am there or who I'm meeting. I don't know if Mr. Parker is waiting for me upstairs or if it will just be Bridget's security team that she mentioned would be here. The elevator ride is slow though I'm sure that's more a result of my nervousness than anything. My hands play with my clutch as I slowly watch the numbers turn red as the elevator rises. When the bell dings, my nerves hit an all-time high but I push them down and take a deep breath before stepping out of the elevator.

"Ms. Rose, you look absolutely stunning," Mr. Parker greets me the moment I step off the elevator.

"Thank you Mr. Parker, you look very nice as well."

He is wearing what I suspect is a tailored black Armani tux complimented with a warm grey tie. Nice is probably the worst word to describe how he looks tonight but my brain isn't able to process anything except nice and hot and sexy. The suit accentuates his broad shoulders and the tie complements his warm blue eyes. He looks absolutely amazing, but I figure nice is the safest option...

"Please, call me Nicholas."

"Only if you call me Kenzie."

"Agreed. Are you ready to head to the gala? It's a little bit of a drive in this traffic I'm afraid, but we should arrive on time."

The elevator takes us to the parking garage in complete silence but it's not uncomfortable. When the doors open in the garage, Carter is waiting and escorts us to a large, black pristine SUV that looks like it was just driven off the dealer lot. He opens the door for me as Nicholas walks around and gets in the other side.

"Do you have any questions about tonight, Kenzie?" Nicholas asks.

"I have reviewed all of the information that Bridget sent me and confident that I can recall where you stand on the issues she shared. I also spent sometime this week researching your company and the information published on your most recent projects."

"You've been busy."

"I wanted to be prepared."

"I assume you saw the tabloid articles?"

"I did. I have to say I struggle to see how people are connecting your personal life to PFS's success."

"I can't either. Frankly if I wasn't concerned about how my employees and people I'm currently doing business with, I would say fuck it and not even do anything to address the articles written. However, when a magazine was found in one of our staff lounges open to the article questioning my ability to manage hundreds of employees, I knew I needed to do something and fast. I have too much at stake to let a few arrogant reporters destroy my life. This," he gestures between us, "is a very small price to pay if it means the nonsense disappears and I can focus entirely on PFS."

"Can I ask you something?"

"Of course."

"I understand why you are doing this from a business perspective, but Bridget had mentioned your family would be in attendance tonight and that they are unaware of our arrangement... "

"And you're wondering why I haven't told them about this?"

"If it's too personal, you don't have to tell me—"

"It's not that. Honestly, it was never an option to tell them about this as far as I'm concerned. If I'm going to fabricate a lie that I need hundreds to believe, the less people who know the truth the better. For the most part the press has left my family alone, but there have been times when they have approached them about my personal life. If they believe the same lie that everyone else believes, there is no chance for them to let something accidently slip."

"I understand, that makes sense."

"Besides, it gets my brother off my ass," he chuckles. "My brother loves to torment me and the fact that the press is giving him ammunition is just pissing me off."

"I could see why," I laugh.

We arrive at the gala few minutes later; I'm surprised at how fast the drive went, the time really seemed to fly by once we started talking. I'm also relieved that for the most part my nerves have calmed. I'm still a little nervous as we pull around the long circular driveway but I'm less anxious than I was on the drive to Bridget's office.

"We're going to get out my door, there will be press, taking our picture as we walk in but once we are inside they won't be permitted. Of course we have to worry about people taking pictures on their cell phones and selling them to tabloids..."

"Don't worry, it'll be fine," I try to assure him.

"Here we go," he takes a deep breath the moment the door opens.

He slides across the seat before stepping out of the car, I follow, taking his offered hand to help me out. Immediately we are bombarded by the press as Nicholas is instantly recognized—cameras are flashing everywhere and I'm momentarily frozen on the spot as I try to take everything in.

"You okay?" he whispers in my ear as he wraps an arm around my waist.

"I'm fine," I take a deep breath as Nicholas leads me through the crowd. We stop a couple of times for pictures but his arm remains around my waist as we stand next to each other for the press. What surprises me is that it doesn't feel uncomfortable to have him touch me like I expected, since we are practically strangers, only really met twice before this. After a few minutes, he leads me to a tented area where he nods to the security team at the entrance before we are permitted to enter.

"Wow," I gasp taking in the view in front of me. Even though I had seen a few pictures from the previous events, nothing compared to seeing the area that had been transformed in front of me. There are several tents set up on the grass with candle-lit tables under them; off in the distance a lighted fountain sprays water from a large display.

"My parents go all-out for this every year," Nicholas looks around almost as if he is seeing it all for the first time.

"It's beautiful."

"Mr. Parker! It's so nice to see you again," a gentleman in a tux approaches us.

"Mr. Jacobson, I'd like to introduce you to my date, Ms. Mackenzie Rose."

"It's a pleasure to meet you," Mr. Jacobson offers his hand.

"It's nice to meet you as well. I understand you are doing some amazing things at the university…"

"Yes… yes I am," he is clearly surprised that I am aware of who he is. "Without PFS's generous support we would not be able to fund our projects, one of which is up for an award this year."

"Yes, I read about that one. Your department patented a way to transform dirty water into drinkable water without electricity, right?"

"Yes! We have developed a PFS funded program and have sent the pilot plans to several foreign countries, we are planning to use the proceeds to send out many more and eventually publish our findings."

"I believe we have a meeting in a few weeks to review the data collected so far if I'm not mistaken," Nicholas speaks up.

"Yes, Mr. Parker, you will be meeting with our research team in two weeks. They are eager to present you with our findings thus far."

"Wonderful, I look forward to it. Now if you will excuse us, I see someone who is trying to get my attention."

"Of course, it was good to see you again Mr. Parker and to meet you, Ms. Rose."

For the next two hours we mingle, well mostly Nicholas mingles and I trail along, every so often contributing to a conversation when something comes up. Most of the discussions surround politics, but those that don't, are focused on projects PFS is currently working on, none of which are public knowledge yet so they weren't included in any of the reading material I found online. I don't mind though—I'm learning more than I thought I would about the key political forces in New York.

"Ladies and Gentleman, if you would please take your seats dinner is about to be served," the DJ announces.

"Please excuse us," Nicholas tells the person he was talking to, though I had to admit that I've already forgotten their name.

"You're doing great," he whispers so no one else can hear as he leads me to the table we were assigned.

"Thank you."

"Nicholas!" A young woman jumps from the table we are approaching and runs towards him, embracing him in a hug. His arm drops from my waist so he can catch her; he twirls her around in a circle before placing her back on the floor in front of us.

"Cara, I would like you to meet Mackenzie Rose. Kenzie, this is my younger sister, Cara," Nicholas introduces.

"It's nice to meet you Cara."

"I love your dress!!!! It's absolutely stunning!! You'll have to tell me where you got it from!"

I immediately feel at ease with Cara—she is probably the easiest going person I've ever spoken to. Once we are at the table, I am introduced to Nicholas's parents, his brother and his date, Cara's date and Nicholas's grandparents. I desperately try to calm my nerves as I sit across from Nicholas's parents, truly hoping I don't do anything to screw this up. I think I'm more worried that his parents will see right through our charade than I am about the press or Nicholas' colleagues.

"So Kenzie, what is it you do?" Nicholas's dad asks me.

"I am currently working at Sweet Dreams Bakery over on-"

"I love that place! They make best muffins, I absolutely love the apple cinnamon ones," his mother cuts me off.

"Well, thank you. I actually make most of the muffins and breads each morning."

"You do? Wow, they are so good!"

"The owner developed each recipe on her own; she has owned the shop for the last twenty years. It's a shame that someone else is going to take it over—"

"What do you mean take it over?" Nicholas asks.

"Ginny, the owner, is retiring so she has put the business up for sale. She suspects a chain place will likely purchase it but she isn't sure yet."

"I hope it's not that donut place that is around the corner from the bakery. Their donuts taste like they are days old."

"Chances are they *are* a few days old. Most places will make large batches in advance and sell them over the next few days. Ginny insists that we make everything fresh every day—anything that doesn't sell by the end of the day is donated to a soup kitchen."

"Good for her," Nicholas' dad smiles.

As dinner is served, I feel much more comfortable around Nicholas's family than when we first sat down. They are all very easy to talk to, allowing the conversation to flow easily around the table as we eat. I learn that Nicholas and his brother Austin, who works with their father at an architectural firm, are teaming up on a project to revitalize a large building downtown for a local nonprofit organization. Austin's date is very quiet and barely says a word throughout the course of dinner. She looks like she feels very uncomfortable and out of place. Cara's date on the other hand is very talkative and has engaged Nicholas' dad in a debate about a recent call at a baseball game. Cara and Nicholas's mom discuss everything that went into planning tonight's gala and already seem to be making notes of things they want to change for next year.

"Kenzie, would you be able to help with the dance auction? One of the girls that was supposed to help me... well let's just say she had too much wine before dinner and needed to be taken home," Cara asks.

"Oh no. Of course, I'll help out," I agree not really sure what I'm agreeing to but I figure how bad can it be?

"Wonderful! Thank you!" she beams.

"You don't have to help out," Nicholas whispers.

"I know, it's fine—I really don't mind."

"Ladies and Gentleman, it's time for the annual dance auction! If the ladies helping with the auction, could please make their way to the stage so we can begin shortly. Gentleman get your wallets and checkbooks ready!"

"Come on, Kenzie!" Cara grasps my hand and pulls me up before the DJ even finishes his announcement.

"Thank you," Nicholas mouths to me as I'm being yanked away.

"So what do we have to do?" I ask as we wait off to the side of the small stage.

"Nothing really. When the DJ announces your name, you walk onto the stage while he tells the audience about your wonderful qualities—"

"What qualities?"

"Oh you'll see," she giggles. "He makes up stuff about each one of us... you know: languages spoken, our careers and so on. Then he opens the bidding until the highest bidder is announced—"

"Wait, so they're bidding on us?"

"Well, not on *you,* silly. They're bidding on dancing with you for the first dance of the night. The winner donates his bid to New Beginnings and in return you dance with him for the first dance. This is our biggest fundraiser of the evening."

"Really?"

"Yup, you would be surprised how much money men are willing to spend to dance with their date or someone that they've had an eye on."

I can't help but feel some regret that I agreed to help Cara with this auction. How will it look if someone takes a picture of me, Nicholas' date, dancing with another man tonight? I could easily see this backfiring on him if the press were to get ahold of pictures from the auction; they would rip him apart, even more than they already have, I'm sure. To prevent that from happening, I'm essentially leaving Nicholas no choice but to spend even more money tonight by bidding on me.

"Don't look so worried; Nicholas will win the auction for you," Cara tries to reassure me, obviously picking up on my nervousness.

"I hope so," I say more to myself than to her.

"I know so. Trust me, I know Nicholas—there's no way he would let another man dance with you. He may have brought other women to these things in the past, but you're the only one he hasn't been able to keep his eyes off of."

"I'm sure that's not true," I disagree.

"We're going to start our auction off tonight with the beautiful Ms. Cara Parker… "

I stop listening to what the DJ is making up about Cara, as she walks onto the stage and my nerves kick in full force. I can't see Nicholas from where I'm standing near the stage although even if I could see him I don't know that it would help me feel better at all. I'll have to hope that Cara is right, that he will ensure he wins the auction for my first dance so there won't be a controversy in the press tomorrow if someone sells pictures of me with another guy.

"And the winning bid is eleven thousand dollars!" the DJ announces as Cara comes off the stage pouting.

"What's wrong?" I ask.

"Next up is the lovely Ms. Mackenzie Rose," the DJ calls me before I can find out from Cara why she looks upset. "Mackenzie is a world renowned architect, having designed some of the most famous sites around the world. She enjoys ballet, the opera and Broadway shows… "

I slowly walk across the stage as the DJ continues rambling useless false information about me before opening the bidding up to the guests.

"Five hundred dollars," a voice I don't recognize calls out.

"Two thousand," someone else calls out.

"Three thousand."

"Five thousand," I can't see Nicholas but I know that was his bid.

"Six thousand."

"Seven thousand," someone counters and I cringe at the high price this is running.

I really just want to cancel the entire auction and run off the stage, forgetting that I ever agreed to help Cara out. Had I known this would be the result, I never would have agreed to help her. I thought I would be helping count bids or helping to show auction items, having no idea that *I* was actually an auction item.

"Fifteen thousand," Nicholas' voice is loud and firm, almost as if he is daring someone to outbid him.

"Fifteen thousand, going once... going twice... Sold to Mr. Parker... next up we have Ms. Cindy Smith..." The DJ presents the next girl for the auction as I make my way off the stage where Nicholas is now waiting for me.

"I'm so sorry! I had no idea... this was not what I was expecting and I didn't—"

"What are you apologizing for? I don't think I've ever had so much fun bidding on an auction here before," Nicholas chuckles.

"Really? I... I thought you would be mad for being put on the spot to bid on me. I was worried that someone else would outbid you and then pictures would be taken and leaked to the press which would—"

"Kenzie, relax," he takes my hand and leads me off to the side of the large tent where we are away from most of the guests but can still hear the DJ. "Austin and I bid every year on the auction, so I was already planning on making a donation through the first dance auction."

"You were?"

"Yes, Austin and I always outbid whatever loser Cara brings to these things. We ensure that the first dance belongs to once of us: it's been our tradition since she was old enough to participate. At first it was because she was barely a teenager and thought of a grown man who wasn't family dancing with her was sickening..."

"And now?"

"Now it's just to annoy her. We promise her every year that we won't outbid her date and every year we do. This year Austin won the bid and will be dancing with her. You see, even if you hadn't participated in the auction, I probably would have outbid Austin for Cara and made a donation that way."

"I had no idea that was what Cara meant when she asked me to help her with the auction."

"I know you didn't. I wanted to warn you before the auction started but I couldn't get away from my grandfather insisting on talking about business."

"I'm glad it's over."

Madison Quinn

"Ladies and Gentleman it's time for the annual first dance. Please claim your prize and bring her to the dance floor for our first dance of the evening."

"Well, that's our cue," he offers his arm and escorts me onto the dance floor. He leads us to the center of the dance floor and soon we are surrounded by eleven other couples. Out of the corner of my eye I see Cara still pouting as I'm sure she would much rather be dancing with her date.

My hand is on Nicholas' shoulder and his on my lower back, our other hands clasped together. Once the music starts, he gracefully moves me across the dance floor in perfect harmony to the music. I'm very surprised at what a wonderful dancer he is; definitely not something I expected. When the music finally stops, he leans down and places the lightest kiss on my cheek before thanking me and leading me off the dance floor.

The rest of the night goes well; we mingle with other guests and of course Nicholas talks a lot of business. At the end of the evening we say goodbye to his family before being escorted to our awaiting car by Carter. When we finally slide inside, I let out a heavy sigh, glad that the night is over and that for the most part I think it was a success.

"Thank you for tonight, Kenzie. I wasn't sure what to expect but you... I think tonight was a success."

Chapter 12

Nicholas

"Playboy Nicholas Parker, breaking his two month stance of not being photographed with a woman, brings yet another new one to an event. Nicholas Parker brought a stunning woman to the New Beginnings Gala Saturday evening, reportedly bidding $15K for her to win the first dance auction. Such a shame, as we know we won't be seeing her again with Nicholas Parker."

A picture of Kenzie and me arriving at my parents' house for the gala is shown, as I knew it would be, since for some reason the gossip sites love to report any move I make in my personal life. Every day this week I have been checking the sites, looking for reports and pictures from the gala but until now hadn't found any. It took them three days to get one up—longer than I expected. However, this is the first step in my own PR campaign to change how the media views me.

I have plans to take Kenzie out in public again, hoping the press will see us on at least a few of those occasions. Then in a couple of weeks this can all be behind me and I can move on with my life. With the press off my case I will be able to focus on PFS, like I need to be doing, without worrying that my employees are questioning my ability. After a few weeks of being seen with Kenzie, I will maintain a contract with her but will likely only request her company for large events when it's expected I bring a guest.

Looking at the picture on the site, I have to admit that I'm surprised we managed to pull it off as well as we did. Kenzie was absolutely outstanding in her performance; she shocked me to hell when she started discussing farming initiatives with the president of the university. It was clear in that moment that she did her homework before that night and reinforced to me that she was taking this contract seriously. I haven't figured her out yet… usually I get a good read on people fairly quickly, but for some reason with Kenzie, I'm having a harder time.

"You made the sites again I see, Parker," Alex interrupts my thoughts by barging into my office.

"I just saw that. Damn fucking vultures can't leave me the hell alone."

"The president of the shipping company is demanding a meeting with you tonight over dinner and drinks—"

"Tonight? What the fuck Alex?!"

"I know… They're insisting they need a meeting with you tonight before they are willing to sign off on the investment."

"What's their sticking point?"

"Their employees."

"We've guaranteed them that everyone's job will be sustained for six months and if at that time their jobs are terminated a severance package will be offered. What's the issue?"

"I don't know. I think they're afraid we're going to go back on our word."

"It's in the fucking contract!"

"I know it is, Parker, I reviewed the contract with them, but I think they are still concerned. They want to meet tonight, dinner and drinks. Honestly, I think he just wants to hear it from you that his employees' jobs are safe."

"Fine… whatever, work with Melody to rearrange my schedule. I expect you to be there Alex, if he is taking away my Friday night, you're losing yours."

"I'll be there."

"Good."

"Oh and Parker, he's bringing his wife. If you could bring someone it might make you appear a little more trustworthy."

"A fucking date will make me appear more trustworthy?"

"Just saying."

"Fine, whatever. You bring Ella and I'll bring a date."

"Later."

These are the fucking things about business I hate: why would bringing a date to a business dinner make me look more trustworthy? The fucking details are in the contract about his employees, but now I have to spend my Friday night at a boring dinner, ironing out, *once again,* the contract details because he doesn't trust me.

"Good afternoon, Wilder Consulting. How may I help you?" a voice answers the phone on the second ring.

"This is Nicholas Parker, I need to speak with Bridget urgently."

"One moment."

Even though the chance of being seen by press tonight is minimal, for my PR plan to work I need Kenzie to be available tonight. I can't go alone if Alex and the other person are bringing dates. I can't bring a different woman or it defeats my purpose of contracting with Kenzie in the first place.

"Hello, Nicholas," Bridget picks up the line a few moments later.

"Bridget, I need you to contact Kenzie immediately."

"Is something wrong? When I spoke to her the other day she indicated the gala went well, but if that wasn't the case—"

"The gala was fine. I need her tonight. I know it's short notice and I'll pay an additional fee for her inconvenience but it's absolutely imperative that she accompany me to a business dinner tonight."

"What time will you need her to meet you?"

"I need her at five, dinner is at 5:30 near PFS."

"I'll contact her right now and will call you back once I get off the phone with her."

"Good."

I wait, and wait, for Bridget to call me back with Kenzie's decision on whether or not she can attend dinner with me tonight. I don't do well with waiting or with things out of my control. If it were up to me, I would have contacted her directly and offered her whatever she needed in order to agree to accompany me tonight. I get that I'm not supposed to do that so we both keep some privacy, but it would have made things so much easier if I could have just picked up the phone and told her what I needed from her tonight. I'm not used to letting someone else take control in my life; I don't do well following orders which is why I started my own company.

An hour passes before I hear from Bridget and I start to panic. How long does it take to fucking call someone and see if she is available tonight? What if she wasn't available to talk to Bridget? How much longer do I wait before trying to come up with another plan for tonight? My only other option is to go to the dinner alone and if someone asks I make an excuse about Kenzie not feeling well. That could work...

"Parker," I answer my cell phone without looking at the caller ID.

"Nicholas, its Bridget—"

"About time."

"I'm sorry, Kenzie needed to see if she could rearrange something before she could commit to dinner tonight—"

"Rearrange? She didn't have another date did she? Because I specifically required her to sign—"

"Calm down, she did not have another date. She signed the exclusivity clause, you know that means I can't show her profile to anyone else."

"So, can she do it or what?"

"Yes, she is available for the evening and will meet you at your office by five."

"Good."

"And next time, Nicholas, try to give the girl a little notice if possible."

"I'll be sure to compensate her for the last minute request in the next transfer I send you."

"I'll see that she gets it."

I sit back in my chair and sigh heavily, relieved that I don't have to come up with an excuse as to why Kenzie is not with me this evening. Although it's unlikely the press would have found out that I was at a business dinner alone, I can't take the risk now that I'm trying to change my public image around. I need to lose the image of being a playboy who is seen with different women all the time. I need the media to think I'm boring and stable so they stop fucking questioning my business practices.

"Melody, get me Carter," I request.

"Yes, Mr. Parker."

Moments later Carter enters my office; as always Melody is very efficient at what she does.

"Melody has informed you of the dinner tonight?" I confirm.

"Yes sir."

"Ms. Rose will be accompanying me tonight and will arrive here around five. Please meet her in the lobby and escort her to my office when she arrives."

"Yes, of course, sir."

"When we are finished with dinner, I want a cab to take her home."

"Yes sir, I'll be sure to have one ready before you leave."

"That will be all."

I dive into my latest financial reports, finally able to focus on work again now that the issue of tonight's dinner tonight is resolved. It really is a waste of time to have dedicated the last 90 minutes worrying about a business dinner, but I have to remain focused on my goal of turning around my public image: one slip up could ruin everything. Back on track now, I spend the rest of the afternoon diving into numbers, spreadsheets and reviewing the performance of several companies that PFS recently brought on. After signing with PFS, the first six months of financial reporting is absolutely key. After that I make a decision whether to continue their contract or to cut ties completely. As usual, I'm easily lost in my work and remain so until Melody alerts me that Carter is here. I tell her to send him in expecting him to need to discuss plans for the weekend or for dinner tonight.

"Mr. Parker—"

"One moment, Carter," I interrupt, needing to spend just another minute reviewing this one line to ensure the calculations are correct. If I stop now, I will probably lose my place and it took me hours to find the one line where there appears to be an error.

"Yes Carter?"

"Ms. Rose sir," I finally look up and realize that not only has Carter been standing there waiting for me to finish looking at my report but that Kenzie has been there as well.

"I'm sorry, I hadn't realized the time. Thank you Carter."

"The car will be ready in ten minutes sir."

"Kenzie, thank you for agreeing to tonight, especially with the incredibly late notice."

"It's not a problem."

"I understand you had to rearrange your schedule, I hope Bridget let you know that you will be compensated for your troubles."

"Really, it's fine."

"You look very nice."

Nice is probably the least descriptive word that I could have come up with to describe how she looks. However, the only other words that come to mind to describe her looks are not appropriate to share with someone that I'm conducting a business relationship with. Kenzie is wearing a black fitted skirt that falls to just above her knee, a light blue button down fitted shirt lays under a black blazer. Her long legs are accentuated by a pair of black heels. My mind immediately pictures her bent over my desk with the skirt pushed up to her waist as I thrust into her.

"Thank you," she thankfully pulls me from my thoughts which I'm grateful: if I kept picturing her like that, she would be able to tell what I was thinking if she looked below my belt. I can't keep picturing her like that... thinking of her like that; this is nothing but a business transaction. She would never be interested in anything more with me and I'm not interested in anything more than a fuck with a woman, something I know Kenzie is too good for. She needs someone who would trust her and I've learned the hard way that hell is going to freeze over before I trust another woman like that ever again.

"Please have a seat," I gesture to the small couch against the windows in my office and sit in the chair across from her.

"You have an amazing building here, the lobby was stunning."

"Thank you. We've been in this building for about five years now; before we moved in I had my brother completely remodel it to fit the image I wanted."

"He did a wonderful job! I don't think I've ever seen anything like it."

"I'll never tell him this, but he blew my expectations out of the water on the design."

"Is there anything I need to know for dinner tonight?" She glances at her watch likely realizing we only have a few minutes before we need to leave. She uncrosses her legs before crossing them again, her skirt riding up just the smallest amount and it takes everything in me not to groan. Her outfit is actually perfect for tonight: it looks very professional but could easily be more casual if she took the blazer off. The skirt isn't too short, but for some reason it's just the right amount of leg for her to look incredibly sexy.

"We have been working with this shipping company for the last several months now, trying to help them avoid bankruptcy. We've made multiple recommendations but they've been hesitant in agreeing to them. The contracts are scheduled to be signed Monday, however at the last minute they demanded a meeting with me, refusing to sign the contract unless I met them for dinner tonight."

"Why?"

"There's a clause in the contract that says all employee positions will remain as is for the first six months. After that, PFS will reevaluate and determine whether or not to continue their positions. If their position is eliminated in the first three years, every employee will be provided with a severance package along with a letter of recommendation."

"Sounds like a good thing?" she's obviously struggling to see why the other party hasn't signed yet.

"It is," I agree. "For some reason, Alex, my vice president, thinks that they are having second thoughts and do not believe that I would hold up my end of the contract."

"But if it's in the contract, aren't you obligated to follow through?"

"Yes and no. There are certain safeguards put in place where I could get out of the clause, if something came up. However, it's a clause that is only used in dire situations. Alex thinks they just want to hear from me that their employees will have jobs. It's a family owned business that has been passed down from one generation to another, but unfortunately the owner's father had a gambling problem and borrowed money from the company. They're barely staying afloat right now and have more debt than they should have. We're offering them a solution where the company remains intact but requires an overhaul in a few areas."

"If you don't mind me asking… why am I needed tonight? It sounds like a business negotiation."

"We won't technically be negotiating, since all that is done already. Essentially, we are meeting to reassure him that the clause in the contract stands, nothing more. As to why you are here… apparently having a date will make me look more *trustworthy,* at least according to Alex. The owner is bringing his wife so I assume the idea is, if I bring a date, I look more like a person and less like a businessman who wants to destroy their company."

"Ah, got it."

"Sir, ma'am, we need to leave now," Carter interrupts us.

"Thank you Carter. Do you have any other questions, Kenzie?"

"No, I think you covered everything."

"I'll apologize in advance: this is probably going to be a very boring dinner for you."

"It won't be a problem."

Carter escorts us to the parking garage where my SUV is waiting. The ride to the restaurant is short since the traffic is light despite the rush hour. I've purposely left early enough so that we are the first to arrive at the table. Over the next ten minutes Alex and Ella arrive followed by Mr. and Mrs. Forrest, the owners of the shipping company. Once again, Kenzie seems to fit right into the group, making conversation easily with Mrs. Forest and Ella while Alex, Mr. Forrest and I discuss business.

The next time I glance at my watch, I'm surprised to see that more than two hours have passed since we arrived. Kenzie sits comfortably next to me, discussing recipes with Mrs. Forrest. I knew she worked at the bakery but I had no idea how much she enjoys baking until I watch her passionately discuss different techniques.

"And that's why Ella does all the cooking, you see, Kenzie, I just burn everything no matter what setting I use on the stove!" Alex laughs as Kenzie finishes a story how one of the girls at the bakery accidently burnt an entire batch of muffins one morning.

"He does, you should see it. He once burnt a pot of boiling water... I ask you: who does that?" Ella laughs.

"Well, I'm sure he was just distracted—" Kenzie tries to defend Alex.

"Yeah, he was distracted by the game that was on TV, or by an email that his boss sent," which earns me a glare, "or by a car that drove too fast down our road or by a ringing phone... you see, Kenzie the list just goes on and on."

"What can I say, I'm easily distracted," Alex doesn't disagree with anything Ella said. Instead, he laughs with her and then leans in to kiss her quickly on the cheek.

"Mr. Parker, Mr. Clark, you will have the finalized contracts Monday morning," Mr. Forrest says a few minutes later when the table falls silent.

"Wonderful, we look forward to them," I shake his hand, sealing the deal.

Carter has already taken care of the bill for our meal, so we quickly say our goodbyes and walk out of the restaurant. Mr. and Mrs. Forrest leave, followed next by Alex and Ella, leaving Kenzie and me on the sidewalk.

"Carter has arranged for a car to take you home: it should be arriving any minute now," I explain, shooting Carter a death glare for not having the cab here by now. Apparently the one he called didn't show up so instead he had to call a car service. This would be so much easier if I could just have Carter take her home, then I would be assured that she arrived safely and we wouldn't have to rely on someone else to get her home.

"Nicholas, it's fine, I could just take the subway. There's a stop just a couple of blocks—"

"Kenzie, I can't let you take the subway home. This may not be an actual date, but I'm too much of a gentleman to let you do that. The car service will take you home tonight and I promise they won't tell me where they drop you off."

On His Terms

"It's unnecessary, but I appreciate it nonetheless."

"Thank you for this evening. Everything went smoother than I expected," I say.

"I'm sure you will be happy when you receive the signed contract on Monday."

"Sir, ma'am," Carter gestures to the car that is slowing just in front of us.

"Thank you again, Kenzie, especially for rearranging your schedule at the last minute to accommodate me," I lean down placing my lips against her cheek gently. I swear her breath hitches when I squeeze her hand in mine just before I pull away from her.

"I believe Bridget has been in touch about next week?"

"Yes, I've confirmed with her that I'm available."

"I'll see you then."

Chapter 13
Kenzie

"So Kenzie… who's your new boyfriend?" Ginny asks the moment I walk into the bakery.

"Huh? What are you talking about?" I'm confused… how could Ginny possibly know about Nicholas? It has to be Nicholas that she is talking about, because I haven't been out with any other guy or even had interest in a guy for years.

"One of the afternoon girls brought a picture of you in—"

"A picture?"

"Here, it's in my office," she leads me back and hands me a piece of paper. On it is a blurry picture of Nicholas and me from the business dinner Friday night. We are sitting next to each other at the table; Nicholas's eyes are on me, but it looks like I'm talking to Ella. I didn't think he was watching me during the dinner but he was probably just making sure that I didn't say something that I shouldn't have, given the limited time we had to prepare. The headline below the picture reads:

"We couldn't believe it either! Billionaire playboy Nicholas Parker is seen for the second time with a mystery woman. Until recently Nicholas Parker had been attending events solo after being seen with half a different dozen women in less than two months. Now, in span of two weeks he is seen with the same one twice! Who is this mystery woman and what spell could she have put on Parker to get him to take her out twice?"

"Oh that…" I stutter.

"You're dating a friggin' billionaire, Kenzie?!?!?" Ruth, one of the other girls who works the morning shift rushes in.

"I… I…" I'm caught completely off guard.

I hadn't expected that part of my life to mix with this part. I thought I could keep them separate: I should have expected that wouldn't be the case if I was seen publicly with Nicholas, the purpose of our arrangement.

"Nicholas Parker and I are dating—"

"For how long? Why didn't you say anything?" Ruth asks.

"Ruth, enough. As long as Kenzie is happy, that is all that matters," Ginny interrupts. "Now, I believe we have some donuts, muffins and breads to make for today."

I want to hug Ginny in that moment, but instead I lead the way out of her office to the kitchen where I start my orders.

I wasn't expecting it to be common knowledge so fast that Nicholas and I were *dating,* but I guess this is exactly what he wanted, what he needed, so the press would begin to paint a different picture of him. I don't remember seeing any press at the dinner the other night, but the little bit I saw of our picture it us looks like it was from someone's cell phone who I can only assume then sold it to the media. The media hasn't yet figured out who I am, but I'm sure it won't be too much longer before my name is leaked to the press, either purposely or through some investigating. I need to remember that at any time I could be questioned about my *relationship* with Nicholas. I need to stay on my toes and be more prepared the next time someone asks about us.

"Kenzie, someone is asking to speak to you about a catering order," Ginny informs me.

"Cara, how nice to see you!" I walk out front and am immediately surprised to see Cara Parker waiting at the counter for me.

"Kenzie, I'm so glad you are working today! I need to talk to you about a catering order," she says.

"Sure, why don't you have a seat at a table and I'll grab our ordering forms."

I gesture to one of the empty tables. Luckily the morning rush has ended, so there it's pretty slow. Had Cara shown up during the morning rush, there is no way I would be able to sit with her and discuss orders. The mornings are hectic no matter what day it is: great for business, but leaves very little time to take care of anything else.

"How are you, Kenzie?" Cara asks when I sit down next to her.

"I'm good, how about you?"

"I'm great! My mom is hosting a morning meeting for a fundraising committee next week and we were hoping you could cater the meeting? It's nothing huge, but everyone just loves this place!"

For the next ten or so minutes, Cara and I discuss the menu for the meeting and what will be needed. She arranges to pick up the order the morning of the meeting, since we don't offer delivery.

"So, I saw you and my brother made the gossip rags again," Cara says.

"I just saw that too," I answer honestly.

"He hates the press. I can't believe they followed him to a business dinner."

"I don't think we were followed. I think someone recognized your brother and took the picture to sell it to the press."

"You might be right. How did you two meet again? I don't remember Nicholas mentioning you before the gala, but then again he doesn't talk much anymore. I can't remember the last time he came to a family dinner... "

"We met at a coffee shop a couple of months ago," I answer with the cover story that Nicholas and I had previously agreed to.

"Oh, I hadn't realized you two knew each other for that long. Well, I have to go. Maybe you can get Nicholas to come to dinner this Sunday?"

"Cara, I don't know—"

"I know my mother would love it. Please... try to get him to come? Of course you come too—"

"We'll see, Cara. No promises, I'm not sure what our schedule is."

"Okay, thanks, Kenzie!"

"Kenzie, do you have a minute?" Ginny asks just as I finish meeting with Cara.

"Of course," I follow her back to her office where she shuts the door.

"I'm only going to bring this up once because it's none of my business. This Parker guy... he treats you right?" she asks.

"Yes Ginny, he's a perfect gentleman."

"Good... you've had enough pain in your life. I don't want to see you have more." That surprises me because I've never spoken to her about my past.

Maybe she just assumes because it was a case worker from the shelter that set up the interview for me. I know my case worker wouldn't have said anything to her about my past—we had talked about it before I agreed to let her arrange the interview for me.

"Listen, you're still the only one here who knows that I'm trying to sell this place and I want to thank you for keeping it to yourself—"

"Of course, Ginny."

"My lawyer called me just now and told me he might have someone interested in purchasing the place."

"That's wonderful! Do you know who it is?"

I'm happy for her, but disappointed that my days here might be coming to an end. I don't allow myself to focus on what will happen if I can't stay on here as an employee. The two *dates* I've had with Nicholas have given my bank account a nice bump; I've even managed to put more away this month that I thought I would since Nicholas really compensated me well for the last minute business dinner. I tried to tell Bridget it wasn't necessary, but she said that Nicholas already paid the money to her so it's mine whether I want it or not. As long as Nicholas maintains the arrangement, I know I'll be able to pay my bills until another job comes along if the new owners don't want to keep me when they take over.

"Not yet. My lawyer says the company is insisting on complete confidentiality about the purchase. I thought it was weird, but apparently it's quite common. Businesses don't want their competitors to know that they are looking to open a new shop in town."

"Oh, that makes sense."

"Right now they're just reviewing our financials, but I wanted to keep you updated…"

"Thank you, Ginny, I appreciate it."

Finally back at my apartment a few hours later, I'm relieved that the morning is over. It a matter of hours, the two worlds that I thought would remain separate have collided. I guess I expected it would be like when I worked at the department store and the bakery at the same time; maybe once in a while customers would overlap but when they did, it was never a big deal and no one really questioned it. I was naïve to think that I could keep this arrangement with Nicholas separate from anything else in my life. I should have known that it was very probable that my coworkers at the bakery would see my picture in the media. I know a few of the girls read those gossip magazines on their breaks so I shouldn't have really been that surprised.

When my arrangement with Nicholas ends, I'll probably find another job to help make ends meet. I don't know if I'll go back to being a personal shopper or not, but I don't think I can see myself taking on another client with Bridget. I think I only feel comfortable with Nicholas because we had met before, although when I think about it, we really only had a few minutes with each other that day on the sidewalk. I don't know why that would make me feel so comfortable with him now. Whatever the reason, I'm not so delusional as to think that I would feel like this with every guy that Bridget sets me up with.

I will say though, it's been nice not working 12 and 14 hour days and actually having a day off each week when I don't work. Before signing on with Bridget and quitting the store, I rarely had a day off. I wouldn't work both jobs every day, but there were plenty of days where I would work one job and not have a day off. Today, I am sort of working two jobs… I have a *date* with Nicholas this evening to attend an exhibit being featured at the museum. Tonight is a preview night exclusive for members including Nicholas, whose donations have made the exhibit possible. I've never been to this museum so I'm looking forward to it. Once again I will be meeting Nicholas and Carter at PFS, but unlike the dinner the other night, we will be leaving together from the museum, since it's likely that people will see us leaving at the end of the evening and we don't want it to raise questions why we are leaving separately.

Ring Ring

"Hello, Kenzie, it's Bridget. How are you, dear?"

"I'm good, Bridget, how are you?"

"Very well. I was just calling to make sure you have everything you need for the date tonight?"

"Yes, I believe so. Stacy helped me pick out a dress with matching accessories. I'm meeting Mr. Parker at PFS and his driver will be taking us to the museum. Afterwards, they will bring me back to PFS before we go our separate ways."

"Did you see your dinner the other night made the press?"

"I did."

"That means that after tonight it's very likely that you and Nicholas both will be in the press tomorrow morning. The media is expected to be at the museum to cover the exhibit opening. I expect you will be pictured very quickly, as this is the third event that you will be seen with Nicholas. I know this is all new for you, so I wanted to check in and see how you were doing with the publicity and to see if you had any concerns before the pictures start coming out tonight?"

"Today was actually the first time that someone figured out the girl in the picture with Nicholas was me."

"Oh?"

"A few of the staff at the bakery where I work figured it out. I guess it was a preview of what's going to happen after we're seen tonight."

"Are you okay with that, Kenzie? Customers may start asking you questions about Nicholas, reporters will probably figure out who you are, and start calling you or showing up at your place of business. I'm not trying to scare you, I just want you to be prepared."

"I appreciate that, Bridget. Today was a shock, but I think it was a good shock. I'm more prepared now; I know what to expect and Nicholas and I have reviewed our backstory so we're on the same page."

"Good... if you ever have questions with dealing with the media or persistent reporters, you let me know. I'm going to send you a slide show in a few minutes which covers some key points in dealing with the media that you might find helpful. Smile, be nice but never give away too much information. No comment is always a safe response if you don't know what else to say. Don't let them get to you, but if they do, don't let them see it. If they find a weakness they will go after it, so stay strong and call me whenever you need to. I'll help you deal with the media if you have a problem."

"Thank you, Bridget; I appreciate everything you've done for me."

"Anytime. Good luck tonight. I look forward to seeing the pictures tomorrow morning."

I spend the next couple of hours getting ready for my *date* with Nicholas. Having never been to an exhibit opening before, I rely heavily on Stacy's advice about what to wear tonight. I wear a red dress that falls just to my knees: a scooping neckline, cap sleeves and a slightly open back. The dress is complemented by black shoes, a diamond tennis bracelet and matching necklace. My hair is curled, letting it fall casually over my shoulders. Somehow between the dress boutique and the salon, they have me leaving my apartment looking like a completely different person than when I woke up.

Tonight I've decided to splurge and request a car service to take me to PFS to meet with Nicholas and Carter. I could have easily taken the subway to PFS, but the thought of walking around in heels on those steps doesn't appeal to me. Right on time, my phone dings with a text letting me know the car service has arrived. I quickly crab my clutch and head to the slick, black sedan waiting out front for me. A few of the people hanging out on the front stoop whistle when I walk by but I ignore them and get into the waiting car.

"Ms. Rose, it's nice to see you again," Carter greets me in the lobby of PFS when we arrive.

"And you, Carter."

"Mr. Parker should be down momentarily."

As if he knew we were waiting, the elevator doors open revealing Nicholas, looking handsome as always. Although we didn't coordinate our outfits, it looks like we did; Nicholas is wearing a black suit with a deep red tie that almost matches my dress perfectly.

"You look beautiful, Kenzie," Nicholas kisses me on the cheek.

"Thank you, Nicholas," I can't help but blush when I see several people in the lobby staring at us. I don't think they expected to see their boss kissing a woman, even if it was only on the cheek.

"Mr. Parker, Ms. Rose, the car is waiting," Carter leads us into the elevator which brings us to the parking garage.

"I'm not sure if you saw, but it turns out we were photographed at dinner last week," Nicholas says.

"So I've learned," I laugh. "One of my coworkers printed out the picture and brought it in, then Cara—"

"Cara?"

"She came to the bakery this morning to place an order and she mentioned seeing the picture. Then Bridget called to make sure I had seen the picture and to remind me that press would be covering the event tonight and that this will be the third time you are seen with me."

"I expect the media to really kick it up a notch after tonight," he sighs.

"That's what you wanted, right?"

"It is, but I just hate that it had to come to this. I would much rather skip these events and focus on PFS, instead of having to spend time concocting lies to keep the media from portraying me as a *playboy*."

"Hopefully, after tonight they will think we are in a committed relationship and will give you some space."

"Let's hope so."

When we arrive at the museum, the press is out in full force as both Bridget and Nicholas had predicted. They are taking pictures and talking to another couple when we arrive, but the moment Nicholas and I step out of the SUV it's as if we are the only people here tonight.

"Mr. Parker, who is your date?"

"What is your relationship to this woman?"

The questions continue, but Nicholas doesn't respond. We pose for a couple of pictures before Nicholas leads me into the museum. Even though the press is not permitted inside, we still have to keep up appearances, especially since we've learned that people will take pictures of us to sell to the media. We walk through the closed museum, taking in each exhibit as our guide describes everything in great detail. Nicholas's arm remains around my waist the entire night. He leans down to whisper in my ear when we talk about the different exhibits, I think playing it up for anyone who might see us.

"Would you like a glass of champagne?" Nicholas asks as a waiter approaches us.

"Yes, thank you."

We take our drinks and move into a room where the mayor will give a speech thanking all the key benefactors who made the exhibit possible. Nicholas takes my hand and leads me to an empty seat in the room where we wait for the speech to begin.

"Oh, I almost forgot, your sister wanted me to convince you to come to a family dinner—"

"UGH, sorry about that. She hounds me every week about going. I wasn't expecting her to bug you about it. I'll call her tomorrow."

"It's fine Nicholas, really. It wasn't a big deal. I told her that I would talk to you about it but that I wasn't sure what your plans were."

"Thank you. I appreciate you pacifying her."

"Ladies and Gentleman, the mayor," our guide introduces.

The mayor gives a lengthy speech, making a point to thank each donor individually for their contribution to the museum. The speech is politically focused of course—discussing the importance of bringing the arts back to the community even when budget cuts prevent the government from providing financial support. The speech makes me think, despite being incredibly successful, Nicholas or PFS makes it a point to donate money to different causes: first the New Beginnings Gala and now to the museum. It's nice to know that not everyone in the world is focused on keeping the money they earn. It's rare for someone wanting to give back to the community the way Nicholas does.

"Are you ready to leave?" Nicholas whispers to me as soon as the speech ends.

"Whenever you're ready."

He takes my hand and leads me to the lobby where Carter is waiting for us; with a simple nod Carter quickly disappears ahead of us while we take in key exhibit pieces in the lobby. A few minutes later Nicholas's phone buzzes. Without looking at it he leads me out the door where the press is once again waiting for us.

"Mr. Parker, who is your date?"

"Ms... Ms... what's your connection to Mr. Parker?"

Once again we ignore the press, instead heading to the SUV that Carter has waiting for us. Nicholas sighs heavily as soon as the door closes, clearly relieved to be away from the press.

"PFS will be issuing a statement tomorrow about us."

"Okay..."

"Essentially, I am going to confirm that we are dating and will ask that they give us privacy. Of course, they won't but according to my PR department this is the best way to answer a few of their questions but still maintain control of at least some of the information that is provided to them."

"That makes sense."

"If any of the press gives you a hard time, I want you to let me know as soon as possible. This is Carter's direct number—you can reach him day or night. If anyone bothers you at home or at work, please call Carter. If needed, we can provide you with security to help you deal with the press. I don't want you to be at risk because of this arrangement."

"Thank you, Nicholas. I'm sure it will be fine, but I appreciate the offer," I take the business card and place it in my clutch.

"Carter has arranged for a car service to meet us at PFS to take you home tonight. If you are agreeable, I would like to have the same car service pick you up for events. They have signed a non-disclosure agreement with us to ensure your privacy. Carter and I both feel it is safest if we only use one car service, as it reduces the risk of someone leaking details about your personal life to the press."

"Oh... okay."

"Thank you for agreeing to this. I know you probably didn't anticipate all of this when you met with Bridget."

"I didn't but so far the press hasn't bothered me. I'm sure that will likely change after today, but I'll be prepared if they start questioning me."

"Thank you again for tonight, I appreciate you attending the exhibit opening with me," Nicholas says when Carter parks the car in PFS's parking garage. A black sedan is waiting next to us which I assume is the car service.

"It was nice Nicholas; I've never been to that museum before so it was a new experience."

"I'll see you on Saturday?"

"Yes, I've confirmed my schedule with Bridget."

Nicholas leans over, kissing me gently on the cheek, letting his lips linger a few seconds longer than they have before. He squeezes my hand just before Carter opens the door but he looks as if he wants to say something. Instead he simply shakes his head and lets go of my hand. Carter escorts me to the awaiting car, introduces me to the driver and then closes the door behind me. We drive out of the parking garage a few minutes later and like that, I'm quickly lost in my thoughts about tonight and this arrangement with Nicholas.

Surprisingly, I've enjoyed the couple of *dates* that we have had so far, I guess I expected them to be boring and uncomfortable like with *him*. I've enjoyed my private life, so the thought of the press learning more about me is unnerving. I knew this was something that would likely happen when I took the job with Bridget. In the back of my head I worry a little if *he* will find me now that my picture is going to be all over the place. *He* only contacted me once after I left, having somehow tracked down where I was working. He made it clear *he* wanted nothing more to do with me. Assuming nothing has changed, I don't expect *him* to try to get a hold of me because I'm pictured with Nicholas but it's still something in the back of my mind. I wish I could just move on with my life and never have to worry about *him* again, but even if the media weren't a concern, he never fails to make an appearance in my nightmares when I least expect it.

"Ma'am," the driver quickly pulls me from my thoughts to alert me that we've arrived at my apartment building.

"Thank you."

I quickly get out of the car and into the building, ignoring the whistles and remarks from the usual crowd gathered on the front stoop. I want to look for a better place to live but with this arrangement still being so new with Nicholas, I'm worried about what will happen if I sign a lease on a new apartment that costs much more than this one does... only for Nicholas to decide he doesn't need me any longer and then I'm left with rent I can't pay. I go to put my key in the lock but the door suddenly eases open without being unlocked.

Madison Quinn

"What the hell?"

Chapter 14
Nicholas

Tonight was another success on the PR image transformation plan that I developed: Kenzie and I were photographed together for the third time in a couple of weeks. I expect our picture to be on several gossip sites by morning if not already. I find myself actually eager to see what the press says about me now. For the first time in two years, they have pictures of me with the same woman attending different events. I could not have planned the business dinner better if I wanted to. I had no idea that someone there would recognize me and sell the picture to the media but I'm grateful they did. I have another date with Kenzie on Saturday, although I'm still trying to determine what we are going to do. I want Saturday to be something not business related, just to ensure that no one suspects that she is only accompanying me to business or PFS events.

"Yes... no I understand... completely off the record... call me tomorrow morning and Mr. Parker will be more than happy to make the donation to the fund... of course... ETA less than 10 minutes."

The one sided conversation Carter is having catches my attention when he mentions my name and more so when he promises I will make a donation to a fund. It's very rare for Carter to promise donations and typically only when the stakes are high which immediately has me concerned.

"What's going on Carter?"

"Sir, that was the New York police department, there has been a reported break in at Ms. Rose's apartment—"

"What?!?! When? Is she hurt?"

"The call was received less than two minutes ago. Ms. Rose called the report in herself. No requests for medical attention were made so my contact doesn't believe she is hurt."

"Get me there now, Carter!"

"Yes sir, we should be there in less than 10 minutes."

"How did they know to call you?"

"I alerted the captain of Ms. Rose's association with you when you first… when this arrangement began. I've had some concerns about the area she lives in so I requested he alert me to any police activity in or immediately around her building."

"I assume the donation I am making tomorrow will ensure that this is kept out of the press?"

"Yes sir, everything tonight is off the record. Officers responding will not make an official report unless Ms. Rose insists on it—"

"I'll ensure she doesn't."

Damn it! Just as my plan was going perfectly, some fucker has to go and screw things up! I can't have Kenzie living in an unsafe place; once the media find out who she is, it will only be a matter of time until they figure out where she lives. What will they think if they learn that I'm dating someone who lives in that type of neighborhood? How can I possibly protect her if it's as bad as Carter says it is? She needs to move out of that building tonight! I can't have her at risk of being injured or becoming a victim of a crime, especially not because of me. This may be a business arrangement, but I would never forgive myself if she were harmed because of our arrangement.

"Carter?"

"Two minutes sir."

Looking out the window of the SUV, I can see the evidence of the crime intensity as we drive past many abandoned buildings. Cars are on the road sitting on cinder blocks, windows of buildings are broken or boarded up, graffiti nearly covers every building and I worry that we haven't even reached the area where Kenzie lives. How is it I let her go home to this neighborhood after our dates? Why didn't I insist that Carter have someone follow her? Why didn't I insist that she move into a safer area when we began our arrangement?

"FUCK!" I'm so frustrated and angry with myself for not preventing this from happening. I should have thought this through better. I'm normally on top of all these small details during business negotiations but this transformation plan was like nothing I've ever done before. It never occurred to me that a woman I contracted with through Bridget would live in such a horrible area.

"We'll park here sir, her building is just ahead," Carter announces a few minutes later.

We see a police cruiser in front of a graffiti covered building. The building is suspiciously quiet which I'm sure has something to do with the police presence. We walk up the front steps, I look for a doorbell to ring for Kenzie but Carter stops me and pushes the door open; it hadn't been locked to begin with. Knowing that anyone can just walk into the building infuriates me. Without a locked front door anyone can get into the building, hide out and attack a resident. The thought of someone harming Kenzie upsets me more than I expected it to and I'm not sure why. I don't know that her break-in was necessarily caused by her association with me, yet I can't help but feel responsible.

"If you think of anything, please give us a call," I hear a police officer say as he steps out of a doorway just down the hall.

"I'll speak to him and make sure that he has spoken with his captain about how to handle this situation sir," Carter says.

"I'll check on Kenzie and convince her that she can't stay here."

"Yes, sir."

After a brief introduction to the police officer, I find myself standing outside Kenzie's door waiting for her to open it. A few seconds after I knock, the door opens a crack to reveal a very surprised Kenzie.

"Nicholas? What... what are you doing here?" she asks.

"Kenzie, can I come in for a moment please?"

"Ummmm..."

"Please Kenzie..."

"Okay."

Thankfully she slowly opens the door to let me enter her apartment; it hadn't occurred to me on our way here that she wouldn't want to see me. I had completely forgotten that per our arrangement I'm not supposed to know where she lives but none of that matters right now. All that matters right now is that I find a way to fix what has happened.

I close the door behind me and walk into her "apartment," if it can be called that. Essentially it's two rooms from what I can see, one of which I assume is a bathroom. Her main room holds a day bed, a dresser with a small television on top and there appears to be some sort of a "kitchen" along the wall which consists of a dorm size fridge, hot plate and a coffee pot. The room has obviously been completely torn apart: there are clothes everywhere, her mattress has been flipped over and sliced down the middle, her fridge door is open and the contents are now on the floor, her television now has a hole through it.

"How did you know?" she asks.

"The police captain called Carter as soon as the call came in. We turned around and headed here as soon as he called."

"You didn't need to come; Nicholas everything is taken care of. The police officer gave me the name of a locksmith that can come tonight to fix the lock. I was just about to call him when you knocked... "

"Kenzie, you can't stay here, it isn't safe."

"It's fine, I've lived here for over a year now and no one has ever bothered me before. I'm sure this was just random—"

"I don't think it was random."

"Why would someone target me? I don't have anything here with stealing Nicholas."

"*They* may not think that. Someone who lives here could have recognized you from our pictures in the press, they may assume because we're dating that you have money."

"You think?" her voice is barely above a whisper as the reality hits her that someone may be targeting her specifically.

"It's very likely."

"Shit," she sighs, leaning against a small end table for support. I walk over to her, wanting to comfort her but I'm not sure what I should do.

"I can't stay here. I'll wait for the locksmith and then... there's a motel a couple blocks away I think. They probably have a room I can get for a few nights. I can starting looking for a new place in the morning—"

"Kenzie..." I try to interrupt but it's obvious she is more talking to herself than to me as she tries to figure out her next step.

"I'll lose my security deposit here... but I should have enough to cover a new one if I can find something quickly."

"Kenzie," I grab her hand to get her attention and she finally stops talking and looks at me with these sad, lost eyes that I've never seen on her before now. "You can come to my place tonight, we'll figure out something—"

"No!" she quickly exclaims. "I... look, that's very generous of you, but I'm sure I can find a place to stay tonight."

"Really, it's not an issue. I have several guest bedrooms that you could stay in—"

"Nicholas, please... I would rather not."

"Okay..."

I swear I've never met anyone like her. Any other woman would jump at the chance to be invited into my apartment even if nothing else but to get their hands on something valuable that I own. Yet, here is Kenzie, with no place but a crummy motel to stay in, refusing to sleep in one of my spare bedrooms. The woman completely baffles me and that's not something that happens often. Suddenly an idea dawns on me, one that might be the perfect answer to our situation.

"I'll figure something out, Nicholas, it's really nothing for you to worry about."

"PFS owns several condos in the city that we use for employees who relocate to New York from out of state to work for us. Alex and Ella just moved out of one they had been staying in when they were waiting to close on their new place. It's completely vacant and no one is scheduled to use it any time soon. Why don't you stay there?"

"I can't... "

"The condo isn't being used anyway—it's fully furnished and within walking distance of the bakery for you."

"That's a very nice offer, but I could never afford something—"

"You don't need to worry about money, the condo is paid for and all the bills are sent directly to PFS."

"I can't let you do that."

"Kenzie, on the way over here I realized that once the press learns your identity they are going to figure out where you live very quickly. I don't know why I didn't realize it before, but you are going to need full time security—"

"What?"

"I'm sorry, but we need to assume that this break in was tied to our *relationship* becoming public knowledge. You're going to need security to help you if the press becomes too much, we need to make sure that something like this doesn't happen again."

"I... I..." She just looks around the room probably trying to make sense of everything. "I don't have anything worth stealing, Nicholas. There's nothing here... I don't...
"

"They don't know that, Kenzie. They probably see you as an easy target because as the press has pointed out, I am worth quite a bit of money. They probably assume you have jewelry, electronics and money lying around here."

"I suppose."

"Please, the condo is sitting empty and would be a safe place for you to live. The building has 24/7 security at all times plus the unit itself has a state of the art security system. You wouldn't have to worry about someone breaking in."

"I... I don't know how I feel about this. I feel like I'm taking advantage of you."

"Kenzie, it's very likely you're in this mess *because* of me. Please let me do this for you, let me protect you."

I can't remember the last time I said *please* so many times. I don't beg for anything, yet here I am begging Kenzie to let me keep her safe. Again, this is something most women wouldn't even question: I am offering to put her up in a luxury condo, completely expense free and she is worried about taking advantage of *me*. This is the woman I first met on the sidewalk a few months ago who tried to refuse my offering to replace the clothes that I had ruined. It's hard to reconcile this woman with the one who receives a paycheck for going on dates with me. Looking around her small apartment, I begin to see why she might have been tempted to agree to Bridget's offer. If this is all she could afford working two jobs, what chance did she have to get out of here?

"Okay," her voice is barely above a whisper, but it's there.

"Great, thank you. Please take only what you absolutely need; the apartment is fully furnished and I can replace anything you don't want to bring. I'll have Carter arrange for a member of my security team to wait here for the locksmith so that anything you don't take tonight is safe. We'll arrange for someone to get the rest of your items tomorrow."

"Nicholas, I don't have very much. They destroyed most of furniture, the jewelry is gone," she looks sadly at her bed and television. "Just let me throw some things into a garbage bag."

"Of course, whatever you want. I'm going to speak with Carter for a moment but I'll be right outside the door."

"Nicholas, he can come into the apartment, you know," she chuckles before opening a drawer and pulling out a bag.

"I'll let him know."

I close the door as I leave the apartment, noting that it barely latches shut. It's obvious someone kicked in the door to gain access. I let out the breath I didn't realize I was holding, relieved that I was able to convince her to move out tonight. I don't know what I would have done if she continued to refuse to leave or had insisted on staying in some flea bag motel tonight. Even though no woman I've ever dated has ever been in my condo since I bought it, I find myself oddly disappointed that she didn't take me up on the offer to stay in one of my guest rooms. After *she* moved out and I sold that condo, I vowed to never let a woman get that close to me again yet here I was offering Kenzie to essentially move in with me.

"Sir?" Carter pulls me from my thoughts before I can figure out why it bothers me that Kenzie said no.

"Kenzie has agreed to move into the vacated condo that Alex and Ella were in. Can you arrange for a locksmith to fix the door tonight and have Hunter wait here until they arrive?"

"I've already contacted someone and they will be here within the hour to fix the lock; Hunter should be here momentarily as well."

"I would like Hunter assigned to Kenzie full time beginning, tomorrow."

"Yes, sir."

"She is bagging up a few things to take with us but if there's anything left that should be saved, can you arrange for it to be delivered tomorrow? She didn't think there would be anything as most of the furniture was destroyed by whoever broke in."

"I'll arrange for someone to dispose of anything left behind."

"Did the police have any leads?"

"No, there were no prints and this building obviously doesn't have any security cameras, so there was nothing to go on. They suspect it was someone who lived here though. A few of the residents apparently made comments about seeing Kenzie getting into a high end car a few times—"

"The car service?"

"That's my guess. Bridget had a car service bring Kenzie to PFS for your last two… dates. I'm guessing a car like that probably stood out when it picked her up."

"So it this was my fault…"

"Sir, I don't think—"

"Kenzie told me to tell you to come inside rather than standing outside her door."

"Yes sir."

"Kenzie?" I call before opening the door all the way not wanting to startle her.

"Over here," she's bent over trying to pull the small fridge out from underneath a countertop.

"Ma'am, please allow me," Carter quickly offers.

"Thank you Carter, if you can just pull it out a little, there's something behind it I need to get," she explains.

Carter pulls the small fridge out from under the counter, and as soon as it's out a few inches, Kenzie indicates that he can stop. She reaches behind the fridge and after a few minutes of searching pulls out a beige envelope that must have been stuck to the back of the fridge.

"Carter if you wouldn't mind, could you help me pull the dresser from the wall? It shouldn't be very heavy, they... most of the drawers are empty now."

Just like with the fridge, Carter moves the dresser away from the wall a few inches and Kenzie reaches behind to pull out another beige envelope. I'm about to ask her what is going on but Carter shakes his head at me, indicating that I shouldn't ask.

Knock knock

"That will be Hunter; what can we take to the SUV for you, Ms. Rose?" Carter asks.

"Just that black bag, I can grab the duffel back and my purse—"

"We'll take the duffel bag and the other bag ma'am. I'll come back up for you both in a few minutes," Carter quickly grabs the two bags before Kenzie can protest and leaves the apartment.

"If there's anything you think you overlooked, Hunter can bring you back here tomorrow to get it—"

"Hunter?"

"He's going to be your CPO—"

"I'm sorry, my what?"

"Close protection officer—he's assigned to your security. He will take you wherever you need to go and will ensure the press don't bother you."

"He's going to follow me around?"

"Yes, I know it's a lot to take in but trust me, after a little while you will barely notice him."

"I doubt that."

"His job will be to make sure something like this doesn't happen again, Kenzie. He's there to keep you safe."

"I know, I'm sorry if it sounds like I'm being argumentative—"

"Not at all, I know this is a lot to take in all at once."

"It's just not how I expected to be spending my night tonight," she sighs and shakes her head, looking around the room one last time before Carter indicates that the SUV is ready for us to leave. I take her hand in mine and lead her out of the apartment; she follows me but doesn't say a word as I'm sure she tries to come to terms that she is leaving. It may not be much, but I get the impression that Kenzie liked the place. When we get into the SUV, she stares blindly out the window...

"Why did the police call you, Nicholas?"

"When we... when we started our arrangement, Carter spoke to the captain in this precinct and requested they contact him if there was any police activity in or around your residence."

"So you knew where I lived?"

"I didn't, no. I have maintained my ignorance of that aspect of our contract until tonight," I assure her trying not to ruin the little bit of trust that I think she has in me.

"But Carter knew where I lived?"

"Yes."

"Bridget told me the information wouldn't be included in my background check; that you wouldn't know where I lived or know how to contact me."

"She didn't give Carter that information. Carter ran a background check—"

"What the hell is it with you running background checks on people without them knowing?!?!"

I've never heard Kenzie raise her voice or curse, so I'm taken aback by her reaction.

"Kenzie... It's standard protocol to run a background check on anyone I come in contact with because of who I am. I have never looked at the report though, Carter gave me very basic information on what was in it."

"Gee thanks," the sarcasm is evident in her voice.

"I'm not going to apologize for the fact that Carter ran the report. It my line of work, it needs to be done. Everyone is considered a risk to PFS, to my family or to me until we have a thorough background report completed."

"I understand that, but don't you think that people like you should at least ask someone before they go diving into someone's past?"

"People like me?"

"Bridget did the same thing! Before she called me about this… about her business, she ran a background check on me. Again, without my permission."

"Kenzie, unfortunately it's how people are weeded out and how risks are reduced."

"I'd like a copy of the report."

"Of course… Carter, please send Ms. Rose a copy of her background report when we return to the condo."

"Of course sir."

"I don't suppose I need to provide you with my email address Carter?"

"No ma'am, I have that information already."

"Of course you do."

"Kenzie… I don't know what to say."

"I think I just want to call it a day and deal with everything tomorrow if you don't mind, Nicholas. It's been a very long day and I'm exhausted. I've been awake now for more than 24 hours so I'm probably not handling this the right way."

Kenzie doesn't say a word for the remainder of the drive, but just before we approach The Accord she takes my hand in hers and squeezes it gently. The subtleness of this gesture makes me smile and despite everything that happened, for the first time in a couple of hours I feel relaxed.

Chapter 15
Kenzie

Finding my apartment torn apart when I arrived home from the exhibit with Nicholas was the very last thing I expected. I was just beginning to try to piece together what had happened when Carter and Nicholas knocked on my door surprising the hell out of me. I never would have thought that Nicholas would suggest, well insist, that I move out of my apartment and into a condo that his company owns. I hate the idea of having to be dependent on him for this apartment; he could terminate our arrangement at any time and I would essentially be homeless again.

What happens if he decides he doesn't need me any longer? I wonder if he would at least give me a couple weeks to find another place? If I save all my money from Bridget and from the bakery I could have enough to cover the cost of a hotel room for a few days or a cheap motel for longer until I found another apartment to rent. I think that's what I'll do… I'll save as much as I can so when Nicholas does end our arrangement and I lose the apartment, I will at least have saved enough to pay for another place.

"Kenzie? We're here," Nicholas pulls me from my thoughts just as I think I have a plan for moving forward.

"Sorry," somehow I was so lost in my thoughts that I hadn't realized that Carter had not only parked the car but was holding my door open. Just before I slide across the seat I realize that Nicholas is holding my hand. I'm surprised by the gesture especially considering our "date" ended several hours ago. We walk through an underground parking garage with Carter following behind us.

"Where are we?" I feel stupid for not asking but I hadn't paid attention to where we were driving. That in itself surprises me because I've never done that before. I never let my guard down so completely as to not know where I am going and where I will end up.

"We are two blocks from the bakery in a building called Accord Towers. The condo is on the fifth floor and then I live a few floors above it—"

"You live here?"

"Yes, however I want to assure you that you will still have your privacy. I don't have a key to this place, only Carter does, but no one will enter the condo without your approval. This will be your place, Kenzie. It won't change anything about our arrangement..."

"But it does..." I sigh. "It changes everything."

"No, it just changes where we meet for our dates and where you are dropped off at afterwards. I will not come into your space Kenzie; the condo is yours," Nicholas explains as we take the elevator from the parking garage.

But... for how long?

"Mr. Parker, Ms. Rose," Carter ushers us through a doorway into a beautiful living space.

"Holy shit," I gasp taking in the space before me.

The door opens to a small tiled entryway but just beyond that is a large living room, completely furnished as Nicholas said it would be. There is an oversized loveseat and a larger couch in the room, plus a coffee table, two end tables and an entertainment center, yet the room still looks incredibly large. The apartment is completely open, but unlike my last space this actually has defined rooms, and several of them. There is a small dining room with a table that can seat four next to a large kitchen with what I can tell even from here are top of the line appliances.

"There are two bedrooms just down the hall, one is set up as a fully equipped office. There is a guest bathroom in the hallway, then the master bedroom with a separate bathroom and walk-in closet. Feel free to change any of the furnishings while you're here—"

"Nicholas, I'm sure—"

"The space is yours, Kenzie, if you want to paint the walls, get new furniture or anything else, please do so. The kitchen is stocked with dishes and cleaning supplies though I'm not sure what is left in the pantry from Alex and Ella—"

"Mr. Parker, Ms. Rose, if I may interrupt," I somehow hadn't noticed Carter standing in the entryway just sort of watching or waiting for us. "The pantry and fridge should be stocked with kitchen essentials and there are a few prepared meals in the freezer until you go food shopping. If there is something you need in the meantime—"

"No, I'm sure whatever is in there is fine, Carter. I hadn't expected anything remotely close to this, so thank you," I'm taken back that all of this was somehow arranged in such a short period of time.

"The meals are delicious, Julie has a way of cooking things so they never taste like they were frozen," Nicholas says.

"Julie?"

I know Nicholas doesn't have a girlfriend in public, but could he have someone that he keeps out of the media spotlight? He said he didn't have time to date but what if that wasn't true and he was just protecting her from the media? I'm not sure why, but suddenly the idea that he is with another woman bothers me. Our exclusivity clause actually only applies to me.

"My housekeeper and personal cook. She keeps my freezer stocked with prepared meals so that I don't starve on the weekends when she is off or on the rare occasion she goes away. There should be instructions on each container as to how to heat it."

"That's very nice of her, please thank her for me." Relief floods me before I have a chance to understand why.

"Of course. Is there anything else you will need tonight?"

"I don't think so…" Who could possibly need anything else in a place like this?

"Ms. Rose, here is the security code to the apartment and instructions on how to change it. This key is for the ground level entrance, here is the code to the parking garage needed to gain access from the outside or from the elevator and then this is the key to the apartment. You should find a list of all the building amenities in the office, now accessible to you. I know Mr. Parker gave you my number if the press bothers you but if you need something please call me at any time. This is Hunter's cell phone number, please contact him in the morning and let him know your schedule for the week. I ask that you not leave the building without him; he will escort you anywhere you need to go, even if it's in the middle of the night."

"I'm sure that won't be necessary but thank you. I'll call him tomorrow and let him know my work schedule: it's pretty much the same every week so it's easy to plan around."

"I'll let Bridget know the details for Saturday once they are confirmed?"

"Sounds good. Thank you again, Nicholas… this… thanks for, well all of it," I lean up on my tiptoes and kiss him lightly on the cheek. I don't know whether I'm out of line or not; technically our date ended hours ago but I feel I need to show him my appreciation somehow.

"It was nothing, Kenzie…"

"Good night Nicholas."

"Night."

With that I'm left alone in this incredibly large, elegant apartment that I know I could never afford. Despite now being awake for more than 24 hours, I find myself full of energy and can't help wanting to explore my new home, even if it's only a temporary new home. I walk through the living room, wanting to head straight for the kitchen but I stop in front of patio doors that I discover open to a small but cozy patio complete with a two chairs and a small table. There isn't much of a view, you kind of look across the street to another building but the thought of just being able to step outside for a few minutes without having to step around or over drunk/high people is perfect for me. I love the sound of the hustle and bustle of the city below me, yet the patio makes it seem like I'm far enough away from all of that.

Back inside, the kitchen is more impressive than I ever could have imagined. There is a full size gas range, a dishwasher, a small walk-in pantry and a full size fridge. The kitchen itself is easily as large as my last apartment. As Carter mentioned, the fridge and pantry are stocked with what you would expect to find in a kitchen: spices, flour, sugar, milk, eggs, cereal, snacks, fruit, vegetables, soda, beer and wine. I could not shop for a couple of weeks and not starve, but I'm actually eager to go food shopping—I can't remember the last time I was able to cook an actual meal. Despite trying, I quickly discovered there are only so many things you can cook on a hot plate that end up tasting halfway decent.

Finally pulling myself away from the kitchen, I go down the hall to discover the office is set up for someone to be able to work completely from home. There's a large desk with a printer, scanner and fax machine, a small filing cabinet and even a laptop which looks brand new.

Next to the office is the bedroom, which is even larger than the living room is. The bed must be a king size which seems ridiculous for one person, but I can't help but throw myself on it, and I'm immediately engulfed by the thick blankets. I didn't think my bed at the apartment was too bad, but after lying on this even for a few minutes I realize just how uncomfortable it truly was.

Just off the bedroom is a large, empty walk in closet that I don't think I could ever own enough clothes to fill. Next to the closet is a bathroom that would be every girl's dream: there is a separate walk in shower, a large soaking tub with jets and a double vanity.

Never in my wildest dreams would I have ever dreamed of living in a place like this. I thought the house I moved into with *him* was impressive, but compared to this, that place was nothing. I can't help but worry that at any moment I'm going to wake up and find out all of this was just a dream and that I'm still back at the crummy apartment building listening to my neighbors fight over who took the last pill.

Needing to put tonight behind me, I take a quick shower in my new bathroom, vowing to spend some time in the soaking tub tomorrow and change into a shirt to sleep in. Despite the energy burst, I fall asleep the moment my head hits the pillow.

Flashback

"You're nothing! We open our house to you and this is how you repay us??? No wonder your mother didn't want you! I bet she doesn't even know who your father is!"

"I'm sorry…"

Slap

"Get out of here! Go to your room and don't come out! I don't want to look at you! I'll be calling tomorrow; I need you out of here. You're just like your mother… a fucking slut! I bet you were fucking him tonight weren't you?"

"No! I swear—"

Slap!

"You will only be good for a fuck… no one will ever love you! Get out of my sight!"

End Flashback

Ring Ring

I wake up twisted in blankets, and covered in sweat to the sound of my cell phone ringing somewhere in the apartment. Glancing at the clock I realize I slept until almost noon; I can't remember the last time I slept for so long. I quickly make my way to the living room and find my phone on the coffee table where I must have left it last night before I went to bed. I see I have a missed call from Bridget. I hit the send button to return her call.

"Kenzie, dear, how are you? Nicholas told me what happened at your apartment last night, are you okay?"

"I'm fine, thank you, Bridget. I'm staying in one of PFS's condos for now, Nicholas insisted—"

"He was right to, dear. The press loves the fact that Nicholas is being pictured with the same woman and will probably come after you even stronger now. I don't know if you've had a chance to check, but your picture is already on several different websites—"

"What? Why?" I immediately panic that the press somehow found out about the break in last night.

"From the art exhibit you attended, dear. Pictures were apparently leaked of you two from inside the exhibit last night, plus you were pictured going into the exhibit."

"Oh. I'll have to check out the sites later today."

"So far it seems mostly positive, although a few sites are placing bets on how much longer you will be by Nicholas's side. You don't need to worry about them though. Nicholas told me he was very satisfied with this arrangement so I think the press will be disappointed when you continue to be seen with him. He asked me to confirm the details of your date for Saturday night if you have a few minutes to talk?"

"Of course."

"He would like to pick you up at five on Saturday and take you to dinner. Seeing as you both live in the same building now, unless you object, he will pick you up at your apartment door."

"No, that's fine."

"The date Saturday will be just the two of you—"

"Oh?"

"Mr. Parker thinks it's important to be seen with you casually so as to not raise any suspicions that you might only be accompanying him to public events. Although there won't be any press around you Saturday, it's likely someone will recognize you and it will be reported to the media."

"I suppose that makes sense."

"Do you have any questions about Saturday, Kenzie?"

"No, I don't think so."

I spend the rest of the day lazily enjoying my temporary new home. I soak in the luxurious jetted tub and watch movies on the incredibly comfortable loveseat. The food that Nicholas's housekeeper left me was amazing, just like he said it would be... you would never know that it was made previously and then frozen. I don't know how I could ever thank Nicholas for everything he and Carter did for me last night; not only did he provide me with a place to live temporarily, he made sure everything was taken care of back at my apartment.

I know I need to apologize for how I reacted about the background check and read what Carter sent me. It contained pretty much what I knew it would. I should have understood why someone in Nicholas's position would need people to have background checks run on them; for all he knew, I could have been some gold digger after his money. I

On His Terms

get it and still don't like that it was done, but I should have reacted differently. I vow to apologize on Saturday night when I see him for our next date. The last thing I want is to seem ungrateful for everything he did last night.

Chapter 16
Kenzie

I broke down and called Hunter this morning so I could go food shopping, something I had put off as long as possible because I thought it would be weird. He immediately offered to go to the store and pick up whatever I needed but I couldn't let him do that. It's hard enough to get used to the idea that I *need* someone to drive me places and accompany me through the grocery store. I can't let him actually *go* food shopping for me that would be too much. Surprisingly it was not as awkward as I thought it might be. We left as soon as I woke up and the store was pretty empty so we didn't have to worry about any press.

Last night before I went to bed I searched the gossip pages for information about me and Nicholas. As he said, PFS released a statement confirming that he was in a "serious relationship" with someone and they asked for the press to respect our privacy. What surprised me was the statement did not release my name or really anything about me, which I suppose was purposely done to try to maintain my privacy a little longer.

When I was shopping with Hunter, I picked up a few items that I would need to bake Nicholas a basket of goodies as a way to thank him for everything he did last night. The kitchen is not only stocked with most of the basic staples you would find in any pantry, but it also has a large mixer, a handheld mixer, baking pans, muffin tins and more utensils than I could ever imagine using. I start baking as soon as we get back to the condo and manage to have a couple different varieties of muffins and cookies made before lunch time which was my goal. I don't expect that Nicholas is going to eat all of these but I figured he could share them with the people who work for him; besides, you really can't just make one muffin…

"Good morning Ms. Rose," Hunter answers the phone before the first ring even stops.

"Good morning, Hunter. I have something for Mr. Parker's office, so do you have a few minutes to take me there?"

"Um… of course. I'll meet you in a few minutes."

"Thank you!"

It's obvious from Hunter's response that going to PFS was probably the last thing he expected from me which makes me wonder if perhaps I shouldn't go there. I've met Nicholas at PFS twice now for *dates* so I just assumed it would acceptable for me to drop the basket off today, but Hunter's response has me second guessing myself. If he's busy or can't see me for some reason I'll just leave the basket with Carter since he is with him during the day. By the time Hunter knocks on the door, I feel a little less nervous but still unsure if I should be going to PFS.

"We've arrived Ms. Rose," Hunter announces after a very short drive. I hadn't realized until now just how close the condo was to PFS. I'm actually looking forward to not having to wake up so early for work tomorrow because I won't need to take the subway and then a bus to get to the bakery. If it weren't for Nicholas insisting that Hunter take me to work, I would probably just walk the couple of blocks to the bakery. The condo really is convenient to everything.

"Ms. Rose," Carter greets us in the lobby.

"Carter, I wanted to drop something off for Nicholas but if he's busy—"

"I believe he is in between a meeting and phone conference at the moment. He probably only has a few minutes to spare, but he should be in his office."

Carter escorts me to the elevator and just before the doors close I see a few women in the lobby whispering and looking back at me. I look down at what I'm wearing: a simple pair of black dress pants and a button down shirt which I thought would be suitable to drop off something but after seeing those women I'm doubting my attire completely. When we finally arrive on Nicholas's floor, I'm greeted by another one of his employees who is impeccably dressed, almost as if she walked off a designer's photo shoot. I silently vow to add at least one or two outfits to my closet that I could wear here if we weren't going to on a date so I would at least look like I fit in a little more.

"Melody, is Mr. Parker free?" Carter asks.

"Yes, he is… but—"

"We'll only be a minute," Carter quickly dismisses her and escorts me to a large door across from the reception desk.

"Yes," Nicholas's voice booms from behind the closed door.

"Go on," Carter chuckles when I make no move to open the door.

"Nicholas?" he hasn't looked up since I entered his office; his is obviously focused on whatever he is looking at. There are papers strewn all over his desk plus several more in his hand. I immediately regret coming here, as it's obvious that I've disturbed him.

"Kenzie? What are you doing here? Is everything okay?" he drops the papers onto his desk and immediately stands up to greet me.

"Everything is fine... I'm sorry to have bothered you," I apologize quickly.

"Nonsense, I needed to step away from this stuff anyway," he shrugs as he looks at all the papers on his desk. "Everything is okay though? The condo... it has everything you need?"

"Oh yes! It has everything I need and many things that I don't need," I laugh. "I wanted to thank you... and well apologize for my reaction the other night—"

"Kenzie, that's not—"

"It is. I overreacted to the situation, as I was caught off guard and then took it out on you when you told me about the background check. I wanted to apologize for that. I understand why Carter would run a background check on me and while I don't like the idea that it was done without my permission, I understand nonetheless. Regardless, blowing up at you was wrong and I'm sorry. I baked you some muffins and cookies to apologize for my behavior but also to thank you for what you did the other night."

"I didn't—"

"Nicholas, I know very few people who would have stepped up and helped someone who is practically a stranger—"

"I wouldn't say that you're a stranger."

"You're probably right, I wouldn't say we're strangers but still... there aren't many people who would have rushed over to help someone they barely know. I just wanted to thank you for coming over to my apartment that late at night and then arranging for me to stay in the condo. It was very generous of you."

"Kenzie... it was nothing, really. I'm just glad you're in a place where you are safe. You didn't need to come here to thank me, but if those are the delicious muffins that you make at the bakery, I certainly wouldn't refuse one."

"Mr. Parker, you're appointment is here," the receptionist alerts Nicholas through his phone intercom.

"I know you're busy—"

"Melody, show them to the board room and let them know that my previous call ran over so I'll be in with them in a few minutes."

"I don't want to make you late for your meeting—"

"They can wait a few minutes; I haven't had a chance to eat lunch yet so you have perfect timing after all."

Nicholas and I sit at a small table for a few minutes while he eats one of the muffins. When I suggest he share the remaining with his staff, he balks at the idea and says he would probably eat them all before he left for the day.

"Mr. Parker," the receptionist interrupts us again.

"I'll be there in a minute, Melody," Nicholas informs her.

"I should let you get to your meeting. I wasn't sure what your schedule was and didn't mean to make you late for anything."

"It's fine; it's a boring meeting anyway. Thank you again for the basket, Kenzie, it was very thoughtful."

Nicholas walks me out to the reception area where Carter and Hunter are waiting for me. He kisses me gently on the cheek before heading down a hallway which I assume leads to the board room where his meeting is. Hunter brings me back to the condo so I can finish unpacking before going to buy an outfit my dinner date with Nicholas tomorrow night.

****

My morning has flown by much faster than I expected. I was able to sleep a little later this morning since I didn't have to figure the subway into my commute time. The bakery is busier than normal for a Saturday morning; usually weekdays are busier than weekends but today for some reason was different. We are so busy that I end up getting no more than a five minute break before Ginny asks me to come back and make another batch of breads so we wouldn't run out. I have no idea why the morning is so busy, but it makes the hours fly by.

I thought it would be weird having Hunter there with me or that my coworkers would ask questions but no one did. I spoke with Ginny when I first arrived and let her know about Hunter; of course her only reaction is asking me over and over again if I'm safe. I assure her I am fine and that Hunter is with me to make sure I *stay* safe. For the most part he sits in the corner of the bakery not bothering anyone; I nearly forget he's there when I start to leave for the day and he rushes to my side to escort me to the car.

Back at the condo I finish unpacking the few items I have and watch a little television. Before I know it, there is a knock at my door and a quick glance through the peephole confirms that it was Nicholas. I quickly set the alarm code before meeting him in the hallway.

"You look... very nice," Nicholas says as I turn around from closing the door.

"Thank you, you look nice as well." He is dressed impeccably as always.

Tonight he is wearing a pair of black dress pants and a light blue button down shirt that complements his eyes. Nice isn't the right word at all... he looks stunning and sexy but I can't bring myself to actually use those words. I find myself wondering what he would look like in a pair of jeans... in the few times we have been out thus far I have never seen him casually dressed.

"I made reservations for us at the Lake View Restaurant," Nicholas informs me.

"I've never been there but I've heard good things about it."

"It's mostly known for the view; the restaurant is built right on the edge of a lake so when you sit in the dining room, you have a perfect view from all angles. As expected, they serve a lot of seafood but they have a variety other items if you don't care for that cuisine."

"Seafood is fine."

"Did you work this morning?"

"I did. We were busier than normal."

"Oh?"

"Usually the work week is the busiest time; most of Ginny's business comes from catering and people coming in for breakfast on their way to work. Weekends tend to be slower but today it was much busier than normal."

"I think I heard there was something going on at the convention center this weekend—if that's the case it might explain why you were busier than normal."

"That's probably it. I've tried to tell Ginny she needs to look at these things online when she is making the schedule, but she's not very big on using the internet so I don't think it's a priority."

"Sir, ma'am," Carter pulls us from our conversation, alerting us that we are approaching the restaurant.

Nicholas escorts me inside and as soon as we arrive we are seated at a table beside the windows overlooking the water. The view really is incredible; it actually feels like you're sitting on top of the water while you eat dinner. The lights from houses across the lake can barely be seen from the restaurant but even those that can be seen just add the ambiance of the place. Every table in the room is occupied yet the tables are set apart enough that you don't feel like it's crowded.

"This view is incredible," I say in awe after we order our dinner.

"It is," he looks out the window as if he is taking in the view for the first time. "So tell me about yourself, Kenzie."

"Um... what do you want to know?" I can't help but feel nervous at his question.

"I don't know... tell me something about you that I don't know. During our first meeting you said you wanted to go back to school. Does that mean you started college at some point or...?"

"Yes, I was actually less than a year away from graduation when I had to withdraw."

"Why? I mean you were so close to graduation, why stop then?"

"I... I didn't have a lot of money for college but I was lucky enough to receive several grants and scholarships that covered my tuition, room and board plus most of the supplies I needed. Unfortunately right before my senior year, I was notified that one of the scholarships I had been awarded had lost funding and would not be renewed. Naturally, it was the largest of the scholarships that I had received; I didn't have enough money saved to cover what that scholarship did so I had to withdrawal from the university my final year."

"Why didn't you take out a student loan to cover the difference?"

"If I could, I would have. Unfortunately by the time I learned my scholarship would not be renewed, I had missed the application deadline for student loans. I had hoped to take only a year off so that I could work and save every penny to go back to school... "

"What happened?"

"Life... it just got in the way."

"What were you studying?"

"Elementary education: I had hoped to become a teacher one day."

"Is that what you're hoping to do now? Finish that degree and go into teacher?"

"I don't think so. I've been looking at some online classes through a community college but haven't decided what I want to take. I could finish my degree in only a couple of classes, but I don't know that I want to go into teaching any longer."

"What do you think you might want to do?"

"It sounds silly… but I think I'd love to take a few culinary classes. Maybe one day open a bakery like Ginny did—"

"Ginny?"

"She's the owner of Sweet Dreams."

"Oh."

"What about you? Did you know that you always wanted to run a large successful company like you do?"

"Kind of," he chuckles. "I knew early on that I didn't want to work for someone else. I'm not good at doing what other people tell me, so going into business for myself seemed like the perfect solution. I received my undergraduate degree from NYU and probably should have continued further, stopped after that."

"How come?"

"It just wasn't for me. I had enough of sitting in classrooms after the first four years, so I couldn't imagine doing it any longer."

"How did you start PFS?"

"I've always had a knack for looking at a problem and coming up with a solution, even when others thought one wasn't possible. My parents insisted I get a job as soon as I told them that I wouldn't be returning to NYU. I started working at this small telecommunications company; my primary responsibility was to show them ways to save money. However, the company was very poorly run with far too many staff being paid to sit around and be unproductive. I was there less than a year before they ended up being forced to close their doors. It was a good thing though."

"How so?"

"I learned what I wanted to do in that moment; when I graduated I wasn't sure exactly where in the financial world I wanted to settle. However, after working there I found a passion in wanting to help companies before they got to the point of having to close their doors. I wanted to work with them on investing their profits in areas that could help sustain them long term."

"So what did you do?"

"My parents refused to loan me the money to start up a business on my own. Well, I shouldn't say they refused; they agreed to lend me the money if I worked for a few years in the field at other companies. They questioned my ability to be taken seriously without more experience under my belt. I had no desire to work for someone else; I wanted to get out in the real world and start making changes. I didn't want to work with only one company when I could be working with several at the same time making a difference."

"Where did you end up getting the money to start PFS then?"

"My grandfather, my mom's dad, loaned me the money I needed to start up PFS. I paid him back, with interest of course, within a year."

"Wow… you're lucky you had someone who believed in you enough to loan you that much money even when your parents said no."

"I understood where my parents were coming from. They wanted me to have work experience to fall back on in case the company didn't succeed."

"Have you ever thought about returning to school?"

"Not really. I mean, I've gotten this far without it; PFS is obviously a success so I don't know that an advanced college degree would make much of a difference. I've thought about taking *a* class here or there, especially in technology as there are times when I struggle to understand some of the spreadsheet equations and how they were generated. Maybe someday I will, but right now I don't think I have the time to sit through classes, homework and projects for hours each week. PFS takes up nearly all the spare time I have as it is."

"I bet."

"So… you grew up on the west coast you said?"

"For the most part; I moved around a lot when I was a child but pretty much stayed around that cost."

"Do you have family in New York?"

"No."

"Ah, so you must have moved here with a boyfriend?"

"No."

"Okay… " I'm sure he can tell this is a conversation I would rather not have. "Do you have any siblings?"

"No, I'm an only child."

"I take it you're not very close to your family?"

"Let's just say I didn't have the best childhood. I would rather leave that door closed, if you don't mind."

"Of course, I'm sorry."

"I… my father died shortly after I was born. I don't remember him and I was never really close to my mother."

"I'm sorry, Kenzie."

We spend the next few minutes in silence, both of us picking at our food, not really knowing what to say to each other.

"The shrimp is really good," I finally decide to break the silence.

"I'm glad you like it. This place is nice because it offers a nice selection besides seafood, even though that's what most people come here for."

"I can see why."

Thankfully, the former conversation has returned because some things, *my* things, are better left unsaid.

"Can I ask… how do you know Bridget? I know her from different fundraising events that we both attend."

"We were strangers until she insisted a store manager hire me one day."

"That's Bridget. She seems like the type who is used to getting exactly what she wants."

"Absolutely," I laugh in agreement. "I helped her with a situation in the store one day and then she insisted the manager hire me and that I be put in charge of her account. I worked there for about a year and a half."

"You quit because of Bridget?"

"Yes and no. I could have probably continued working, although it would have been a scheduling nightmare since I primarily worked evenings and weekends. I knew I couldn't work three jobs, so one had to go. I really enjoy working at the bakery which made the decision easier."

We spent the rest of dinner talking about and getting to know each other. It was surprisingly comfortable and I was grateful that Nicholas didn't pry into my past—I think he could tell it was a topic I wasn't comfortable talking about. The conversation stayed pretty much on the present, with Nicholas doing most of the talking, especially about PFS and the different projects they are working on. Without realizing it, we talked most of the night away and soon we were the only ones left in the restaurant.

"I guess we should head home," Nicholas glances around the empty dining room.

"They're probably waiting for us to leave so they can close for the night. I hadn't realized how late it was."

"Me neither."

We're both quiet on the way back to The Accord Towers, but it's a comfortable silence. Although, come to think of it, I can't recall a time when I haven't been comfortable with Nicholas, surprising since it's usually rare for me to be comfortable around anyone. Tonight is the first time when we are just Nicholas and Kenzie. There is no looming contract over our heads like during our first meeting, or people watching us when we have attended events together. Tonight is has been about us—different... nice but different. When we arrive back at The Accord Towers, Nicholas escorts me back to my condo, only this time Carter waits at the elevator for him rather than walking down the hall with us.

"I had a nice time tonight, Kenzie."

"Me too."

He leans down to kiss me on my cheek as he has done every time we part, only this time his lips land closer to my lips. I can feel his breath on my cheek—I know if I were to move my head just slightly, his lips would be on mine. It's tempting... so very tempting, but I have to remind myself that this is all for show. This is nothing more than a business transaction; Nicholas is kissing me only for appearances. Not for the first time though, I find myself wondering how his lips would feel on mine. If this weren't a business transaction, would he want to kiss me? Would he even be interested in me?

"Good night, Kenzie," he places one final kiss just next to the corner of my lips before pulling back.

"Night..." We stand there, looking at each other for some time before Nicholas finally pulls away and heads back to the elevator.

I quickly unlock my door, turn off the alarm and close the door behind me before collapsing onto the loveseat in the living room. I can't remember the last time I felt like this: the last time I actually wanted a guy to kiss me. I need to do something because I can't keep thinking about it. This is supposed to be a business deal: a transaction, between two people. I'm not supposed to be attracted to him. He could never want someone like me... he's only interested in me now because of this arrangement. If it weren't for Bridget, he probably wouldn't have noticed me.

Madison Quinn

Chapter 17
Nicholas

Flashback

"Mommy hungry... mommy... wake up," I shake her.

"Go away."

"Mommy, belly hurts."

"Find something; there's food in the fridge."

"No, gone. No food."

"Look in the cabinets then; I'm tired, leave me alone."

The food is gone in the cabinets too; it's always gone. I wish my Mommy would just wake up. I wish Mommy would be like Suzie's mom who bakes cookies and cooks us yummy food. Why doesn't my mommy cook? Why doesn't my kitchen have all the food that Suzie's does?

"Mommy... "

"Go away, you little shit; I'll get up and deal with you later."

Another night of broken sleep though I'm not entirely surprised. I thought tonight might have been different since I fell asleep much faster than normal and didn't toss and turn as much. I should have expected the end to a nice night would be like this.

Dinner last night was anything but uncomfortable. We easily found things to talk about and there really wasn't a time when things were awkward between us. I confirmed last night what I suspected from our first meeting: Kenzie does not like to talk about herself and will do almost anything to avoid talking about her past. I'm curious as to why she does not talk about her childhood, her family or even something simple like why she decided to move to the east coast? People don't just up and decide to leave Denver to move to New York, at least not without a good reason.

When she said she didn't have family out here, I just assumed she followed love: that some guy she was with decided to move here and she followed. She denied that but once again gave me no clue as to why she would move across country. I'm tempted to ask Carter to dig deeper into her background; there has to be something there to explain why she left or what happened to her family. He assured me there was nothing out of the ordinary in her background report but I know she is hiding something.

Either what she is hiding doesn't appear on her background report because it is something that was never reported, or she has managed to find someone to bury certain details of her past which isn't easy and I should know. If it wasn't for this damn contract with Bridget, I would just look at the full background report myself but I gave her my word that I wouldn't pry into her personal information and I'm trying like hell to uphold my end of the contract. Plus, the thought of Kenzie getting mad at me again bothers me, although I don't know why it should. I piss people off on a daily basis in my business and don't think twice. Yet here I am worried that Kenzie will get mad; she was really upset by the fact that Carter even ran a background check on her. I don't know how she would react if she knew I had him dig deeper or that I even read the report.

Trying to push thoughts of Kenzie out of my mind, I take a shower and start to weed through my many emails that came in during dinner. Once again I find myself waiting a reasonable time before I let Carter know I want to go for a run. Running helps pull me from my nightmares; it clears my mind and gets me ready for the day. Of course as luck would have it, it's raining outside and I despise running when it's raining hard. A few minutes later, Carter and I are in the gym of The Towers running on treadmills instead.

I'm listening to music, lost in my thoughts which are focused on trying to find the next big project for PFS to take on. I don't know how long I run but when I finally look up I see an absolutely stunning woman standing next to the pool. One wall of the gym overlooks the indoor Olympic size swimming pool one floor below the gym, but the ceiling of the room extends to the height of the gym. Not too many people use the pool but this morning there is a sexy brunette standing at the edge, almost as if she is trying to decide if she is going in. I can only see her back, but from what I can see, she looks incredibly sexy in the bikini she is wearing. Without warning, she dives perfectly into the pool, swimming the entire length before lifting her head up for air. She swims several times back and forth without stopping. I don't know why, but I can't seem to stop watching her. It's almost like I'm drawn to her.

After several minutes, or perhaps longer, the beautiful brunette climbs out of the pool once again giving me a perfect view of the profile of her body. She has long legs that seem to go on forever; a small ass but one that I could see filling my hands perfectly. I can tell from this angle her stomach is completely flat and firm. Her breasts are perfect just like the rest of her: not too big, but not too small either. I imagine what she would look like naked beneath me. Fuck, she wouldn't even have to be naked, she could stay in the bikini she has on right now.

I wonder what it would be like to walk into the pool area, push her against the wall, move her bikini bottom aside and thrust into her. I would hold her wrists in one hand behind her back, the other would be gripping her firm ass as I fuck her hard against the wall until she begs me to make her come. No one would be able to see us but the idea of fucking her in public arouses both of us further. We use each other; taking from each other what we both desperately need, a quick hard fuck. I nearly groan aloud as I picture finding my release inside her flat against that wall. Opening my eyes, I'm absolutely stunned at the sight before me.

Kenzie.

Fuck!! Kenzie is the beautiful woman who was swimming in the pool.

What the fuck?!?!? I can't be picturing fucking her! I can't complicate our perfect arrangement by finding her attractive! FUCK!!!! I knew she likely had an incredible body; some of the dresses she has worn have made that obvious but I never expected to see her in so little clothing as she is wearing right now. I know without even closing my eyes that the image of her in the bikini is burned into my mind. How the fuck am I ever going to look at her again without picturing her like this?

FUCK... FUCK... FUCK... FUCK...

Not only am I now left trying to figure out how to burn the image from my mind, but I'm stuck with a fucking hard on in the middle of the gym! I slow the pace down on the treadmill, close my eyes and begin picturing all sorts of unattractive images in my mind. Finally after several minutes, I am able to get myself under control and thankfully when I open my eyes she is gone from the pool area.

"Let's go, Carter."

"Yes, sir."

Returning to my condo, I immediately take off for my shower to wash the sweat from my body before breakfast and ultimately another day of work, even though it's Sunday. My mother convinced me to come to dinner tonight so I only have a few hours to get work done before I need to leave. I strip my clothes off and enter the hot shower, letting the water wash away the grime of the gym. I make the mistake of closing my eyes, the image of fucking Kenzie against the wall in the pool room immediately returns. Unlike at the gym when I was only picturing a body, this time I'm imagining it's her against the wall. I'm picturing her arms behind her back, her ass in my hand, her pussy gripping me tightly and her moaning in my ear begging me to fuck her harder.

I'm picturing everything I want from her, which is absolutely nothing she would want from me. She is not the type of woman who gets fucked hard against a wall. She is the type who expects to be made love to—something I could never give her. She deserves so much more: she deserves better than me. If nothing else, hopefully this arrangement gives her what she needs to improve her life so she can find someone who is right for her... someone who is not me.

Although I know she would never want it, I'm still picturing myself thrusting into her warm body against the cold, hard wall tile. My hand grasps my dick, stroking it as I'm imagining her sex stroking me. I can almost feel her breath against my ear, panting, as I bring her closer and closer to her release. I begin stroking myself faster as I wonder what she would look like when she came. Would she open her eyes? Would she scream my name? Is she quiet or loud when her orgasm finally hits?

"Fuck, Kenzie!" I hiss as I come at the mere thought of how she might look as she comes.

DAMN IT!!

I need to stop thinking about her like this; picturing her naked isn't going to help our arrangement, in fact it will only make it worse. How the fuck can I kiss her goodnight on the cheek after a date if I'm picturing her naked against a wall? How can I tell her how beautiful she looks in a dress when I'm imagining what I now know is underneath it?

DAMN IT!!!

I drag myself from the shower, just as my dick is beginning to twitch yet again at the thought of Kenzie's body against mine. It was hard enough last night after dinner to kiss her on the cheek, especially when she looked up at me with her beautiful brown eyes and I couldn't help but wonder how her soft lips would feel against mine. What the fuck am I going to do the next time I see her? How am I going to keep my hands or lips off her? I need to do something or not only will I break the terms of our contract, but I will risk losing the perfect solution to my public image situation as I know she doesn't think of me the way I'm thinking of her right now.

I force myself to focus on work the remainder of the day, pushing her as far away from my mind as possible. It's the only thing I can do, because if I sit and think about her much longer, I'm tempted to take the elevator down the few floors that are separating us right now and do something she will hate. For the first time I understand why Bridget's contract insists that our addresses remain private; it would be so much easier if I didn't know she was only a few floors below me...

"Sir?" Carter pulls me from my thoughts which have once again become nearly entirely focused on Kenzie.

"I'll be ready to leave in five."

Thankfully the ride to my parent's house is not focused on Kenzie. I have a slew of emails from Alex, providing me with details about several companies requesting our assistance. The fact that Alex and I are both working on a Sunday afternoon doesn't surprise me—a successful business doesn't get built by working only Monday through Friday, nine to five. Especially when some of the companies we work with are all over the globe, which means in they are in different time zones. Alex knows just as well as I do that our business requires "nontraditional" hours and thankfully he has no problem putting in these hours.

Before I realize it Carter has stopped the car in front of my parent's house, I quickly finish my last email and let Alex know that I will be unavailable for the next couple of hours. My parents hate it when I spend dinner on my phone so when at all possible I try to respect their wishes and not respond to emails unless they are urgent. He knows the routine and will call if something comes up and I don't respond right away to his email.

"Nicholas!" Cara races out the front door to great me before I reach the door.

"Cara… One day you're going to knock me to the ground," I wrap my arms around her and lift her off the ground.

"Where's Kenzie? I was hoping you would bring her tonight," she pouts

"I told mom, Kenzie was busy tonight and not able to make it to dinner," I lie.

"I know… I was still hoping you would bring her."

"Another time, perhaps."

"We were just looking at the picture of you two from last night, which is why I was hoping you would bring her."

"Picture?"

"From your date…"

"Are you sure it's from last night? It might be from—"

"The story said it was from last night. You were at Lake View right?"

"We were… I didn't know anyone got a picture of us."

"Come inside, I'll show you."

Madison Quinn

I quickly great my parents and Austin while Cara grabs her ipad to show me the article that was posted today. I've made it a habit of checking the gossip sites every day for anything new written about me but somehow today I forgot.

Is Nicholas Parker becoming a romantic?

A source dining at the Lake View Restaurant last night captured Nicholas Parker, billionaire playboy, out to dinner with the woman that PFS has referred to as his romantic interest. Our source captured this grainy picture of the two sharing dinner overlooking the lake at what is one of the most romantic tables in the entire dining room— sought after because of the incredible views.

According to the source, Nicholas Parker and his date spent several hours at the restaurant apparently lost in their own world. "They barely looked up from each other when the waiter brought their food," our source says. "They were the last customers to leave; the entire dining room was empty by the time they finally pulled away from each other.

They've obviously known one another for some time; they looked very comfortable together." According to our source, they walked out of the dining room holding hands and got into the same car. So New York... how long do you think our Playboy will be able to commit to one woman? We all know he hasn't been seen with the same woman since...

I immediately stop reading the article, not wanting to taint the night by thinking about what happened the last time I trusted a woman enough to let *her* into my life. If nothing else this article is a reminder that I need to be careful, reinforcing the fact that I need to keep the arrangement with Kenzie strictly professional. While it seems like my image transformation is working, this reporter is quick to remind everyone that they still think I'm a playboy at the core. If only the media knew the true story; I was never a playboy... even before *her* I wasn't a playboy. *She* was a mistake; *she* is the reason I keep my personal life confined. *She* is the reason I will never again fall for a woman. *She* is the reason I could never be more than a business transaction to Kenzie.

Chapter 18
Kenzie

I haven't seen Nicholas in almost a week; tonight will be the first time we've seen each other since our dinner at the Lake View Restaurant last weekend. Bridget called to confirm the details of our *date* tonight for an awards banquet that Nicholas is attending but she said otherwise he didn't have anything he needed me for this week. I suppose I shouldn't be surprised; he had mentioned that he was working on a several large projects when we had dinner, I'm sure one of those consumed his time.

I've spent most of the week working; one of the girls that usually works weekdays, ended up quitting unexpectedly which meant I had longer hours. I'm looking forward to this weekend, it's the first entire weekend in probably more than a year at least that I've had off. I'm going with Nicholas to the awards dinner tonight, but tomorrow I signed up for a weekend culinary class at the community college. It's nothing big, but I'm excited to finally do something for myself. I was thrilled when Ginny said I could have the weekend off to take this class and half expected her to change her mind since we've been short staffed all week but she confirmed this morning that she didn't need me. I can't remember the last time I was able to do something for *me*, something that didn't involve paying for bills or trying to save money just in case I needed to leave suddenly again.

For tonight's dinner, Bridget told me the dress code is dressy but not formal. I'm wearing a simple floor length dress that has a slit up the side to add just a hint of sexiness to it. According to Bridget, the banquet is being hosted by a local community group to thank several of their major sponsors and should have minimal press coverage given the quaintness of this event. Of course she was quick to remind me that even when the press aren't present, we need to act as if we are a couple since we have been photographed several times already by people who then sell our picture to the gossip websites.

"Good evening, Kenzie, you look stunning," Nicholas greets me at the door right on time as always.

"Thank you." For some unknown reason I blush at his complement which surprises me.

"Shall we?"

"Just let me set the alarm," I quickly punch in the code and lock the door behind me.

"How was your week?" he asks on the drive over.

"It was good... busy but good."

"Oh?"

"One of the girls quit without warning so I've been helping to cover her shifts. I've worked every morning this week, but thankfully I'm off this weekend at least."

"Do you have plans for the weekend?"

"Sort of... I signed up for a culinary class at the community college—"

"That's really great! I know you mentioned wanting to go back to school."

"It's not much... it's just a weekend class—not part of a program or anything but I'm looking forward to it."

"It's all weekend?"

"Six hours tomorrow and then six hours on Sunday. I was worried that Ginny might say she needed me this weekend, but she said her approval for my time off stands."

"Good for you."

"Thank you." *Why the hell am I blushing again? I don't think I've ever blushed this much in my entire life!* "How was your week?"

"Busy... I was out of town for a few days. We've been working on a long distance deal and I needed to fly out this week to review some things on site."

"Is it moving forward?"

"I believe so."

"Wow, that's wonderful."

"Do you have any questions about tonight? I assume Bridget filled you in on the details of the event?"

"She explained that you were being given an award for some of your charity work around the city by a local community based organization that is also recognizing several sponsors. She doesn't expect there to be much press coverage as this is a relatively small event."

"I assume you saw the picture of us from the Lake View?"

"I did… it was obviously taken from a cell phone, the quality wasn't the greatest."

"It's possible the same thing could happen at tonight's event, especially now that our picture appears on more of the sites."

"Is there anything I should know for tonight?"

"I don't think so. I normally don't attend this dinner; Alex usually handles the smaller awards banquets for PFS, but unfortunately he is away this weekend which is why we ended up here tonight. He warned me ahead of time the food isn't the greatest, so don't be surprised if we leave and you're still hungry. We can always stop and grab something on the way home if the food is that bad—"

"I'm sure it won't be—"

"I wouldn't bet on it," he chuckles. "From what Alex has told me, there will be a speech by the organization's founder, we'll have dinner and then the awards will be given. I should be one of the first awards, but we'll stay for a few of the others before making an excuse to leave. I have no desire to stay longer than we need to, but I want it to look like we've been there long enough for appearances."

"Okay, just let me know when and we'll go."

A short time later, we arrive at a chain hotel where the awards banquet is being held and are ushered into a large conference room with about thirty or so tables set up and small stage on one side. Nicholas leads me around, introducing me to various people who all seem to be heads of different businesses.

He keeps me close to him as he walks around the room; his arm is around my waist, his hand set on my hip as we walk. Before we approach anyone, he whispers in my ear who they are so that when he introduces us I know a little about them ahead of time. I'm grateful for this small gesture as it helps me make small talk with some of the guests after introductions are made.

"Ladies and gentleman if you would please find your way to your tables we would like to begin in a few minutes," a voice comes over the speaker system.

"I think that's our cue," Nicholas leads me across the room to a table just off to the side of the stage.

"Ladies and Gentleman, I would like to introduce you to the founder of Children First, Ms. Samantha Richardson." Everyone rises and claps as an older woman takes the stage.

"Thank you all for taking time out of your busy schedules to attend our dinner this evening. As you know Children First started more than twenty five years ago as a grass roots effort to provide free activities to children in our community in an effort to keep them off the streets after school. Each of you has contributed to our organization over the last year, allowing my dream to continue. As government funding is reduced, we are forced to rely on private donations like yours to keep our mission going.

"When I almost lost my oldest son to a drug addiction more than twenty five years ago, I knew something needed to change. I was a single parent, struggling to work enough hours to keep a roof over my children's head and food in their stomachs. I was so busy worrying about these things I failed to see what was happening to my own child. By age twelve, my son began experimenting with street drugs and by fourteen he moved onto prescription drugs. By the time I learned about his drug use, he was in deep.

"It took many months, but I was finally able to get him into a good rehab center, one that focused on children instead of adults. I am proud of the man that my son has become today but seeing what he went through scarred me for life. I knew in that moment something needed to change. I was a single parent with no family support—I was busting my ass at minimum wage jobs trying to make ends meet. I couldn't afford after school programs, so my children were left home alone often late into the evening until I got home from work.

"Children First aims to help these families... Through your donations, more than seventy-five children have, free of charge, a place to go after school until their parents can pick them up. Through your donations, these children receive a warm meal, help with homework and socialization with peers their own age. Through your donations, these children are staying off the streets and off drugs! Tonight we thank you for recognizing our mission as something this community needs!"

The room erupts once again in applause and everyone stands as the speaker applauds the audience. I was truly moved by the speech and silently vow to look into the organization when I get back to the condo to see if there is some way I can help. Obviously I don't have money to contribute, but perhaps I can find a few hours to donate time to one of the after school programs.

"Chicken or Pasta miss?" A waiter pulls me from my thoughts.

"I'll have the pasta please," I answer.

"Sir?" he asks Nicholas.

"I'll have the chicken."

As Nicholas talks business with a few of the people at our table, he takes my hand in his. I'm grateful for these small gestures; it reminds me that even though he is discussing business, he hasn't forgotten that I'm with him tonight. When he shifts in his seat to face someone on the other side of the table his leg rests against mine and I find that he is leaning closer to me. As I take a breath, I realize just how good he smells. It's a mix between what I'm sure is a very expensive cologne and probably aftershave or soap from his shower.

My mind immediately jumps to what Nicholas might look like in the shower, and I feel my face becoming flush. I have no idea why my mind suddenly went there; perhaps it's because I don't recall being this close to him before. I quickly try to focus on the conversation that he is having but with him this close to me I can't seem to focus on anything other than him. I try thinking of anything to keep my mind blank but when his thumb starts rubbing the bare skin of my shoulder, it becomes a lost cause.

I glance his way but his attention is entirely focused on the man who is sitting a couple seats away from me. I don't know if he realizes his hand is on my shoulder, his leg resting against mine or that he is *this* close to me or perhaps he *does* realize it and this is all part of the image he wants to portray. The reminder that this is only a business transaction is like a bucket of ice being thrown at me... I'm immediately brought back to our contract. I know that everything that Nicholas is doing right now is for appearances only. If it weren't for Bridget and our contract, Nicholas never would have looked in my direction. He would never be sitting here like this; he wouldn't be touching me or paying me any attention.

"Your dinner," the waiter from earlier once again pulls me from my thoughts.

We eat our dinner in relative silence; a few of the guests at our table comment about how good the food is. I nod in agreement although the pasta is incredibly under cooked and the center of the ravioli is cold. It looks as if Nicholas's dish isn't much better, he has some type of chicken with what looks like spinach and cheese on top. He hasn't touched his rice that looks dry and has only eaten half of his chicken.

"Well... was I right about the food?" he leans in and whispers to me.

"Definitely," I grin, remembering our conversation from the car.

"We'll go somewhere after this and have a real meal."

We both manage to finish about half of our dinners before sitting back in our chairs. A few people at our table have finished their meals, but there are several plates half full like ours.

"Ladies and Gentleman, as we wrap up dinner I would like present our first award of the evening. Parker Financial Services has been a major contributor to Children First for the last five years. They always answer our call for donations and this last year their management team spent an entire Saturday out of their busy schedules to help us clean up our newest community center. Without their generosity, less than half of the children we served would have had a place to go after school. We are fortune tonight to have the CEO and founder of PFS with us... please join me in thanking Mr. Nicholas Parker for their incredible generosity over the last five years."

Nicholas rises, as does everyone at the table and places a quick kiss on my cheek before taking the stage next to Mrs. Richardson who hands him a plaque in recognition.

"Thank you, Mrs. Richardson. It is your dream and incredible hard work over the last twenty-five years that has made tonight possible. Parker Financial Services is a proud member of this community; we have been incredibly fortunate in that what we do has allowed us to support such incredible, life changing organizations as yours. I know all too well the impact that a less than ideal living environment can have on one's life and believe that if we can provide the proper supports to children early on, their adult lives can be different.

"Children learn coping skills very early in life; if they do not have them by the time they reach adulthood they will not suddenly develop them. These adults are less likely to seek help because they never had help growing up. These adults are less likely to accept help for the same reason.

"One of the things that drew me to Children First was that not only do you keep kids off the streets after school but you also strive to surround them with positive role models. I love that your community programs operate 24/7 so that no child is left out because of an odd schedule their parent may work. You obviously recognize the needs of our community; providing a hot meal to children who would likely go without at night has a tremendous impact on them.

"All too often, they receive free meals at school but then go home to an empty fridge. How can we expect these children to focus on school work if they don't have food in their stomachs? The pain that comes with not having enough food to eat is unbearable and not something that can be ignored. I'm grateful that you are one of the few organizations in our community that understand this.

"I love that you continue to provide outreach services to children when they leave your program. We need more organizations like yours that also strive to support children in improving their lives. It is not enough to provide them with the support to help them graduate high school. It's time we start thinking about how we can help beyond high school. How can we support them in attending a training school, community college, university or in job placement? If we can support them in these areas, they can not only help themselves out of a bad situation but also help their families including younger siblings.

"I want to encourage each of you here tonight, to go back to your companies and think of ways that you can offer financial support to a child who is graduating high school this year and has dreams to pursue something more. PFS will personally be providing a full scholarship to one graduating senior this year for up to five years of undergraduate education with the possibility of extending the funding for an additional three years of graduate school. I am committing tonight to awarding this scholarship to one student each year for the next five years. If PFS is unable to fund a scholarship one year due to performance, I will personally pay the tuition bill out of my pocket to ensure that child isn't forced to stop attending college."

Holy Shit.

I am beyond stunned by Nicholas's speech. There was so much unexpected in it. I guess I just assumed it would be a business speech, focusing entirely on the facts in addition to thanking the organization for recognizing PFS's contribution. I was shocked that he took this opportunity to deliver an obviously personal speech, leaving me with so many questions. How does he know about the impact of a less than ideal living conditions can have? When did he have a poor living environment? Was he talking about his own kitchen when he spoke about not having enough food? I remember reading somewhere in an article before our first event that he was adopted by the Parkers but had spent some time in foster care before that. Could he be referring to his early childhood in this speech? I find myself wanting to know more, needing to know what made him the man he is today.

The end of his speech shocked me almost as much as the beginning, especially when his eyes sought out mine. I have no doubt that he added the last part of his speech, offering to pay a tuition bill out of pocket, because of the reason I had to drop out of college. I don't like to think about it, but I know my life would have been very different had I been able to graduate. I wouldn't have taken the crappy job as a waitress where I met *him;* I wouldn't have spent a year of my life living in hell with *him*. I wouldn't have had to return to the house that I was so eager to escape that I jumped at the chance to live with a man I barely knew.

My entire life could have been different but I will never really know how different it could have been since I wasn't able to finish my degree. I had no idea that Nicholas had paid that much attention to what I told him, or that it impacted him to the point where he put it in a safety net to make sure that students awarded the scholarship from his company wouldn't be stranded if PFS wasn't able to contribute to the scholarship one year.

The room is applauding loudly for Nicholas and everyone is on their feet as he shakes hands with Mrs. Richardson who is wiping the tears from her eyes. I have no doubt that she was as unprepared for his speech as I was and like me, was moved by his

Madison Quinn

incredible donation. A few minutes later Nicholas leaves the stage, making his way through the crowd, stopping along the way to shake several hands before he finally makes it back to our table.

He takes my hand as soon as he approaches the table. Without giving it a second thought I lean up and kiss him. Unlike every other kiss, this time my lips are on his and they are just as soft as I imagined they would be. His hand wraps around my waist as he takes a step closer to me, pressing his lips more firmly against mine but neither of us deepen it. A few seconds later, Nicholas pulls back just enough so that his eyes find mine. I immediately blush at the realization of what I just did and then guilt washes over me, knowing that I just violated the contract we signed with Bridget. Nicholas doesn't say anything; he simply pulls out my chair and sits down next to me once again. His hand is still holding mine but his eyes are fixed on the stage as Mrs. Richardson begins to introduce the next sponsor.

I struggle to focus on the next couple of speeches, sort of just going through the motions of clapping after each award is presented. I worry about the kiss… I have no idea what possessed me to do something like that. Well I do know… it was Nicholas's speech. I was so focused on the speech itself and the generous donation he was making that I forgot for that brief moment about out contract. I forgot that this was nothing more than a business transaction, that our *relationship* truly only exists in a contract stipulating our individual roles that we both signed. I forgot that we weren't two people enjoying each other's company tonight. My stupid lapse in judgment may have changed everything between us.

As another person finishes their speech, I try to take my hand from Nicholas's to clap but he grips my hand tighter. I look at him for the first time since my stupid move and realize that Nicholas doesn't look right. His face is paler than I have ever seen it and his leg is shaking under the table. I don't know what's wrong but I can tell something isn't right with him.

"Nicholas?"

Chapter 19
Kenzie

"Nicholas?" I lean against him and whisper his name. "Are you okay?"

He shakes his head indicating he isn't. I move my chair a little closer to him and place my hand on the back of his neck. I try to make it look casual to anyone who would notice, although I'm sure it looks a little off. The moment I place my hand on his neck I can feel the heat radiating from his body and I quickly realize that he has a fever.

"I'll have Carter get the car ready and we can leave," I pull out my phone as he nods in agreement.

Nicholas isn't feeling well. Can you get car ready to leave? Will meet you out front? –Kenzie

Will meet you in back of building, you're closer to that exit. Leave room, go down hallway, exit will be on the left. – Carter

I'm thankful that I had thought to program Carter's phone number into my phone after Nicholas gave me his number when he was worried about the press bothering me.

"We're good," I let Nicholas know.

"Ladies, Gentleman, if you will excuse us something has come up at PFS that requires my attention," Nicholas announces to the table before standing up. He wraps his arm around my waist as we make our way across the room and for the first time I don't think this gesture is for appearances but rather to help ground him. When we exit the conference room, I wrap my arm around his waist just in case he suddenly needs more help walking.

"We're meeting Carter this way," I gesture down the hall when Nicholas begins to head towards the front of the building. He closes his eyes briefly before nodding and following me slowly down the hallway. It takes us much longer than it should to finally reach the rear exit where I'm thankful to see Carter waiting with the car right in front of the door. He quickly rushes to us when he sees us approaching. As soon as the SUV door is open, Nicholas gets in and slides across the seat, placing his head against the window. I climb in next to him before Carter closes the door behind me.

"Are you okay? Can I get you anything?"

He just shakes his head and closes his eyes; Carter gets in the front seat and we pull out of the hotel parking lot.

"Mr. Parker... do I need to take you to the hospital?" Carter asks.

"No... home," he mumbles.

"Are you sure?"

"Home... call my mother, Carter. See if she can get there tonight."

"Yes sir."

I sit next to Nicholas who still hasn't opened his eyes. I'm not really sure what I can do for him but I feel a strong need to do something. I ask Carter for a bottle of water, thankfully he has a couple cold on the front seat with him. Even though Nicholas didn't ask for it, I open it and give it to him, encouraging him to take some. He takes a small sip, but quickly gives the bottle back to me, shaking his head.

"Sir, your mother said she would meet us at home and should get there just after we do. Kenzie, she asked to speak to you after she meets with Mr. Parker as she is concerned this could be food poisoning."

"Oh... we didn't eat the same main course, but I'll talk to her just in case."

We arrive at The Accord Towers a few minutes later and with Carter's assistance we manage to get Nicholas to the elevator where he leans against the wall for support. He looks weak and he has barely opened his eyes since we left the hotel. I'm worried that I should insist Carter take him to the hospital instead of back to his apartment. He looks like he should be in a hospital. Maybe his mother could convince him to let Carter take him there tonight?

I barely notice the elevator stopping; the doors open into a large foyer and I'm immediately taken aback when I realize that this must be where Nicholas lives. Carter wraps his arm around Nicholas's waist, as he leans on him for support as we walk across the vast tile floor. I follow Carter and Nicholas down a hallway to a large bedroom that is easily triple the size of the master bedroom in the condo I'm staying in. Carter helps Nicholas to sit on the bed before leaving the room, I assume to wait for Nicholas's mom.

"Can I help you take your jacket off?" I offer.

He shakes his head but when he struggles to coordinate his movements, I take over and slip the jacket off his arms. He falls back onto the bed, groaning when his head meets the pillow. I glance around the large room for a bathroom and spot a door next to the bed but when I open it I embarrassingly realize it is a large walk in closet and not a bathroom. There's another door across from the bed where I finally find an incredible bathroom: a girl could seriously live in a bathroom like this. There's a large tub that is just begging for someone to soak in, a walk in shower with dual shower heads and of course a double vanity with an area for a woman to apply her make up.

In a few of the articles I read about Nicholas it referenced a woman he previously lived with who I assume probably fell in love with this bathroom the moment she saw it. I don't know why but the thought of picturing him with another woman bothers me even though there is no reason it should. Our arrangement is purely business; I wouldn't be surprised if he had a woman that he keeps away from the press— he is a man after all. I quickly shake my head, pulling myself from thoughts of him with another woman and go in search of what I came in here for. Looking around I spot a basket filled with washcloths; I wet one and bring it back into the bedroom. He shudders when I place the cool cloth on his forehead but doesn't say anything.

"Ms. Rose, Dr. Parker is here," Carter announces from the doorway.

"Dr. Parker, it's nice to see you again—"

"Please, no one calls me *Dr.* Parker unless I'm working dear," she chuckles.

"Of course, Mrs. Parker—"

Yes, we met at the New Beginnings Gala but we didn't have much of a chance to talk with everything going on that night. This is the first time I'm really talking to Nicholas's mom and with him practically passed out on the bed, it's a little unnerving.

"How about you call me Vivienne?" she suggests.

"Vivienne… thank you for coming so quickly."

"Tell me what happened and more importantly what Nicholas ate tonight," she requests as she sits on the bed next to him to take his pulse.

"He had a chicken entrée for dinner, I think there was spinach and cheese on it. He ate about half of it—I don't think he touched the rice. He gave a speech just after we finished dinner then we sat through two other ones. That's when I noticed he suddenly looked pale. His leg was shaking and he was… his neck seemed hot when I touched him. I tried to get him to drink water but he really hasn't had much."

"Okay, thank you."

"If you don't need anything else, I'll wait for you outside."

"Thank you."

"Ms. Rose," Carter greets me as soon as I leave Nicholas's room.

"Dr. Parker… I mean Vivienne is with Nicholas."

"I want to show you around the main floor quickly," I look at him confused as to why he would think I needed a tour of Nicholas's apartment right now. "If Dr. Parker suggests you talk in the kitchen or Nicholas's office it might be a good idea for it to appear that you have been here before."

"Oh! Yes, you're probably right."

Carter quickly gives me a tour of the main floor: there is a large great room, also a room that is probably any man's dream complete with a pool table and dart board, a large dining room with a table that seats at least 10, Nicholas's office, a guest bathroom and a chef's dream kitchen. I could easily live in just the kitchen itself… it's easily double the size of the one in my condo and has everything a chef could ever need.

"Would you like a cup of tea, coffee or a glass of wine?" Carter offers.

"A cup of tea would be nice thank you."

Carter quickly makes a cup of tea for me and joins me at the large island in the kitchen while we wait for Vivienne to finish with her son. He points out the pantry and another door that I'm surprised to learn is another small apartment that he and Julie share. Nicholas's main floor is so large, I can't imagine how much more remains up the stairs that I saw in the foyer. How much space can one man possibly need?

"Carter, Kenzie," Vivienne enters the kitchen.

"Dr. Parker, can I get you something to drink? Tea, coffee—" Carter offers.

"No thank you Carter. I can't stay long, I'm scheduled to work a double tonight at the hospital," she says. "Kenzie, how are you feeling?"

"Fine… Nicholas and I didn't eat the same meal tonight thankfully."

"Good. I am pretty confident that Nicholas has a case of food poisoning, but I'm taking some blood to the hospital just to rule out anything else. I don't think it's the flu, given the sudden onset, but I want to rule it out just to be sure."

"So he's going to be okay?"

"Yes, in a few days he should be fine. He probably should be in a hospital, but my son is incredibly stubborn just like his father and refuses to go. He's more worried that someone might think he is weak by being admitted into a hospital than he is about his own health. He's stable for now, but I've warned him that if his condition worsens or if his blood work shows something more serious then I will call for the ambulance myself to bring him to the hospital."

"What can we do for him?"

"Unfortunately, there's not much you can do but keep him comfortable. I've given him something for fever and nausea which should help. Someone will need to check on him every couple of hours through the night; dehydration is a big concern. Tomorrow if Julie can prepare some chicken broth—"

"Julie is away for the weekend Dr. Parker," Carter interrupts.

"Oh... perhaps you can pick something up from a restaurant? It needs to be bland, my only concern with ordering it from somewhere."

"I'll make sure we have something for him in the freezer."

"Tonight, we need someone to check on him every two to three hours. If his temperature spikes above 103.8, I will need to be contacted immediately and if I'm not available then someone needs to call an ambulance. He needs medication around the clock for the next 48 hours to keep his fever down and prevent him from vomiting any liquid he takes in. As I said, dehydration is my concern: if he doesn't take in enough liquids, his body could begin shutting down. I cannot stress enough the importance of someone monitoring him around the clock this weekend. If Julie is not available, will one of you two be willing to do this?"

"Unfortunately, I'm scheduled to fly out in a few hours to meet Julie at her niece's wedding. I can try to arrange a later flight... maybe I can stay for a few hours in the morning—"

"I can come by tomorrow afternoon to check on him, but unfortunately I'm scheduled to work a double tonight and then the overnight shift tomorrow night. Theodore is out of town helping someone with a project. Cara left this morning for a weekend trip with a few friends. Austin... well let's just say Austin wouldn't be the ideal person to take care of someone who is ill."

"I'll stay," I offer.

"Are you sure, Kenzie?" Carter asks.

"It's not a problem," I assure him.

"Hunter and Ben are scheduled to work this weekend, either of them can run out for anything you might need," Carter adds.

"I'm sure we'll be fine. I can make the chicken broth that you recommended, Vivienne; I'm sure Julie has everything I would need. If you let me know about the medication I can make sure he takes it as you say."

"Wonderful, thank you so much! Nicholas is very lucky to have you. I'm thankful that you didn't have plans this weekend; I'm not sure what we would have done if you weren't available. He probably would have had no choice but to go into the hospital where he would have been most unhappy."

"It's not a problem, I'm glad I can help."

"Here's some medication to get you through the night. Carter, I've called in a few prescriptions to the pharmacy, so can you arrange for someone to pick them up first thing in the morning?"

"Of course, Dr. Parker."

"He needs this one every four hours to keep his fever down. I left a forehead thermometer on the nightstand in his room and recommend checking his temperature every two to three hours. At the same time you'll need to get him to drink something. Here's a few packets of an electrolyte drink; just mix it with cold water and it helps prevent dehydration. Carter, this is another thing that should be picked up at the pharmacy tomorrow morning. They may not have it in powder but they should have it in liquid form."

"I'll be sure Hunter or Ben picks everything up as soon as they open."

"If you have trouble waking him up, or his fever spikes, you need to call me right away, Kenzie. Here is my cell number and the hospital number where you can have me paged if I don't answer my cell. If you can't reach me, call an ambulance and have him brought in. Don't worry about him getting mad at you, I'll take full responsibility. His health is more important than what the media might think of him."

"I'll call for an ambulance if I can't reach you, I promise."

"He might start feeling better late tomorrow afternoon. If he feels up to it, you can add some noodles and vegetables to the broth. He shouldn't eat anything heavy at least until Monday and even then, it needs to be small amounts. He may tell you otherwise, but it's important that you monitor him all weekend. Even when his fever finally leaves, he isn't out of the woods, as it can come back at any time over the next few days. Just keep an eye on him once the fever drops, make sure he keeps drinking and eating. Drinking is more important than eating so don't panic if he doesn't eat anything. Just don't let him convince you that he is fine."

"I won't. I promise, I'll stay until you say it's safe to leave."

"Julie and I are both scheduled to fly back on Monday afternoon so we can take over then if he still needs someone," Carter offers.

"By Monday hopefully, he will be out of the woods. It's the next two days that we really need to focus on, but Monday should be the final day. And Kenzie, don't let him do too much work when he does start to feel better. He needs his rest, so try to get him to just rest. His body can't recover if he is using the little energy he has to sit in front of a computer and stare at spreadsheets all day."

"I'll try," I agree despite knowing that it will probably be very difficult to get Nicholas to stay away from work.

"Unfortunately, I need to get going. I'm already late for my shift at the hospital. Kenzie, I appreciate you staying this weekend; if I wasn't scheduled to work or could find a replacement I would stay myself—"

"It's fine. I don't mind," I assure her.

"I'll call in a few hours and check on him. Maybe you can text me so I have your cell phone number?"

"Of course, I'll send you a text in a few minutes."

"Take care; don't hesitate to call me at any time. Even if you just have a question about the medication, just call."

"I will and thank you again for coming tonight."

"*Thank you,* Kenzie. I really appreciate this; I'm sure it's not how you envisioned spending your weekend," Vivienne gives me a quick hug goodbye before heading to the hospital for her shift.

"Carter, I'm going to run to my apartment quick and grab a couple changes of clothes," I realize that I'm going to need a few things if I'm going to be staying here this weekend.

"Of course, I'll contact Hunter and Ben to let them know what is going on."

"I don't know that we need both of them this weekend if Nicholas and I are both here. I mean, it's just a thought…"

"No that's a good point. Originally Ben was covering for me as Hunter was going to be assigned to you for the weekend. I'll have Ben remain on call that way, if something comes up, he can come in. Hunter will be here all weekend and will pick up anything you might need."

I take the elevator to my condo and begin to pack a small bag to bring back to Nicholas's. I grab a couple changes of clothes, pajamas and toiletries to, adding the charger to my phone and a book I started reading the other night. I'm not sure what else I might need but since I'm only a few floors below, I know I can always run down here if I forget something.

I check the email on my phone and see the registration confirmation for the cooking class I was supposed to take this weekend. I quickly send a reply email notifying them that something has come up and I won't be able to attend the class this weekend. I know I'll lose the deposit for the class as it was nonrefundable but seeing that no one else was available this weekend, there was no way I could still go to the class without feeling guilty. With everything that Nicholas has done for me, the least I can do is take care of him this weekend.

The community college is offering another weekend cooking class in a couple of months; I'll call Monday and have them transfer my payment to that class which means I should only lose the registration deposit. In the end though, I'm not upset. Nicholas helped me after the break in at my apartment and moved me in the middle of the night to this condo when he could have easily looked the other way. Canceling my plans this weekend is a small price to pay as a way to repay him.

"Ms. Rose, would you like me to put your bag in one of the guest rooms?" Carter greets me as soon as I step off the elevator.

"Yes, thank you."

"At the top of the stairs, there is a guest room on the right that I'll put your bag in."

"Okay, I'm going to check on Nicholas and look over the stuff that Mrs—Vivienne left."

I knock on Nicholas's door, but of course he doesn't answer. I wait a couple of minutes just in case he is in the bathroom. I don't want to walk in and make it awkward. When he doesn't respond I open the door a little but upon seeing him still in bed, I open the door more and step into the room. Nicholas is lying in his bed, another one that is entirely too big for one person I decide, and is still sound asleep. His breathing is soft and steady as he sleeps but his coloring looks a little better.

I quietly walk over to his nightstand and look at everything Vivienne left for him. I replay her instructions as to what I need to do this weekend and realize that I probably won't be able to sleep in the guest room upstairs where Carter just put my bag. I'm not about to sleep in the same bed as Nicholas, so I try to come up with another solution. Looking around the dark room, I see a chaise lounge in the corner so I move it closer to the bed and decide that this is where I will sleep tonight. It will keep me close enough to

On His Terms

Nicholas to check on him throughout the night but not too close that either of us will be uncomfortable.

I'm not sure how he will feel about me staying here this weekend. When he and Carter moved me into the condo, Nicholas told me he also lived here but now I obviously know exactly where he lives. Not only do I know where he lives, but I'm staying with him for the entire weekend. I hope that he isn't mad that I'm invading his privacy by staying here; I don't think there was really another option to avoid him being admitted into a hospital.

Chapter 20
Nicholas

I feel like I've been hit by a fucking Mac truck!

My body aches, every fucking muscle hurts; like I was hit by a fucking truck or something! What the fuck is wrong with me? I try to open my eyes but FUCK, even doing that hurts! I can barely focus on the clock next to my bed… 2:03 it reads. My room is dark so it must be two in the morning. I manage to push myself into a sitting position but fuck if just sitting up doesn't hurt. What the fuck happened last night? I scramble my brain, trying to figure out why I feel like I-want-to-die-and-but-I'm-afraid-I-won't. Kenzie and I went to the dinner; I remember the dry chicken that had no taste whatsoever. I gave a speech… Kenzie kissed me.

Kenzie fucking kissed me.

Kenzie kissed me… on the lips.

Kenzie's lips were on mine.

God, I was so shocked, I think I just stood there without doing anything for a full minute. I knew she would rightly assume that the scholarship portion of my speech was written because of her. When I was writing that part earlier in the week, I couldn't help but think about her. I have been fortunate that if something like that happened to me when I was at NYU, my parents would have immediately stepped in and helped me out until I could apply for loans or other scholarships.

Her reaction, however, to my speech was nothing I could have expected. I watched her from the stage, unable to take my eyes off her; I watched her eyes fill with tears as my speech sunk in. I couldn't get off the stage fast enough… I wanted to go to her and do… something. I don't know what but I just remember thinking that I didn't want to see her cry because of a speech.

When I finally made my way back to the table, Kenzie was standing there waiting for me. I immediately took her hand in mine, relieved to see that there were no tears in her eyes any longer. I don't remember what I was thinking, but the next thing I knew her lips were on mine. I swear it took me a minute to realize it wasn't my all in my head—I've imagined what her lips would feel like for weeks now... hell probably since the first time I saw her.

I shake my head to push past those thoughts and try to figure out what the hell happened afterwards. It takes me a few minutes and multiple tries but I finally manage to get out of bed. When the room finally stops spinning, I decide to head to the bathroom, hoping that if I splash water on my face it will help.

FUCK

I walk right into the chair that is normally in the corner of my room. What the fuck is that doing next to my bed? Why the fuck would I have moved a chair last night? There's a throw blanket from the great room lying across the chair... did I sleep in the chair last night? Why would I move it next to my bed to sleep in it? Why wouldn't I just sleep in my own bed? I shake my head again; nothing seems to make sense tonight. I use the bathroom, splash water on my face and decide to head to the kitchen to get a bottle of water. I'm confused when I open my bedroom door as the apartment is very bright; my room was nearly pitch dark but now I realize that someone must have closed my curtains.

I slowly make my way down the hall to the kitchen and am shocked again at what I see and confused even more. Kenzie is in my kitchen, with her back to me, cooking something on my stove. I try to figure out how the hell she ended up here last night but for the life of me I can't remember anything. God, I would think if I fucked her I would remember it! But that doesn't make sense... I can't see either of us jeopardizing our arrangement like that, no matter how much I've thought about it since I saw her in a bikini. So if I didn't fuck her, what the fuck is she doing in my kitchen? Why is she in my apartment?

"Kenzie?"

I finally give up trying to remember what the fuck happened last night and figure asking her is the only way to find out. Of course, my voice comes out as barely above a whisper but she must have heard me because she immediately turns around and gasps in surprise.

"Nicholas! You're not supposed to be out of bed! Sit down, let me get you some water," she rushes around me pulling a bottle of cold water from the fridge and handing it to me. As she runs over to the stove to turn the heat down on whatever she is making, I realize how odd it is to have her here. Other than Julie and my mother, no woman has stepped foot in this kitchen, yet Kenzie is comfortably moving around as if she has been here multiple times... as if she belongs here.

"How are you feeling? Do you feel like your fever is back? It shouldn't be—you're not due for more medicine for another two hours…" she glances at her watch while rambling.

"I don't think I have a fever, why would I?"

"Do you remember what happened?"

"Not really… I mean, I remember the awards dinner." Her face blushes and I can tell she must be remembering the kiss as well. I hold off bringing it up until I figure out exactly what the hell happened. "I remember I started not to feel well after my speech, but I can't seem to remember much after that."

"Drink the water and I'll tell you what happened," she eyes the still full bottle in my hands. "Your mom will be mad at me if you don't drink enough."

"My mom?"

"Drink," she commands and I reluctantly open the bottle and take a few small sips which I admit feels really good on my sore throat. "We stayed for two speeches after yours but by the second it was clear something was wrong. Your face was very pale and your leg was shaking. By the time we got into the car you were pretty out of it—you kept your eyes closed the entire ride and didn't say much. Carter offered to take you to the hospital but you refused—"

"Good."

"He called your mom who came shortly after we got back here. She had asked to talk with me when she came to see you—"

"Why?"

"She suspected food poisoning and to see if I was at risk of coming down with it. Since we ate different meals the chances were slim that it would hit me as well."

"Food poisoning? That's what's wrong with me?"

"Unfortunately, as all of your other blood work came back clear."

"Why are you here though? Where's Julie or Carter?"

"I…" she looks upset and I realize that what I said came out completely wrong.

"Shit… I'm sorry, Kenzie. I didn't mean it like that. I was just surprised to see you here."

"Julie is away for the weekend... at a wedding I think. Carter left very early this morning to catch a flight to meet her."

"Oh that's right, I forgot they were off this weekend."

"Hunter is here and Ben is on call. Hunter went to the pharmacy as soon as they opened this morning and got everything your mom requested for you."

"What are you making? Something smells really good," my stomach growls suddenly.

"It's chicken noodle soup. Your mom said you should start with broth first but if you are able to keep that down you could move to chicken and noodles. I'm making a large batch of it, figuring you could freeze it in case you get sick again."

"I don't get sick... well not usually."

"Do you want to eat here? Or somewhere else?"

"Here's fine."

She brings me a bowl of hot broth a few minutes later before getting herself a bowl with chicken, noodles and vegetables in it. I look at her bowl with envy; it looks so much better than mine does. I'm surprised when I taste my broth though; it doesn't taste like colored water like I expected.

"I appreciate you making this for me, but it wasn't necessary. I'm sure Ben could have gotten something from a restaurant, but thank you."

"Your mom was concerned it wouldn't be bland enough. It wasn't a big deal; I haven't made chicken noodle soup in a long time."

"You said that Carter left early this morning?" She nods. "So you've been here since he left?"

"No... I... actually..." she stutters and for the first time since I've met her, she actually looks nervous, almost deathly nervous.

"What is it?"

"I've been here since last night."

"You slept here?"

I'm shocked... beyond shocked. I swore I would never let another woman, well one who wasn't family, into my personal space again. Swore I would never let someone get this close to me again. To say that I'm conflicted right now is an understatement. I've thought of Kenzie being here, hell I *wanted* her here, but now that she's actually here, in my home, I don't know what to think. A few hours is one thing, but fuck she's been here the entire night. It's not that I don't trust her, I do… but it's hard not to be skeptical after what *she* did.

"Your mother wouldn't agree to keep you here unless someone agreed to spend the weekend taking care of you. If I hadn't agreed to stay, she was going to admit you to the hospital."

"I'm sure someone—"

"Your mother was on her way to the hospital to work a double and is scheduled to work overnight tonight, your dad and Cara are out of town and your mom felt Austin wasn't the right person—"

"No, he probably isn't."

"With Julie and Carter away…."

"No, that makes sense. Look, thank you for staying with me but I'm sure you have things to do—" I don't want to keep her here; I have no doubt this is the last place she wants to spend her weekend.

"Actually, I can't leave."

"Why not?"

"Your mother made me promise to stay here until she cleared you to be able to stay by yourself."

"I'm sure that's not necessary, I'm fine."

"I… I'm sorry, Nicholas, but I gave her my word I would look after you this weekend. She said you would probably start to feel better this afternoon but she was concerned that you fever could come back."

"I'm sure my mother is just overreacting—"

"I can assure you I am not overreacting, Nicholas," I hear my mother's voice before I see her walking down the hallway in her hospital scrubs.

"I was just explaining to Kenzie—"

"I heard you," she cuts me off and turns to give Kenzie a hug which absolutely shocks me. My mother is not a very trusting woman when it comes to people in my life, especially females. "How are you, Kenzie? Are you still feeling okay?"

"I'm good, Vivienne, thank you."

Vivienne? My mother is letting Kenzie call her by her first name? Well that's a complete shock as well. My mother insisted *she* call her Mrs. Parker; it was never an option for *her* to call my mother anything else. When the truth came out about *her* my mother told me she never liked *her* but I guess I was blind to how much my mother truly didn't like *her*. Seeing her interact with Kenzie is completely different—I can tell my mother actually likes Kenzie.

"Any problems since we spoke this morning?" my mom asks.

"No, I just finished making some soup. Would you like a bowl?"

"I'd love some, thank you," and sits on the stool next to me while Kenzie rushes to the stove to get another bowl ready. The entire scene before me seems off... like I'm on the outside looking in, or like it's a TV show I'm watching but missed a large chunk of it. "How are you feeling, dear? You gave us quite a scare last night."

"I did?"

"Your temperature rose pretty high several times throughout the night. You are very lucky to have a woman in your life who cares so much about you. I know for a fact she barely slept last night; if she got more than a couple of hours, you would have missed your medication and your fever would have spiked. You were dangerously close to being admitted into the hospital and if it wasn't for Kenzie, I would have called the ambulance myself."

"Vivienne, it was—"

"Don't argue, Kenzie. I know how little you slept and I have the text messages to prove it," she gives Kenzie a look that basically prevents further argument. "I'm just saying dear, you have a wonderful woman here. Don't let her get a way."

"I won't, mom." I'm taken back by my mother's words. I can't recall her ever saying that to me before.

"I see you're eating soup; you're feeling okay?"

"I'm going to..." Kenzie nods towards the hallway, clearly wanting to give us privacy.

"I feel like I've been hit by a truck honestly. My entire body hurts," I admit.

"I'm not surprised, Nicholas. You were pretty sick last night. The test results all came back clear, so I think this is a case of food poisoning. According to the ER nurse who was on last night, they had several people come in with food poisoning. Looks like you weren't the only one who had the chicken dish last night."

"UGH, I'm never going back to that hotel."

"I know you probably don't want Kenzie to see you like this, but it's important someone is here with you the rest of the weekend. Just because you're feeling a little better now doesn't mean you're going to keep feeling so good. As you begin to eat and drink more, you could become sick again as your stomach might not be ready to handle food just yet. Dehydration is a major concern with any type of illness but especially with food poisoning. So either you allow Kenzie to stay here until Carter and Julie come back on Monday or I call for an ambulance and have you admitted to the hospital so I can keep an eye on you."

"Is that really—"

"Yes it is," her voice is firm and lets me know that I will not win this argument. I have no desire to be admitted into a hospital; the last thing I need is for the press to start leaking stories that I'm dying or have some debilitating illness that prevents me from running PFS.

"Okay, Kenzie can stay the weekend," I say with resignation.

"Now, was that so bad?" she raises an eye brow chuckling. "I need to get going, been working far too many hours and need to get some sleep before my next shift. Let Kenzie know I said goodbye. I'm serious, Nicholas, don't let this one go. It's very rare to find a woman who is as selfless as she is. Last night should have proved to you just how much she cares for you."

"Thank you Mom, I love you," I kiss her on the cheek before she walks out of the room.

I'm shocked that Kenzie volunteered to stay the weekend with me; she could have easily said she had plans and let my mother arrange for me to be admitted into the hospital. Our *date* ended last night, she didn't need to agree to stay beyond the dinner. She could have told Carter and my mother that she wasn't able to stay. Why didn't she? Why would she agree not only to stay the weekend with me but if what my mother said was true, stay up most of the night to make sure I was okay? Maybe she thought if she didn't stay with me I would get mad? That I would terminate our arrangement?

"Did your mom leave?" Kenzie walks into the kitchen quickly pulling me from my thoughts.

"She did, she wanted to get home and to nap before her next shift."

"I'm sure she's tired."

"Kenzie... I don't want you to think that I'm ungrateful—"

"No, I don't think—"

"I know I sounded ungrateful," I interrupt her quickly. "I appreciate you staying here last night, more than you know. Thank you for this weekend; thank you for keeping me out of the hospital. This... what you did... it's more than I ever would have expected."

"I'm just glad I could help," she shrugs it off, obviously uncomfortable.

"And the soup was delicious. I'm looking forward to having more later, if I'm still feeling good."

"I'll leave it on the stove to keep warm; it'll make a good light meal later tonight if you get hungry."

"So... Did you want to watch a movie or something?"

"Sure, that would be nice."

We settle into the only room in my apartment that has a television. I don't have much free time, so watching television is something I rarely do. In my billiards room, I have a large flat screen TV on one of the walls with a large couch in front of it. Originally Austin convinced me to get it so we could play video games on it but then Cara insisted I get a movie streaming subscription so she could order movies when she is here. I rarely use the service, but it's here. There's no way I could concentrate on PFS work right now, even if I wanted to. My body is too sore and my head feels like it's in the clouds. I doubt I could respond to an email right now, let alone do anything productive. At least with the TV in here, it gives Kenzie and me something to do since she's stuck here all weekend.

"What type of movies do you like?" I ask her as we both sit down on the couch in front of the TV.

"Something funny would be nice, but really I'll watch anything."

I flip through the on screen guide until I reach the comedy section and slowly scroll through the movies, most of which I've never heard of until she speaks up.

"Oh, can we watch that one? I saw the previews when it was in the theater but never got a chance to see it."

"Sure, whatever you want."

"Oh, let me grab my phone. I need to set the alarm for your next medicine."

She jumps from the couch before I can offer to get it and returns a few minutes later with a prescription bottle and her phone. She presses a few buttons before placing the phone on the arm of the couch next to her. Just as I hit play on the movie, I see her putting the throw blanket that was on the chair next to my bed over her legs. Suddenly I realize that not only did Kenzie sleep here last night but that she slept in my bedroom. God, I hope I didn't have a nightmare. She hasn't mentioned me having one, so hopefully last night was a rare night.

"Nicholas? Nicholas?" I hear Kenzie's voice and realize I must have fallen asleep at some point during the movie.

"Sorry... how long was I out?"

"About three hours. I wasn't going to wake you but you need to take your medicine," she hands me a couple pills and a bottle of water.

"I should get up anyway," I stand up but realize I must have stood too fast because the entire room goes black and I feel dizzy again.

"Sit back down," Kenzie's by my side immediately, her arm around my waist helping me back onto the couch.

"Thanks... I must have gotten up too fast."

"Maybe try and wait a few minutes before you get up again?"

"Yeah, probably a good idea."

I sit back on the couch and close my eyes, willing my body to return to normal. I hate being sick—I especially hate letting someone see me like this. She shouldn't have to deal with me being sick; if I wasn't afraid my mother would follow through with her threat to admit me into the hospital, I would insist that Kenzie go home. She shouldn't have to stay the entire weekend with me, worrying about medication schedules and cooking soups. I'm sure this is the last thing she imagined doing this weekend, she was probably—

"Your cooking classes," I realize aloud.

"I sent them an email last night letting them know I wouldn't be able to attend—"

"Oh Kenzie, I'm so sorry. Perhaps you can still go tomorrow? I'm sure—"

"It was a two day class; you needed to commit to attending both days when you registered for the class. Really, Nicholas, it's not a big deal; they're offering another weekend class in a couple of months so I'll arrange for them to transfer my payment to one."

On His Terms

"I completely forgot. I assure you, had I remembered I would have figured something else out so you could still take your class."

"Nicholas, it's fine really; you needed someone to stay the weekend with you and I could arrange my schedule easier than anyone else could, it was a simple decision. There will be other classes that I can take, so please don't give it a second thought."

Well now I feel worse than I did earlier; I feel like a dick for not remembering that this weekend was the cooking class she signed up for. I could tell she was excited about it when she told me on our way to dinner yesterday. I feel like such an ass for not remembering. When I can think more clearly, I need to find a way to repay her for everything she has done this weekend. Giving up her class, rearranging her life, is more than I think anyone would have done in the same situation. Allowing myself to think back to my life a few years ago, I can honestly say that no one in my life outside of my family would have done something like this for me. *She* never would have given up something *she* wanted to do to take care of me. Not for the first time, I can't help but wonder what the fuck I was thinking.

Chapter 21
Nicholas

"What should the sleeping arrangements be tonight?" Kenzie asks.

"What do you mean?"

"Well... last night I slept in your room—"

"You did?" I had a feeling this was the case, but hearing her confirm it still surprises me, even if it shouldn't.

"It made sense... I had to check your temperature every couple of hours, then give you medicine and water. It didn't seem feasible for me to sleep upstairs. I know it probably wasn't ideal, but I moved a chair next to your bed and slept there so I could keep an eye on you."

"I was wondering how the chair moved there."

"I'm sorry, I meant to move it but I didn't want to wake you—I guess I forgot about it."

"No, it's fine. When I woke up and saw it there, I thought I moved it there but couldn't figure out why I would have done that."

"Your mom said you probably won't need anything tonight but that I should keep an ear out just in case. Carter put my bag in a guest room upstairs but I don't think I would be able to hear you from there."

"Kenzie, I don't think you have anything to worry about. I'm feeling much better, especially after having more of the soup you made."

"I know... I would just feel better if I were closer just in case."

"If it makes you sleep better tonight, how about if I sleep in the guest room next to the room you're in tonight?"

I immediately regret the suggestion the moment the words leave my mouth. If she is sleeping in the room next to me, it increases the chance that she could hear my nightmare. If by some chance I managed to not have one last night when she was in my room, it almost definitely guarantees I will have one tonight. UGH, I should have thought of another option. I can't have her hearing me. I don't need her asking questions about why I have them. She doesn't need to know about that part of my life; we don't need to cross that line. I don't want to see her looking at me with pity the way anyone does when they witness my nightmares. She's one of the few people who don't look at me like that.

"Really? That would be a great idea. Are you sure you don't mind? I could always sleep on the couch or something—"

"Kenzie, I'm not going to have you sleep on the couch. It's bad enough you had to sleep in an uncomfortable chair—"

"It wasn't—"

"It's much less comfortable than a bed would have been I'm sure. I can't ask you to sleep on the couch tonight."

"Thank you, I appreciate that. I just want to be close enough that if you need something or if I have to call your mom… "

"It's fine."

"I think if you don't mind, I'm going to get ready for bed. I'm pretty beat and that bed upstairs is calling my name," Kenzie says a few minutes later.

"Of course. There should be everything you need in the bedroom, but if something is missing, let me know and I'm sure I can figure out where Julie keeps whatever it is you might need. The bathroom should be fully stocked as well. I'll be in the room just to the left of your room. I'll be heading up in the next few minutes as well."

"Thank you Nicholas. Is there anything you need before I go upstairs?"

"No, I'm fine. I'll take a couple bottles of water up with me and my medicine."

Kenzie takes our glasses to the kitchen before heading upstairs, while I sit back on the couch for a few minutes and try to figure out how the hell I'm going to get through tonight without having a nightmare. After a few minutes I realize there is nothing I can do, I go to my room and change into something I can sleep in. Before heading upstairs to the guest room, I stop in my office and grab my laptop, taking it upstairs with me. I don't know that I'll be able to get much work done, but perhaps if I can distract myself, I might avoid having a nightmare.

When I get to the top of the stairs, I pause at the closed door of the room Kenzie is sleeping in tonight. I don't know why I stop but I find myself wanting to go into her room. Walking into the room next to hers, I shake my head. I turn on the laptop and wait for it to start while scrolling through emails on my phone to see what I have missed in the last 24 hours. Of course, I have dozens of emails that I haven't read, let alone responded to since I left for the dinner last night.

I'm reading through an email from Alex about a company that we've been considering taking on for over a month now, when I hear the shower water start. It takes me a moment to realize that Kenzie must be getting into the shower in the ensuite just on the other side of my room. Immediately my mind goes into overdrive; knowing she is in the shower I can't *not* picture her naked in there. I imagine her standing under the hot water, her pale skin turning pink from the heat as it cascades down her beautiful body. It takes everything in me not to rush into her room, open the bathroom door and walk into the shower with her…

I wouldn't bother to take my clothes off but would wrap my arms around her waist, pulling her against me until she could feel just what she does to me. Unlike the kiss at the awards dinner, I take full control of this one: my lips are firm against hers, she gasps in surprise as I take advantage and slip my tongue into her mouth. I explore her mouth while my hands explore every inch of her body that I can reach. She tugs at my hair, pulling me closer to her as she becomes more aroused.

My hands find her perfect breasts; she moans against my lips when I tease her hardened nipples. She tugs my pants down, freeing my dick that begs for her attention. I groan into her mouth when she takes me in her hand… I'm so close to coming, it takes everything in me to hold it back. I haven't been this out of control since I was a teenager. I've never been so turned by a woman; I want nothing more than to plunge deep inside her and stay there all night.

Reminding myself that Kenzie deserves more than that, I force my attention back to Kenzie. My gaze goes down her beautiful body, taking her in completely for the first time. I touch her everywhere and it's still not enough. Her body is screaming for me, begging me for attention. My fingers leave her nipple and slowly move down to her pussy. She gasps when I apply the slightest pressure to her clit. Her back arches, pushing her tits against my shirt covered chest as I slide my fingers through her slick folds. She grips my dick tighter, pumping it as she begins to rock her hips against me. Our breathing is heavy, we're both moaning loudly as we both get closer to our releases.

"Fuck… KENZIE!" I gasp as I come, having been so caught up in my fantasy that I was pleasuring myself, while imagining it was Kenzie's hand on my dick.

The shower water is no longer on. I have no idea how long I was lying in bed imagining her in the shower. I can't remember the last time I had to jack myself off. I can usually control myself. I don't know how to stop thinking about her like this. I need to keep things professional between us and can't risk her finding out that I'm thinking about her like this. The last thing I need is for her to be disgusted by me and cancel our arrangement. I need to find a way to stop thinking about her.

Shaking my head, I head into my own shower, hoping that will clear my thoughts. Getting lost in the water seems to help, at least a little. My thoughts return to the last email Alex had sent about the company I desperately want to work with.

I leave the shower and return to my bed to begin responding to emails now that my mind is more focused. My alarm on my phone goes off, I quickly take the medicine and return to work. I'm glad I'm beginning to feel better, although I really don't think Kenzie needed to stay the weekend. I think my mom overreacted but I can't possibly tell her that. I lose myself in work, responding to emails and reviewing financial spreadsheets until I can't think straight any longer.

"No! Please… I'm sorry… I didn't mean… Ow! STOP!!! Please… please… you're hurting me… "

I jump out of bed, ignoring the dizziness that threatens to force me back down when I hear Kenzie calling out. I can't move fast enough, I race out the door and down the hall to her room. There's less than 50 feet between our doors but it seems like it takes forever to get to her room. Thankfully she left the door unlocked—I don't know that I have the energy to break it down right now and hell if I know where Carter keeps the keys.

"Stop… please… please… " Kenzie is whimpering when I finally reach her bed.

I try calling out to her but she doesn't answer me—I don't know if she hears me. I assume she is having a nightmare because it's obvious no one is hurting her right now. I sit on the bed next to her, trying to determine what I should do next. I don't know if I should wake her, but I can't just sit here and listen to her crying.

"Ow! Ow! Please… stop… I'm sorry, I'm sorry," she cries and I know I need to do something.

I slide myself down, lying next to her and pull her close to me. Her body stiffens at my touch, but I just hold her close to me whispering in her ear that she is safe. It takes several long minutes but finally her crying seems to lessen with only the occasional sob coming out.

"Kenzie… it's okay, baby. No one will hurt you again. I won't let anyone hurt you," I whisper while rubbing her back trying to reassure her that she is safe.

"Nicholas? What… How…?" she tries to pull away from me a few minutes later when she finally wakes up but I don't let go of her.

"You had a nightmare."

"I'm sorry I woke you... I... it was probably from that movie we watched earlier."

"It wasn't from the movie, Kenzie."

"Uh... I was reading a book—"

"Stop," I plead.

I look down at her but she doesn't meet my gaze. I gently lift her chin until I can see her face. I'll never forget the look in her eyes: fear, shame, embarrassment and sorrow stare back at me. She silently begs me not to ask her about the nightmare, but I don't know how to just let it go. Someone hurt her and that's not something I can ignore, even if that's what she wants.

"Kenzie... who hurt you baby?"

"No one."

"Someone hurt you. Your nightmare was real—it wasn't from a book or a movie, was it?"

She shakes her head and tries to look back down but I hold her chin up, not letting her shrink away. I've never seen her like this; the Kenzie I know is strong, confident and even when her apartment was broken into—she is resilient. The Kenzie looking up at me now is like a shell of that person: the person looking back at me is not the one I've gotten to know these last few weeks. My heart, which I swore would never exist again, breaks as she looks at me with pleading eyes.

I don't know what to do; I don't know how to handle this. Put me in a board room and I can take on anything that comes my way. Put Kenzie in my arms, sobbing after she relives someone hurting her and I don't know how to act. God, I want to find out so badly what happened to her. I want to beg her to tell me who did this to her and then I want Carter to find him so I can ruin him.

"You're safe, no one will ever hurt you again, I promise," I vow. Even though I don't know who hurt her, I know I would do anything to keep her from being hurt again.

She doesn't say anything but a single tear rolls down her cheek. She licks her lips as she shudders against me. I don't think about what happens next; it's almost as if my body has a mind of its own. Holding her chin in place, I lean down until my lips hover just above hers. I close my eyes and wait... I wait for her to push me away or tell me she doesn't want me to kiss her. When she doesn't say anything or push me away, I close the gap between our lips and envelope mine over hers. I wrap my arm around her waist, anchoring her to me as I deepen the kiss, not knowing how else to comfort her right now. She tentatively reaches up, running her hand through my hair providing the encouragement I need. I suck her bottom lip into my mouth; she moans in response and tugs at my hair just enough to make my dick start to stir.

As I feel it twitching and threatening to make its presence known, I realize we need to stop before we both do something we would regret. As much as it kills me, I pull back from Kenzie's soft lips but keep her pressed against me. My heart beats wildly; my breathing is heavy, almost as if I just finished running a marathon. God, I hope I wasn't wrong for kissing her... the last thing I want is for her to feel like I took advantage of her when she was upset.

"Kenzie, baby... tell me who hurt you."

"No one."

"That's not true and we both know it. Who. Hurt. You?"

"Nicholas, please let it go."

"I can't. Someone hurt you and I want to know who. I need to make sure whoever did this can't hurt you again."

"He can't. He doesn't even live here; he can't hurt me again."

"He lives on the west coast?" I suddenly realize that she didn't run to New York for love; she ran to get away from someone.

"Yes."

"He's the reason you left—the reason you moved to New York."

"Yes."

"Who was he?"

"No one."

"Baby... "

"He was just a stupid guy who I thought loved me."

"He was your boyfriend?"

"Fiancé technically."

"You were going to marry him? Someone who hit you?"

"Please, Nicholas. It's a part of my life I don't like to think about. I was young and incredibly stupid."

"Why would you stay with him? You deserve so much better; no one should ever hit you."

"I didn't think anyone would ever love me—he was the first guy who acted like he cared about me. He would apologize after hitting me and tell me how much he loved me. I was stupid. I believed him. I believed that I deserved it every time he hit me. That I didn't deserve anything better."

"Why would you think that? You're such a wonderful, loving, caring person. You deserve someone who treats you as such."

"I... that's not what I was told growing up. When you hear something often enough, you end up believing it."

"Oh Kenzie..."

"It's the past... I don't like to think about it."

"What made you finally decide to leave? I'm grateful you finally did but—"

"He almost killed me one night."

"WHAT?!?!"

I'm fuming... I'm seeing red... I'm going to kill the son of a bitch. What kind of fucking piece of shit almost kills the woman he supposedly loves? What type of man hits any woman?

"Please, *please*... I don't want to talk about it. I finally woke up that night, left him and worked with a wonderful group who helped me move out here. They made sure nothing from that night appeared in my medical records and helped me find a group in New York that could help me get my life back together."

"Kenzie... if he ever tries to contact you again I want you to tell me. Please, promise me you will tell me if you hear from him."

"I... I will."

"Do you often have nightmares?"

"Not really. It's not like I have them every night. I wish I didn't have them at all, but they always seem to hit when I least expect it."

"I know what you mean."

On His Terms

"You do?"

I don't respond, not wanting to admit that she's not the only one who suffers from nightmares. Unlike Kenzie though, my nightmares occur almost every night. It's rare to go a night without one and I've learned to function on very little sleep. I never would have expected Kenzie to have suffered from nightmares and never would have guessed the reason for them. I'm left with more questions unanswered than were answered tonight. What the fuck did this guy do to her? What did her mother do when she was growing up to make her think she didn't deserve to be loved? Who the fuck is this low life who hurt her?

I need to have Carter dig into her background. I need to know who this fucker was. I need someone on him to make sure he can't hurt Kenzie ever again. I don't give a shit what happens in a few weeks when our arrangement ends: I'll pay any cost to ensure that this fucker stays far away from her. People like that shouldn't be allowed in society; there is no place for men who beat women.

"Nicholas," Kenzie moans softly, pulling me from my angry thoughts.

I look down and realize that she is fast asleep, still wrapped in my arms. She moaned my name in her sleep... and even though I have no idea why she did this, it makes me smile. I should leave, go back to my room and sleep in my own bed. I should leave things alone so they don't become awkward between us. Having Kenzie here isn't good— we have crossed too many lines this weekend. The right thing to do would be to go to sleep in the room next door and pretend that I never came in here. The right thing to do would be to forget everything she just told me. The right thing to do would be to forget how great it feels to have this woman curled up next to me. To forget how amazing it feels to have her sleeping in my arms.

Unfortunately I've never been good at doing the right thing.

Chapter 22
Kenzie

I'm hot... like I'm lying next to a scorching fire. I force my eyes open needing to figure out why it's suddenly so hot in here. I can't sleep when it's this hot. When my eyes finally focus, I immediately realize why I'm sweltering and it absolutely floors me. Nicholas, a shirtless Nicholas no less, is lying next to me, sound asleep. His leg is wrapped over mine and his arm rests across my stomach. It takes me a minute to remember how he ended up in here with me.

I panic remembering the nightmare I had last night that brought him into my room. I never wanted to him to know about my past, never expecting there to be a reason for him to know about my nightmares. I never thought we would ever be sleeping under the same roof so in my mind there would never be a chance for him to find out about my ex. You just don't randomly bring up that you dated an asshole who liked to hit you over dinner one night with someone you barely know. You especially don't discuss things like that with a guy who is paying you to go on dates with him. That is not part of the contract. He wants and needs someone who is complication-free; he doesn't want to sit and talk about someone's horrible childhood or the stupid mistakes they made as an adult.

I take one last glance at him, one last deep breath inhaling his scent, before I slide myself from his grip. I immediately feel... alone. I can't remember the last time I had someone's arms around me like that. I can't remember the last time someone cuddled me after a nightmare; hell I can't remember the last time someone just held me. I would love nothing more than to stay in bed, wrapped in his arms all day, but unfortunately I know things are going to be awkward enough when he wakes up. I don't want to give Nicholas any more of a reason to cancel our arrangement.

I look back at him sound asleep in the bed that I was in only moments ago, before I resolutely step into the hallway and close the door behind me. I head down to the kitchen, determined to make breakfast and a pot of coffee before Nicholas wakes up. I need to wrap my head around everything that happened last night.

God, it felt so good to sleep in Nicholas's arms. I don't know why he came into my room when he could have just ignored my screams. I don't know why he laid in bed next to me when he could have just called my name or shook me awake like they used to do at the shelter. I don't know why he held me even when I'm sure I fought him... I don't know why he kissed me. His soft lips felt amazing against mine—the kiss was so different than the one at the awards dinner. It was full of emotion, which doesn't make sense because this is just a business transaction. Nicholas doesn't have feelings for me. He probably just felt sorry for me. Perhaps that's what I felt in the kiss... sympathy.

And then he stayed in my bed... all night. He slept next to me the entire night when he could have easily gone back to the guest room he was supposed to stay in. Why didn't he go back to his room? Maybe he was going to return to his room but accidently fell asleep? Maybe he thought I would be mad if he left? The dinging of my phone forces my attention away from him.

Did Nicholas have any problems during the night? –Vivienne

No, his fever remained down and he ate a bowl of chicken noodle soup with veggies before bed without a problem. – Kenzie

Good to hear! He might not have a bad case since he didn't eat all of the chicken – Vivienne

What can he have for breakfast? Should we stick with soup or can he have something else? – Kenzie

Something light should be okay. Nothing greasy or too heavy though. –Vivienne

Great, thanks! –Kenzie

I'll stop by later this evening to check on him. If he holds down breakfast without a problem and his fever doesn't return, I don't see the need for you to stay another night. – Vivienne

Thanks –Kenzie

I'm relieved that Nicholas is feeling better but when I first read her text, I felt disappointed as it means I would need to leave soon. I don't know why, but I was kind of looking forward to spending more time with him especially now that he is on the mend. I learned a lot more about Nicholas yesterday, than I did over the few dinners and events we've been to together. I knew after the night my apartment was broken into that he was caring, but last night just went beyond anything I could have imagined. Nicholas comforted me in a way that no one has ever been able to. In all the years I've had nightmares, no one made me feel as safe as Nicholas did last night. No one made me feel protected the way he did.

I suppose it's a good thing that my stay here is coming to an end earlier than originally planned; we've crossed quite a few lines this weekend, that are going to be hard to uncross. Do we just pretend like this weekend never happened? I saw a side of him that I had no idea existed under the CEO façade he puts on every day. I've caught a few glimpses it, but last night, I realized Nicholas really is nothing I ever expected.

I briefly consider talking with Bridget but quickly decide against it. What if she determines that I violated the contract with Nicholas and fires me? What if she ends the contract between me and Nicholas? I don't even know what I would say to her. I don't know how to explain what I'm feeling or even what I'm thinking.

"Something smells good," Nicholas's voice pulls me from my worries.

"Your mom said you could try a real meal this morning as long as it was light and non-greasy. I was just finishing an egg white omelet with veggies and a little cheese."

"It smells really good, but you didn't need to cook for me, Kenzie."

"I was up so it wasn't a big deal. Do you want to try coffee? Or maybe tea?"

"Coffee would be wonderful. I'll get it."

The coffee pot is next to the stove putting Nicholas close to me. I can feel myself blushing immediately, at the memory of how it felt to have his body pressed against mine last night and wrapped around me this morning. When he returns to the breakfast bar the air around me suddenly feels cooler and I find myself wishing he hadn't left the spot where he was standing.

"If you don't like it—"

"Kenzie, you haven't made anything that I haven't liked, so I have no doubt this will taste just as good."

"Your mom said she would stop by later this afternoon to check on you but that if you keep breakfast down and your fever doesn't return, you won't need me here any longer."

"Oh... that's good. I'm sure you have things to do."

We sit in silence finishing our breakfast; both of us seem to be avoiding the topic of last night. I don't know what to say to him. Do I apologize for having the nightmare? Do I thank him for waking me? For holding me all night? For comforting me? For kissing me?

How the hell does someone handle this?!?!

I don't know that there is a protocol for how you deal with someone the morning after they wake you up and hold you all night. I suppose this would be different if we were friends or lovers—at least then we would be emotionally invested in our relationship. This is different because we're not emotionally invested in this business transaction… at least Nicholas isn't. I think I could be…

"Do you return to work tomorrow or are you off?" Nicholas pulls me from my thoughts.

"I'm scheduled to work in the morning. What about you? Are you going to PFS tomorrow?"

"Probably not, I think I'll work from home tomorrow. My office is set up so that I can work from here so my assistant will only need to rearrange any face-to-face meetings I had scheduled for tomorrow. I think I'll spend one more day here before braving the office. I don't need my employees concerned that I'm sick. It's the reason I didn't want to go to the hospital. Periodically I work from home so it won't raise any red flags for anyone if I spend the day here tomorrow."

"It's good that you have that flexibility."

"It is. I usually work a lot of evenings and weekends from here so having a fully equipped office is essential."

"Do you ever *not* work?" I can't help but laugh. It seems he works constantly: long hours at the office only to return home to work more hours. No wonder he said he doesn't have time to date…

"Not really. Even when I've taken a vacation, I don't completely disconnect from the office. I can't… when you run your own business like I do, a day off means a risk that something could happen. I've taken a day here and there, of course, but even then I've never been entirely unavailable to my staff. Alex always knows how to reach me if something comes up."

"What do you like to do when you *are* able to take a day or two off?"

"I love spending time on the open water. I have a boat that I don't get to use nearly as much as I should. There's something so calming about being on the water, don't you think?"

"I wouldn't know. I've never been on a boat before."

"Never?" I shake my head. "Wow… you have no idea what you're missing. I don't know if it's the rocking from the waves or just the fact that you can look for miles and see nothing but blue… whatever it is, it's relaxing. You should try it sometime."

"Maybe."

"What about you? When you're not working, what do you like to do?"

"I like to read, so I spend a lot of time at the library. I've always loved to cook and bake although the last apartment I lived in wasn't really conducive to do either. Since I moved… since I've been staying downstairs, I have been cooking a lot more. I love to try new recipes or make up ones on my own. There's something very satisfying about making an entire meal from scratch."

"I wouldn't know. Unfortunately I can't cook very much. A frozen pizza, spaghetti and anything that can be prepared in the microwave is pretty much the extent of my cooking skills."

"I'm sure you could follow a recipe—"

"Nope. I can barely follow the instructions Julie leaves me on the food she freezes for the weekends when she is off. I get too distracted: I'll start following a recipe or the heating instructions and then end up engulfed in emails or something work related. The next thing you know whatever I was making is burned to a crisp."

"I guess I could see how that could happen."

We spend the next few hours learning more about each other as we lounge on the couch in the great room of Nicholas's apartment. I find out he plays the guitar beautifully— I even talked him into playing an incredibly moving piece for me. I have absolutely no musical ability so watching someone play so easily is amazing. I learn more about Nicholas's family, although he doesn't talk about the time in his life before he was adopted. I don't ask about it because, not only is it really none of my business, but I want to respect his privacy in the way that he is respecting mine. At no point during our conversation does he ask about my nightmare or even about my childhood. It dawns on me that he is likely purposely omitting those questions.

"Nicholas?" I hear Vivienne's voice from the foyer.

"Mom? What are you doing here?"

"I told Kenzie… Oh hi Kenzie! I wasn't expecting you to still be here," she quickly hugs me hello when she realizes I'm sitting on the couch. "Are you still not feeling well Nicholas? Is your fever back? Is your stomach—"

"I'm fine Mom. Kenzie and I were just talking," Nicholas quickly interrupts her.

"Oh good. I was hoping you didn't start feeling bad again," she sighs.

"I'm going to gather my stuff," I quickly excuse myself, wanting to give them some privacy.

I make my way back to the guest room upstairs; the bed is still in complete disarray from last night. I quickly make it, not wanting to leave it a mess for Julie when she comes back tomorrow. I take a quick shower and stow the few belongings I brought with me on Friday when I packed in a hurry to stay the weekend.

"Nicholas?" I walk into the great room expecting to see Vivienne and Nicholas still talking.

"In here," his voice comes from his office.

"I was thinking I would get going—"

"Can you come in here for a moment?"

"Sure."

"Have a seat."

I sit in a chair across from a stunning mahogany desk that is covered with papers and files. I glance around the room, three of the walls have floor to ceiling bookshelves that are filled. The other wall has a long table against it filled with different office equipment including a printer, shredder, scanner and a fax machine. I suppose he is truly set up to work completely from home like he said.

"This is for you," he hands me a small white envelope. I open it, confused as to what it might be, and a wave of emotions comes over me when I take it in.

"What is this?" I look at the check in complete disbelief.

"Since we didn't make arrangements for this weekend through Bridget, I didn't feel it was necessary to send the payment through her. If you would prefer that—"

"Payment?"

"For this weekend. I calculated your hourly rate by the number of hours you spent here this weekend. I added in a little extra since this was last minute and you had to miss your cooking classes—"

"I... I can't accept this."

"Why not?"

"Nicholas... this weekend... we weren't... "

I'm completely mortified that he would give me this check. I don't understand why he suddenly reverted back to our business arrangement. Was it because I said I needed to leave? Was he always planning on paying me or did something happen to change his mind? I don't think anything could have happened—

"You spent the weekend with me; why would you not accept this?"

"I… I didn't do it because of our contract, Nicholas."

"Then why did you do it? Why didn't you tell Carter and my mother that you were busy? You had plans, Kenzie. You were supposed to attend that class—"

"You're right I was. But I changed my plans. You needed someone here with you and I was able to rearrange things to be that person."

"Which is why you should take this," he hands me the check that I laid on his desk.

"No."

"No?"

"No. I'm not taking this. We didn't go through Bridget to arrange this, meaning this is outside our contract—"

"Which is why—"

"No. I refuse to accept this money, Nicholas. I didn't do this because of a stupid contract."

"Then why did you do this?"

"Because you needed someone!"

"But why you? You could have walked away. I don't understand why you would do something like this and then not let me pay you!"

"Then I guess you don't know me at all."

"I know you need money, which was the reason you signed up with Bridget to begin with. You wanted to better your life. You wanted to go back to school and finish your degree. You wanted a safer place to live. Take this money and use it for that, Kenzie. Please… you earned it this weekend."

"I earned it?"

"Yes… you took care of me this weekend. You made sure I stayed hydrated, you gave me medicine round the clock, you stayed up half the night and you cooked for me."

"And what about you?"

On His Terms

"What about me?"

"Should I pay you?"

"*Pay me*? For what? What would *you* pay *me* for?"

"For last night... should I pay you for the time you spent... comforting me?"

"What?!?! No, of course not! That was different!"

"Why? Why was it different?"

"I... I don't know it just was," he answers quietly.

"I'm not taking this money, Nicholas. This weekend had nothing to do with our contract with Bridget and if you think that's all this was..."

"Then why did you do it?"

"Good bye Nicholas."

Chapter 23
Nicholas

What the fuck just happened? Did she really just walk out on me? I thought I was doing the right thing; I thought I was doing what she expected. Why the fuck would she not accept the check? Who the fuck turns down twenty thousand dollars?

Earlier

"How are you feeling Nicholas?"

"I'm good Mom. Kenzie made me an omelet this morning and I had about half a cup of coffee. My stomach feels fine and my fever hasn't returned."

"That's such a relief, dear. Most of the people who attended the dinner with you are still in the hospital and are struggling to keep even liquids down. It probably helped that you didn't eat all of the chicken they served or you would be in the same boat."

"I don't know how anyone finished that dinner, it was so bland. Kenzie and I were even talking about stopping somewhere for dinner after the awards ceremony since we were both still hungry."

"You're really lucky to have Kenzie, son. Not a lot of women would have given up their weekend to take care of their sick boyfriend."

"I'm very grateful she was able to keep me out of the hospital."

"Why haven't you brought her to Sunday dinner yet? She really is a wonderful woman, a real breath of fresh air."

"I know, I will. We've been busy and our schedules don't always match up," I hate lying to her but I never expected this arrangement to become so personal. Obviously I knew Kenzie would meet my parents at the gala and possibly other events, but I never expected my mother to take such a liking to her. I never pictured her attending Sunday dinners at my parents' house, hugging my mom... that she would fit in so well.

"She is so much better than—"

"Don't say her name."

"I'm just saying, there's no way 'she' would have given up her weekend to take care of you. I don't think that bitch ever cared about anyone other than herself."

I'm floored... I can't remember the last time I heard my mother curse. She doesn't use that type of language, not ever. We were never allowed to curse growing up and even now she is quick to reprimand us if we use that type of language in her presence. How did I not see how much my mother hated her?

"I never realized how you felt about her."

"You were blinded by her and unfortunately only saw what 'she' wanted you to see. No one liked her; it wasn't just me. Your dad, Austin and Cara... no one could stand her. Don't you remember how uncomfortable those dinners were when you would bring 'her' over? I suspect she felt it and why she suddenly started making plans every Sunday night."

"I guess she did."

"She never would have done what Kenzie did for you this weekend, son, you have to know that. She would have asked what was in it for her. She would have expected something in return. People like her don't do things for other people if there's nothing for them to gain."

"Kenzie did—"

"Kenzie's nothing like 'she' was, anyone could see that. Kenzie loves you—"

"No—"

"She does. I'm guessing you two haven't told each other that yet, but I can see it every time you two are together. She gave up her weekend to move in here with you, and despite what she says, I'm sure she had something to do—"

"She was registered for a cooking class this weekend."

"Yet she didn't blink an eye to give it all up for you, son. I'm assuming she expects absolutely nothing in return either. She's just that type of person. She's good for you, Nicholas, and I just don't mean because of this weekend. You stayed the entire night at the New Beginnings Gala, something you haven't done since you were a teenager and I forced you to stay. You just seem happier with Kenzie; happier than I think I ever saw you with..."

I don't know what to think anymore. I thought I was doing the right thing by compensating her for the time she spent here this weekend. I assumed the only reason she stayed on Friday night rather than say she was busy was because she saw a way to make more money. I know she wants to go back to school and those cooking classes couldn't have been cheap. Even without paying rent on an apartment, she still has bills to pay. Was it completely wrong to assume she saw a way to make money and put some aside? Her bank account barely had a couple hundred dollars in it when Carter ran her background check. How could she not see this as an opportunity to make a large amount of money all at once? As a way to build up her bank account so she could afford to go back to school? How could I know that my mom might have been right? That Kenzie never expected a payout for this weekend?

I replay the conversation with Kenzie before she left my office and try to figure out what I missed or where I went wrong.

FUCK! FUCK!! FUCK!!

I fucked up... I fucked up big time.

I never considered how she would feel about me coming into her room last night after her nightmare. We both avoided talking about it— I thought was a good thing. I thought I was keeping things separate. I thought I was keeping things from becoming awkward between us. Since she didn't bring it up, I assumed she didn't want to talk to about it. I went into her room last night to comfort her; I couldn't stand the thought of her being in pain even if the pain was only in a nightmare. I didn't do it because I thought she would pay me for doing it! How could she think—

FUCK!!!!!!!!!!!!

Oh fuck... oh fuck... oh fuck...

She agreed to stay with me Friday night because she wanted to comfort me; she wanted to take care of me the same way I wanted to take care of her last night. FUCK!!!!!! How the fuck do I fix this? How fucking stupid could I be? I should have known that she wouldn't have wanted the money. I should have known that she wouldn't have expected to be paid for taking care of me. I need to find a way to fix this. *How the fuck do I fix this?* I should call her... FUCK... I don't have her phone number. All part of this stupid contract with Bridget so we both can keep our privacy; I don't think privacy matters anymore, we fucking slept in the same bed last night!

God, it felt so good to have Kenzie in my arms last night. I woke up a few hours after we both fell asleep and just watched her sleep for a little while. She looked so peaceful; it was hard to believe that the woman in my arms was the one who thought no one would ever love her. I don't understand how Kenzie could have such a low opinion of herself. This is the woman who gave up everything for me this weekend so I wouldn't have to go to a hospital. This is a woman who agreed to help Cara with a dance auction without even knowing what that would entail.

I eventually fell back to sleep but not until she rolled over and snuggled back into me so her back was against my chest. It was as if she was seeking me out in her sleep. I've never slept with a woman before, not all night... I would leave after they fell asleep and go back to my room. I never shared a bed with *her*; the risk of having a nightmare was always too great. I would never forgive myself if I accidently injured *her* during a nightmare, although after what *she* did, I might reconsider that notion. Thinking back to that time in my life, I don't know that I ever really wanted to sleep with her. She was a good fuck but I never wanted to hold her or sleep next to her.

Yet last night, I couldn't bring myself to leave Kenzie. Even when I was awake and watching her sleep, I knew I should have left to keep things professional between us yet I couldn't bring myself to do that. I have never felt this way about someone before. I'm not sure what it means feeling like this with Kenzie last night.

I don't know what to do. The lines are getting blurred; this weekend has changed everything. I had a hard enough time keeping my thoughts professional after seeing her in that bikini but after this weekend I don't know how I can still see her as a business transaction. How can I look at her and only think of our contract? How do I forget what it felt like to have her body against mine?

But more importantly, how do I fix what happened tonight? I may not fully understand why Kenzie would give up her entire weekend, including the classes she has been looking forward to, just to take care of me, but I now know it wasn't about the money. Perhaps, she just did it because that's the kind of person she is and to her it meant nothing. But what if by some chance it *did* mean something? What if she is having trouble with the blurred lines between us, too? Maybe the kiss at dinner the other night wasn't just for show...

If Kenzie feels that way, I'm even more fucked that I thought I was. I can't have her thinking of this arrangement as anything more than a business transaction. I'm the last person she needs to be falling for. I'm no good for her... I'm nothing that she needs in her life. She needs someone without baggage, without complications and I come with a truckload of shit.

"Good evening, Mr. Parker," Carter pulls me from my thoughts a few hours later.

"Carter... I wasn't expecting you until tomorrow morning? I thought your flight was Monday?"

"It wasn't but Julie and I were able to take an earlier flight. How are you feeling, sir?"

"Much better, thank you. Kenzie left a few hours ago after my mother gave me the all clear. I think I'm going to work from home tomorrow and will return to the office on Tuesday."

"Very good, sir. Is there anything you need?"

"I need to send flowers to Kenzie. Can you arrange for someone to deliver her a bouquet tomorrow when she gets home from the bakery?"

"Of course sir. What would you like the card to say?"

"*I'm sorry, please call me*. Have it signed with my first name and my cell phone number."

"Yes sir."

"Oh and Carter… I want a more thorough background check done on Kenzie ASAP."

"Anything in particular I should be looking for?"

"She had a fiancé before she moved to New York. I suspect he's the reason she left Denver though she hasn't even confirmed that she lived there yet. I want… I need to know who he is. He… he beat her. According to her, one night he almost killed her—"

"There was nothing that would have suggested an abusive relationship in her medical records—"

"She said she worked with a group who made sure those details from that night didn't make it into her file. Was there anything in her medical records that maybe were documented as something else?"

"Give me a minute. I'll grab her file from my office."

Carter quickly returns. Thankfully he is as organized as I am and can find anything immediately. Carter has been working for me for a number of years now; he was the first person I hired when it became obvious I needed security outside of PFS. I have never regretted hiring him, even if we butt heads at times.

"Well…"

"What is it?"

"She had an emergency room visit a couple years ago: she stated she fell down the stairs but the injuries could suggest something else."

"What type of injuries?"

"A few broken ribs, a gash on her arm requiring stitches, bruises on her cheek and a bump on her head. The notes in the file indicate that she had several older bruises at the time but she attributed them to bumping into things around the house. The hospital staff treated her and sent her home in a few hours. It isn't noted that anyone suspected anything other than the fall."

"I need to know who she was with at that time and then I want to know everything about him. Once you find him, I want his whereabouts tracked. He should be residing in Denver or somewhere he could easily commute to the city from. I want to know if he leaves the state at any time. Check surrounding states if you don't find him in Colorado."

"Do we consider him a threat, sir?"

"We haven't received a threat from him yet, but I want to do everything we can to ensure he never comes near Kenzie again."

"Has she stated if she heard from him since he left?"

"She didn't say and I didn't ask."

"You said she ended things with him when she moved here?"

"Yes, she said she left and moved to New York to get away from him."

"And we assume he is still in Denver?"

"I'm assuming so... why? What are you getting at Carter?"

"She moved here... roughly two years ago. If he hasn't contacted her since she left him, you have to wonder why not? Abusers typically don't let their women just walk away from them."

"What are you thinking?"

"The only reason he would stay away is if she has something she can use against him. Something that could ruin him if it were ever discovered. She agrees to keep it out of the press in exchange for him letting her go."

"Those envelopes... the day we moved her from the apartment, remember she had two envelopes hidden that she insisted she take with her?"

"That's what gave me the thought when you said she was abused. First, I assumed they were childhood mementos or maybe paperwork she wanted to keep safe but now I wonder if they weren't her insurance policy."

"I assumed the same thing."

"I'll start digging into who her ex might have been and will let you know as soon as I find something on him, sir."

"Very good. And Carter... thank you for returning a day early."

"Of course, sir."

The next few days pass by slowly. Kenzie doesn't respond to my flowers even though I have Carter sending them daily to her apartment. I know she received them; Hunter confirmed that she has them. Why hasn't she called me? Did I fuck things up that badly with her? What if she has decided she needs to end our arrangement? The thought of not seeing her again makes me feel... I don't know what. As luck would have it, I have nothing on my schedule this week that I need Kenzie to accompany me to so I can't even use that excuse to see her. I'm tempted to schedule something anyway, to call Bridget and ask her to arrange for a private *date* with Kenzie, but what if that just fucks up things even more between us?

Want to grab a drink? –N

Sure... what's up? –A

The Scorekeeper? – N

I'll see you in 15 –A

"Carter?" I call out knowing he's somewhere nearby and can hear me.

"Yes, sir?"

"I'm going to go to The Scorekeeper for a few drinks." If Carter is surprised he doesn't show it. The Scorekeeper is a sports bar, not far from the office where Alex and I have gone a few times after work to grab a drink. It's not a bad place, but why leave the condo when I have access to finer liquors than a sports bar would have?

I need to talk to someone about this mess and how the fuck to fix it, but I'm limited who I can talk to because of how Kenzie and I are involved. I can't go to my mom; not only would she not understand why I'm doing this, but then she would know that I've been lying to her. My brother is destined to forever be a bachelor: he has no desire to commit to one woman so he's probably not the greatest option either. I could probably get advice from Cara, but I don't know that I trust her to not slip and accidently tell someone about the contract I have with Kenzie. So that leaves Alex. He's proven himself over the years and I trust that he wouldn't share this with anyone else. He knows the shit I went through two years ago after that fucking situation blew up in my face and nearly ruined me.

"Nicholas," Alex nods as he walks over to the table where I already have his favorite beer waiting.

"Alex."

"What's up?"

"I fucked up Alex… big time. I need you to tell me how to fix it. I've been sending her flowers… something I've never done! They aren't working, though. I thought all women wanted flowers?"

"Whoa… who are you sending flowers to and why?"

"Kenzie."

"I'm not a mind reader, Nicholas… you're going to have to give me more information if we're going to sort through this."

I spend the next few minutes giving him the very basic information about our arrangement; I leave out Bridget's company, letting him think that the contract is just between Kenzie and me.

"Fuck, Parker," he laughs. "You took my advice."

"Your advice was to hire a prostitute," I growl. "Kenzie is not a fucking prostitute."

"Relax Parker, my advice was to hire someone—you *inferred* I was talking about a prostitute."

"You meant something like this?"

"I've heard about people using similar services before."

"Why didn't you suggest that?"

"After the way you reacted? I figured the last thing you'd consider would be to hire someone to be by your side. I was going to give it a little longer and if the press didn't start backing off, I would have said something privately to you."

"Can you help me figure out how the hell I fix this?"

"Why me?"

"You've been with Ella fucking forever; you must have learned a few things over the years," I shrug. "Look, I need advice and don't know who the fuck to talk to because I can't have this arrangement with Kenzie leaked."

"Ella might disagree and say I have no idea what women want sometimes," he laughs. "But tell me what you did to fuck up."

"We went out Friday night to the awards dinner. I gave the speech… and then she kissed me."

"This was the first time you've kissed, I assume?"

"Yes… she initiated it."

"Does that bother you?"

"No… yes… I don't know."

"Okay, then what?"

"I came down with food poisoning from my meal. Carter and Kenzie brought me back to The Accord and my mother saw me. She wanted to admit me into the hospital but agreed to let me stay at home if someone was there the entire time to watch over me. Carter and Julie were off for the weekend—they were attending Julie's niece's wedding or something like that. I was really out of it, I think I was sleeping or passed out when it was decided Kenzie would stay the weekend with me."

"Okay…"

"So things seemed to be fine, I was shocked when I woke up on Saturday and learned that not only was she spending the weekend in my apartment, but that she had slept in my bedroom."

"Get to the part where you fucked up man…"

"Anyway, we spent the day together just hanging out in my apartment. My mother stopped by and refused to allow Kenzie to leave, threatening me if I told her to go home that she would admit me into the hospital. Finally, on Sunday, my mother came back and cleared me and said Kenzie could leave, that I no longer needed someone to watch over me. That's when I really fucked things up with Kenzie."

"What'd you do?"

"When she said she was going to leave, I asked her to come into my office and I gave her a check for twenty thousand dollars. She refused to take it, Alex! Can you believe it?"

"Fuck, I'll take a check, Parker, if you're handing them out. Why didn't she take it? I assume the twenty thousand was above the rate you agreed to because it was last minute."

"She said she didn't do it because of the contract we had. I tried telling her that I was just trying to compensate her for the time she spent taking care of me but she wouldn't hear of it."

"How did things end?"

"She told me the reason she stayed had nothing to do with the contract we have. I asked her again why did she stay then. The first time she told me if I didn't know the answer to that then I didn't know her very well at all."

"And the second time you asked that question?"

"She said goodbye and walked out of the apartment."

"Shit."

"I've sent her flowers every fucking day, apologizing and asking her to call me. She hasn't responded! Not once! I don't know how to make her forgive me, Alex! Tell me what I need to do! I thought all women wanted flowers! I need to fix this! I can't have her end our contract!"

"Why not, Nicholas? You told me this arrangement was only going to last a few months, just long enough to get the press of your back about your personal life. It's been… what… two months—"

"Almost three."

"It sounds like the time was approaching to end the contract anyway. Did you want to be the one to end it… is that what this is about?"

"No."

"Then why would it bother you if Kenzie ended the contract now?"

"Because I don't want to break the contract," I finally admit aloud.

"Why not?"

"Because our arrangement works. I get the press off my back and Kenzie gets the money she needs to go back to school. It's a win win situation for everyone."

"They have backed off but is that the only reason you don't want to end the contract with her?"

"No. I enjoy spending time with Kenzie. I learned a lot about her this weekend and enjoyed having her with me. I think… we've become friends."

"Have you told her that?"

"No! Why would I?"

"Maybe she feels the same way?"

"I... I don't know. I guess."

"Why do you think she stayed with you this weekend, Parker? You're the smartest fucking guy I know; think about what you just said."

"Because she thinks of me as a friend?"

"It sounds like she cares for you."

"My mom thinks we're in love," I shake my head, remembering the conversation with her in my kitchen that day.

"Shit, really?" he sits back in his seat, the surprise evident on his face.

"She says she can tell by the way we look at each other. I guess Kenzie and I are just better actors than I thought we were."

"Is it—"

"No!"

"Why not?"

"This is business, Alex. Nothing more than a contract between two people. I'm not fucking going down that road again. I'm not opening myself up and letting someone... I'm not repeating my past."

"And you think Kenzie is like—"

"No, of course not. The fact that she didn't take the money proves that she isn't."

"Is that what it was about?"

"What do you mean?"

"Was the money a test?"

"No! Of course not!"

"Are you sure? You offered her a very large amount of money after she spent the weekend in your home, caring for you. Is it possible that you needed to find out if she was just like—"

"Don't fucking compare Kenzie to that bitch! Kenzie is nothing like her!"

"And her not taking the check proves that, doesn't it?"

"Yes! I mean no... it's not just that."

"It's not?"

"No! Kenzie couldn't be more different than *she* was!"

"Yet, you thought she stayed with this weekend because of money."

FUCK, could Alex be right? Could I have been testing Kenzie without knowing it? I thought I was just doing the right thing: I thought I was helping Kenzie out after she helped me.

"Do you think that's how she saw it?"

"I don't know. She could have felt like you were trying to be nice, she could have felt that you were trying to buy her off, or she could have felt like a whore—"

"What?!?! Don't you talk about Kenzie like that!"

"Parker, you're an idiot sometimes." The bastard is fucking smirking at me! "Have you thought about it from her perspective? You kissed for the first time and spent the entire weekend together. Then as soon as your mother said you didn't need her there any longer you offer her money and essentially kick her out."

"That's not—"

"Yeah, it is."

FUCK! Does she really feel like I treated her like a whore? That I was ungrateful for what she did?

"How the fuck do I fix this, Alex? I can't have her thinking that about herself. Tell me what to do; tell me how to fix this."

"You need to talk to her, moron. Flowers are wonderful, but it sounds like Kenzie is not the type of woman who wants, or needs, material items. You need to talk to her."

"How can I fucking talk to her if she won't call me?"

"Find a way Nicholas. Get her alone and talk to her. Maybe you should tell her about what happened two years ago. She needs to understand why you thought that she wouldn't have stayed just because she cared about you."

"Everyone always wants something from me... anyone else would have expected something from me for what she did."

"Your parents wouldn't have."

"Of course not but Kenzie's not my family; she isn't obligated to take care of me!"

Madison Quinn

"You're right, she choose to spend the weekend with you, without expecting anything in return."

"I just wanted to thank her for taking care of me, for canceling her plans and spending the entire weekend in my apartment instead of her own. Why the fuck was that so wrong?"

"Did you say that to her?"

"Yes…" I did… didn't I? FUCK! Maybe I didn't.

"Parker… tell me you fucking thanked her!"

"I don't know. I thought I did, but I don't remember."

"When you gave her the money, what did you say?"

"I told her it was payment for her time." I cringe even repeating those words. I'm embarrassed at myself, thinking back to how I handled the entire situation. How the fuck did I not think to thank her? I mean, I did earlier at some point, but not when I gave her the check, which is when everything changed.

"You didn't fucking thank her, Parker? No wonder she saw this as a pay off! You need to find a way to thank her."

"I've been trying, Alex! The flowers aren't working."

"No, and I doubt they will. I think you need to find a different way to thank Kenzie. Think of something she wants to do or maybe somewhere she would like to go. Don't make this about publicity or your image. In fact, if you can do something alone, it would go a long way in showing her you don't have an ulterior motive."

An idea pops into my head the moment Alex suggests doing something that Kenzie would like to do away from the press.

"I can do that."

"And Nicholas? Don't fucking pay her at the end of the day."

Chapter 24
Kenzie

My apartment is beginning to look like a florist shop! Nicholas has been sending me flowers every day this week; each beautiful floral arrangement comes with the same card that reads *"I'm sorry; call me."* If I knew what to say to him, I would call him. If I thought he knew what he was apologizing for, I would call him. I don't think he understands how or why what he did upsets me. Hell, I don't fully understand myself why it bothered me so much. I've been trying to figure that out all week. On one hand, I can see why maybe he felt obligated to pay me. That was after all what our arrangement has been up until this weekend: it's been about him paying me for my time. Granted the payment was sent through Bridget, but the premise still remains—he paid for my time. On the other hand though, I felt like that weekend went far beyond the arrangement we had until that point. We got to know each other on a much more personal level. Maybe that wasn't how he viewed the weekend?

I haven't spent any real time completely alone with a man in more than two years. When I left *him* that night, I swore I would never place myself at risk again. That I would never trust a man that much ever again, which meant that I would never be completely alone with one.

It was one of my initial concerns I brought up with Bridget when she first approached me about signing a contract. I refused to meet with him alone in his office or go on business trips with someone until I felt comfortable. Yet, thinking back to the conversation with Vivienne and Carter, none of those thoughts ever impacted my decision to stay the weekend with Nicholas. What's more surprising though is that at no point did I feel unsafe or at risk being alone with Nicholas. Maybe it was because I knew that Hunter was nearby…

Beep beep beep

Even though I've already been awake for a couple of hours, my alarm goes off pulling me from my thoughts. After waking up at four every morning this week, my body seems to just wake up at that time naturally. I wasn't originally scheduled to work today… in fact I was kind of looking forward to having a day off since I've been working every day this week. Unfortunately, one of the new girls that Ginny hired needed to change her schedule today, so Ginny asked me to work a few hours. The only nice thing was I didn't need to be at the bakery until ten, meaning I could have slept a while longer

Bridget called me yesterday and gave me the schedule for the next two weeks. Nicholas has a few events he needs to attend that he has asked for me to accompany him. I was surprised that he was still requesting me. When I first saw her name appear on my caller ID, I just assumed she was calling to let me know that Nicholas had decided to terminate our arrangement. In the split second before I answered the call, I started to panic about where I was going to live. In fact, that thought hasn't been far from my mind all week.

Thankfully, because I haven't been paying rent, I've been able to save a decent amount of money that I've received from Bridget. I probably have enough that now I could afford the security deposit and first month's rent on a decent apartment. My concern though is how I would maintain that apartment once my savings account dried up. I don't want to go back to the shitty apartment or one like it that I rented before. I want to live in a place that I feel safe walking into without worrying about people getting drunk or high on my front steps.

Beep beep beep

My alarm reminds me that I really need to get out of bed and get ready for my shift at the bakery today. I'm only going in for a few hours so afterwards I plan to get caught up on laundry and maybe do some shopping for the events Bridget called me about.

I still have to figure out what to do about Nicholas... I know I need to talk to him but I don't know how to explain why he hurt me. I guess it bothered me the most because I trusted him in spending that much time alone with him yet I didn't feel that he trusted me. Trust isn't the right word; of course he trusted me—why wouldn't he?

Now that I think more about it, I may have overreacted to what he did. Clearly he didn't see our arrangement as anything but a contract and he was acting out that part by offering me money. I overreacted because clearly I thought the weekend was about more than the contract. I thought we were developing a friendship and that he would see that I offered to stay with him because we were friends and not because of a contract. Realizing I overreacted, I vow to call Nicholas as soon as I back to the apartment this afternoon. I don't know exactly what I will say, but I know I need to apologize to him.

I quickly jump in the shower and get ready for work. It's really warm out today, so warm that I wish I could wear shorts to work but of course that isn't safe or acceptable at the bakery. Instead I'm stuck wearing jeans and the bakery t shirt with the store's logo on it.

I love that my apartment has a balcony on it; it's convenient to be able to step outside in the morning and have a cup of coffee.

Knock knock

"Good morning Hunter," I greet him at the door after setting the alarm and grabbing my purse.

"Good morning Ms. Rose, how are you?" he asks.

"Are you ever going to call me Kenzie?" I've requested he drop the *Ms. Rose* many times, but he never does.

"Probably not," he chuckles.

"Of course not," I laugh at his admission. "I'm only working until one today, but then I need to do some shopping this afternoon. I'm thinking of stopping back at here for lunch and then maybe going shopping if you are available?"

"Of course, Ms. Rose. I have the car ready for us downstairs."

"I thought we would walk today since I'm not going in til later?" Hunter doesn't think it's safe to be walking just the couple of blocks to the bakery in the wee hours of the morning so we have been driving.

"I'm sorry, I forgot you wanted to walk. I need to drop off something on our way back from the bakery. If you want to walk I can always come back here—"

"No, of course not. We can drive."

While Hunter maneuvers through the city traffic, I take out my phone and read through the latest headlines. Even though I have the alerts set on my phone for anything related to Nicholas, I still search his name on the internet since I haven't received anything recently. There is no reference of our attendance at the awards dinner but I'm not surprised since it was a small event. I think it worked out well that there was no press, considering how sick Nicholas was that evening. The last thing he would need is to have the press get a picture of him leaving the dinner ill. I'm sure they would have had a field day with that.

"Hunter, where are we going? This isn't the usual route," I look out the window observing where we are. I don't recognize the buildings on this street and it seems like we are heading in the opposite direction of the bakery.

"Yes… about thirty to forty minutes out depending on traffic. Yes… I understand," Hunter says into an earpiece.

"Hunter?" I ask when he seems to have ended the call. "I think the bakery is that way."

"It is, ma'am."

"Where are we going?" Now I'm getting nervous… Up until now I've trusted Hunter; the ride to the bakery in the morning takes less than seven minutes so I haven't considered the situation a risk. However, his actions this morning have me doubting my own judgment. I'm seconds away from having a full-blown panic attack… I can't believe that I trusted a man again. I never thought Hunter would do something but what if—

"I have been instructed to bring you to a location where we will meet Mr. Parker and Carter."

"What? Where are we meeting them?"

"I'm not at liberty to tell you, ma'am."

"You're not at liberty? What if I refuse to go? You can't just take me there against my will!" My breathing is increasing, my heart is racing—I can feel the walls pushing in. I need to get out of the car. I need to take control back… I have no control here. I try opening the car door, but it is locked, despite me hitting the unlock button multiple times.

"Ms. Rose… Ms.—KENZIE!" Hunter calls my name loudly. My eyes meet his in the rear view mirror. "If you don't want to go, I will turn around and we can go back to your apartment. Please do not try to jump out of the car. You'll hurt yourself and Mr. Parker will fire me if you do that!"

"Where… where are we going?" I ask.

"We're meeting Mr. Parker and Carter. I promise you are not in danger. Mr. Parker has arranged… something… he wanted it to be a surprise."

"I'm supposed to be at work—my shift started nine minutes ago."

"You actually aren't scheduled to work today at all, Ms. Rose. Mr. Parker had requested your supervisor's assistance in scheduling this trip so you would be surprised. She agreed to put you on the schedule for a couple of hours even though she didn't need you to work."

"He could have just told me about all of this!"

"It's none of my business, but I don't believe you two have exactly been talking this week."

I slowly begin to relax. I feel a little more at ease knowing that I'm going to meet Nicholas and Carter. I can't remember the last time I had a panic attack but the fact that I almost had one a few minutes ago is very frightening. I don't like feeling out of control and I especially don't like feeling unsafe. In the back of my mind I knew Hunter wouldn't have hurt me yet that was immediately where my mind went when I realized we were unexpectedly heading in the opposite direction of the bakery.

"We're here, Ms. Rose," Hunter alerts me to the fact that the car is stopped a few minutes later. I look out the window but all I see is a parking lot which doesn't help me figure out where we are. He comes around, opens my door and I step out into the bright sunlight.

"Kenzie," Nicholas's familiar voice erases the last bit of tension in my body. "Thank you for coming."

"I don't think I had much of a choice," I say sarcastically trying to hide any signs of the panic attack that was creeping up.

"You did... you always have a choice. But thank you for coming. If you're ready, I'd like to start our day."

"I guess. I didn't bring anything with me—"

"I have everything you need, don't worry."

Nicholas leads over to a set of stairs and the view before me absolutely stunning. We are at a marina with dozens of bobbing boats in each direction and beyond them is the open water.

"We're...?"

"I'm taking you out for a day on my boat, that is if you want to."

"Wow... I mean, yes of course!"

We walk down the steps to the dock, past several smaller boats until we reach the largest boat in the row. Nicholas helps me step onto the deck, before having a few words with Carter.

"Ready to take off, Kenzie?" Nicholas asks.

"Yes!"

"We have to go slow until we get further away from the Marina, it's the 'No Wake' rule, but then we'll speed up. If you want to walk around, just hold onto the railing, it can be tricky on a moving boat until you get used to it."

With that, Nicholas climbs up to what I think is called the bridge and starts the motor. As he said we would, we move slowly through the marina but I don't mind because it gives me a chance to take everything in. We pass by dozens of all different sized boats, and then the water just seems to open up. Nicholas accelerates and we start moving through the water much faster. As we go out further, we begin to pass by large, beautiful houses that are clearly designed to take in the view of the water. They are the types of houses that you can only dream of living in but will never be able to afford. As we move further away from the coast, the houses slowly fade away and looking around, the only things that I can see are a few boats and the open water.

Feeling rather silly while he does all the work, I decide to go off and find Nicholas. I stand up and immediately feel a little unsteady on my feet but quickly gain my confidence as I walk further into the boat. I glance down a set of stairs and see what looks to be like a small living room. I carefully head towards the back of the boat where I find Nicholas holding the wheel as he gazes out the window at the endless water in front of us. He seems very relaxed, more so than I ever think I've seen him. I can see why he said he finds it so relaxing; it's almost as if no one else in the world exists. He looks so different than the man I first met to discuss a business contract, yet he also looks different from the man I spent time with over the weekend. He looks like someone who doesn't have a care in the world.

"It's beautiful out here," I say.

"Oh! You startled me; I didn't hear you. Would you like to try steering it?"

"No! I'll crash into something or break it!"

"Kenzie, look around. There's nothing for miles. There's a boat all the way over there," he points to the left of us. "You won't crash into anything, I promise. C'mon, take the wheel."

He puts his arm out, indicating I should step in front of him to take control of the steering wheel that sort of resembles one that you would find in a car. I cautiously step in front of him, still worried that I'm going to somehow break the boat. He steps closer to me and brings my hands onto the wheel. He is standing so close to me right now that I swear I can feel his breath on my neck... I can't help but think about how good it felt to fall asleep with his arms around me last Saturday night. I slept so soundly after the nightmare, unlike most nights when I have nightmares where if I even try to go back to sleep I end up having another one.

"I'll be right back, just hold the wheel steady," Nicholas lets go of the wheel and walks away from me.

"What?!?! Where are you going?"

He doesn't answer me but disappears down a set of steps just to my right that I hadn't noticed before. While he's gone I concentrate on holding the steering wheel straight, which isn't really that difficult. I constantly scan the horizon for boats or big rocks or land or anything else I might crash into while Nicholas is gone. A few minutes later Nicholas comes back up the stairs carrying two glasses of orange juice and a bowl of fruit. He sets everything down on a table near a couple of lounge chairs.

"You doing okay?" he asks.

"I haven't crashed us yet."

"No, you haven't," he chuckles in agreement. "I was thinking we would cut the motor and drop the anchor up ahead to the right. What do you think?"

"Uh… sure. Whatever you want to do is fine."

"Think you can steer us over there?"

"No."

"Sure you can. It's just like a driving car; don't jerk the wheel to hard in one direction. Slowly ease the wheel in the direction you want to move… Yup that's it; hold it steady just like that."

He is right behind me again; one of his hands is on a control that seems to be decreasing the speed of the boat. With Nicholas this close to me, it's hard to think of anything other than the night I slept in his arms. It felt so good to have someone hold me again, to have someone's arms wrapped around me. If we weren't under contract with Bridget, I would turn around right now and throw my hands around his neck and press my body against his, just so I could feel him against me again. I could just imagine his arms wrapping around my waist as he pulled me even closer to him, his lips would slowly come down to reach mine—

"This looks like a good spot… How about this?" he pulls me from my thoughts. My face heats up in the realization that I was just thinking about him kissing me while he was standing right behind me.

"Sure, sounds good," I try to hide the embarrassment from my voice.

Nicholas hits a button and the motor immediately silences.

"I thought we could have some fruit? I can get something else if you're hungry?"

"No, fruit is fine. I had breakfast not that long ago."

He leads me to an area with several lounge chairs and tables where we sit, the fruit bowl and drinks on a small table between us.

"If you get too warm, I brought a change of clothes for you, as well as a bathing suit if you want to swim."

"You did?" Wow, I'm shocked that Nicholas came this prepared for the trip. While the breeze is cool now, I could see it heating up in the next hour or so when the sun is higher in the sky.

"We also have a packed lunch, bottles of water, wine, suntan lotion, towels and probably anything else we might need. I wasn't sure how long you would want to be out here so I planned as if we were going to spend the day on the water."

"Thank you… you really didn't have to go to all this trouble, Nicholas."

"I did," he takes a deep breath and slowly lets it out. He looks very conflicted, as if he is trying to figure out what to say next. "I fucked up, Kenzie… I'm not proud of my behavior towards you on Sunday. I sounded ungrateful and as if I didn't care that you gave your entire weekend up to take care of me—"

"No, that—"

"Please, Kenzie. Don't downplay how I acted. I realize now that I was treated you as if you were an employee rather than as a… friend. I can't imagine how badly I hurt you that day and I'm sorry my stupidity caused that. I realize now that you spent the weekend with me without expecting something in return, without wanting something for yourself. While it doesn't excuse my behavior, you need to understand that having someone like you in my life is a true rarity. Every day I'm surrounded by people who want something from me or are trying to use me to better themselves."

"Nicholas, I would never—"

"I know you wouldn't, I realize that now. At the time though, I couldn't see why you would agree to cancel your cooking classes, rearrange your schedule and practically move in with me for a weekend without expecting something in return. I assumed initially that you did it because you expected payment for the weekend which would be a rather large amount—"

"Nicholas, I never thought that!" I quickly interrupt, immediately pissed off that he would think that was the reason I agreed to stay with him.

"I know that now. I knew it the moment you walked out of my apartment. I know now that you stayed with me last weekend because that's just the type of person you are— that you wanted nothing more than to help me the way I helped you after you nightmare."

"I never expected you to pay me for staying with you Nicholas. The thought never even entered my mind. I could see why you jumped to that though… your mind immediately went to our contract. This is a business arrangement after all," I shrug my shoulders and look out to the water.

On His Terms

"Kenzie, I've been telling myself the same thing. This is a business arrangement and nothing more," he takes another deep breath and I find myself waiting for him to tell me that the contract is over. That he needs to terminate the contract because we've crossed too many lines, that—

"The truth is though, this *has* become more than a business arrangement for me."

"It has?" Okay, not what I was expecting at all.

"I hope you realize it, too. I think this weekend, or maybe even before this weekend, we've begun to become friends. I enjoy spending time with you and I felt like we got to know each other more. It's been a very long time since I've been able to trust a woman; when I feel threatened I immediately go into business mode. It's what I do when things start to spin out of control either professionally or personally. It helps me take control back."

"You felt threatened?"

"Not by you... no that's not true. I guess I did feel threatened by you."

"Nicholas, I don't understand. How could I threaten you? Did I do something—"

"No! You didn't do anything. Unfortunately, I got burned a long time ago by someone I trusted very much—"

"Who was she?"

"Her name was," he takes another deep breath, running his hands through his hair which I've learned he does when he is stressed.

"Harper... and at one time I thought I loved her."

Chapter 25
Nicholas

I can't believe I'm about to tell Kenzie everything that *she* did. I haven't talked to anyone about *her* since the truth came out. Not since the world as I knew it, was completely turned upside down. Everyone knows to dare not mention her name around me. If it were up to me, I would erase that time in my life entirely. It's amazing how things are when you take a step back and really look at what you thought you had. Looking back to that time, I can't figure out how I was so blind to what *she* was doing to me. I pride myself at being able to recognize when people are lying or trying to use me; yet for the first time someone completely deceived me.

"It's been more than two years, but obviously the damage she did still haunts me to this day. It's been a long time since I allowed myself to consider trusting a woman again."

"What did she do to you, Nicholas?" Kenzie sits up in the lounge chair so she can face me.

"She nearly ruined me; she nearly cost me everything," I cringe at the thought of what could have happened. "Harper interviewed me for an article that was to be featured in some small paper. It was supposed to be her first article that she wrote alone. The interview itself sucked: it was boring, her questions weren't unique and the answers could have easily been found on the internet had she typed my name into google. I only remembered the interview because she seemed so full of herself that day, yet was clearly unprepared for the interview itself. She hadn't memorized the questions, she constantly had to refer back to her notes and the recorder she brought didn't work."

"Sounds like a rough interview."

"I didn't see her again for a year or maybe it was close to two years later. We ended up attending the same charity fundraising event that was being held at a hotel downtown. She was there as a guest of her father's, whom I've done business with in the past. We both had too much to drink that night, one thing led to another and before I knew it, we were upstairs in a hotel room.

"From there we... I guess you could say we used each other whenever the need arose. For the first few months, that's all it was... just sex. Eventually though she started staying over at my place and things started to shift between us. Suddenly, she was calling or coming over more; initially it bothered me but... I know this sounds crass... the sex was good and she was convenient. It's hard to look back and think about when things started to change, but somehow we moved from a sexual relationship to something more. We started spending more time together, attending events or going out together. At one point, I remember thinking she was perfect. She did everything to try to please me: she changed her plans to see me whenever something came up, she enjoyed the same things I did... But you know what the weird thing was?"

"What?" Kenzie quietly asks.

"She never argued with me. She never had a different opinion from mine. She never disagreed with anything I did or a decision I made. At the time I stupidly thought that meant we were perfect together. I realize now it was just part of her plan."

"Her plan?"

"Eventually our relationship moved to the next level; she told me she loved me. I had never been in love before, so I thought what we had was real. I believed her when she said she loved me. Looking back I realize now that I only saw what she wanted to me to see. I realize now that the reason she seemed so perfect for me was because that's what she wanted me to think."

"What happened?"

"Looking back, I can see how things changed, but at the time I couldn't and refused to believe that she was doing anything wrong. I was convinced of the image that Harper wanted me to see; I believed she was perfect."

"No one's perfect," Kenzie sighs heavily... I think she is more talking to herself than to me.

"They're not, but at the time I was too blinded to see that. Which is the ironic part: put me in a board room and I can tell you within five minutes who is lying and who is only there for the money. Yet when it came to my personal life, I completely misjudged her and it almost cost me everything.

"I didn't live at The Accord back then, I had a condo that was a pretty decent size but one that didn't have guest quarters for Julie and Carter. Carter would stay in one of the spare bedrooms and Julie would come during the day but leave after dinner. One day Julie came over earlier than normal, which I had known about but didn't tell Harper about because she wasn't supposed to be there at that time either. Julie walked in on Harper going through my office. Julie said she was working on my computer and going through my files. The computer didn't surprise me—I had given her the password one day when she was having issues with her laptop and she needed to order something for her dad. I blew off what Julie said about her going through my files. Why I didn't think she was snooping on me then I have no idea...."

"Because you trusted her."

"I did. I was stupid and thought that when someone told you they loved you that they wouldn't do anything to hurt you. A couple weeks later, the head of my financial department demanded a meeting with me. This doesn't happen often, so I know when he asks for a meeting, something major is going on. Only it wasn't just my head of finance there, he also brought my head of IT at PFS. My finance guy said that over the last three months there was evidence of small amounts being withdrawn from several of my business accounts for expenses that couldn't be reconciled. My initial thought, of course, was that an employee in one of those departments was stealing from me. I demanded answers immediately, with photographic proof of who it was, so we could go after them."

"It was her, wasn't it?"

"Yes," I shake my head still amazed to this day how stupid I was. "Carter knew I would want photographic evidence of the thief so he had already secured that with my head of IT beforehand. He had several pictures of Harper making purchases using credits cards that were designated to certain departments within PFS. They were small purchases; nothing that would immediately raise red flags... a few hundred dollars here, a thousand or so there... I know it sounds like a lot of money but you have to remember that we literally have hundreds of employees who hold PFS issued credit cards... "

"How did she get the credit card?"

"That took some more digging, because we have systems in place at PFS to prevent things like this from happening. All credit card applications require two signatures: the head of the finance department and mine. I often bring work home so it's not unusual for these types of documents to be in my home. I never once considered it would be an issue. I've worked with Julie and Carter long enough now that trusting them isn't ever a question. When I first hired them, I would make sure everything was locked up before I would leave the apartment. But over the years they have proven that I could trust them, so I stopped locking as many things up."

"She stole one of the credit card applications from you?"

"She did. She somehow changed the name on the application and the mailing address. Asher, my head of IT at PFS, tracked the purchases; accessed security footage from the stores where the credit cards were used and found out it was Harper who was using the cards. In total, over the three months, she spent more than sixty thousand dollars on various purchases for herself."

"Holy shit."

"That's not the worst part."

"What could be worse than that?" Kenzie asks in complete disbelief.

"When confronted with the photographic proof of Harper stealing from me, I was left with the decision of what to do. On one hand, this was the woman I supposedly loved and who loved me. On the other hand, there was no disputing the evidence that she was in fact stealing from me.

"I dismissed my team and told them I needed to think before I could figure out how to proceed. Part of me wanted to call the police and have her arrested, but the other part of me was still trying to figure out why she would do something like that. That's the part that to this day I still don't understand. You see, Harper is from money—her parents are very wealthy, so she didn't need it. Everything she has ever wanted has been handed to her. Her full education was paid for by her parents, she was given a brand new condo and high end car at graduation, credit cards of her own her parents paid off monthly... she didn't want for anything. Yet she stole sixty thousand dollars from me... to buy things that her parents would have bought her: a new laptop, gas for her car, plane tickets, hotel rooms, rental cars..."

"What did you do?"

"I cancelled my plans with her for that evening; I lied and told her I needed to work late or something, I think. I knew I needed time alone to process what just happened before I could determine my next moves. A couple of hours later, Carter had Melody... you met her at my office, she's my personal assistant." Kenzie nods. "He had her clear my schedule then came into my office and said we needed to get home immediately. That's where things got worse... "

"What did she do to?"

"Julie has a very strict schedule she follows when it comes to cleaning various parts of the house. What I learned that day is that every three to four months she pulls all the furniture away from the walls in the spare bedrooms to vacuum behind them. Harper typically used one of the spare bedrooms when she came over... although we didn't live together, she was there often enough that she had a few items in the closet and the bathroom.

"Anyway, Julie moved the dresser away from the wall and found an envelope containing a thumb drive on it. I suppose Julie was leery of Harper ever since she found her in my office. Julie never voiced her suspicion to me after finding her there, but I think she knew something was going on even then. Anyway, Julie took the thumb drive and brought it to PFS and asked Carter to have it broken into since it was password protected. Carter had Asher break the password and when they discovered what was on it, they decided I needed to be away from PFS when I found out."

"What did she put on the drive?"

"It seems she was preparing to sell me out. She was writing a book about her time with me, documenting nearly everything we did. She had pictures saved of… when we were together. She gave detailed descriptions of our sex life. If that wasn't bad enough, she had notes on business decisions I made including formulas I used to determine whether companies were worth taking on or not."

"How did she find all that out?"

"Up til then, I never thought about how much I stored in my home office, so I imagine she learned most of it by snooping on my home computer or through my files there. A few times she was at PFS and Melody let her wait in my office alone if I was running late, so she could have dug then too. Afterward Carter went through our security footage and found her essentially tearing apart my office looking for information. The thumb drive had details about my family and things about me that if leaked could have serious consequences for PFS. We believe she was going to write a tell-all book and sell it."

"Wow… I can't believe someone would do anything like that."

"Neither could I… Well, I guess I could, but I thought those things happened to other people, not to me. When I saw the thumb drive, I lost it which Carter knew would happen and why he insisted I come home before being told about the drive. I got really drunk; I can't remember the last time I drank so much.

"I called Austin, who has had more than a few issues with women; he came over to drink with me. By the end of the night, we had finished almost every ounce of alcohol we could find in my apartment, but we had a plan. When we woke up the next day, with incredible hangovers mind you, we went to see a lawyer and took the evidence of her stealing from me with us. I purposely did not bring the thumb drive; there were pictures on there that one's family should not see. And while it was an invasion of my privacy, I didn't want to risk that evidence getting out to the public. Her stealing from me was one thing, but the stuff she had on that thumb drive were things that could seriously damage my career.

"After much discussion with the attorney, we decided the best course of action was to pursue criminal charges for theft. My family has very close ties with the district attorney and managed to keep everything out of the press. We entered into a private agreement with Harper and her attorney which resulted in the records from the preceding being sealed. She agreed to plead guilty to the charges in exchange for a decreased sentence. She served about 18 months in prison, but her parents arranged for her to be sent to one of the nicest ones out there. The type only people with money go, places where you don't feel like you actually lose your freedom. She was required to sign legal documents that prohibit her from every speaking about our relationship to anyone and she is banned from ever working in the media industry again."

"Wow… I know I keep saying that, but wow, Nicholas. I can't believe someone would do something like to you. She took complete advantage of you and then was about to expose you to ruin your business. Why would someone do something like that?"

"To make an easy buck, Kenzie. A book about my secrets and how I run my business would sell, very quickly, no doubt. She could have probably made a couple hundred thousand dollars from books and then more from talk shows, magazines, etc…"

For the first time since I started talking I look at her, sitting back in her lounge chair and staring out at the water. I can only assume she is taking in everything I just told her. I can't help but wonder what she is thinking. Does she think I was stupid for allowing *her* into my life? Does she think less of me because of the decisions I made? Is she wondering what was on the thumb drive that I was so worried about or does she think it was mostly business details that I was worried the most about? I originally planned to leave out the fact that there were pictures on the thumb drive, but once I started talking, everything just came out.

"I get it," Kenzie breaks her silence a few minutes later.

"You get what?" I can't say I'm not confused by her response.

"I get why you gave me the check last weekend. I get why you thought I expected that in return."

"You do? Because honestly, Kenzie, I don't know why I did it. Alex thinks that I was testing you, but I'm not sure I buy that—"

"No, I think he's right. It's obvious now that Harper was only with you because of your money, and she saw an easy way to make quick money with you. After what you went through, I could see how you could expect people to be like that with you. But Nicholas… you have to know that I would never… *never* do what she did to you. I don't know that you will ever be able to trust me, but—"

"Kenzie, that's what freaked me out the most about last weekend. I started to trust to you, even without knowing it. After everything blew up in my face with Harper, I swore off women. I swore I would never trust another woman—"

"Nicholas, you can't—"

"Why not? It's been working for me for the last two years—"

"Has it?"

"Of course it has. I moved out of that apartment, got rid of all the memories of *her* and moved to The Accord Towers with Carter and Julie. Until last weekend, the only women who stepped foot into my condo, besides Julie were my mother and sister. You were the first woman who has ever been there; you were there the entire weekend and... I let my guard down. Honestly, that scared the shit out of me. I worked so hard over the last two and a half years to ensure that my guard was always up so something like that didn't happen again."

Kenzie's gaze is once again on the water; I'm beginning to think she understands why I find being on the boat so relaxing. I don't know what's going through her head right now, but I don't ask. I'm afraid to ask... I'm not sure I want to know what she's thinking right now. It's been a long time since I've opened myself up to anyone like this. I don't do vulnerable... I don't do weak and right now I know this is exactly how I look to her.

"I hadn't been alone with a man, in more than two years, before I walked into your apartment that night," she finally says, albeit very quietly, almost as if she's afraid of what she is saying.

"What do you mean? I'm sure we—"

"We haven't, not really anyway."

I think back at all the times we've met before our *dates* and realize she is right: each time Carter was present. We spent a few minutes once in my office when she brought muffins and cookies when I moved her into The Accord after her apartment was broken into. That was maybe... ten minutes I think; I had to rush to a meeting so she couldn't stay very long. Hunter has driven her to the bakery but that's only a few minutes drive each way.

"Yet, you still volunteered to stay the weekend with me." I'm even more shocked now.

"I did," she shrugs. "Like you, I swore I would never trust a man again. I swore that I would never put myself at risk again. Our ex's aren't that different when you think about it, really. They both deceived us into believing they were the person they wanted us to see, but we both ended up finding out that it was all a façade.

"When Bridget approached me about this arrangement, my safety was my number one concern. I let her know that I would never agree to be alone with someone; I would never agree to meet you at your office after hours if no one else was going to be working. Although she mentioned possible business trips, I let her know that would have to be discussed at a much later date because in all honesty, I never thought I would see myself spending days in the same hotel room with a man. I swore I would put myself at risk again, that I would never let my guard down and trust someone again."

"Yet here we are," I can't help but point out the fact that we are entirely alone on a boat in the middle of open water with no one around us for miles.

"Yes, even though I almost didn't make it here."

"What do you mean? Did something happen on the way here?"

"I'm surprised Carter didn't tell you. I'm sure Hunter called him and told him he thought I was going crazy."

"I doubt Hunter would say something like that and if he did, he knows he would be fired. What happened, Kenzie? Did Hunter do something—"

"No!" she quickly interrupts. I trust Hunter nearly as much as I trust Carter. I can't picture him doing anything unprofessional. "I... I guess you could say I kind of freaked out when I realized we weren't going to the bakery—"

"Oh, Kenzie... I'm sorry," FUCK I feel foolish now. "I had no idea... I... you weren't talking to me, I didn't know how else to talk to you."

"You could have come to the apartment," she points out the obvious solution but I don't think she realizes that I didn't want to invade her privacy by doing that.

I may know where she lives now but I refuse to take advantage of that. The stipulation in the contract is there for a reason. Even though we have blurred some of the lines in the contract, I don't want to take advantage of that one. Her privacy is important her just as mine is to me.

"I nearly had a panic attack in the car with Hunter when he wouldn't tell me where we were going. I tried to open the car door to jump out, but of course it didn't open—"

"Kenzie, I'm so sorry. I never thought... I didn't think... "

"Why would you? I never told you about my trust issues and it's not like I didn't know Hunter—he's been with me for weeks now. I freaked out and my first thought was that I was at risk."

"What happened?"

"Hunter must have seen that I was freaking out because the next thing I knew we were pulled onto the side of the road and he was turned around calling my name. He told me that if I wanted, he would turn the car around and take me back to The Accord. I only began to calm down when he told me he was taking me to you and Carter."

"I'm sorry. I swear I'll never do that again. I should have known that it would have frightened you not know where you were going—"

"You had no reason to know, Nicholas. We've gone out plenty of times now; sometimes I don't know all the details of the evenings and I've never had an issue with it."

"Because we were never alone," I realize.

"Exactly, and today I was suddenly alone in a car with Hunter."

"But you had no issues coming aboard the boat today?" I point out.

"I know," she sighs and looks back out at the water. "And I had no concerns about staying the weekend at your apartment when it was obvious no one was able to. As scary trusting me is, it's just as scary for me to trust you."

Chapter 26
Nicholas

In that moment I realized how little I truly know about Kenzie; I know now her ex abused her, but I don't know what her time with him was really like. She is very closed off about her past, although given the little bit I do know, it makes sense that she would have difficulty trusting men. I should have realized that having Hunter bring her here today instead of to the bakery where she expected to go would have upset her. All I wanted to do was to get a chance to talk to her alone—she wasn't responding to the flowers I sent, so I really didn't know what else I could do. Alex told me to talk to her alone, to take her somewhere and do something just the two of us… yet he didn't tell me how the hell to get her attention when she wouldn't talk to me!

"Can we go swimming?" Kenzie pulls me from my thoughts.

"Of course! Come with me and I'll show you where everything is," I stand and take her hand to help her up from the lounge chair where we've been sitting for the last couple of hours. I hadn't realized how much time had passed, until I looked at my phone and realized it was well after noon. After the heavy discussion, I think a swim sounds like a great idea. With her hand still in mine, I lead her back through the main area of the boat and down the steps to the bedrooms.

"I'll give you a quick tour while we're here," I offer. "Obviously this is the kitchen; it has all main features of a home kitchen but on a much smaller scale. After we go swimming I'll bring up the lunch that Julie packed and we can eat if you're hungry."

"Sounds good."

"Through here is a small office, over there is a guest bedroom and bathroom and then this is the master bedroom."

"Wow, Nicholas, this is amazing! I had no idea so much space was down here. I mean, the boat is obviously big but… wow!"

"In the bag you'll find a bathing suit, a cover up, a pair of flip flops, shorts and a top—"

"You bought all of this?"

"Yes... well technically a personal shopper at Neiman's arranged all of this. I gave her your picture and she based the sizes from that, so I'm hoping they fit—"

"Thank you... You definitely didn't need to do all of this, but thank you."

"Kenzie, I just want you to know again how sorry I am—"

"Nicholas, you've apologized; you're forgiven. I overreacted as well, and like you, I didn't know how to fix things. The flowers you sent me, which were absolutely beautiful by the way, were your way of trying to reach out to me. I wanted to call you so many times, but I didn't know what to say, because I don't think I even understood why it bothered me so much that you thought you needed to pay me."

"Because you recognized before I did, that this was more than a business arrangement. I don't know when it happened, but it did."

"Do you think that's okay though? I mean... Oh, I don't know what I mean."

"Kenzie, I'm sure Bridget has clients who have developed friendships and probably even relationships from these arrangements. I think when two people spend a lot of time together, it's a natural reaction. It just didn't take as much time for us."

"I suppose."

"I'm going to change in the guest room; how about we meet on the deck in a few minutes? Anything you might need should be in the bathroom just through that door."

"Thank you Nicholas... again for all of this."

"You're welcome."

I slowly close the door and walk across the small hallway to the guest bedroom, closing myself in the room before I sit on the bed. I never expected to tell Kenzie so much about what happened and thought I could gloss over all the details, just giving her the gist of it. I never thought I would tell her as much as I did. I'm relieved I did though; I may not have realized it at the time but I'm really glad she didn't accept the money I tried to give her. I wouldn't have thought any less of her if she did, but when she didn't, it... it just reinforced what I already knew, that Kenzie was nothing like *she* was.

When I hear the bedroom door open and shut across the hall I realized I need to hurry up and get changed. I quickly don a pair of swim trunks and T-shirt to swim in; while I hate swimming with a shirt on I'm not about to take the chance that something could happen.

When I make my way up to the deck, I stop dead in my tracks at seeing Kenzie. She is standing at the end of the boat, holding onto the rail and looking out over the water.

She's wearing nothing but the bikini that I purchased for her and combined with the backdrop of the blue water, makes her looking incredibly beautiful.

FUCK

I should have told Neiman's to give her a one piece bathing suit. Hell I should have "forgotten" the bathing suit and taken swimming off the agenda for today. My mind immediately goes to all the things that I could do to this gorgeous woman right now. There is no one around for miles, I could fuck her right now, right where she is standing and no one would ever know. I could walk up to her, tease her senseless and then pull her bikini bottoms to the side, plunge into her and fuck her against the railing of the boat without giving it a second thought.

But I won't and I can't. I can't jeopardize our arrangement and more importantly I would never hurt her. I'm not what she needs, what she deserves and I don't think I ever could be. She deserves someone who comes without baggage, someone who won't have issues trusting her completely. The realization that I could never be that man is the equivalent of having a bucket of ice dumped down my swim trunks.

"It's beautiful out here isn't it?" I say, approaching Kenzie.

"Absolutely stunning; I see why you enjoy coming out here. Do you spend much time on the water?"

"Not as much as I would like to unfortunately. If it were up to me I would be out here every weekend…"

"What stops you?"

"Work typically; then there are various social events but mostly it's work."

"If I could get away from everything, I would take advantage of it whenever I could. Being out here makes you forget… everything," she muses wistfully.

Those simple sentences make me realize she truly gets why coming out here means so much to me. She may not know that she gets my reason, but her statement alone tells me she feels the same way I do when she looks out at the water. For some reason it is so easy to lose yourself in the waves when all you see is blue in all directions.

"I put some of the suntan lotion on, but I couldn't reach my back. Do you mind?" Kenzie asks.

"Sure, of course," I take the bottle from her as I step closer to her. "Is it okay if I untie the bottom strap? It might be easier—"

"Sure," her hands immediately go to the fabric covering her breasts, holding it in place.

Despite the earlier realization, I find myself wishing she would have let the top fall off. I squirt some of the lotion onto my hand and slowly apply it to her back. She jumps when I first touch her, probably from the coldness but immediately relaxes as I rub the lotion on. As I smooth it down her back, for the first time I see scars. They're small and light, barely noticeable unless you're close to her but they are there.

"Kenzie?"

"I scar easily..." She shrugs and I have to force myself to continue what I'm doing rather than focus on the scars. There are a easily two dozen of them, all different sizes and shapes but they cover from the middle of her back to her waistline at least from what I can see.

"Kenzie..." I don't know what to say, what I should say. I hate the fucker who did this to her and want nothing more than to find a way to destroy him for hurting her. I can't imagine any man wanting to do something like this to a woman, let alone one that is as beautiful and perfect as Kenzie is.

Perfect?

"Don't Nicholas... please. It was a long time ago—can we just forget about it?"

Her voice is shaky as she tries portraying the strong image I know she wants me to see. I'm suddenly confronted with an overwhelming need to hold her, to comfort her and to tell her that everything will be okay, no one would ever hurt her again. But I don't. Instead, I tie her bathing suit back into place and step away.

"Thank you," her voice is barely above a whisper and I have no doubt that she is thanking me for more than putting sun tan lotion on.

"Do you want to swim here or should we move the boat?" I suggest.

"I like it here, if you don't mind."

"No, here is perfect."

We go to the back of the boat where there is a ladder and a small stand to sit on, but Kenzie surprises me and dives right into the water from the deck of the boat. I chuckle as she splashes me with cold water from her jump. She swims out quite a distance before turning around and swimming back to the boat without coming up for a breath of air.

"Aren't you coming in?" she asks.

Feeling the need to lighten things up, I stand up and cannon ball into the water only a few feet from her.

"Nicholas!" she giggles and tries to splash water at me but I sink under before it hits me.

We spend the rest of the day just like that, swimming and having fun. Gone are the heavy conversations and the many unanswered questions that remain between us. Instead, we keep things light and current rather than talking about our pasts. We enjoy the chicken salad lunch that Julie prepared for us before heading back to the marina late in the afternoon.

As I stand behind Kenzie, watching her steer the boat back towards the marina, I find myself surprised at how nice today turned out. I was prepared for anything to happen today, anything but this. I pictured her refusing to get on the boat with me, or cursing me out for trying to give her the money, or worse yet, even pictured her ending our arrangement because of what I did. Never did I dare to hope that today would have gone as well as it did. I actually had fun... I can't remember the last time I could say that. Hell, I can't remember the last time I spent the entire day with a woman.

It's weird, but when I think back to being with *her,* I realize just how off things were between us. I never spend an entire day with *her...* sure a few hours here and there but that usually was it. *She* never wanted to come on the boat, claiming the water made her sick. Today, Kenzie and I spent more than six hours on the boat... just the two of us. The only time *she* and I spent six hours together would be at a function with hundreds of other people around. Although it wasn't always *her* fault because I was always busy with PFS. Looking back at it now, I could have made more of an effort to spend time with *her...* if I had wanted to.

It didn't take much to spend the day out here with Kenzie; just a few meetings and calls rearranged and some work pushed off until tomorrow. At the time I thought *she* just understood how busy I was, but now I see that it was all part of the façade that she wanted me to see.

"Nicholas... Nicholas!" Kenzie pulls me from my thoughts as we approach the marina.

"You're doing fine, we're going to head into the third row—"

"No! You need to do this! I'm going to hit another boat, or the dock or someone!"

"You'll do fine, keep your hands firm on the wheel," I put my hands on the wheel on either side of her body essentially making it impossible for her move. Her body is tense around me but I'm not worried; she has been steering the boat for the last hour, navigating around several other boats with complete ease. Besides, my hands are on the wheel, I can easily correct anything she does before anything were to occur. She may be scared, but I think secretly she is enjoying having this control.

"We're going to start to turn left just after we pass that boat, do you see it?" I ask.

"Ye... yes," she's nervous but I'm not.

"Perfect... yup... just like that."

"I can't believe I did that!" She exclaims happily when I cut the engine at the dock.

"I told you that you could do it!"

She turns and throws her hands around my neck pulling me close to her before she rests her face in the crook of my neck. My hands automatically go around her waist, holding her close to me.

"Thank you, Nicholas... thank you for today," she whispers against my neck so softly that I can feel her lips move against my skin.

"Anytime, Kenzie."

She pulls back slightly from me until her face is only a couple inches from me, her hands are still wrapped around my neck and mine around her waist. My eyes find hers and immediately I feel like she is looking at me differently. I feel like she can see right through me, as if she can see deep into me. Suddenly, I feel... exposed.

"Nicholas," Kenzie whispers when I look away as if I'm afraid if she continues looking at me the way she is right now, she will be able to see it all.

"Thank you... for telling me everything today; thank you for trusting me," she leans up just enough to place her soft lips against mine. Her eyes close the moment our lips touch, but I can't bring myself to close mine. Her fingers run through the ends of my hair at my neck; my hands find the bare skin just beneath the back of her shirt. As she becomes more certain of herself, or maybe of what she's doing, Kenzie deepens our kiss – changing it from a kiss between two friends to one between...

BBBBBBBBBBBBBBBBBEEEEEEEEEEEEPPPPPPPPPPPPPPPPPP

We both immediately pull away from each other at the sound of a boat's loud horn not far from us. On one hand I want to kill the fucker who stopped Kenzie from kissing me, but on the other hand I know it's probably for the best. If she had continued to kiss me like that, I don't know if I would have been able to stop myself. My dick is already stirring with her body pressed up against it.

"Carter will be waiting to drive us back to The Accord unless you need to go somewhere else?"

"No, that's fine."

As we head towards the front of the boat, I see Carter waiting for us on the dock and I have no doubt that he just saw what transpired between us. Thankfully, I don't need to worry about him saying anything—unless I ask Carter for his opinion, he rarely gives it. I tell Kenzie to wait on the deck for me so I can get off the boat first. I toss Carter a rope and he quickly secures the boat to the dock as I step off. Kenzie takes my hand, not releasing it as we walk towards the car.

"Mac will see to it?" I ask Carter.

"Yes, he is already here and waiting."

"Mac?" Kenzie asks.

"He's... my boat guy, I guess you could say. He gets the boat ready when I want to take it out and like today, he will see that it's shut down completely and secure it for the night."

The ride back to the city is quiet, but Kenzie doesn't let go of my hand the entire ride and I don't stop holding hers either. When we get back to The Accord, I walk Kenzie to her apartment door and kiss her on the cheek as has become our tradition after *dates*. I am more than tempted to kiss her on the lips again. I want nothing more than to feel her body against mine and her lips pressed up against mine. In the end I know nothing good could come of that... if my image-changing mission is to be successful, I can't give her a reason to break the contract. A night with me fucking her would almost guarantee that.

Chapter 27
Kenzie

I've enjoyed staying at The Accord Towers but the fact remains that it is Nicholas's apartment. I think I would feel more secure if I had a place of my own—some place that I couldn't lose without any notice if Nicholas suddenly decides to end our arrangement. The issue I know I'm going to have though is finding a place that is safe so that while Nicholas and I have this arrangement press can't get to me, at a price I can afford. Right now, I think I can afford a small apartment in a decent area but I'm concerned when the arrangement ends what will happen. I don't think I could sign another contract with Bridget.

If this arrangement with Nicholas has taught me anything, it's that I can't be involved with someone without emotional attachments. He was right when he said that our arrangement has begun to go beyond a business arrangement and we've sort of become friends. We're not the type of friends who call each other or text, but when we go on *dates* we share things about our lives. I don't know how I will feel when he ends this—I think it will feel like losing a friend and it's been a long time since I've had someone I considered a friend. I quickly shake my head from those thoughts; I need to just focus on keeping things status quo between us which means not kissing him again. I can't be the reason he decides to end our arrangement.

Nicholas and I were supposed to go to dinner earlier this week but he ended up having to cancel because of a last minute business meeting he had to fly to. We're going to dinner at his parents' tonight; I'm not sure how I feel about this. Although I've met Vivienne and talked to her several times now, I can't help but feel nervous spending the evening with them. From what Bridget told me, Nicholas's entire family will be there which I assume includes Austin and Cara.

Bridget also confirmed that next week Nicholas has a busy schedule and has requested I accompany him to several different events including a charity fundraising dinner and a business. When I was talking to her I found myself wondering if she knew about our day on the boat or the weekend that we spent together. I feel guilty that we did these things without going through her as stated in our contract. However, I know if we had for either of these things it would have resulted in a payment from Nicholas—obviously not something I want. Since I don't expect us to be spending more time together outside of our actual arrangement, I decide against informing Bridget about the weekend and the day on the boat.

I struggled with what to wear for dinner tonight; Bridget said that Nicholas told her that the dress code would be casual for dinner. What the hell is casual though to a family that has the amount of money that the Parkers have? I end up spending an hour at Stacy's where I eventually choose a halter style sundress that falls just to my knees with a pair of dressy sandals. I think it's a little more than casual, but I hope that it will fit in with what the Parkers expect for tonight. I was a little surprised when Bridget scheduled this dinner. I had assumed I would only see them at different events. I guess I wasn't expecting to see them in such an intimate or personal setting…

Knock knock

Thankfully Nicholas pulls me from my thoughts and overall worry about how tonight is going to go. I quickly grab my purse, set the alarm and open the door where he is waiting for me. For the first time since I've met him, Nicholas is wearing jeans which surprises me. I immediately second guess my outfit for tonight, wondering if I shouldn't go back inside and change into something more casual.

"You look… very nice," Nicholas says.

"Do you think I should change?"

"No! Why would you?"

"Bridget mentioned the dress would be casual for tonight, and you're in jeans… "

"I assure you Cara will not be dressed in jeans, if that's what you're worried about. I'm not sure that girl owns a single pair. I can't remember the last time I even saw her in jeans. You look perfect… you don't need to change."

"If you're sure."

We walk down to the elevator where Carter is waiting and escorts us to the SUV. Nicholas is busy typing away on his cell phone without a care in the world, meanwhile I'm a nervous wreck about tonight. Meeting Nicholas's family at the gala was one thing, but meeting in their home at a family dinner is completely different. It feels so much more personal—

"Are you okay?" Nicholas pulls me from my thoughts.

"Fine."

"Are you nervous?"

"Yes."

"Why? You've met my family before."

"But not like this. This is… different. At the gala there were so many other people there or things going on to distract everyone. This feels… more personal."

"You have nothing to worry about, Kenzie. My mother already loves you —"

"I doubt that—she barely knows me. We texted a few times and talked at your apartment for a few minutes, but that was pretty much it."

"Trust me, my mother likes you."

"You don't know that."

"Kenzie," he takes a deep breath and runs his hands through his hair before continuing. "Do you want to know how I know my mother likes you?" I nod. "She lets you call her Vivienne—"

"She told me—"

"I know she did. But… she's never let… *Harper* call her by her name," I can hear the disgust in his voice as he says Harper's name. "She was always Mrs. or Dr. Parker to *her*. My mother never texted her, never talked to her except to be polite and pretty much hated her."

"Oh."

"Yeah, oh. So, just trust me, my mother likes you. If you've won her over, you've won over my dad by default. Cara loves everyone and Austin… well Austin will do anything to avoid confrontation, so you don't have to worry about it."

"Is there anything I should know about for tonight?"

"I don't think so. Just be yourself."

"Sir, ma'am… we have arrived," Carter alerts us. I have no idea how long we've been parked in the driveway but I'm thankful for these few minutes.

"You ready?" Nicholas asks.

"Yes," I say trying to force some confidence in my voice.

Although we were here for the gala, the house looks completely different without all the lights and press around it. Nicholas opens the door and leads me into the very large foyer where he takes my jacket and purse to hang them with his own in the closet. I immediately look up–the ceiling above us is so high it almost makes me dizzy. There's a beautiful chandelier above and a curved stairway to our left.

"Nicholas! Kenzie! I thought I heard the door open," Vivienne rushes in to greet us, first hugging Nicholas and then me.

"Vivienne, it's nice to see you again," I say.

"I'm so glad that you could make it tonight, Kenzie! I've been after Nicholas to bring you by for two weeks now; I'm glad your plans changed and you are able to join us."

"I'm glad it all worked out," I reply, not entirely sure what Nicholas has told her so I play along.

"Come, everyone's in the great room," she leads us to a large room just off the foyer where Nicholas's dad, Austin and Cara are all talking.

"Nicholas!" Cara runs towards him and practically jumps into his arms to hug him.

"Cara!" he chuckles at her reaction.

"Kenzie! I'm so happy you could come!" She hugs me next before taking my hand, to lead me to the couch.

"Kenzie, it's nice of you to join us for dinner tonight," Nicholas's dad says.

"Thank you for inviting me Mr. Parker."

"Please it's Theodore; I'm only Mr. Parker at work."

"Kenzie, I love your dress! Where did you get it? Oh! Better yet, can you take me there? Are you going to the dinner next weekend? If so, maybe we can go shopping together this week?" Cara fires off tons of questions catching me off guard.

"Cara, give the poor girl a minute to think," Austin warns as he smiles at me.

"Um… I think we're going to that dinner," I glance at Nicholas who nods in indication that we are. "I haven't had a chance to shop for a dress yet, so if you want, I'd love to go shopping with you for one."

"Fantastic! I'm so excited! When can you go? Do you work every day this week?"

"How about Wednesday? I work a few hours in the morning but by early afternoon I should be free."

"Perfect! I can't wait!"

I try to catch Nicholas's eye to see if I did the right thing by agreeing to shop with her, but he doesn't seem to notice me. I hope he doesn't get mad that I'm spending time with Cara; she caught me completely off guard. I couldn't figure out a way to say no without sounding rude; agreeing just seemed like the appropriate response.

"Dinner is ready," Vivienne announces a few minute later.

Nicholas takes my hand as we stand up before leading me into the beautiful dining room. The long table is set up like something out of a magazine, with wonderful smelling dishes around a floral centerpiece. Like the perfect gentleman he is, Nicholas pulls my chair out for me, then gently pushes it in before taking his seat next to me.

"You're doing fine, stop worrying," he whispers and puts his hand on my knee which I hadn't realized was shaking until that moment. His hand is hot against my cool skin; I can feel my body temperature rising just from his touch. I don't know if he notices because he quickly removes his hand a few seconds later.

"So Kenzie, how's the bakery?" Theodore asks.

"It's good. It seems as if the owner has found a seller for the bakery—"

"She did?" Nicholas asks surprised.

"Yes, Ginny just told me about it this morning." I forgot to mention it when we spoke on the ride over here.

"Tell me it's not one of those chain places," Vivienne pleads.

"I don't think so. Ginny said that she had to sign something that prevents her from telling anyone specific details about the sale until a certain date—"

"That's fairly common, Kenzie, I don't think it's anything you need to worry about," Nicholas says.

"She did say that the owners have agreed to keep on all staff who have had solid performance reviews for at least six months following the date of the announcement," I explain.

"That's really good news," Nicholas says.

"I'm sure you must be relieved," Vivienne adds.

"I am. I hope the new owners keep the feel of the bakery; Ginny has a lot of personal connections with so many of the customers who come in, so it would be a shame to lose that."

"I hope they keep the same recipes!" Cara exclaims.

"I second that," Austin agrees.

"I've signed too many business deals over their muffins for have them change their recipe now," Nicholas chuckles. "Melody manages always know exactly what to order for my meetings."

The food is passed around as conversation flows easily amongst everyone. I sit back and watch what is going on around me. I don't know that I've ever seen a family dinner like this one. It's not only Theodore and Vivienne asking questions about their children's lives, but it's Cara, Austin and Nicholas that seem to know everything that is going on with each other. It amazes me how close everyone is… not just close in the sense that they are family but that they actually care about what is happening with each other.

"Would you like some wine?" Nicholas asks.

"Yes, please."

"White or red?"

"White, thank you."

Nicholas puts his hand on my shoulder, squeezing it gently before he walks into the kitchen. I continue to just watch everyone; interestingly I don't feel uncomfortable like I expected to. Every so often someone asks me a question, making sure like I don't feel like an outsider. Nicholas comes back to the table a few minutes later, handing me a glass of wine before draping his arm over my shoulders as he sits down.

Out of the corner of my eye I see Vivienne watching us and smiling; for the first time since Nicholas and I started this arrangement I feel guilty for deceiving everyone. Well maybe not everyone—I don't feel guilty for deceiving the press so they leave Nicholas alone and he can focus on his company. I think I just feel guilty about deceiving Nicholas's family since they think we are an actual couple like everyone else does. I understand why he didn't want to tell anyone else about our arrangement but…

"How about we move into the great room? Dessert will be ready in a few minutes—I'll bring it in for everyone in there," Vivienne suggests.

"Would you like another glass of wine?" Nicholas asks.

"No, thank you," I quickly answer.

"Anyone else need another drink while I'm in the kitchen?" Nicholas asks everyone.

"I'll help you," Austin jumps up.

"I'd like another glass," Cara requests.

"I'll have another beer," Theodore adds.

"You sure you don't need anything, Kenzie?" Austin asks.

"I'm good, thanks," I answer.

Theodore and Cara immediately engage in conversation about a fashion design class that Cara is currently taking. I gather from the conversation that she has had a difficult time deciding what she wants to do with her life. I envy her; her parents seem to support her as she takes different classes rather than pushing her in a certain direction or worse not supporting her education at all. I'm surprised that Theodore seems genuinely interested in Cara's description in her class the other day despite the fact that I'm sure he could care less about fashion design.

A couple of hours and far too much delicious dessert later, Nicholas and I say our goodbyes to his family. I've exchanged phone numbers with Cara, having confirmed our shopping plans later this week for next weekend's charity dinner.

Austin, Nicholas and Theodore discussed an upcoming baseball game that they are going to in a few weeks. This led to Vivienne suggesting I join her and Cara for a girl's day at the spa when the guys go to the game. I give a non-committal answer promising to check my schedule, not because I don't want to spend the day at a spa (who wouldn't?) but because I don't know how Nicholas wants me to respond. We hadn't discussed our arrangement overlapping with his family life or how he would feel about me spending time alone with them. I've already agreed to shop with Cara later this week, so I don't want to commit to anything else without talking with Nicholas first. Vivienne accepts my answer without blinking an eye.

"I told you that you had no reason to worry," Nicholas says as Carter pulls away.

"It went much better than I thought it would," I admit.

"Can I ask you something?" he requests after a few minutes of silence.

"Okay, sure," I'm not sure what to think about the uncertainty I hear in his voice.

"How come you don't drink? I mean, you drink, of course, but I don't think I've ever seen you have more than one drink when we've gone out. Do you not like to drink?"

"It's not that," I sigh realizing that Nicholas is right—I haven't had more than one drink of alcohol anytime we have been out together. "I hadn't realized that... I guess old habits die hard."

"What do you mean? Did you... do you have a problem with alcohol?"

"No! Gosh, no. I've only ever been drunk once and that was freshman year in college. I drank way too much at a fraternity party and spent the rest of night with my head over the toilet bowl. That was the last time I ever got drunk."

"Then why only have one drink?"

"I…" UGH! I can't imagine what Nicholas will think when I tell him the real reason I limit myself to one drink. Unfortunately, I can't come up with a good enough lie and even if I could, after how open he was with me on the boat, I don't know that I want to lie to him. "It was one of the rules."

"Rules?"

"My ex… Image was important to *him*; he believed I was a direct reflection on *him*. He would… pick out my outfits, order my food and basically control everything when we went out. There were a lot of rules: what I could talk about, who I could talk to and how much I could drink. Even though I had never been drunk around *him*, I was only ever allowed to have one drink when we were out."

"Kenzie… I don't know what to say. You don't seem like the person who would just let someone control their life like that. I mean—"

"No, I get it. Trust me, I'm not the person I was when I met him. I've grown a lot in the last two and a half years. I've learned a lot about myself and about the person I was back then. Today? No, I wouldn't let someone control as much of my life as *he* did. This… this arrangement with Bridget? I had to think long and hard about it about not only of my safety but because to a degree I knew I would give up some control. I knew there was a chance that I could be with someone that would pick out my clothing for events or who would tell me what I can and can't talk about or to whom. But, to me I was willing to pay that price, because it was only over a very small part of my life. It was no different in my mind than wearing a uniform to work. I'll never go back to that type of control; I will never allow someone to control my every move the way he did."

"You deserve so much better than that, Kenzie. I hope you realize that."

"I don't know what I deserve… but I know that I don't want what I had."

"Someone really did a number on you growing up, didn't they?"

"What do you mean?"

"You don't see… you don't see yourself."

"Sure I do—"

"You don't, Kenzie. If you don't recognize that you deserve better than that asshole, you don't see the wonderful person you really are."

"I may not know what I deserve, Nicholas, but I know without a shadow of a doubt that history will never repeat itself. I will never allow someone to control my life like he did or treat me the way he did."

"I'm glad, really I am. I just wish... you could see... who you are," Nicholas sighs and runs his hands through his hair. "Who told you that you didn't deserve any better than that asshole growing up? Who led you to believe that someone wouldn't love you?"

"I... I... I don't want to talk about this anymore," I panic, trying to push away the memories that are threatening to take over. "Please... leave it alone, Nicholas. My childhood wasn't a happy one: I didn't grow up in a nice house with loving parents who cared about what I did every day. Just forget about it."

Fighting the tears that are threatening to spill out, I turn away from Nicholas and stare out the window. I can feel him watching me but I don't turn back. It's bad enough that he knows even a little about my ex; he doesn't need to know everything else too. I can't open myself up to him, tell him everything, when he has the power to end our arrangement and walk out of my life at any moment.

The elevator ride to the floor of my apartment is quiet. I'm not mad at Nicholas for asking about my childhood but I just didn't expect him to be able to read me so easily. It's as if he could see right through me: as if he could see parts of me that even I can't see. I don't know why he cares whether or not I think I deserve better than my ex. Isn't it enough that I swore I would never end up with someone like that again?

"Kenzie, I'm sorry. I over-stepped and I didn't mean to upset you," Nicholas apologizes as we stand awkwardly at the door to my apartment.

"It's not you, it's me. There are certain times of my life that I just don't like talking about—"

"I get it, really I do."

"Thank you for inviting me to dinner tonight, I had a nice time with your family," I desperately need to change the subject before things become even more uncomfortable out here.

"Thank *you* for coming. I know my parents were glad you came as well. I believe Bridget has been in touch about this week?"

"Yes, the business dinner and then the charity dinner over the weekend."

"I'll have to check with Melody, but I think there is something next week too."

"Sure, no problem."

"Good night, Kenzie, and again I'm sorry that I over-stepped earlier; I didn't mean to upset you."

Before I can respond, Nicholas surprises me by kissing me… on the lips this time. I'm caught so off guard, I just stand there trying to make sense of the fact that his soft lips are against mine. I'm just about to wrap my arms around him when he pulls back from me. He places one last quick kiss on my lips before turning around and to head to the elevator where Carter awaits. With a heated face, I unlock the apartment door and turn off the alarm.

I put my stuff down, take a quick shower and get ready for bed. Surprisingly sleep quickly finds me, although I have to force myself not to keep thinking about how Nicholas's lips felt against mine or to think about why he kissed me tonight.

Flashback

"You're such a fucking liar! I know you were with him today; I know that's why you're late!"

"No, I swear I wasn't. I… I left school late, I had to talk to my teacher-"

SLAP

"Don't lie to me! Why did you need to talk to your teacher? Did you do something wrong?"

"No. He asked to see me about working on the school newspaper. He wanted me to write an article—"

"That's a lie! All you ever do is lie! You're just like your mother—a fucking liar who is good for absolutely nothing! You're going to end up just like she did: alone and miserable. No one will ever love you; no one will ever put up with your lies. You will never amount to anything. I'm done. I knew the moment I was called about you, that you would be nothing but a piece of shit like your mother was. You've caused me nothing but problems since you came here. I'm calling tomorrow, I want you out of here!"

"I'm… I'm sorry. Please… I didn't mean—"

"You didn't mean what? To ruin my life? Well congratulations, you have! Yet again I've had to clean up your mother's mess and I'm fucking tired of it! Get the fuck out of here. I don't want to fucking see you again!"

"Ow!" I yelp in pain as I wasn't fast enough to dodge whatever she threw at me that just hit me in the back.

Madison Quinn

"Get the fuck out of here! Stay in your room the rest of the night. Don't you dare come out for dinner either. You're not getting anything tonight!"

She's throwing things down the hallway as I desperately try to make my way to my small bedroom. It's nothing more than a closet that they put a small mattress in on the floor; my clothes are hanging on the rod above me. It's tiny and dark, but I don't mind—in here I know I'm safe. She never comes in here. I scream as something else hits my back when I stop to open my door but don't turn around to see what it was. I throw myself into my room and close the door quickly behind me. I turn on the small lamp that sits on the floor next to my mattress. The blood is already seeping through the back of my shirt when I pull it off.

Chapter 28
Nicholas

"I can't do this anymore, Nicky." Mommy's crying again. She's always crying.

"It's okay, Mommy. Don't cry," I beg her.

"It's not okay, it's never okay. Get in the tub, Nicky."

I don't want to make her cry again so I get in the bathtub but the water is too hot. I cry out—she slaps me across the cheek.

"It's fine."

"It's too hot, Mommy."

"No it's not, get in the god damn tub."

"Mommy," I sob but do as she says.

I don't want to make her mad again; last time she was mad, she locked me in my bedroom and I didn't eat all day. The water turns my skin red and it hurts, but I don't cry. I can't make her mad again.

"I'm sorry I'm not the Mommy you need, Nicky."

"You're my mommy." I don't understand what she's saying.

"But I'm not a good Mommy, Nicky."

"You are—"

"No, I'm not: I yell at you too much, the apartment is always dirty, I never have enough money for food, I... I lost my job again. We're going to lose this apartment Nicky, we're going to be homeless."

"Homeless?" I don't know what that means.

"Homeless; the man who owns this place says we have to move out of here by tomorrow."

"Where will we go Mommy?"

"That's what being homeless means, baby, we have nowhere to go."

"But where will I go to sleep? Where is my bed going to be?"

"It doesn't matter Nicky, after today, nothing is going to matter."

"Mommy?"

"Why don't you lean back so I can wash your hair?"

I lay on my back and close my eyes, but when Mommy doesn't do anything I look up to find her staring at me. She has a funny look in her eyes, she smiles at me, mumbling something I can't hear, and puts her hand on my chest and pushes down. My face goes underwater! She knows I don't like having water in my eyes. Why did do that? I try and try to push her hand away but she's too strong.

FUCK!

I wake up sweating with my blankets thrown off the bed; I can't seem to catch my breath and or stop my body from shaking. This nightmare is always the worst; I'll never forget that day. I'll never be able to rid myself of that memory. Most days though I can keep myself from remembering it but then this fucking nightmare brings it right back to the surface. The clock next to my bed lets me know it's barely three in the morning, once again too fucking early to wake up Carter and go for a run. I know there's no point in trying to go back to sleep tonight—there's no way I'll be able to close my eyes and not picture that bathroom. I weigh my options as to what the hell I can do at this hour of the morning. I'm too tired to get an real work done. I can at least recognize that it's not safe for me to go running in the middle of the night without Carter so that's also out. I decide to head to the gym downstairs and hit the treadmill to see if that helps. It isn't ideal, but at least it's something.

I change into clean work out clothes and head down to the gym; I'm not worried about not telling Carter because after he realizes I'm not in the apartment he will check the security feed and see that I didn't leave the building. It's no surprise that the gym is empty at this hour of the morning. I put my ear buds in and start a playlist on my phone before setting the speed on the treadmill. I quickly lose myself in the rhythm of running and my thoughts begin to slowly fade away from that horrible day so many years ago.

After an hour, I finally feel like my head is clear enough to start my day. I slow the treadmill down to a walk and look around me. The gym itself is still empty but there is one woman swimming in the indoor pool below the gym. It only takes me a brief second to recognize the beautiful woman swimming is no other than Kenzie.

I'm surprised to see her in the pool at four o'clock in the morning. I know she is off today from the bakery so that isn't the reason she is awake this early. I immediately worry that the reason she is in the gym so early is because she also had a nightmare. The idea of her having one like the one she did when I was sick, bothers the hell out of me. My gut clenches as I remember her screams and how she kept apologizing, begging her ex to stop hurting her.

Without giving it a second thought, I jump off the treadmill and head out of the gym. Arriving at the elevator, instead of punching in the security code for the penthouse, I enter the access code for the pool. I let out the breath I didn't know I was holding when I see that Kenzie is still swimming laps in the pool and hadn't left before I could get here. I sit at the edge of the pool with my feet in the water and just watch her swim. I don't know why I'm here; I don't know what I'm even going to say. It's like I'm drawn to her or some shit. It's the same feeling I had last night after listening to the fucking *rules* her ex made her follow. I've never heard of someone having rules for their fiancée like that. I could see cautioning her about certain topics that could be a hot button for someone at a business dinner, but limiting what she could drink and choosing what she wore?

When she was describing it last night on our way back home, all I wanted to do was destroy the fucker who did that to her. He fucked with her so much so that even more than two years later, she still doesn't allow herself to have more than one drink when she is out with someone. I doubt that she even realizes she is still following his rule about that. Our car ride back last night also made me realize how little Kenzie thinks of herself. She honestly does not see the wonderful person she is; she wouldn't even admit that she deserve better than the asshole who used to hit her. How the hell does she not see that? Shit, even I know I'm not good enough for her!

"Nicholas! You scared me!" Kenzie finally comes up from the water and sees me sitting there. I'm kind of embarrassed that I have no idea how long I've been watching her swim back and forth.

"I was in the gym and saw you swimming down here. What are you doing here so early?"

"Couldn't sleep," she shrugs, as if not wanting to admit the real reason she is down here at this hour. "What about you? Why were you in gym this early?"

"Couldn't sleep," I smirk, repeating her vague answer.

"Touché," she laughs.

"You like to swim?"

"I was on the swim team in high school for a little while; before I moved... *came* here I hadn't been swimming in years. I forgot how relaxing it is."

When she gets out of the pool I nearly groan; she's wearing the bathing suit I had purchased for her last weekend. She walks past me, over to the lounge chair where she had a towel waiting. I watch, almost fascinated, as she dries the dripping water off her body. I can't help but wonder what it would be like to lick each drop of water off her.

"Nicholas?" Thankfully, Kenzie pulls me from my naughty thoughts before my dick decides to make them obvious to her.

"Sorry, I have a big meeting this morning I was thinking about," I lie.

"I asked if you wanted to come back to the apartment for some breakfast? But if you have a meeting..."

"No, breakfast would be nice. Let me run up to my place to change; I'm kind of sweaty from the treadmill."

"Okay, I'll see you in a few minutes?"

"Sure. Thank you Kenzie."

She gets off the elevator at her floor while I ride the rest of the way alone to my apartment. When the doors open I'm greeted by silence which is no surprise. Typically Carter doesn't come out of his apartment until closer to five and Julie not until six when we are due back from our morning run. I quickly take a shower and change into a pair of jeans and a casual shirt before heading to Kenzie's apartment. When I approach her door, I'm immediately reminded of standing here last night when things were still a little awkward between us after her confession in the car.

I remember the pain in her eyes when she looked up at me. I didn't know what to do but once again I found myself overwhelmed with the sudden need to comfort her. She is the only person I've ever felt such a strong protectiveness for, well, outside of my family, of course. I didn't know how to comfort her last night, so I did the only thing that came natural to me. I kissed her. For the first time since her nightmare, *I* kissed her on the lips. And it felt... it left me needing a very cold shower when I finally got back to my apartment. All I really wanted to do was take her into her apartment and fuck her senseless until she forgot everything that that bastard did to her. Thankfully I realized how that would only fuck things up royally and just end up hurting her more, which is why I walked away.

I'm surprised to find myself standing outside her door again, surprised that she invited me to breakfast and more surprised that I said yes. My response came without hesitation or thought, a rarity for me. I could have easily declined her invitation, returned to my apartment and began preparing for my day ahead. Instead, I'm once again standing outside the door to her apartment. I take a deep breath and knock on the door.

"Come in. Breakfast is just about ready. Would you like a cup of coffee?" Kenzie greets me a few seconds later.

"Yes, thank you."

I follow her into the kitchen area where she hands me a cup of hot coffee and encourages me to sit at the table in the dining room. I look around the apartment since this is the first time I've been here since she moved in. Looking around, I realize the apartment looks exactly same as it did the last time I was here. The walls a bare except for a few landscape pictures that I had Melody order for the space in an effort to make it feel more comfortable to the employees who stayed here while they looked for a new place to live. The kitchen counters are bare, even the fridge is free of magnets or papers hanging up. It doesn't seem like Kenzie has done very much with the space since she moved in at all.

"I hope you like blueberry pancakes," Kenzie puts a plate of hot pancakes in front of me.

"I do, thank you."

She takes a seat across from me with her plate and cup of coffee. We eat in a comfortable silence for a few minutes before my curiosity gets the better of me.

"You know you can redecorate or paint in here if you wanted to," I suggest.

"Nah, it's fine just the way it is. Actually I'm starting to look for my own place so—"

"What?" I'm really hoping I didn't just hear her correctly.

"I... I've begun the process of looking for an apartment. I have calls into a few places that I'm hoping to look at in the next couple of weeks—"

"Kenzie, if you don't like something about this apartment—"

"No! Gosh no, Nicholas, this place is perfect!"

"Then what is it? Why do you want to move out?"

"Nicholas... this is *your* apartment, not mine. This move was temporary, it was never a permanent arrangement for me. I could never afford to live in a million dollar condo like this."

Two million, but I don't correct her.

"Kenzie, before I moved into The Accord, I looked at a number of different places. This condo has the highest level of security available; every other building you look at will fall short."

"I don't doubt that," she shrugs and sighs. "The reality is I can't afford even a studio apartment in this building, and that's okay. I won't be going back to where I used to live that's for sure. I'm hoping to find a place with decent security—"

"You won't. That's what I'm trying to tell you; nothing you look at will compare.

"I know, what I find won't be The Accord, but it will be safer than where I was before here."

"Why do you want to move? If there is something you don't like about this apartment we can change it—"

"Nicholas, you don't get it," she shakes her head as if I'm missing something obvious. "This is *your* apartment, not mine."

"It's yours for as long as you need it."

"I *needed* this place after my last apartment was broken into; I can afford my own place so I no longer *need* this apartment."

"Okay, *need* was the wrong word. This place is yours for as long as you want it, Kenzie. Stay here; the building is secure, you don't need to worry about someone breaking in or the press bothering you and you have access to all the amenities that it has to offer."

"For how long? Any way you look at it, this apartment is temporary."

"For as long as you want to stay! I don't need the apartment—"

"And what happens when you do? What happens when you hire someone who needs a place to stay while they relocate?"

"We have other condos that PFS owns, so that's the least of my concerns. I want to keep you safe, to keep the press away from you, and here I can do that."

"And what happens when this," she waves her hands between us, "ends? I'll have nowhere to go; I will have no place of my own. I'll have to settle for whatever I can find at that moment which will probably mean I'll end up in a hotel for a little while until I find a place. I won't do that again. If I find my own place now, then when this ends I'll still have my own place."

"Is that what you're worried about? Do you really think I would just kick you out when this arrangement ends?"

"I don't know," she shrugs and avoids looking at me which answers my question more than her words do. I'm completely taken back that she would think I would just kick her out when we're done.

"Kenzie…" I sigh trying to figure out how to convince her that would never happen. Hell, I'd fucking give her the apartment, if I thought that was what she wanted, but I learned my lesson the last time I tried to offer her money.

"Look, I get it… you need something of your own; you don't want to be completely dependent on me."

"Yeah," she whispers but still doesn't look at me.

"I would hope that by now you would know me well enough to know that I wouldn't put you on the street just because our arrangement ended; I know part of you knows that." She attempts to interrupt but I don't let her. "But I also know because of your ex, you have doubts. What if we put together a legal contract that gives you the right to stay here if we ended things? You would have a place to stay that is safe while we're in this arrangement together but when it ends you would have the time you needed to find a place of your own?"

"You would do that?" She finally makes eye contact with me, immediately I feel relieved.

"Of course, Kenzie. I'll have my legal team draw up a contract that says if our relationship is ended by either party that you have the right to remain in the condo for up to six months. I want you to be safe and this place has the best security possible. The press hasn't bothered you too much yet but that could change at any time. Will you consider staying?"

"I'll think about it," she agrees.

Thank God. I don't know what I would have done if she had insisted on moving out. Short of buying her a house somewhere outside of the city, no one can offer the security that The Accord Towers has. That was the reason I choose to live here after leaving *her*. I knew I needed top security to ensure she couldn't access my apartment ever again. The Accord guaranteed that. Having Kenzie here means I can guarantee the press won't bother her but also that there is no chance of anyone from her past getting to her.

"I've got to get going; I have an early meeting that I need to prepare for," I realize that my meeting starts in thirty minutes and I'm not even dressed yet for the office.

"Thank you for having breakfast with me, Nicholas."

"Please think about what I've said. Can I email you the contract my legal department draws up?"

"Yes, that would be fine."

"I'll see you later this week?"

"Yes, for dinner."

I lean down and kiss her softly on the cheek before leaving her apartment and to head back upstairs. When the elevator doors open, Carter immediately walks into the foyer but doesn't say anything. I have no doubt that he knew where I was since he didn't call my phone.

"Will you need breakfast sir?" he asks.

"No, I'll be ready to leave in ten minutes," I confirm.

"You may want to check your email when you have a moment."

"Any email in particular I should focus on? I'm sure I have dozens right now."

"From me, sir; it contains a link to something Asher found online about you this morning."

Is New York's infamous playboy single again?

It's been more than three weeks since Nicholas Parker and Mackenzie Rose were seen together; has their time together ended already? Did she run like all the other women in his life? Did she find out the dirty secret that he tries to hide from everyone? Once again, we have to wonder if Nicholas Parker can't keep one woman happy, how on earth can he keep hundreds of employees and clients happy? How much longer will PFS be successful at this rate?

Chapter 29
Kenzie

This week is turning out like nothing I could have expected. I've had to take some time off from the bakery because the press has been hanging out there, trying to talk to me. It started the day after the article came out questioning whether or not Nicholas and I are still together. The first day the press was manageable; Hunter was able to keep them out of the bakery but by the second day the number of press there had doubled. Even after Hunter requested additional security from Carter they were barely managing. Even worse, the reporters were keeping away some of the regular customers.

"Kenzie, dear can I see you for a moment?" Ginny asks just as I'm about to take my break.

"Of course Ginny."

"Look Kenzie… I don't know how to say this…"

"What's wrong Ginny? Is everything okay with your daughter?"

"Oh goodness…. yes, thankfully everyone is fine," she takes a deep breath before continuing and in my gut I know this isn't good news. "Kenzie, I want you to know how happy I am for you. You deserve the best life has to offer, especially after… everything. I'm so glad that you finally let someone in, someone who can make you happy. I haven't seen you smile this much in all the times I've known you. I'm really happy for you."

"Thank you, Ginny." I feel a big but coming on.

"The thing is… the press…"

"I know. I'm so sorry that they won't leave; I don't know how to keep them away."

"Unfortunately, Kenzie, I'm sure you've noticed that they're is keeping our business away. If it were up to me I would just ride this out and wait for them to leave. Unfortunately, this isn't only about me. The sale was finalized just the other day so I have to think about the new owners. While they aren't aware of what is going on yet, I'm sure once *our numbers start coming in for this week, they will question the drop in sales. What I'm trying to say is... I think it might be best if you took some time off—"*

"Are you... firing me?" I gulp even saying the words.

"NO! Of course not. No matter what happens, you will always have a job here as long as I have a say in the matter. I'm just suggesting that perhaps you need to take some time off until this all dies down. Maybe just a few days until they move onto a different story? I'm really happy that you found someone who loves you, really I am. I just wish the press would stop following you around to report your every move."

"I know, I feel the same way but unfortunately the press seems to love reporting everything in Nicholas's life... including me right now."

"I wish I didn't have to ask this of you, but—"

"No, it's fine. I understand, really."

"Hopefully, in a few days, this interest in you will disappear and you can come back without the press."

I never expected this whole thing with Nicholas to impact my job at the bakery. I never thought the press would hound me the way they have been this week. I guess up until now I've been lucky that the press had left me alone. After the article earlier this week highlighting the fact that Nicholas and I haven't made a public appearance together in a few weeks, the press just started hounding me nonstop. More articles have been written this week, actually reporting what each of us do every day. Tonight, Nicholas and I are going out for a business dinner and I'm sure there will be press there. Tomorrow, I'm going shopping with Cara and Hunter has already let me know that we will be bringing additional security with us since there will be two of us and only one of him.

The one thing I don't understand is why the press gives a shit about what Nicholas does in his personal life. I gave up reading most of the articles, and just skim the headlines now. Some of them hint the reason Nicholas is pictured with so many women is because he is actually gay and hasn't come out of the closet yet. That one doesn't make sense to me at all since there are so many pictures of Nicholas with his ex. Does the press think that was all for show or that he discovered his sexual preference after her? Some articles suggest he is hiding something that causes women to run away when they find it out. For the life of me I can't figure out what they think Nicholas is hiding. They act like he is a horrible monster in private, when just the opposite is true.

Knock knock

Shit! I was so lost in my thoughts I hadn't realized the time.

"Would you mind coming in for a minute? I just need two more minutes—I'm running a little late."

"Of course, take your time Kenzie."

With Nicholas in the living room, I quickly dart into the bedroom to put on my strappy sandals. Tonight I'm wearing a simple black fitted dress that has a few large red roses on it. I have a red wrap that will cover my bare shoulders in case it gets chilly tonight. I'm not sure what tonight's dinner is about, but the dress seems like the perfect mix between business and casual.

"Sorry about that, I'm ready now."

"You look very pretty," Nicholas puts his hand on my back as he leads me out of the apartment.

"Thank you."

"I heard the press was bothering you this week," Nicholas says once we are seated in the SUV.

"They seem to have really come at me full force this week," I admit. "I was really surprised that they followed me to work."

"I know," he sighs and runs his hands through his hair. "I wish this wasn't my life, but unfortunately this comes with the territory I suppose. Are they still bothering you at work?"

"No... but that's probably because I'm not working right now."

"What? What happened?"

"Ginny suggested I take some time off until things calm down. Unfortunately, it was impacting business: regular customers who have come in daily for years stopped because the reporters were asking them questions about me."

"Oh, Kenzie. I'm so sorry. I'll fix this—"

"There's nothing you can do, Nicholas. Once the press dies down, Ginny has assured me that I will still have a job, so I just need to wait it out. I'm sure they will stop once they realize they aren't getting anything from me."

"I'll start having a weekly check deposited into your bank account—"

"You'll WHAT?!?!"

"For your lost wages, I'll cover them of course."

"Um, no you won't."

"Kenzie, you're not working because of me; it's only fair that I cover your lost wages."

"No."

"No?"

"No. You have given me a place to stay completely rent free and already pay for the time we spend together, I will not allow you to give me money every week too."

"But—"

"No. Thanks to this arrangement I already have good amount of money saved—"

"But that was so you can go back to school—"

"And I will. I have minimal expenses and probably won't even need to tap into my savings account."

"I just don't understand why you won't let me do this. If it wasn't for me you would still be working at the bakery."

"Yes, that's true. But if it wasn't for you I would be living in a shitty apartment right now, that is raided by the police every other week. Where I have to step over people who are drunk or high just to get into my building and where the electricity was routinely turned off by the owner. I prefer staying here over that."

"Kenzie… you really are like no one I've ever met," he sighs heavily but I'm not sure if it's in frustration or anger.

"I'll take that as a compliment," I say, although I'm not sure if that's how he meant it.

"You should."

"So tell me what tonight is about. Bridget just said it was a business dinner."

"It's a celebratory dinner; we just closed a deal with this company and Alex thought it would good to take them out to celebrate. We signed with the company under the disguise that we hope to be able to help them avoid bankruptcy."

"But?"

"Bankruptcy is inevitable: they can't keep going as they have been and no amount of change will fix that. What will fix it though, is merging it with a larger company that is what we're going to recommend in two months after we've had a second look at the books."

"Why not just tell them up front that you intend to recommend they merge with another company?"

"Because then they wouldn't have agreed to sign with us if we told them the plan ahead of time."

"And you wanted to sign the company?"

"It made good financial sense: the company I want them to merge with is also under PFS and is in a position to offer this company's employees higher pay and better benefits. It will also make both owners a significant amount of money long term."

"Why didn't they do that to begin with? It sounds like they could have walked away with more money in their pockets."

"Most people don't see that as an option. They were reluctant to even sell but unfortunately once we built the trust with them and we demonstrate that in a matter of months the banks will begin foreclosing on their buildings, they begin to consider our recommendation."

"Sir, ma'am, just to warn you I believe we were followed when we left the condo," Carter alerts us.

"Reporters?" Nicholas asks.

"I believe so."

"Unfuckingbelievable! All this over a fucking dinner," Nicholas shakes his head.

"Think of this way, maybe it will be the confirmation the press needs to know we are still together."

"Maybe."

The moment we pull up to the restaurant, reporters are snapping our picture. We barely make it out of the car before they start screaming questions at us.

"Mr. Parker! Mr. Parker! Are you and Ms. Rose still an item?"

"Why haven't you been seen together in three weeks?"

"What are you hiding?"

"What do you say to reports that PFS is suffering because of your personal life?"

"I say that my financial reports indicate otherwise," Nicholas snaps at the young reporter who dared ask about PFS.

Carter and Hunter lead us through the crowd of reporters who continue to snap pictures of us and question our relationship status. Nicholas's arm is wrapped firmly around my waist, anchoring me to him as we try to make our way to the front of door.

"Ladies, Gentleman," Nicholas addresses the crowd before we go into dinner. "Ms. Rose and I are here to celebrate a successful business deal. I am aware that there are reports that we haven't been together in the last few weeks. However, as you can now see, we are very much still together. Now, if you will excuse us we have a dinner reservation to keep."

Seconds later we are inside the warmth of the restaurant and my ears finally stop buzzing from all the questions being yelled at us. We are escorted to our table where we are the last ones to arrive which I know disappoints Nicholas. Had it not been for the press outside, I'm confident we would have been the first.

"So Kenzie, how are you enjoying being famous?" Alex asks as I sit next to him.

"UGH, I don't get why they care so much about what Nicholas does."

"New York's youngest billionaire, who just happens to be good looking and single? Can you blame them, Kenzie?" Ella asks.

"I get that part, but still they act like his personal life has some bearing on his business decisions."

"That part pisses me off," Alex agrees. "His track record should stand for itself."

Dinner goes well, I chat with Alex and Ella while Nicholas talks with the owners of the company. I try to make small talk with them, but they aren't very talkative, so I stick to chatting with Ella and Alex who make me feel very comfortable. Less than two hours after we arrive, dinner is over and everyone says goodbye. Unlike when we arrived, Nicholas and I are escorted by Hunter to a rear entrance where Carter is waiting with the SUV. The press doesn't see us leave and we're get back home without being followed.

"Thank you for coming to dinner with me tonight, Kenzie. I'm sorry the press has been bothering you so much," Nicholas says as we stand outside the apartment door.

"Well at least the food was good," I joke.

"That it was."

"Oh, I'm not sure if you remembered but I'm going shopping with Cara tomorrow—
"

"She has made sure I haven't forgotten," he chuckles.

"Oh?"

"She's texted me several times this week reminding me that you two planned to go out tomorrow. She's very excited about it."

"I hope you don't mind; when she asked me—"

"No, it's fine. I mean, if I'm completely honest, I wasn't expecting so much overlap between this arrangement and my family." I nod in agreement because I knew he wasn't expecting it. "But my family really likes you, so if this makes them happy, then I'm fine with it. Unless you mind—"

"No! Not at all," I quickly interrupt. "It's been a long time since I've gone shopping with someone, so I'm looking forward to it."

"Here's my card," he pulls a black American express card from his wallet and hands it to me.

"What's this for?"

"For tomorrow."

"I'm not following… "

"Kenzie, you're going shopping for the charity dinner this weekend right?" I nod. "Normally I would be paying for your outfit for the evening anyway so Bridget sends me a bill for your purchases and I pay for them. However, since you can't very well tell the store to charge it to Bridget, here is my credit card for the purchase."

"Nicholas… I don't know that I feel right having this."

"I trust you with it. Buy your outfit for the weekend and treat my sister to lunch. She'll be expecting you to whip out my credit card for the dress anyway."

"Why would she expect that?"

"She just would. You're going with me to the dinner, so it's only natural that I would pay for your outfit."

"I could pay for it myself."

"You could, but you won't, and she won't suspect anything. If you paid for it yourself, she would probably flat out ask you why I'm not paying for it. Don't worry about it. It's no different than when you go to Stacy's and have it charged to Bridget."

"I guess."

"Stay with Hunter and Ben tomorrow. I have no doubt that the press will follow you when you shop. If it gets out of hand, just come back here. I can always have someone send over dresses for you to shop from home and not have to deal with the press. In fact, maybe we should do that instead."

"Nicholas, we'll be fine."

"Just stay with them, please, I don't trust the press."

"I will."

"I'll pick you up on Saturday?"

"I'll be ready."

"Good night, Kenzie."

"Night, Nicholas."

When he leans down to kiss me the air seems to shift between us; his eyes lock onto mine and his face stops only inches from mine. He moves a piece of my hair to just behind my ear, a sweet move that surprises me, just before his lips find mine. The kiss is soft at first, but his lips become firm against mine as he wraps his arm around my lower back, pulling me against him. My arms go around his neck, my fingers weaving through the back of his hair as I completely lose myself in the kiss. I gasp in surprise when I feel Nicholas's tongue against my lips. He cautiously enters my mouth, almost as if he is afraid of my reaction, but I don't push him away or stop him. I am completely caught up in this, just as I think he might be. I can't remember the last time I was ever kissed so… passionately.

Ring ring

"Fuck," Nicholas pulls away at the sound of his phone ringing from his pocket.

The phone stops a few seconds later. Our heavy breathing is the only sound that can be heard in the hallway, which is when I suddenly remember that we are standing in the middle of the hallway. What's worse is that Carter is only a few feet away at the elevator, thankfully though, with his back is towards us.

"Kenzie… " His eyes find mine and I'm pretty sure I see regret in them.

"Good night, Nicholas," I kiss him on the lips softly one last time before I turn and enter my apartment.

I lock the door, reset the alarm and collapse on the loveseat, trying to make sense out of what just happened. Things seemed to have been going well between us tonight. But then why did Nicholas suddenly look like he regretted kissing me? Did he regret blurring the lines? Did he think he made a mistake? Did he think I didn't want to kiss him?

I couldn't just stand there; I knew the next words out of his mouth would have been an apology. I didn't need to hear him tell me he was sorry for kissing me. Not when for the first time in years, I felt… alive. No one has ever kissed me like Nicholas just did. No one has ever made me lose myself in a kiss. I've never felt like I did a few minutes ago and I couldn't stand there and let him apologize for that. I didn't want to hear that he regretted what just happened because of the stupid rules of the contract. I reread the contract the other week after I had kissed him, and it does not say that we can't kiss. The only thing it exclusively prohibits is sex, so we have done nothing wrong. I'm sure Nicholas, being the knowledgeable business man that he is, would know this. If he regretted kissing me, it wouldn't be because he was worried we violated some part of the contract.

I give up trying to figure out his motives and get ready for bed. Unfortunately sleep doesn't find me easily and I'm in the pool by three thirty, desperately trying to swim the memories of the nightmare away. I keep looking for Nicholas, expecting to see him by the pool like he was the other morning but he never appears. Part of me is disappointed but part of me is also relieved: I'm not sure what I would say to him if he were here this morning.

Since I won't be seeing Nicholas again until the charity dinner on Saturday, I figure I have two days to figure out if I should say something to him or just forget that it happened or wait for him to bring it up. Vowing not to think about the kiss again today, I spend the morning doing laundry and getting ready for my shopping trip with Cara.

Knock Knock

"Are you ready, Kenzie?" it took weeks, but I've finally convinced Hunter to stop calling me Ms. Rose.

"All ready," I confirm. "Are we picking up Cara?"

"We're meeting her at Neiman's; Ben is picking her up."

When we arrive at the department store, Cara is there waiting for us and immediately engulfs me in a huge hug when she sees me approaching. I'm surprised that Nicholas has arranged for us to have a private dressing room for the entire day along with a personal shopper. Cara doesn't bat an eye at the arrangements, so I assume this is pretty typical for her when she goes shopping for events like this.

"Kenzie, you have to try this on!" Cara holds up what can only be described as gaudy… I desperately try to come up with the words to tell her that there is no way in hell I would be wearing that to the dinner on Saturday night, without hurting her feelings.

"Oh my God! You should see the look on your face!"

"I thought you were serious!" I join her in laughing.

"I hate trying on dresses, so I like to mix it up and try on silly ones. It helps pass the time and makes the trip more enjoyable."

"Ah, makes sense. In that case you should try on this," I hold up a neon pink beaded dress that looks like something out of the 50's.

Over the next hour, we have managed to hand the personal shopper dozens of dresses to be hung up for us in the dressingarea. The room is a large room with two areas closed off with curtains to provide privacy while we change. The entire room is reserved for us so as Cara and I try on outfits, we take turns modeling them. I'm trying on the third dress when I hear my phone buzzing with a text. Cara apparently decided to send Nicholas and me pictures of the dresses we have tried on so far.

Sorry for the texts while you're at work. I hadn't realized Cara was going to send you the pictures –Kenzie

 Up until now I haven't had Nicholas's cell phone number, so I hope he doesn't mind me texting him. I'm sure he is swamped at work and the last thing he needs or wants is to receive texts from Cara as we play dress up. When he doesn't respond I stick the phone back in my purse and continue on with our modeling show.

A couple of hours later, Cara and I have both found dresses for the charity dinner on Saturday. As Nicholas predicted, Cara doesn't bat an eye when I hand the personal shopper his credit card as a payment for my dress. Hunter arranges the delivery of the dresses while Cara and I discuss lunch plans. We settle on a small bistro a few blocks from the department store, but the minute we step out of the dressing room we are blinded by the flashes of cameras.

"Right this way, ladies," Hunter leads us through the crowd while Ben follows closely behind.

"Where's Nicholas Parker?"

"Is he aware that you two are out shopping?"

"What event are you shopping for?"

"Mackenzie, what do you say to the rumors that Nicholas Parker can't keep a woman happy?"

"Cara, why do you think all the women in your brother's life run away from him? Is he hiding something?"

"Why don't you all just leave my brother alone? It's none of your business what he does with his personal life!" Cara exclaims just before we split up to head towards our cars.

Thankfully, only a few minutes later, I'm safe inside the SUV, although a couple reporters continue to snap pictures of the car. Honestly, I don't understand what the big deal is: I went shopping with Nicholas' sister—this is news? With everything else going on in the world, reporters decide they need to focus on what we bought for a charity dinner?

Lunch another time? – Cara

Definitely –Kenzie

"How did they know where we were, Hunter?"

"We suspect one of the employees tipped off the press after recognizing you. We are trying to determine who notified the press so it can be addressed."

I shake my head in disbelief; while I worked as a personal shopper I never would have dreamed of calling the press if a client was there. Granted, I never worked with anyone I think the press would care about, but still, I wouldn't have invaded someone's privacy like that. When we reach The Accord, I'm once again thankful for the security in the building as we pull into the private underground parking garage that can only be accessed by a key card.

If the paparazzi were following us, they wouldn't have been able to make it into the garage. This week has forced me to realize that I need to accept Nicholas's offer to stay here through the duration of our arrangement. I realize I could never afford to live in an apartment with this level of security, which means I would be dealing with the press on my own every time I left my apartment or tried to come home.

Change into a pair of comfy yoga pants and a fitted T-shirt when I get back, I curl up on the loveseat with a book. Unfortunately, the lack of sleep from the previous night catches up with me and I soon fall asleep. I must have slept for a couple of hours because when I wake up the room has darkened, since I didn't leave any lights on. I grab my phone to check the time and realize I have a text message from Nicholas.

I need to talk to you. Are you free tonight? –Nicholas

Yes, I'm free. Home now. –Kenzie

Do you want to come to my apartment? – Nicholas

Or, if you would rather, I can reserve a private room somewhere? – Nicholas

No, I'll come up. –Kenzie

Madison Quinn

I know why he offered the private room, but at this point, it's not necessary. I spent the weekend at his apartment and then we spent an entire day on his boat in the middle of nowhere. I no longer have any worries about spending time alone with him. Plus, I know we're not truly alone in his apartment since both Julie and Carter live there. I quickly use the bathroom, throw my hair into a messy bun and slip on a pair of shoes before setting the alarm to head upstairs.

"Good evening Ms. Rose," Carter startles me as soon as I open my door.

"Oh! I wasn't expecting you, Carter."

"The security codes have been changed since you last used them; the one you had is no longer active," he explains.

"Oh."

A few minutes later, the elevator doors open to Nicholas's expansive foyer.

"Mr. Parker is in his office," Carter ushers me down the hallway to Nicholas's office.

"Mr. Parker, Ms. Rose has arrived," Carter announces.

"Thank you, please come in, Kenzie," Nicholas gestures for me to sit in the chair across from this desk. I'm immediately reminded of the last time I was in here. If Nicholas tries to give me money again, I swear I'm going to scream. I really hope he doesn't think he needs to pay me for today—

"Kenzie... we need to talk."

"Okay..." Well this wasn't what I was expecting and Nicholas's uneasiness is alarming.

"I.... I...." he runs his hands through his hair and takes a deep breath before continuing. "I think we need to end our contract with Bridget."

On His Terms

Want more of Kenzie and Nicholas's story?

On Her Terms will be available Fall 2018!

Did you enjoy On His Terms?
Please share a review on your favorite site.
Recommend their story to your friends!

Keep up to date with upcoming release, giveaways and opportunities to win prizes by connecting with me on Facebook!
https://www.facebook.com/madison.quinn.71697

Also, sign up for my newsletter for exclusive ARC opportunities!
http://madisonquinnauthor.com